THE *Role* OF A LIFETIME

A Woman Reinvents Herself … for Good … and Bad!

JAMES B. FLAHERTY

iUniverse®

THE ROLE OF A LIFETIME
A WOMAN REINVENTS HERSELF … FOR GOOD … AND BAD!

iUniverse books may be ordered through booksellers or by contacting:

iUniverse
1663 Liberty Drive
Bloomington, IN 47403
www.iuniverse.com
844-349-9409

ISBN: 978-1-5320-3099-4 (sc)
ISBN: 978-1-5320-3100-7 (hc)
ISBN: 978-1-5320-3098-7 (e)

Library of Congress Control Number: 2017916852

Print information available on the last page.

iUniverse rev. date: 02/08/2024

CHAPTER 1

The Flawless Bettina Richardson Isn't So Flawless, but Only She Knows Who She Is … and Isn't

A nd her platinum-edged husband, Dillworth Richardson, did not know she was actually Bethel Sokoloff, daughter of a mediocre Bronx tailor. Heir to a multifaceted fortune too vast for a calculator to contain, Dillworth knew Bettina only as she had presented herself— the only child of a refined family, properly grounded and educated, left penniless by the private plane crash that snuffed out the lives of her parents.

Bethel had worked very hard to become Bettina. There were ten months of diction lessons, paid for by working as a barmaid in a waterfront bar. It's hard to erase fluid Bronx from a voice. She memorized and practiced how a department store beauty salon did her hair, makeup, and nails. A legal name change to Bettina Marshton, a fake résumé, forged references, and a splendid nose job, plus a lease at a proper residence hotel for young women, helped her obtain a position selling at Tiffany's.

It all paid off. Dillworth was smitten by her gentle and genteel vulnerability and, after a couple of false starts, succeeded in convincing her he was honorable and trustworthy. Meanwhile, Bethel—pardon me— Bettina never stopped studying. She would walk along Fifth or Madison Avenue and watch the women born to wealth. How they dressed. How they walked. How they wore their hair. And when they paused, how did they stand?

After a year and a half of nerve-racking role-playing, Bettina and Dillworth (she called him Dilly) were married in one of those social weddings that attracts guests from the Hamptons, Palm Beach, the Cape, Europe, and any other address deemed fashionable at the time. A three-week Caribbean honeymoon ("Mummy and Daddy never took me to the islands. They didn't care for … well, you know, the people."), and then they settled into Dilly's Fifth Avenue apartment, with a converted barn in Short Hills, New Jersey, for weekends.

Bethel, or Bettina, as the world now knew her, had ample sexual credits but allowed Dillworth to "teach" her the techniques of passion, although it was a full year before she could engage in "mouth sex," as she called it, to Dillworth's amusement. The real amusement was that the old Bethel didn't have to be taught anything, even though sex had never been a paramount influence in her life.

CHAPTER 2

Dilly Was an Orderly Man, Not Taken to Snap Decisions or Unlikely Turns in His Life, but He Remembered Distinctly the First Time He Saw Bettina

He was shopping at Tiffany's for his mother's birthday. He was staring into a counter of diamond and sapphire pins and bracelets when a musical and gentle voice kissed his consciousness. "Good morning, sir. I mean, good afternoon. It is afternoon, I believe." He looked up to see a timid, embarrassed smile, encased in a very special gathering of features and flesh and hair. "Now that we've established the time of day, may I be of service?" Something touched Dilly. He smiled back, and somewhere chimes tinkled. He swears he remembers chimes. She looked ... vulnerable. The clothes were ultraconservative, but she managed to look glamorous. She probably didn't realize she was glamorous-looking. He suspected it was something that just happened to her, slowly over the years, so she never came to accept it as a quality of her own. He made the purchase, which was, Bettina remembers clearly, the equivalent of half a year's salary for her, and while he waited for the package to be gift wrapped, he managed to ask information-gathering questions, the answers to which she had long rehearsed. "No, sir, I haven't lived in New York very long at all."

"Unfortunately, there's no family in the area, so I live in Heraldon Hall, the young women's residence in the Upper East Side." "No, no married couples can live there, only unattached women."

Bettina loved the questions. And she answered each one with a hint of *Is this proper for me to be speaking to you about these things?* After all, this is what she had been training herself for. There had been other, clumsy attempts at communication from other male shoppers, but she refused to be bullied into a confrontation with someone whose wife "doesn't understand me, just because she was lonely. She had been waiting for Mr. Right to ride up on a white horse or, better yet, in a Silver Cloud Rolls, and here he was. And besides that, he was beautiful-looking. He even smelled good.

There were cocktails—usually champagne at Windows of the World; glorious flowers sent to her hotel; intimate dinners at flawless restaurants. Thank God she had studied food magazines for a full year, reading every word, checking pronunciation, and she knew which fish were *in* and which were *out*. She, quite honestly, denied any knowledge of wine, saying, "I know you'll make the correct choice, and I would make a fool of myself pretending." He was enchanted. At the Carlyle Hotel, after four months of dating, a horrifically nervous Dilly sweetly and gently eased his newfound flower into bed. She succumbed, after tearfully admitting that the sex act had been forced onto her some five years prior and that he probably wouldn't want to have anything more to do with her, knowing that. He wanted to kill the aggressor in her life and make sure his gentleness would make her forget the unhappiness of five years earlier. It was sweet, if not exciting, and she kept her remarks to the minimum, especially touching him with "Oh, Dilly, when I'm with you, every day is my birthday; every day is Christmas. I'm so very happy and feel so protected." In his own eyes, he grew strong and muscular. They stayed there, sleeping together that night. She forced herself to wake at five thirty in the morning and went to the bathroom and rejuvenated her face, her hair, and her breath so that he woke to find his new, adoring goddess at his side, gazing at him tenderly.

Even though Bettina—still Bethel in her head back in those days—was enjoying the sex, she decided there had to be very definite limits. What was the old saying? Why buy the cow when you get the milk for free? So the courtship continued at a gentlemanly pace, now and then spiced by coupling, which, while not exotic, was growing in interest enough to keep Dilly fascinated with the thought of her. During this period, she often thought perhaps she'd just opt for the status quo. He showered her with good things and gifts and a good life and was hinting about finding her a lovely apartment somewhere. She knew the alternative was the jackpot—getting married. But she also knew that meant meeting the family. And although she had worked hard and was becoming accustomed to being Bettina, she also knew the family would not be blinded by sexual attraction. Would they see through the facade? It all came to a head one evening while they were dining at Le Bernardin, touted, with good cause, as one of the world's finest restaurants.

"Bettina, there's, um, something I've been meaning to discuss with you."

"What, my darling Dilly?"

"This arrangement—wrong word—relationship of ours is, uh, missing something."

Her heart skipped a beat. *Is he ending it?* "Not from my standpoint, Dilly. Being with you is everything good that could ever happen to me. If I'm letting you down in some way, please tell me, and … and I'll do whatever I can, make any changes I can." The tears that glistened in her eyes were real, even though the emotion of her words was false; she honestly feared losing him.

"Oh God, Bettina, please don't cry. You're perfect, and I'm just stumbling here because I've never asked someone to marry me before. Here—I think this might help explain." And he gave her the small, understated blue Tiffany box.

"Dill … Dilleee …" Bettina's tears spilled down her cheeks, and she stood up, jostling the table where they were dining, spilling her champagne, and reached across the table to kiss Dillworth Richardson and said, "Yes, yes, yes. I love you and will marry you."

Dilly presented her with a 3.6-carat marquise-cut diamond ring—from Tiffany's, since he was grateful to Tiffany's for introducing them. He would have bought her a larger ring but thought it would be vulgar. It was, she decided, very cute the way he handled it. It was Dilly all the way.

Edwina Richardson Wasn't Just Dillworth's Mother; She Was the Supreme Court—a Blue Chip Icon of Correctness, of Right versus Wrong

"You're bringing *who* to meet me?" Mrs. Richardson closed the book she had been reading without marking the place, she would discover later, and made a never-before gesture, which her son noticed, lightly scratching her right shoulder. She was not given to physical gestures of any sort because she found them distracting and common. "What is her name, and tell me again why it's important that we meet."

"Her name is Bettina, Mother, and I've asked her to marry me."

The shoulder scratching had migrated to pulling lightly on the left earlobe and an almost imperceptible side-to-side shake, as though she was refusing to believe what she was hearing.

"Just like that I'm told you've invited someone to join the family whom I have never met. I think that's rather appalling, Dillworth. What if I find this … this person—"

"Her name is Bettina, Mother."

"Very well. Bettina. What if I find this Bettina unacceptable?"

"No chance of that, Mother. Good heavens, you don't think I'd fall in love with just anybody."

Fall in love! My God, it's probably too late. "I suppose in the current vernacular of relationships that you have already consummated this ... um ... friendship?"

"A gentleman would never discuss his private relationship with a woman. You taught me that eons ago."

Mrs. Richardson played her role well. She got her scratching and ear pulling gestures under control and, with a series of calculated questions, elicited information about the magical Bettina—information she could use to check out her background.

"In short, Mother, Bettina has found some part of me I didn't know existed. My pulse races; my heart beats faster; I'm almost breathless when I see her."

"Sounds to me like a coronary occlusion. Pardon me, dear, I'm just exercising my wit. I'm sure Bettina is charming. Why don't you invite her for an evening a week from this Saturday? It will be only the two of you, your father and me, and your sister and her husband."

"I don't want you to frighten her, Mother."

"Frighten her! What do you think we are, Dillworth? Ogres? We are your family, and if she has been invited to become a member of this family, I think we all have a right to meet her—as a family."

CHAPTER 4

Dilly, as a Young Man, Had Been One of Those Sons Who Other Parents Held Up as an Example to Their Own Children

Not that he was a saint, but Dilly's sense of propriety, his awareness of being a Richardson, of belonging to a correct society kept him from any public embarrassment. His memories, as well as the actuality of his adolescence, were all normal. He never strayed too far from the norm for that period. His awareness of the opposite sex came to him gently, and his courteous self-awareness kept him from experimentation until his third year in college. Even then, it was sex without passion. He was wise enough to recognize it as such and in the ensuing years, he exercised his sexual rights and needs only when he felt it would be unhealthy to abstain for any longer.

Dillworth's relationship with his parents was like the rest of his life—proper and nonchallenging. His father, who had been left a sizeable fortune, had built it to staggering proportions. Although they weren't particularly close, father and son appreciated each other's sensibilities. He knew nothing of his father's highly confidential sexual couplings. Had he known, it would have offended him greatly.

His mother, on the other hand, was not to be ignored. The type who always turned her cheek and kissed the air, she was not overly demonstrative but always demanding with her son. "Why are you taking these courses in college, Dilly? Give me your personal rationale for each course, and tell me why you feel it has value to your education." The questions she asked were never simple. "You no doubt have noticed Bill Rodgers is going to marry that simpleton he brought home from some college weekend. Considering what will be expected of Bill in terms of his family business, what is your opinion of men marrying women who are neither their social nor mental equals?" She, in turn, approved of her son, although secretly wished he had more fire from within. He never displeased or disappointed but also never overwhelmed her with his excellence. He was pleasantly predictable. Considering the alternatives, she was more than content with the status quo. There were moments when she worried about his seeming lack of interest in women. There were two or three who would have been fine as the other Mrs. Richardson. But after a while they disappeared, and a new candidate would appear.

Apparently, he had known Bettina for a while, quietly shoring up the foundations of their relationship. And by the time she was introduced to the family, he was enamored of her, and it was too late for Edwina to undermine the relationship. Their marriage stunned her. But she put on her best public face and went through all the motions, promising herself that when the time came, she would expose her new daughter-in-law as a sham. She was sure she was a sham. And certainly, time would prove her correct.

Dilly, while neither devious nor an empty shell, had always harbored doubts about himself. In his most introspective moments, he considered himself somewhat of a phony. Even back in college days, maintaining a decent low honors average, he wondered how much he really knew. Were his grades simply a result of his organized mind? Or did he honestly grasp all the new concepts presented by his professors? They liked him. In fact, everyone liked Dilly. He was attractive, which never hurt anyone. He had and has a slender, angular face, with skin and tissue handsomely arranged on an aristocratic gathering of bones. Even his hair cooperated. Just blond enough but not so blond to be showy or vulgar. It was thick but lay flat, quickly responsive to a brush, and with a tendency to move with his head movements. His nose was what we call patrician, just a tiny bit too long, but it didn't matter. The eyes, wide apart, deep set, were gray-green and were accented by healthy eyebrows, startlingly black. His mouth always hid a smile but with a little encouragement would flash into a broad smile that was both genuine and likeable. Occasionally, people stopped him for an autograph because of a definite resemblance to the actor Jeremy Irons. He was refined and handsome and looked as though he should live in the elegant homes of his family. As to be expected, his grooming and manners were impeccable. And he had a quick wit, a seemingly facile mind, and that engaging smile. He even smelled good, having taken an early interest in good and expensive men's colognes. That use of fragrance could easily be interpreted as an affectation, considering the solidness of Dilly's personality, but in truth, he enjoyed the subtle presence of a fine fragrance. It certainly wasn't a closeted feminine trait but simply a personal expression. His two favorites were by Jean Laporte—Mechant Loup and Premier Figuier. Now and then, for variety, he'd use Armani. His clothes looked like Polo, whether they were or not. It was old-money dressing, sensible, not splashy, richly conservative, and it suited him. He was remembered by both sexes in college as a "terrific guy," "dependable," and a "solid citizen."

The girls he dated would fall in love with him for a few minutes. His money was sexy, and he was certainly cute enough. But his lack of passion made all those relationships fade away. He seemed to date the same girl. She was always slender, never sloppy, with straight or just barely curled blonde hair. Her curves were always minimal, and her posture and taste in fashion impeccable. His deflowering, now barely a memory, was in the off-campus apartment and arms of Jillian Montrose, a twenty-year-old junior from Bloomfield Hills, Michigan, president of her sorority, honors student, and an aficionado of rough sex. Had Dillworth even heard the term *rough sex*, he would have paled, but following his own biological time clock, he had determined it would be unhealthy for him to abstain longer, and with a little encouragement on her part, he found himself nibbling on the bare breasts of Ms. Montrose and shortly thereafter doing what comes naturally in the missionary position. He remembered the incident with some embarrassment, recalling his ineptitude and wishing that it would end, not enjoying the sighs and her penchant for uttering such C-novel exclamations as, "Give it to me, Dilly … give me more of you … deeper, deeper." He remembered thinking, *Surely, this isn't what everyone's so excited about?* In retrospect, it was agreeable but certainly not something that would or could guide his major decisions in life.

Once the necessities of college life had been dealt with, and he had his BA from Northwestern University and the MBA from Yale in hand, Dilly entered the high-anxiety world of McKinsey and Company, the corporate analysts. He came to love the drama of living with a company for a certain period and then analyzing all its strengths and weaknesses. His coworkers found him to be a tower of energy. His disciplined nature served him well in the high-pressured halls of McKinsey. There were demands and deadlines, reports, and recommendations, and the future of companies often were in the hands and heads of these young, dynamic corporate analysts. Dilly's point of view was highly regarded by his peers and seniors. He knew it stemmed from his ability to interpersonalize the problem, to mentally make himself part of the company, to mentally install himself as the CEO, and then make all his decisions from that viewpoint. His high percentage of correct decisions paid off, and he moved up through the company in relatively few years and was made a partner.

Dilly knew he did not have to make his own career. The corporations, factories, and industrial complexes that the family owned and controlled would have to be managed. It was certain his sister, Elizabeth, had zero interest in controlling any of it. She just wanted to maintain her $3 million annual allowance and was delighted to turn it all over to her younger brother, who, she realized, was probably smarter than Dad, was one of God's good people, and would never stoop to injure his sister, emotionally or financially. She was right. But he stayed with McKinsey long enough to learn everything he wanted to learn about other industries because he knew there were huge opportunities that his father was overlooking. But he wouldn't countermand his father until he was given the right and the opportunity to do so.

If Anyone Had Asked Bettina, "What's the Tallest Mountain You've Ever Had to Climb?" She Would Have Named It Edwina

ven now, though accepted by the world at large as Mrs. Dillworth Richardson, every moment of that evening remained etched in Bettina's memory. "Well, Bettina, how nice to finally meet you."

"Thank you, Mrs. Richardson. It's so good of you to invite me."

Tsk-tsk. She sounds as though she's auditioning for the lead in Pygmalion. *Perhaps I should ask her where it rains in Spain.* "What a lovely dress." *A cheap knockoff of a good design, but she does have a good body, and the color complements her.*

"I'm Elizabeth Catarsi, your future sister-in-law, and that tall, handsome man over there is Teddy, my husband. I like your dress too. That color is *wow* on you but would wash me out."

Bettina turned to see Dilly's face, softened by a slight roundness and a splash of mahogany hair. But even better, there was a warm smile and laughing eyes, which helped Bettina thaw from the laser coldness of the mother's icy welcome. "Hi, Elizabeth. This is very exciting and a little scary, meeting all of Dilly's family at once."

Elizabeth was a godsend. As she walked Bettina into the room, she quietly advised her, "Mother will play twenty questions with you. Just look her in the eye and answer her as direct and simple as possible. We'll protect you if the going gets tough."

Bettina stopped hyperventilating internally and turned to greet the senior Mr. Richardson, Roland Hughington Richardson, who was examining her with open curiosity. She felt no animosity in his appraisal, but she did feel stripped bare. He smiled. "Hello, my dear. Welcome to the family." He gently pulled her hand to him and bent slightly to brush his lips to her knuckles. She felt he was conquerable. Mother was still a high hurdle, and she didn't feel strong enough to clear it tonight. "Teddy, come over here and meet Dilly's beautiful treasure."

She recognized Teddy's expression totally. She'd have to be careful to never be alone with Teddy. He wanted her naked and was sure he was the only man alive who could make her happy. What a pig. Married to the beautiful and desirable Elizabeth wasn't enough. He wanted more. And his refined brother-in-law had that something more. "How do you do, Teddy. I'm so glad to meet you and Elizabeth."

"That goes double for us," he said, while massaging her hand.

She reclaimed her hand and turned back to Mrs. Richardson, who looked as though her son had brought a native Eskimo into the parlor. "I'm delighted to meet the family, Mrs. Richardson. Dilly—Dillworth—has told me so much about each of you, I feel as though we've already met."

"Well, then, my dear, you're well ahead of us. That naughty son of mine has kept you all to himself. Now that I've met you I can understand his infatuation."

Dilly, who hadn't uttered a word yet, butted his words right up to his mother's, with—was that a slight edge to his voice? "I'd say it was a bit more than infatuation, Mother. Bettina has consented to marry me, and we've selected this September 17 as the date."

"So soon, Dilly? Don't you think—"

"No, Mother, I think there's plenty of time for invitations and all the wedding plans. For the first couple of years, my apartment will do nicely for us until we decide precisely where we want to reside."

My God, it's fait accompli. Very well, I'll endure it for the moment, but I'll find a way to pierce your armor, Miss Bettina Whatever-Your-Name-Is. And I don't believe the Bettina part, either. "So, Bettina, tell us about your family."

By contrast, the Spanish Inquisition was a musical comedy. Mrs. Richardson parried and thrust, again and again, and Bettina found within her enough adrenaline and spunk to answer the questions, with a lighthearted smile or embarrassed giggle, even though many of the queries bordered on cruel and made Dilly and his sister flinch. Dilly's father was enchanted, and sister Elizabeth, not believing all that she was hearing, didn't care. She liked Bettina. She admired her goal-line stand with mother. She would be her friend. Whether she would ever know the true Bettina didn't matter, at least not right now. She was beautiful. Dilly adored her. And she had balls, something she and Dilly hadn't had to grow, as long as their behavior, both public and private, was within the realm of acceptability by Mother.

Edwina thought Bettina was unnaturally perfect, her gestures too studied, the walk too practiced, the demure turn of the head or lowering of the eyes too theatrical. She kept a close watch for chinks in the veneer. She also kept her doubts to herself, not just because she didn't want to interfere with her son's choice but also because she feared his turning to call girls, as his father had, to accommodate his nastier sexual needs. The elder Richardson never knew his wife was aware, and she had convinced herself it wasn't important. But she did care about Dillworth, who thus far hadn't given her any major concerns, except, of course, in his choice of Bettina.

CHAPTER 6

Bettina Understands the Meaning of Being between a Rock and a Hard Place

Bettina recognized "Mama's" doubts. And one night, after going "all the way" with "mouth sex"—because "I love you more each day, my daring Dilly"—Bettina told him she had had a nightmare. "Something happened to you, and your mother, who always treats me nicely, threw me out into the streets. It was so real, Dilly, I just lay awake for hours, crying." Dillworth, having seen his mother querulously eyeing Bettina, thought it could be true and generously signed over $10 million to his bride in an unusual postmarital agreement. It was hers to do as she wished.

"Oh, Kiki, you are too much," Bettina giggled into the phone, thinking what a total asshole Victoria King Van Holten really was, "and of course you're right, as usual. Her paintings aren't worth the canvas they're painted on, but yes, I'll be at the opening. Looking forward to seeing you, you gorgeous, mean creature. Toodle." *Toodle, ugh. I may throw up. Since I have the ten million, how many years do I have to keep this up? I know—forever. Because there's another hundred million if I wait around. Not bad pay for playing my part.* Emerson, their butler, interrupted her conversation with herself as he presented the mail. "Thank you, Emerson. Would you please bring me some tea? The mint would be nice."

The one envelope was irresistible. On the outside, it read, "We know what you're thinking and what you would like to be doing." The letter inside reached out at Bettina, opening old wounds, bruising tender spots. It was divine revelation. Whoever Madame DeSantis was, she existed for one purpose—to elevate Bettina to a newer and higher level of being.

The letter read:

Dear Bettina,

Like all of us, some days are better than others. The difference for me is there are no bad days, just good days and wonderful days. Today is one of those wonderful days. I am looking through my tarot cards and thinking about you because your birthday is approaching soon. I drew a nine of cups. Alas, the card was upside down. A robbery is in the making, which you could prevent by being more cautious. You think you're insulated from day-to-day crimes, but that isn't so. Next, was the Tower, also upside down. This is serious. You could temporarily lose freedom, just because you are vying for material gain. You must be cautious, Bettina, or you will bring trouble down upon yourself. And there is so much more I can tell you, not just today but every week and every month ahead. I hesitate to tell you about the third card. It can be read two ways. But I know what it means in terms of you.

I am Madame DeSantis. For three decades, people of great wealth and position have relied on me to tell them what lies ahead and which way to turn. I have served princes of industry, one president, many cabinet members, and yes, even royalty, whom I cannot name. Movie stars and bankers and world-famous surgeons have all turned to me. Why? You may ask yourself that very question.

You have heard that we are all merely pawns in the hands of fate. That isn't true. You are master of your own destiny. The difference is knowing which path will lead to a new opportunity or help you avoid a possible catastrophe.

I know the secrets that you hide. And you should have no shame for them. I know what you want. I too have wanted the very same things. We are both unusual women, Bettina Richardson. Your life is a two-edged sword. One edge cuts through the undergrowth and red tape of life, leaving you in golden sunshine; the other side can cut you deeply, leaving you in deep pain, with your tenderest parts exposed to the world. You must know which side to wield.

If you use the coupon enclosed in this message, my first reading to you will be for a negligible twenty dollars instead of the normal fifty dollars. And besides the reading, I will reveal to you the third card I drew while thinking of you. Ah, Bettina, do not delay. There are many forces bearing down on you. They are both good and bad, and I want you to emerge glorious and victorious in the golden sunshine. Meanwhile, I am both your friend and your humble and obedient servant.

With ever-lasting affection,
Madame DeSantis

Bettina read the letter at least five times, and each time the message became more intimate. It no longer spoke to the mythical Bettina but to Bethel, a name she had so pushed out of her mind it was nearly forgotten. She rushed to write the check and send it to Madame DeSantis after having no success finding her by telephone. This was what she needed. Madame DeSantis would help her survive—in grand style.

CHAPTER 7

You Don't Know Me. My Name Is Kenneth, and I'd Like to Introduce Myself by Telling You about My Childhood and How I've Come to Influence This Bettina Person You Just Met

First, my childhood—my mother had painter's eyes. That she was a horror among womankind is another story that I will share with you. But I thought first I'd lull you into believing this to be a story of familial bliss by telling you the solitary positive gift she left me. Even though I still damn her memory, the legacy of her eyes almost makes me want to forgive. While she wouldn't lift a brush due to ennui or unadulterated laziness, she saw beauty or at least line and form in the commonplace. She was especially moved by ever-changing skies. Even now I study the sky every day. I'm eager to wake up early so I can greet the sunrise and share its mythical pleasures. And a fiery sunset seduces me, as it turns late day clouds into gold-touched jewels.

I am touched by the memory of her stopping the car and telling me to "Look to the horizon, Francis [more about my name later]. That's the straight-line way off in the distance. And those bumps in the line are little towns populated with people who realize their dreams. "People"—and I remember her voice growing acidic "people who don't have to live with the likes of your father." So much for my memory. Thanks be to a higher power, whoever he, she, or it may be, Mother is long dead.

For some unexplained reason, today's sky was taking me back to one of many troubled childhood days. Giant cumulus clouds had blossomed in a too-blue sky, following a horrific storm, which painted the landscape pure white, gray in the shadows, with hints of mauve. And in the early morning and late daylight, it was splashed with yellow gold. Midday, with a blazing sun overhead and the temperature in the single digits, branches of the trees created a jigsaw across the snow. Walking, it creaked and squeaked, and on the trees the snow was transformed into puffs of newly picked cotton—every branch and twig so artistically adorned it appeared hand-done, instead of art directed by Mother Nature.

The policemen came to the door, their eyes gentle, full of sloppy sentiment. "Son ... son, there's been an accident." The roads were slippery that day, and I visualized my parents' car spinning out of control, Mother screaming, my father panicked, turning the wheel pointlessly, yelling at her to shut up as the car dropped over the side of a trestle bridge, hurling them to sure death. I bit my lower lip and tried desperately to look frightened. One of the cops stooped beside me, took my two shoulders in his hammy lower-class hands, and looked at me with his stupid wrong-side-of-the-track eyes, and said—shit!

It was only fantasy. They came home that night for yet another evening, another year, another lifetime of bickering. Strange how I can remember that one afternoon among so many lonely, cold, haunted afternoons. Had I been able to speak at birth, I would have told my parents how much I hated them. For starters, Francis was a stupid name for a boy. I was taunted and teased and soon learned to live by my wits. My name should have been Richard the Lionhearted. Or Beowulf would mirror some of my inward passions. When I finally escaped my parents' ungenerous grasp, I summarily dropped the hated Francis. I had been named after an obscure uncle they had hoped would leave them something. My middle name was Kenneth, which was good enough.

I guess I never knew jack shit about life, but what the hell did one learn about life when one lived in *Lost* Angeles. If the sun didn't make you mushy-brained, the layers of bougainvillea and the bastardized Spanish architecture would dissolve your hard edges before you ever developed any.

So I didn't have a clue—so what? There were private things I knew. Things I had no right to know for my age. Naw, I wasn't precocious. That word's too cute. And God and Aunt Jemima knew I wasn't gifted. I guess, I guess, I was wise. A young, wise old man. I remember my childhood, painfully and permanently etched in my memory bank. My peer group was moronic. As all suburban children do, they played sandlot football and baseball. I hated the physical aspect of football, and baseball was like watching grass grow. When not beating up on one another, they built tree huts and wasted their days fantasizing, first about castles, then about cars, and finally about girls. I participated to the extent necessary to cover my disdain for them.

But even then, I realized how easy it was to manipulate people. How willing individuals were to turn their lives over to anyone with a strong point of view. I was only a kid, but even then, I knew the world was full of suckers. Little did I know I would become an adult lollypop full of instant gratification with sweet promises of more to come.

Perhaps I came by my gifts naturally. My father, Donald Monroe, never did an honest day's work. If there was a way to goldbrick, shirk, slack off, and malinger, he would find it. Over the years, he sold dictionaries, mainly to people who would never crack a book; vacuum cleaners, which gave him an opportunity to clean up in numerous women's bedrooms, according to my suffering mother; and telephone pitches, followed by personal visits to sell snake-infested rock-quarry land in Arizona to unsuspecting retirees. If he had an ethical bone in his body, it had dissolved in his own acid years before. He was shallow but noisy.

I suppose he was good-looking if you didn't see past the surface. He had one of those small, trimmed mustaches that seem to go hand in hand with an unctuous personality. He was rangy, tall, and, without a drop of exercise, possessed a fatless body, which, topped with wind-blown curly hair, gave him an almost sexy, almost athletic look. It's difficult for me to praise any facet of old Dad, since my recollection of him produces a moldy portrait. Added to his ample list of minuses were his excesses. Ever present was an unfiltered cigarette, evident in his stale breath and stained fingers. And now, older, I realize alcohol was a constant companion. How they afforded these excesses—for I will make no effort to whitewash my unsainted mother—I cannot tell you. Their foundation was quicksand; their dreams were borrowed from the misfortunes of others. I suppose they managed somehow.

Was there ever time for me? Do I remember walking hand in hand with Dad? Did I build sandcastles with my mommy? Did someone tuck my head in the soft curve of his or her neck and rock me, crooning lullabies? Not even close. I was an impediment. A mistake resulting from drunken coupling, something to push aside. And to ensure a lasting influence of their negligence, three years after I made my unwelcome arrival, they had the gall to further insult the reproductive process by bringing Annette the Hun, my cursed sister, into a beleaguered world. I didn't know an older brother existed until years later.

But where, you may ask, is the mother of this picture-perfect group? To praise Ethel Annabel Monroe would be tantamount to electing Typhoid Mary as Mother of the Year. Forgive my unkind, un-son-like description of Mom. I remember her as chicken-breasted, with the thin legs that so often accompany incipient alcoholism, and determined mouse-hewed hair that curled across one side of the face, as unflattering as her artificial Hollywood voice, a direct steal from early Olivia de Havilland and Joan Bennett movies. She was a horror. With better looks and more courage, she might have also been a whore. Did she cook? No, she opened cans. Did she keep a clean house, a nest for her brood? Hah! She trailed debris. We entertained no one. She and Dad just faced off with one another, night after night. Strong amoral wills in a battle for supremacy.

Why do I tell you all this? Do I want your sympathy? Perhaps I insist that you recognize why I am who I am, why I do what I do. It's not necessarily a gift as much as a defense mechanism. It's in my genes. Fuck 'em first; ask questions later.

Strange, looking back, to realize my first scam was a harbinger of what was to come. I found an old Gypsy, down on her luck, scratching out the barest kind of existence, reading palms and spouting all kinds of guessed crap for a couple of dollars a throw. I asked her if she knew anything about drawing up an authentic-sounding horoscope or making predictions based on numbers. The old asshole really believed in herself and told me it was all true. I signed her up with a guaranteed minimum income, almost as minimum as she had before, and I started selling "professional, personal readings by a mystic … totally authentic … without the needless embarrassment of a personal call to your home or to the mystic's home. Monthly (or weekly) guidance for only twenty dollars each reading, a minimum of two readings required."

I didn't have too much hope for this scheme. Wrote up the pitch, and arranged for it to be delivered to every mailbox in Manhattan's silk-stocking district, personalized to the mailing list. I still find it hard to believe all that happened.

Mind-boggling. Four thousand suckers each sent $20—$80,000. I had made a deal to pay "Madame DeSantis," alias Ruby Schmidt-Feller, $1,000 but decided it was worth it to give her $1,500, bighearted guy that I am, so we could personalize all these mind-fucking messages. Even after all the postage and printing, that first mailing was good for more than $50,000 profit. With a little luck, I could turn that $50,000 into a bonanza. And I was lucky. I just didn't know how lucky.

We were swamped by the emotional waterfall immediately following that first mailing. Bettina Richardson, now so dear to my heart, was just one of many. Empty people desperate to be filled with promises, no matter how hollow, promises of money, of long life, of dreams.

But the letter from Mrs. Dillworth Richardson couldn't be ignored. The notepaper itself was easily $2 a sheet, with raised gold engraving, and gold-washed edges. I had a friend run a D&B on Richardson and found he was on the Fortune 400 Richest list. Society books had little on his Mrs., other than her maiden name and vague references to having been educated in the Midwest.

She had requested a personal meeting and reading with Madame DeSantis and offered to pay $500 for the privilege. "Alas," I wrote back on some hastily printed Madame DeSantis stationery, "to interrupt my solitude and to meet personally, the fee is $2,000. And even then, there are no guarantees. The madame has to feel the necessity of a meeting." Bettina's answer was in the return mail. Besides the $2,000 in her note, Bettina said she would rent me, alias Madame DeSantis, a suite in the Waldorf for two nights. I (we) answered, and a date was set.

Next was how to make Ruby (i.e., Madame DeSantis) more appealing. Her normal drag was right out of Barnum & Bailey. Her hair was a deep henna rinse, pulled tight to the back of her head, with a braided bun laced with silk scarves. She had Cleopatra eye makeup, for God's sake, and big, showy, campy '40s glasses. And the outfit! Layers of color and print, with a wide belt with signs of the zodiac, moon earrings, crystal-ball rings on two fingers, and Moroccan-style felt slippers. Pure crap. I found a woman who specialized in makeovers and hired her for $300 to do a complete makeup job and costuming and said that I would pay for the costume. That ran another $350, but it was worth every cent. Old Ruby looked terrific. Her washed-out gray hair, now sans henna, was still pulled tight to the back of the head, with a zodiac stick pin as a quiet accessory. Dignified woman CEO makeup, which looked perfect with new gold Ben Franklin wire glasses, replaced the Cleopatra eye makeup. And the outfit was pure genius. Subtle and perfect. Gunmetal flannel, high-necked, long-sleeved, midcalf length, with a line of black braided buttons from the shoulder to the hem. The belt, more of the black braid. One small pin, a gold crescent moon. We even kept one of the crystal ball rings. A black felt low-heeled pump over dark, not black, hose. You'd vote her in as prime minister.

We rehearsed everything and anything she might be asked and what to say. Bighearted me promised her another $200 if all went well.

And me? What role was I to play? How could I be there and exert the necessary control? The answer came to me about a week later. I bolted upright in bed and turned on the light and began scribbling notes before the thought faded. What could be more appealing or irresistible? I would be Madame's disciple, a devoted follower who had followed her advice and gained stature and now was assisting her in her efforts to impart wisdom. Perfect.

And best of all, no disguise was necessary. I could be me, spruced up to appear prosperous, and God knows I knew all the right moves. Role-playing was my life, and this was a role I was born into. The big question was whether Mrs. Dillworth Richardson would buy it—hook, line … and checkbook.

The nights were the worst for me. Sleep wasn't in the cards. Just thoughts of the upcoming meeting and the opportunity it presented kept my motor running. I couldn't turn off. What if old Ruby blew it? What if this Bettina Richardson had a brain after all? I know, I know—I'm projecting. Cool it, Kenny. Kenneth sounds good. No more Francis, no more Kenny. I'm now Kenneth Monroe, a disciple, a believer, and a follower of Madame DeSantis.

Maybe I wouldn't have made the cover of *GQ*, but little children didn't run screaming when they saw me. Maybe it was my lack of self-esteem, but the person I knew in the mirror didn't turn me on. But maybe it wasn't all bad. Even though my hair was a dead-mouse brown, it was thick and only needed some daily care. My nose was slightly long, and it just traveled downward, except for one slight lump to one side, a reminder of a boyhood spat. But my eyes were something else. When I taught myself to stop looking away so people wouldn't say I looked shifty, I had almost bottle-green eyes. When I learned they had an almost hypnotic quality, I learned to drill everyone I spoke to … or listened to. My mouth was pensive and my lips soft, almost effeminate, and emphasized every expression as weak.

But trust me, friend, weak I wasn't. That I looked vulnerable suited me fine. How could anybody who looked as gentle as I be dangerous? Even though anyone I ever "helped" would never forget me. All in all, I was pleasantly forgetful, except for my eyes.

It was fun. I had money in my pocket and took my five-foot-eleven acceptable body to Saks Fifth Avenue. I knew I didn't look like I belonged there, and for a long time none of the salesmen would approach me. Finally, one nice looking gent in his fifties asked if I needed help. I explained I was in the market for at least two suits, perhaps a sport coat, some slacks, shirts, and a couple of ties. Let me tell you, friend, clothes may not make the man, but they don't hurt. The new Kenneth Monroe, right down to his Ferragamo slip-ons (I splurged), wasn't quite so forgetful. A good haircut, some Italian tortoise-shell glasses, and I looked like a man who was on a big winning streak. A woman even eyed me as I was buying a good, manly, citrusy fragrance from the Armani counter. How long had it been since there was a woman in my bed? I didn't want to think about it. Someday, maybe soon, I'd be able to buy what I wanted as a bed partner. But first, Bettina, whoever you are, let's make beautiful music together. I'm ready; are you?

CHAPTER 8

Bettina Was Ready for Something, but She Didn't Know What ... or Why

Why touch something that didn't need to be touched? She knew she had the ten million, and the rest would eventually be hers if she stayed in character. Why this need to delve into her own secret self? She was increasingly aware of her growing boredom with her socialite husband and, at the same time, questioned her own boredom. Dilly was good and decent, and God only knows why he loved her. But she convinced herself to privately mock his manner and gestures, all of which he was born into. She stifled yawns during the sex act, yawns he didn't deserve. Although never overly promiscuous, the men in her world were not inclined to romantic coupling; she had known only rough, hard sex. She thought once, and the thought had frightened her, how nice it would be if Dilly died. When he took the occasional business trip, she uncharitably wished the plane would fall from the sky. Bettina only wanted what she wanted. There was no room for generosity or caring. But now she spent the day thinking of the mysteries soon to be revealed to her.

Emerson, both butler and captain of the house, who very secretly thought the young Mrs. Dillworth was common, although she didn't treat him badly, wondered what was gnawing at her. Bettina wandered through the Sister Parish-decorated, twelve-room unit on Fifth Avenue, facing Central Park. She might have been in a furniture showroom as she paced from one room to another, now and then perching on some spindly antique or huddling up with herself on an overstuffed sofa. She wasn't aware what she was doing, but Emerson saw it and wondered what the hell she was looking for.

In the library, she doodled cocktail glasses and bottles of champagne, even though she wasn't much of a drinker. During her visit to the morning room, with its silk walls and empire furnishings, dominated by a fine Monet, she filled in one word in the *New York Times* Sunday puzzle, something she never played. The kitchen lost a celery stick during her trek, and she devoted thirty-five minutes in her bedroom, rearranging all her fragrances. Her husband's study lost a small bronze but gained a pair of crystal Steuben animals. The Biedermeier dining room, with its deep red walls and splashy Frankenthaler paintings, was untouched. No, the floral arrangement in the center of the table was replaced with a collection of silvered bronze figurines, which, obviously too small for the scale of the room, were replaced by a collection of unmatching crystal candlesticks. Meanwhile, every room gave Bettina an opportunity to look at a different facet of her life.

What did she want besides the $10 million? Was she through with Dilly? Would she be better off in Europe? Were her needs sexual? Or purely financial? Was she bored with her life? Did she need something that was just for her? *I mean, what's-her-name paints. Maybe I should become a painter.* Social work is too, too … dirty. Unpleasant. Sick people. Poor people. Wrong. Could Madame DeSantis expose her? No, no, no. *She will be my friend. I need a friend who knows me for who I am.* Had she been able to foretell the future, she never would have answered that letter. A living scam herself, Bettina was a natural and willing victim.

CHAPTER 9

Madame DeSantis Was Destined to Play a Major Role in Bettina's Life

"Ruby—I mean, Madame—let's go over it again."

"Kenny—I mean, Kenneth—this is all bullshit. You think this rich lady is so batty in the head that if I tell her to fork over a million dollars to spread the word of Madame DeSantis that she's going to do it? You're batty in the head. I look like Strom Thurmond's maiden secretary. She's going to take one look and run like hell, let me tell you. You are a mashugana. And if it works, you're gonna owe me more than any crappy two hundred dollars."

I really thought I was going to lose it, dealing with this old sack of shit, trying to make her understand what was in the offing. What a turd brain she was. "Ruby, haven't I paid you well until now? Took you off the fuckin' sidewalk and got some decent food in your belly and moved you to better digs. Isn't that true, huh, huh?"

"Big fucking deal. A scam is a scam. At least it was clean, and if I didn't feel like working, I didn't work. Now all of a sudden, it's 'Ruby, do this, Ruby, do that.' Why don't we just hang out a shingle that says, 'The Madame is in. Open every day ten to six.' It's all so much shit, Kenny."

"It's Kenneth, remember?"

"Kenneth, how could I forget? Now if I can only remember my own name. Schmidt-Feller has more sex appeal than DeSantis."

"Ruby, dammit!"

"Aaaah, forget it, Ken-neth. 'Ah, my dear Mrs. Richardson, and I know you will not object to my calling you Bettina. Let me have your hand. Mmmm, wonderful. So much has happened to you, and it is all nothing compared to your future.' And then while I'm studying her palm, my expression changes. I squint my eyes and furrow my brow—that's your word; I don't know what the fuck furrow means. And when she says, 'What's wrong? What do you see?' I force a fake smile back on my face, turn her hand over, and say, 'No, no, it's nothing.' She'll probably say, 'I can see it's something—not just nothing.' And I will turn to her with a look of real affection and reassurance, and say, 'It's nothing that we have to deal with now. I promise you. In time, in time. Not now. Now we're going to talk about what Bettina wants out of her life, and how Madame DeSantis is going to help make it all come true. But first, some tea. It's very special hibiscus tea, and it will open doors in your mind as we speak.'

"Somewhere during all this first part, she is going to notice you—you, sitting silently in one corner of the room, observing us and now and then staring out the window. When that time comes, I will explain who you are and why you are with me."

Bettina was more nervous than when she went on trial before Dilly's mother. She changed outfits three times, finally settling on an Oscar de la Renta suit. It was a curly mohair in a deep bronze color, with a military lapel flap that buttoned over the front, just showing a hint of blouse, which was apricot-colored satin. Burnished gold low-heel pumps and tailored gold jewelry completed the look. It was rich, underplayed, good taste in every aspect. Bettina looked her part and was prepared to play her role perfectly.

Madame DeSantis didn't look like Madame DeSantis—she looked like Bettina Richardson's mother should have looked. Very dignified, composed, peaceful. But immediately Bettina felt touched and moved by her presence. *God, she saw something in my hand, something bad, but . . .* "Madame, pardon me for asking, but who is the gentleman in the corner?"

"Oh, forgive me, dear Bettina. Kenneth, my dear Kenneth, come forward so I can present you to Bettina. Bettina, this is Kenneth Monroe. He came to me ... how many years ago, Kenneth?"

"Five, Madame."

"Yes, five years ago, contemplating suicide, a completely unacceptable premise to me, and to say he was down on his luck would have been a gross minimization of his problems. We studied together; he did all that I asked and became a man of such importance, of such stature that I was thrilled for him and with him. Knowing that my job is to be a parent with special insights, once he was positively heading in the right direction, I let him go."

Kenny moved toward Ruby and knelt beside her chair. He smiled at her warmly and turned to speak to Bettina, who was hypnotized by the physical exchange between them. "Money didn't matter. I had all that I would ever need. I suddenly realized that what Madame did for me she can do for so many others. And here was my opportunity to pay back, to give back, to a world that had given me so much. Despite her telling me to do whatever I wanted—I returned ... to be her disciple. I also make sure those she helps do not hurt her ... for, as you know, not everyone is trustworthy. I am her business manager."

"He makes it sound as though I'm a prizefighter. Business manager—*phaah.*"

I was getting ready to belt Ruby. She was straying from the script, but she redeemed herself. She took my hand, turned the palm over, and lightly kissed it.

"His belief gives me strength to go on, to continue resolving the lives of those whom I have touched. People like you, Bettina, who in turn have touched my heart." It was Academy Award time. The old bitch came through so good I could have kissed her. I promised myself to give her a bigger cut. Not too big, but bigger.

"And now, my beautiful Bettina, tell me your story, and I will tell you what I see inside of you."

CHAPTER *10*

Hah! Bettina Telling Her True Story Wouldn't Thrill Anyone Unless He Was a Student of the Dirty, the Downtrodden, and the Hopeless

Bethel Sokoloff was one of three children, each notable for his/her lack of specialness. Bethel was probably the least attractive of the trio, although with adulthood, her face caught up to her features, except for her nose. Not just a nose, it was, to the cruel neighborhood boys, "a studio apartment." A Jewish girl's nightmare. All the jokes about Jewish noses in one climactic statement, right in the middle of Bethel's face. A nose job during her transformation took care of that problem. The result? An adult face that bordered on perfection, self-trained to have expressions of arrogance, disdain, or idleness. Her eyes were gray/mauve, an unusual color that she accented with careful eye shadows in the same color. The hair was just blonde enough and had just enough body that a once-a-week visit to an expensive salon kept it looking flawless. Now and then, like today, she french-twisted it; other times let it fall casually, rich-girl style, to her shoulders. It always looked good. God gave Bethel trim ankles and good skin, and the rest she gave herself. From sloppy early eating habits, she had whittled her body down to a lithe size 6 or 8, which looked perfect on her five-foot-seven frame. And she kept it there. Admitting that she adored every form of junk food ever created, she banished those tastes from her mouth, probably forever, and ate only what was necessary to keep herself alive. At this point, truthfully, it was no longer an effort to avoid bad foods; it was the way she was.

Her parents, Moishe and Ruth, weren't bad people. They were just what they were. Lower-middle class, bordering on low, without the emotional or mental resources to do more than provide the basics for their children. They didn't scream at one another. They weren't problem drinkers, although one of Bethel's memories was of her mother sitting in a kitchen chair, rolling bourbon around in her mouth.

Moishe was a tailor, and she could see him still, with pins between his lips and the perpetual sad-eyed look that characterized his generation and his class. At least they didn't beat their children. They were just boring. Bethel's memory of them was a story without a plot. Monotony on top of monotony. A monotone chorus singing a one-note song.

Siblings Sam and Mickey (Michelle) were another story. Other than Sam making Bethel jerk him off when she was eleven and he was twelve, Sam was her idol. Big brother was tough, street-smart, and destined to do great things. Their genders kept them from sharing all the important stuff, like dreams, but Bethel knew that Sam had something special going for him. His death at age nineteen, while attempting a peanut-size robbery of a deli, ended life in the Bronx, if you could call that life, as they knew it, for Bethel. Nothing was the same, and it was at that point that she started looking for the nearest exit.

Mickey, her baby sister, found reward and importance in the sex act. The boy would feel he was in charge, but in truth she manipulated all of them. On her sixteenth birthday, she told her sister matter-of-factly, "I've fucked every Jewish boy in the high school. They think they've fucked me, but they don't know shit." Mickey had clap once ("Big deal—two shots and adios") and one abortion ("That hurt. I hope his dick falls off") and suddenly, at age eighteen, started dating the son of the rabbi. To Bethel's total disbelief, she married the boy and became a pillar of the temple. All the boys who stayed in the neighborhood always referred to her— privately, not in front of the rabbi or his family, who were big time in the neighborhood—as "Mrs. Saul Nussbaum, the tightest pussy on Grand Concourse." Mickey, now only called Michelle, never mattered. She was nonexistent from Bethel's standpoint.

Bethel herself? She worked at one meaningless job after another, hoping each one would be the beginning of the big break. She tried a real estate office, seeing the possibility of big commissions, and they gave her slum buildings to rent, dealing with pimps, whores, and drug addicts. Her boss, Arnie something-or-other, was a gross pig who weighed in around 375, who, when she came in to cry about her plight, offered relief, but she should start on her knees, right then, right there, in his office. Alas, poor misguided, poor stupid nothing that Bethel was, she acquiesced. She kept her eyes closed, and if his big belly hadn't kept hitting her forehead, could have imagined he was someone else. She never told any of them that she liked it. But given the options, she preferred "mouth sex," as Mrs. Dillworth Richardson would say, to the missionary position or variations thereof. She didn't want them lying on top of her. She didn't want the pushing, the grunting, and the inane comments. Cock sucking was neater. And what was it that famous writer Capote said? Oh yeah, cock sucking was the only way to maintain a firm jawline.

After real estate, she was a sales representative for a shop-at-home decorating service, a division of one of the big department stores. She told her supervisor she would do better selling to the male customers who called in, saying at the time, "I have the right head to deal with men." She certainly did. The commissions were fractionally more than what she would have earned pushing coffee and doughnuts over a Chock full o' Nuts counter.

Then she signed on for her self-designed intensive training course. On her days off, she'd walk down Madison Avenue and watch all the women. They were beautiful, whether they were beautiful or not. They knew how to walk, how to dress, and how to tilt their heads when they laughed. Their hair wasn't sprayed hard, like Bethel's. The colors of their clothing were subtle, except now and then there would be a rich-toned accessory. They had backgrounds; they had a future waiting in the wings. They didn't chew gum. They were everything she wasn't. But she watched, studied, read magazines, and watched TV shows about them. She found a reasonably good plastic surgeon in the Bronx—old but still practicing—and did him in his office, arranging a very special rate. That ended the nose problem forever.

There was no barter for the diction lessons. And to learn how to walk and dress properly, she had to rely on her own powers of observation. Neighbors thought she was strange. They'd hear Bethel, knowing she was alone, speaking in a soft, well-modulated tone about a world that didn't exist. "I'm crazy about the Miro show at the museum—just divine, really." "Did you read the review of Sondheim's newest? It sounds frightful." "There's the most marvelous bistro on First Avenue. You can't believe the food. I felt I was back on the Left Bank."

The Tiffany job let her take her show on the road. She also left the Bronx for the first time in her life and moved to a women's residential hotel ... a place where decent young women lived in New York. She never allowed herself to even think that she was bored. And when she caught herself thinking about going down on the elevator operator, she mentally slapped herself.

"So you see, Madame, I had a rather modest upbringing. We were comfortably middle class, which isn't terrible, certainly not poor, but modest by comparison with the standards by which I live now. After my parents' unfortunate passing, I came to New York and obtained the position selling at Tiffany's, and it was there I met Dilly—I mean, Mr. Richardson."

"Well, my dear, good things had to happen to you. Had I known you way back then, I could have told you all these riches would come to you. It was foretold in the stars and in your hands!"

Kenneth interrupted the exchange between Bettina and the Madame. "But why are you here? Why did you have to meet with Madame? What did you hope to find?" He leaned far forward, his arms crossed across his midsection as though he had a stomachache. His eyes never wavered from Bettina's. The intensity of his gaze unnerved Bettina. She got up and paced, unaware she was doing it.

"I don't know," she almost whispered. "Your letter said you know what I want and know that good things can happen to me and bad things, and maybe I need to know all that you know. Maybe I am living a lie. Maybe I will be robbed. Maybe I ... maybe ... maybe it's not enough."

"What's not enough, child?" Madame DeSantis had walked over to Bettina and put a protective arm around her waist, encircling her arm. "Open your heart, and you will find a good and caring person inside, and we, together, will make sure that person is given the opportunity to live life to the fullest."

I was flabbergasted with the poise and polish of old Ruby. She could bring a tear to your eye. *My God, Ruby—Madame—is wet-eyed. She can cry on cue. Holy shit!*

"Come, child ... come sit with Madame, and let's peel away the layers that keep you from feeling the warmth of the sunshine."

CHAPTER *11*

Madame DeSantis, Nee Ruby Schmidt-Feller, Was No Longer Role-Playing in the Strictest Sense

Without warning, Bettina had triggered memories buried so deep they never surfaced, even during her most introspective moments. Bettina was her Gila, reincarnated. Gila, her beautiful daughter, who probably was dead because of her neglect, or was it just bad luck? Now, could it be, was someone giving her a second chance? Her tears weren't a result of good acting. She approached this young woman with her heart, determined to protect her and guide her through a maze of human deceit.

Decades had passed since Ruby and Karl had migrated to New York City to find fame and fortune. They were young, in love, so being poor didn't matter. They knew that even though the streets weren't paved in gold, they would find real riches. And for a while, it seemed possible. Their New York wasn't the glitter of Manhattan; it was a cheesy apartment with linoleum as old as their parents, a miniscule refrigerator that barely cooled water, in a loud echo-chamber building that smelled of urine in the stairwells, with the arguments of fellow tenants ricocheting up and down the stairs and through the hallways.

Even then, New York was a city on the make. Sure, there were plenty of people doing the straight-and-narrow thing, the Christian work ethic, all that, but for every one of those there was a street-smart semicriminal mind looking for an easy buck or a determined immigrant who refused to stay poor. Back then, way back then, Ruby and her Karl fell in the latter category. Ethnic slurs didn't stand in the way of classified advertising in that period. "We Want German Girls to Clean Houses … we know how hardworking you are, and how clean you are … we have jobs for girls who can clean house as well as their mothers could." Within three days of arrival, Ruby was working. She was paid ten dollars a day for an eight-hour day. She was ecstatic. New York's dream was coming true. It was tougher for Karl to connect. With no special skill, he finally found employment on a construction gang, earning something equivalent to Ruby. He wasn't thrilled. He knew there had to be more and was determined to find it.

As Bettina stumbled through her story, Ruby, drowning in the painful memories that flooded Bettina's eyes, could think only of Gila, knowing she would be about Bettina's age. For the first time in twenty years, she recalled her pregnancy—the early months of extreme morning sickness, Karl's impatience with her poor health, her own delight in seeing her stomach begin to grow, the magic of feeling the baby moving and kicking, the discomfort of the final month. It was August, horribly hot; she had gained nearly fifty pounds and continued working because it was necessary. By the end of the day, the five-flight walk-up to their unbearably hot apartment left her trembling—weak, frightened, no more enthralled with pregnancy, and both anxious and afraid for it to end. Sitting there in the Waldorf Astoria, she could once again feel the water run down her leg as the water broke, all alone, for Karl was out drinking with the men, or so he said, not wanting to stay home with a cow. She managed to move her bulk downstairs one step at a time and, with a few dollars she had saved, took herself to the nearest hospital. God intervened. On duty was a Dr. Reiner, one generation removed from the mother country. Seeing her fear, he moved her into an emergency ward, delivered the child—a female, miraculously healthy since it had been deprived of prenatal care—and managed to keep Ruby there for three days until she left the hospital with the baby, without money, without knowledge, to go home to what? A husband who did not want a child? The good doctor had done all he could. She fell on her knees before him and kissed his hands, and he sent her on her way, placing a ten-dollar bill from his pocket in her purse, cursing his own life, not feeling strong enough to play God with people in this way.

Bettina, seeing the love in the older woman's eyes, told more truths than she had anticipated telling. Her parents weren't killed. They were merely poor, detached, who gave her nothing, emotionally or financially. She allowed as how she was a self-created aristocrat. Ruby heard it all through the morass of her own memory landslide.

"I don't know if it matters, Madame, but I am not what—or who—my husband thinks I am. You mentioned that I could be robbed? Who would rob me? Why?"

Kenneth resisted rubbing his hands together. *Honey, you're sitting right here in a room with the robber baron.* If she could have done it, Ruby would have sent Bettina running from the room, but she knew Kenny might hurt her, and besides, he already knew too much. Somehow, she would find a way to protect this child.

"What is the problem, Bettina?" Kenneth was standing in the shadows of the farthest corner, not wishing to physically crowd his pigeon. "Do you want your husband to make you financially independent?"

"That's already happened, Kenneth … if I may call you by your first name."

"Of course."

"My husband settled a … an … adequate … amount of money with no strings."

"He sounds generous and kind."

"That's a good description of Dilly. Kind, generous. You could also add boring, predictable, flat. I would fight with him, but he wouldn't even understand fighting. He'd just think I had gone crazy and probably have me committed."

"Do you love him, child?" Ruby patted her shoulder.

"I guess not. But I can't give you one good reason why. I thought I had everything I wanted until your letter came, and I suddenly needed something else."

Kenneth had strolled over slowly and casually. He plopped down beside her on the sofa and held his hands in a prayerful clasp under his chin. Looking downward, he said, "You sound just like me. Is this all there is? Is life one possession after another? Money for the sake of money? Pleasures for all the senses, except the soul? And the soul is the only sense that makes sense. Not in some religious, hocus-pocus way but to know that you exist for a purpose. And that's what that letter did, and that's why you came to Madame." He turned and took both of Bettina's hands. "Oh, Bettina, I know that you and I together can do magnificent things for a world that needs Madame." He looked at her and then turned toward heaven, his eyes drinking in some vision up there, and Bettina looked for it herself and found her heart beating faster. The moment passed, and Kenneth again looked at her. "Forgive me, my dear Bettina. I was lost for a moment, but I know when that feeling washes over me, I must respond to it. Oh ..." As he leaned forward, their clasped hands were pressed between their chests, and he touched his cheek to hers. Then abruptly, he let go of her hands and returned to the far corner of the room, gazing out of the window, leaning against the wall as though exhausted from the "happening."

After a long silence, Madame spoke. "Well"—she breathed deeply through her nose—"I believe we have all said and experienced quite enough for today. We need time to let new thoughts form, time for these new experiences to become memories. I want you to return home now, Bettina, and I will contact you when I feel strong enough to give you the kind of guidance you seek."

"Yes, yes, Madame. Both of you, I can't tell you ..." Bettina's eyes filled with tears. "I'm sorry, I ..."

"Sweet child." Ruby leaned forward and barely brushed her lips against Bettina's forehead. "Go in peace and think of a world that awaits you."

Five minutes, at least, passed, while Kenny paced, and Ruby sat sphinxlike. "I'll kill you if you hurt that girl, Kenny."

He was incredulous. "What the fuck does that mean? I was just thinking what a classy job you did, and now you threaten me? Fuck off, lady. We have a live one on our hands, and if we handle it right, we're both going to be living better than we ever did, in this or any earlier life." He mimicked Ruby's protective pose, with arms folded across her chest, and said, *"I'll kill you if you hurt that girl, Kenny.* Hah! I'll kill *you* if you let the pigeon go."

Ruby Schmidt-Feller, alias Madame DeSantis, was fighting the demons of hell, green and yellow vipers, hissing and snapping at her. One slid in behind her and sank his fangs into her neck. "Aaargh." She bolted upright in her bed, sweat soaking through her nightie, that moment of panic when one tries to determine if the dream is reality or just a dream. She sat there, almost panting, exhausted by the fear, and finally turned on her bed light and moved into the small closet kitchen and poured some milk into a saucepan. *Warm milk will help.* With the milk now warming her favorite mug, she moved into the sitting room part of her studio apartment and sat there, not hearing the night sounds of the city, hearing only the cooing of her baby. *"Guten Morgen, liebchen,"* she heard her own voice say as she bent over the corrugated box that held her infant. And looking up at her was Bettina's face. Ruby wept.

Kenny lay smiling at the ceiling in the darkness of his bedroom. *I know we lose if I move too fast. So I'll let her simmer in her own emotional juices. Ah, my sweet, delicious, rich Bettina, you and me—correction, you and I—are going to do so many good works. All we need are my brains, your willingness to be mind-fucked, and all that nice money the family was good enough to give you. Wonder how much? Two million? Five million? More? I'm going to remember you in my prayers every night. I want to make sure you don't get hit by a bus.*

CHAPTER 12

Bettina Knew She Had Changed. Bethel Had Faded Away. Beautiful Bettina Had Replaced Her. She Felt This Must Be the Way Women Felt and Looked when They Were Having an Affair

Her skin glowed, and her arresting mauvey-gray eyes seemed to have specks of gold. The Museum Ball was about as important a social gathering as there could be. Dilly was being added to the board, probably because he'd written a $5 million check to the museum a few months ago. She knew most of the women would be wearing black. It was the dead of winter, and while she usually planned on disappearing into a mass of chic people, tonight she wore Arnold Scaasi's jonquil-yellow satin ball gown. An enormous satin bow fell over one shoulder, leaving the other shoulder bare. It fitted her nicely curved bodice to the waist and then blossomed out in overlapping petal shapes. The color was startling, and the total effect of her blonde hair and sizeable yellow-diamond earrings made her a standout. Even the blasé Dilly noticed and commented, "What a lucky, lucky fellow I am." She pursed her lips at him and blew a kiss, smiling warmly and thinking what an asshole he was, but it didn't matter; nothing mattered. Now she had Madame DeSantis in her life, and wonderful things were going to happen.

"Oh, Anne, you look fabulous. That skiing in Vail does such things for you. I wish I had your talent and energy for sports." Bettina beamed and gushed and held both of Anne Danafours's hands, knowing as she said it that Anne's best talent and energy was in bed and that having run though most of the social register—and Bettina didn't care if that included Dilly—was now, in her boredom, turning to women, an idea that Bettina found ridiculous and physically repulsive. "Now, Harry, I don't want a big hug. Your beard gives me razor burn, and Dilly would be forced to take you out on Fifth Avenue and fight a duel."

Dilly was delighted to see Bettina participating so willingly. Usually reticent and not terribly social-minded, she not only looked the part tonight but was acting it as well. He wondered if his mother had noticed.

Lucy Terrington said, "She's really quite smashing, Edwin. I'm sure you agree."

"You're sure I agree about what?"

"Not what, dear, who—your daughter-in-law. Look at her. She's a standout tonight. I know she's not your favorite cup of tea, but surely you can't fault her tonight."

"Lucy, I can fault her anytime. It's strictly *entre nous*, but class is something you're born with, or it's a coat or hat that doesn't quite fit. Bettina, if that is her name, doesn't wear *our* class well."

Handsome young men of debatable sexual leanings passed "mahvelous," "scrumptious" hors d'oeuvres. And four bars, each with four bartenders, kept high spirits flowing. The dinner was just another catered dinner, although food-minded guests credited the museum's chef for having unusual side dishes, and besides, what you ate wasn't important. It was who saw you and what you said to whomever you said it. Show-and-Tell for high society.

One of the men at Bettina's table told a mildly risqué story, and everyone tittered appropriately, and Bettina thought of the stories she could tell. Eyelashes would drop into the soup, watches would stop, dogs would die.

She now and then sent wifely loving smiles across the table to Dilly, who was entranced by his wife tonight, who had everyone's eye.

Dilly was better than usual that night in bed, and Bettina allowed herself to be just a tad more physical, saying that the evening had keyed her up. Later, as she lay beside the sleeping Dilly, she realized that during the climax of the sex-making, the face of Kenneth Monroe, Madame DeSantis's manager, flashed before her. Strange.

CHAPTER 13

Kenneth Plans to Rob Bettina, While Ruby Plans How to Save Her

Kenneth paced, talking to himself. Ruby waited and watched, trying not to incite his anger, all the while trying to figure out how to extricate Bettina from the scam. "Okay, lady, so what do I tell you to make you loosen up the purse strings? What does Madame need money for? It's got to be a good enough reason. . . . uh, she's setting up a foundation to help people who have lost their way get back on track. Not bad, even if I say so myself. But naw, it's all too pat. That Bettina baby might see through it. She has more behind her than silver spoons and nannies. She might even be smart. Screwed up big time but not dumb. Why are you just sitting there playing dumb, Ruby? Make a contribution. This is your one-way ticket to Easy Street."

Ruby sighed. This didn't feel good. "Why don't we tell her I'm going under and need some financial help, maybe fifty thousand dollars, and you can keep forty-five thousand of it for yourself, and then . . . then we'll convince her to give a few million dollars to the poor. That would be the right thing to do, Kenneth."

"Ruby, Ruby, Ruby . . . you're dumber than dog shit. *We*, you and I, are the poor. Ms. Bettina is rich. And we—correction, I—am going to figure out a way to make it all right for Bettina to give me—that's us—at least a million dollars and maybe a couple. If you want to stay poor, that's okay by me, lady. But the game is underway, and you're already in it, so don't drop the ball, Ruby. Just follow my lead."

Herman Warshon, shortened from Warshonsky, was a small, unattractive man who had amassed a large fortune by ladling out dishonest legal advice for a piece of the pie. His clothes weren't even an attempt at fashionable knock-offs. Just cheap polyester, with spots here and there, attesting to his lousy table manners and lack of interest in dry cleaning. Behind the Ben Franklin glasses, there were mean eyes that looked at you with unmasked disgust. The scowl lines that ran from the sides of his nose downward could have been tattooed they were so prominent. His breath was stale, his complexion blotchy. And Kenneth hung on every word as though it was the Sermon on the Mount. "It's very interesting, Kenneth. You have a live one. I understand that. But the big question is how to fleece her. And the other big question is how much of it is mine? The answer to the second question is 40 percent."

"No way. I have the pigeon. I've set her up. I've done all the thinking, and—"

"Correction. You've done all the thinking up to now. You've thought as far as you can go. Now you need me. May I remind you of some simple arithmetic? Sixty percent of ten million is more than 100 percent of five million. Admit it, boy, you're out of your league. And you don't know how to pull it off. I do."

Kenneth hated Herman and hated the necessity of Herman. And if he could, he would dump Ruby right now, but she was a key player in this drama. He just had to make sure it had a profitable ending, even if nobody lived happily ever after except him.

CHAPTER *14*

Once Bettina Found the Madame, She Wasn't about to Let Her Too Far Out of Her Sight

There were little notes, flowers, and, once, a private invitation to lunch, to which Kenneth put a halt, not trusting Ruby to be alone with Bettina. From Kenneth's side, there were gentle notes from Madame DeSantis, never pushing, never asking for anything, just general advice. In turn, without asking, there were checks for $1,000 tucked in Bettina's return letters. She was completely hooked, and Kenneth was playing hard to get—not impossible to get but just out of reach, as Herman advised.

Just thinking about the Madame and the helpful advice she was getting had wrought a change in Bettina. She had more energy, was more focused, more cheerful. Dillworth noted it and approved. He wanted his bride to be happy and productive. Although they certainly had enough money to do anything they wanted, he worked hard. The Richardson empire was sprawling and, under his direction, constantly growing. Most of his days were spent with boards of directors or huddled with chief operating officers, determining the best course of action in a reactionary economy. As much as he loved Bettina, and he did, he didn't have the energy to cope with a floundering wife. Her new point of view pleased him. He asked her about it one night, and she said she was on a self-improvement kick. Besides cooking lessons, there were singing lessons, and she attended some lectures on managing one's finances. He applauded her and said there was nothing she could improve on, but secretly he was happy about the new Bettina.

The private investigators hired by Mrs. Richardson came up with zero about Bettina's past. There was no record of her parents or the plane crash that supposedly made her an orphan, and her schools didn't know her. It was as Mrs. Richardson had suspected. Bettina didn't exist. She was a created person. But who was the real woman behind the facade? Beyond the nonexistent past, the investigators said they had a couple of other ideas they wanted to pursue. Meanwhile, Mrs. Richardson kept the news of Bettina's history to herself, waiting for the right moment to expose her phony daughter-in-law.

Bettina had chosen the day carefully. None of the servants were on duty. The house was empty. She didn't think she could handle lunch on her own, so she had the Four Seasons send over a cold chicken creation, a light salad, and a mousse. She didn't want to appear too showy in front of Madame and Kenneth. She hoped her apartment didn't appear ostentatious. These were good people who did rich things without the accoutrement that one accumulated with actual riches.

"My child, what a treat this is. Kenneth and I usually have broth or tea and crackers for lunch. And oh, how lovely is your home. But that doesn't surprise me. Anything that is part of your life has to be gentle and loving." It was delivered to Bettina as if it were a blessing. Because it was heartfelt, Bettina responded in kind, with a teary-eyed hug of the older woman. Kenneth was amazed. *There's an unmistakable private bond between these two women, but who gives a shit?*

"Bettina, it's so nice of you to include me." Of course, Ruby had had to insist that Kenneth be invited. He told her if he didn't go, neither did she.

"My goodness, what a beautiful place this is. Madame and I, well, we live so modestly because the only thing to do with money is to help others, right?"

Bettina turned to Kenneth, her eyes bright with the fervor of being a part of something bigger and more meaningful than the day-to-day tedium of her life. The afternoon passed in a dizzying swirl of emotions. Of little importance, a tour of the home; more importantly, Madame's reaction to every subtlety, both spoken and otherwise. At times, Bettina wasn't sure whether Madame had spoken aloud or if her thoughts were just being transferred through some private telepathic channel.

"So, you see, Bettina, Madame DeSantis has provided an important service for humankind. Her advice to those more fortunate than the average person has resulted in charitable organizations and good will foundations and is already breeding a next generation of good works and good workers. But together, she and I are working on a concept that's so exciting, so— gosh, amazing—that I'm afraid to talk about it." *Not bad, Kenny, whatever it means. I sound pretty believable. And Bettina, or whatever the hell her name really is, is just lapping it up.*

"Oh, Kenneth, I want so much to be part of it all and to learn everything I can about Madame's favorite enterprises. Perhaps I can participate, both personally and financially."

Can you? Oh, baby, do fish swim? Do bears shit in the woods? I'm going to make your every wish come true, big-time. "Golly, Bettina, you're wonderful to make that offer. We'll see how our plans come together. But thanks so much."

> 2815 Chatham Rd. Apt. 4G
> Bronx, NY 10134
> Dearest Bettina:
>
> Beginnings are so difficult, especially when I don't know where I want to end up. I have dreams about you. I see you as a child, whatever that childhood was. I see into your fantasies. And now I find myself frantically looking for your future, afraid for you, wanting to protect you from evil influences. We must secret ourselves away some day and speak with open hearts about these things. Forgive me for taking this seemingly circuitous route, but I felt the need to write you right now. As always, I am your friend.
>
> Madame DeSantis

Ruby sealed the letter and mailed it before she could back down. Would Bettina understand that she might be in trouble? Would this help guide her out of any trap that Kenneth and that horrible Warshon man might be setting for her? Au contraire. The diffused, convoluted message only made Bettina's heart beat faster, convincing her that Madame was going to advise her to choose a correct path. She struggled to find the right words to communicate her understanding and devotion to Madame.

Madame:

I was thrilled to get your letter. Just knowing you have my past and present in your sight makes me feel secure. My fantasies and my future plans are tied, hopefully, to a new direction you will help me find. I know it was fate that brought us together, and your caring for me will carry me to a place I've never been. Whenever there is a moment when we can speak privately, you know I will be available. Thank you for calling me your friend …

Bettina

Meanwhile, Mrs. Richardson Continued Her Sleuthing, and Finally There Were Some Results

"We only got one thing, Mrs. Richardson, but it may be the break we was looking for."

Why, Mrs. Richardson thought, *must all private detectives speak as though they were raised in a B novel?* "What is it, Mr. Andragliemmo?"

"When this Bettina was working at Tiffany's and living in that woman's residence, she made a few phone calls to the same number in the Bronx, and we've tracked it down and know the names of the people who live there. They're not what you'd call social register. The old man, he's a no-talent, no-money tailor; his wife is some nothing slob, and we understand they had two or three kids, all grown now. Do you want us to continue investigating the individuals there or what? It's all typed up in this report."

"No, gentlemen, you've done very well. I'll read the report, but let's stop for the moment. Do you have a bill ready for your services to date?"

"Yes, ma'am. It would be great if we could get a check today."

"That's no problem. Please wait here, and someone will bring the check out. Thank you again for your services." Mrs. Richardson exited the room with a triumphant inner smile. *Now, Miss Bettina, I'm going to find out who you really are.*

Bettina, or at least her money, was the sun, and everyone else was in orbit around her. Herman Warshon was finalizing his plans for a magnet to grab her money. Kenny stayed focused on prompting Ruby, training her to be the con artist she had to be. Ruby spent sleepless nights worrying about her Bettina and how she could lead her from danger.

Dilly observed his wife as she toyed with a soft-boiled egg and skim-read the morning paper.

Feeling his gaze, she looked up and smiled. "Am I ignoring you, darling? If so, I apologize."

"No, my sweet bee"—a new nickname he had adopted for Bettina— "there's something I want to discuss with you."

"Oh?"

"I have a lengthy business trip to make—at least three weeks—mostly to Europe. First, I can't stand the thought of being away from you for three weeks. And second, I wondered if you'd like to join me the second week in Paris."

Thinking rapidly, worrying about Madame DeSantis's need to speak with her, Bettina also realized she could not deny her husband her company. Besides, it was time she took her act on an international stage. Handling the rich and powerful in this country was one thing but Paris! "How exciting. And romantic. Of course I'll come to Paris. Just give me the travel dates, and I'll be ready."

Dilly grinned like a schoolboy, took her hand, and leaned across to nuzzle Bettina. "You really please me, Bettina. I do love you, more every day."

The tears that moistened her eyes were real, Bettina realized with a start. *My God, maybe I'm honestly falling in love with Dilly, or who knows? I'll discuss this with Madame.*

Mrs. Richardson had been busy too. She called the name given her by the detectives—Moishe Sokoloff—and set up an appointment to bring some clothes that needed tailoring. The difficult part was appearing natural. She went to K-Mart, secure that she would not be seen by anyone she knew, bought a simple housedress, cheap shoes, and even some costume jewelry. She scarfed her head, hiding the hairdo. She wore only lipstick. She took a cab.

After looking at the old, casual slacks from her husband's closet, the sad-eyed man behind the counter said, "Sure, lady, these are all do-able, but it'd be better if I could measure them on your husband. You know, it's fine you say they need to be shortened by an inch and a half, but it might look different on him, you know."

"Yeah, Mr. Sokoloff. [*Yeah? My God!*] But he won't have them shortened, and I'm tired of them dragging. Boy, husbands and children are really something. I guess you're a husband, but did you ever have children?"

"Oy, did I have children. Two girls and a boy—but he's dead."

"I'm so sorry."

"So am I. Sam could have been sumpin. But you know, the wrong crowd, young toughs. He got shot."

"Oh dea ... gosh. That's too sad."

"Was it ever. And then my two girls. One did good for herself, married the rabbi, became a big deal in the neighborhood. She's okay, has a couple of kids, calls us maybe once a month to make sure we're okay. And then there's my Bethel."

"Bethel?"

"Yeah, a really different kid. I don't know. You know she never wanted to be what she is or what we are. So I guess she just decided to be someone else. You've heard stories like this before. Your kid grows up, does the usual dumb-kid things, then says she's gotta get outta here, and she does. Damn if she doesn't have a few bucks now and sends us money on a regular basis, which we can use but don't need, and offered to buy us an apartment in a better part of the city. But you know, we've lived here thirty-five years, and we ain't about to change now. You know what I mean?"

"Yeah, Mr. Sokoloff, I do know what you mean. What does this Bethel do now?"

"Hey, whatta I know? I think she's married to some swell. We don't have her phone number or address. She came one day with new winter coats for her mom and me, and she looked ... really good. You know, like those girls look in Midtown. The clothes weren't flashy, but I could tell the tailoring was, and I thought her earrings were real gold. Hey, it could be worse. I don't think she's doing anything dishonest."

Except living a lie, Mr. Sokoloff. "Golly, I'm taking too much of your time, Mr. Sokoloff. But thanks for everything."

"It's okay Mrs. . . . Mrs. . . ."

"Franklin."

"Okay, Mrs. Franklin. Your stuff'll be ready in a week."

"Thanks . . . a lot, Mr. Sokoloff. You're . . . a nice man."

He smiled his weak smile, peering at Mrs. Richardson over his half-moon glasses. "I try to be. Thanks for saying it. Bye-bye."

Strange, thought Dilly's mother. *I did like Mr. Sokoloff. And I'd bet money, even though betting is vulgar, that Bettina Richardson is really Bethel Sokoloff, an ambitious Jewish girl from the Bronx. But I'll save it 'til I need it.*

CHAPTER *16*

Paris Was a Superb Challenge for the New Bettina

Bettina wasn't mentally prepared for Paris. Without previous experience and not enough personal foundation to imagine the unknown, she was overwhelmed by its exquisiteness. Dilly had reserved a suite in Le Crillon, an eighteenth-century palace turned hotel. Even though she had become accustomed to their own lavish lifestyle and residences, the elegance of Le Crillon made her gasp.

Every moment of that week was touched with magic. One day, they drifted through the chateaus of the Loire Valley. Another day they focused on visiting all the treasures of the Louvre. There were unforgettable dinners—the one at Arpege especially stood out. There were aperitifs in cozy bistros and shopping excursions in stores more refined than anything stateside. And there was Dilly, enjoying her wide-eyed joy at being seduced, as everyone is, by this most beautiful of all cities. There was one spectacular side trip out of Paris. They took the high-speed train to Dijon, surrounded by fields of the yellow mustard blossoms. Bettina was amazed to find even the tracks were clean, which was anything but true on the American train lines. In Dijon, they rented a car and drove through the beautiful vineyard-sprinkled fields of Bourgogne. They lunched at one of France's culinary jewels, Georges Blanc, in Vonnas, about half an hour from the extraordinarily beautiful village of Beune. That luncheon, which took slightly more than three hours, was, according to the well-traveled Dilly, "the best meal I've ever had in my entire life."

Adding to the enchantment of this two-day excursion, they stayed in Chateau de Gilly, a relais chateaux of such magnificence they were both a bit in awe. It was a Norman castle, complete with moat and turrets and towers and arched stone passageways, and richness of décor unequalled in the finest American establishment. Their own room was unbelievable in scale. Besides two queen-size beds, there was a living room suite of elegant furniture in front of the huge fireplace and still enough room for a full pool table, which wasn't there but could have been. There was a small entrance hall sitting room to the suite, and the bathroom was approximately six hundred square feet, with inlaid marble and rich wood paneling. Bettina tried to take it all in stride, but she found herself saying *wow* to herself. Dilly made her laugh. He said he'd buy the place and change the name to Chateau de Bettina.

The trip home on the Air France Concord was pleasant enough, but anticlimactic compared to the lush, sexiness of Paris and the richness of the Bourgogne countryside. Bettina was enchanted. And Dilly had been . . . very loving. Bettina found herself studying him as he slept, seeing not his bankbook but his gentle yet strong face, even in repose. Her feelings toward him were confusing. Madame would help her sort them out.

CHAPTER 17

As Much as Kenny Hated Herman, He Had to Admire the Man

What a devious but brilliant thinker. He had to admit the plan was excellent. The Center for Self-Fulfillment. Herman knew of a piece of land we could show the pigeon as the future site and insisted on spending a few thousand dollars having a scale model made of "the Center" so she could visualize all the niceties.

Somehow, through another bad source, Herman found out that Dillworth had settled $10 million on his bride, with no strings attached. Ten million was just right for a "down payment" on something that would never feel a carpenter's hammer.

The ten million didn't seem to be a big problem. Bigger was dealing with Madame. Ruby was obviously fighting a demon from within. Every time Kenny tried to get her involved in the scam, he could see her retreat, even though she said she was right there. He had gentled his approach so as not to alienate her.

"Look, Ruby, when we get Bettina this far, showing the model, you have to expand on each of these functions. This section, for example, is for what?"

"Um, for people with physical problems?"

"No, but there is a section for physically challenged disciples. What else might it be for?"

"Addictions?"

"Hey, good girl, that's it. These are the drunks, the chain-smokers, the compulsive gamblers, and the sexaholics. And what do we do with them in this compound?"

"Well, we have counseling, and twelve-step meetings like AA, with inmates—"

"Disciples."

"Disciples ... sharing their stories to help others."

"And what's your role in this area, Madame?"

"Once a week, I address all of them about the importance of understanding where they are going and what they can do to help themselves get there. And once a month, I have a private audience with each one of them."

"Right, Ru ... Madame. Right on."

"You know something, Kenneth?"

"What's that, Ruby?"

"It really sounds wonderful. Why don't we actually do this?"

She's really losing it, stupid old asshole. "Yeah, I know it sounds very nice, but Ruby, we're not qualified to run something like this. It needs real doctors. It would take a boatload of lawyers to set it up, another ton of money to promote it, salaries to pay. No, no, no, out of the question. But I'm glad you like it so much. It means it looks and feels real to you, and that's what we have to communicate to Bettina."

"Yes, we have to communicate that to Bettina." Ruby was despondent with the thought but didn't know how to get out. She was afraid if she tried, Kenneth and Herman would hurt her.

CHAPTER 18

The New Bettina Was Afraid of Nothing

She carried the image of Madame in her heart and head and consciously passed every decision through her all-knowing friend. The result was an enhanced Bettina. Perhaps the chin was elevated a touch. The smile a trifle broader. The eye contact, where tentative before, reached inside its recipient. Where internally she was always grasping the correct enunciation, now the language flowed. No one really noticed the change, but everyone felt it. Dilly began to see new qualities, as did her social-set buddies. She had arrived.

Only Edwina Richardson wasn't buying it. She acknowledged Bettina was handling her role well, but every time she saw her, she saw Bethel Sokoloff and her sad-eyed father.

"Oh, this is such fun, Lisa. I haven't been to a showing of a new collection in, oh, eons."

"Bettina, dearest new old friend, with a body like yours, you don't have to go to every collection. Anything off the rack looks like it was made only for you. The rest of us, with imperfect hips—God, I hate my hips—too big or too small boobs, upper arms that are starting to jiggle, the PLMs, people like me, are always looking for the fashion that hides the most or accentuates our best. At this point, I think my only best are my earlobes."

"You're a true nut, Lisa, but I love every minute with you."

Lisa turned and looked at Bettina, whose eyes were moist and shining with friendship. "That's one of the sweetest things you or anyone ever said to me. I love being with you too." Lisa Gutwillig was slightly beyond her thirty-fifth birthday and was as natural as a woman of her social standing could possibly be. Always about five to ten pounds over the ideal weight, she dressed perfectly for her height and weight, combed her hair with her fingers, and had dark enough eyebrows and eyelashes that she wore only lipstick during the day and a light foundation in the evening.

When she first met Bettina Richardson, she felt Bettina's vulnerability, her uneasiness with the polished disdain of the social set. She liked her, although she felt instinctually that Bettina was hiding something. She decided that whatever she was hiding, it wasn't important, and the girl needed a friend.

For Bettina, Lisa was a gift from a guardian angel, a chum, and a buddy, someone to speak with every single day. And Lisa wasn't just a stylish spender of a rich husband's money. She was fun and inventive. It wasn't for many months that Bettina found out the big money in the Gutwillig house came from Lisa. That her husband, Frederic (called Fred by Lisa), though well-heeled and certainly gentrified, came from well-to-do but not rich circumstances. They had a fine marriage. He loved to work and increase the family fortune, and Lisa loved living. She was also a very good mother. Yes, there was a nanny and chauffeur and all the niceties that make mothering much easier, but she was a hands-on parent, now with two young teen sons. She went rollerblading with them, played softball, took them swimming, rock climbing, and even on a bicycle trip for two weeks through Province. They were loved, fiercely protected, and strongly disciplined. And they showed it. Timmy and George were deservedly the apples of their mother's eye. It was a whole new experience for Bettina to see and feel the value of familial love.

"Betts, check out this next rag. You'd have to be bulimic and underweight to put it on. And you can't wear panties with it."

"Honestly, Lisa." Bettina laughed, wondering if she would ever be able to see the humor of everything around her and have the mental capacity to comment on the passing scene.

"Aha, here comes the fat-girl stuff. Lots of loose panels that disguise the rolls. That one is kind of neat. Whatta you think?"

"I'd love it on you. I think the tailored look is better for me."

"Gunny sacks would look good on you. And that Scaasi gown you wore to the ball wasn't tailored. You were drop-dead gorgeous that night . . . and every day of your life."

"Stop! I love it, but you're embarrassing me. I'm glad you think I look all right. But I want to see a worthwhile, productive, valuable woman looking back at me from my mirror. Someone like you, although there can't be anyone else that good."

Later, having an aperitif at the Plaza, Lisa studied her friend. "You mean it, don't you? You don't feel you have much value, do you?"

"No, I really don't." Bettina wanted to tell her friend the real story but knew it could never happen. She also couldn't tell her about the Madame, in case Lisa thought that was strange.

"Look, sweet friend, you're still very young and have time to enrich your life a thousand ways. Meanwhile, you've brought so much life to Dilly, who, until you came along, was a real cold fish. And you certainly have value to me. A day without Bettina is a day without sunshine."

Bettina reached across the table grabbed Lisa's hand. She hung her head so the tears wouldn't show. She lifted her head, smiled that brilliant smile, and said, "I'm so lucky. And you're right. I must be valuable. How else could I have a friend like you? Well, what's the latest with Timmy and George, and poor Fred? Is he still working around the clock?"

"And loving every minute of it. I've given him an ultimatum. We're taking a fun vacation a month from now, and hey, why don't you and Dilly come with us? Oh, why didn't I think of that before now?"

"What are you talking about?"

"I've reserved a fifty-foot trimaran—you know, those sailboats with three hulls—to spend a week tooling around the British and American Virgin Islands. It sounds delicious. There's a captain, a mate, and the captain's wife. They do all the care and feeding of us, and now and then we anchor off some perfect little island with snowy beaches and swim and sun and drink as much rum as is legal."

"It sounds like true paradise … but we couldn't possibly interfere with a planned family vacation. That's not fair to all three of your boys."

"Are you kidding? They'd be thrilled to have other people to protect them from their snarly mother. Besides, the boys adore you, and I have a feeling that Dilly might show a whole different side of himself with the kids around. And they are good kids, as you know. And don't worry about Fred. I'm secure enough to put myself out in a swimsuit next to you. He's crazy about you, and I know he likes Dilly. So let's do it! Nail Dilly's feet to the floor when he comes home this evening. The dates are April 19th to the 27th. The kids have spring vacation, so we're not flexible on the date."

"I love the idea. Although I'm not a great swimmer …"

"You can go to the Athletic Club this month and take a swimming course. There's a marvelous hunky instructor there."

"I'll speak with Dilly tonight. Thank you so much. It sounds unbelievably wonderful."

CHAPTER *19*

The "Scammee," Bettina, Was Going for the Hook

Warshon disliked Kenny as much as Kenny disliked Warshon. "Even when you're holding all the cards, you play it close to your vest. The net net is that even if you win, you lose. Playing to win is not for the faint of heart. Look, the pigeon wants to roost. She's dying to roost. And you're wondering how to get some pocket expense money out of her. Stupid! That's what you are. Now here's what you do. ..."

"Why, Kenneth, I think you and the Madame are very sweet to do this for me." Kenny had rented a Lincoln Town Car, not a limousine—too showy—and a uniformed driver to transport Bettina, Ruby, and him to the land site in Pennsylvania, about an hour and a half out of New York City.

"Madame and I are humbled by your gracious acceptance of the project and your willingness to actively participate. We can't begin to tell you what your enthusiasm means to us. Up to now, we haven't unfolded our plans to anyone, but today, we're going to start."

"I'm really interested in knowing who the people are who will come to the Center for Self-Fulfillment."

"People you know, child." Ruby had been well coached and, without seeming too zealous, played her part to a T. "People whose lives have been ruled by addictions. Or people who have never been able to realize their own potential. People who have wasted away because of a dependency on another person—a person who eats at his or her very soul. We all know people like this. Some of them hide their pain better than others. But the pain is there. It's visible, tactile, hurtful to see and experience."

"You know, Bettina, just sitting here listening to Madame, I remember where I was the day I found Madame." Kenny hung his head low.

Bettina thought, *The memory is so painful he can't make eye contact.*

"I had gone to the roof of my apartment building that morning. I was going to jump. There was nothing left, no reason to go on living. I remember going to the edge ..."

"But you see, Bettina, he didn't jump because there was basically a good person there. He saw innocent people below, a woman pushing a baby carriage, and understood that he wouldn't just take his life. He very probably would kill someone else or leave someone with a life-shattering experience. When Kenneth told me that story, I knew he would make it. Because as long as you care about other people, you will become all that you can be. With you, Bettina, that's not even a momentary concern. Your goodness illuminates me." Ruby reached out, all love in her eyes, and gently pushed a loose silken strand of hair away from Bettina's eye. Bettina reached out and embraced the older woman. Kenny was ecstatic.

"So you see, Bettina, this will be the entrance to the Center. Two stone pillars, very simple and classic, to symbolize strength, with an arch, the name carved in stone, the bronze gates always open. We're debating whether to add a bronze sign, maybe with a quote or something right to the point, such as, 'Your Future Happiness Lies within These Gates.'"

"Oh, I like that, Kenneth. Your future happiness lies within these gates. I think that would be very nice."

"Now, on that rise there's going to be an interdenominational chapel."

"I hadn't even thought about that. Of course we need a chapel."

"Absolutely, child. Oftentimes, religion is the best medicine for someone who is on the road to recovery."

"I must confess religion doesn't play as important a role in my life as it probably should."

"You don't have to be actively involved with the church to be a good Christian." Ruby was gazing out toward the hills and heavens. "Christian thinking stems from within. It is immediately with you upon waking. You face your own weaknesses. You acknowledge those moments when you let someone down, and ask that person's forgiveness, and inwardly vow to be optimistic, constructive, helpful, loving, and caring. You consciously tell yourself and your higher power that you want to make someone's day better today, knowing that person will, in turn, make someone else's day better. If only a fraction of the people in this world did that every day, what a happier world this would be."

"Every day, Madame, I'm going to wake up and think about that. And I'll make sure I make someone's day better, every day." The two women melted in each other's smiles.

Kenny was amazed. Ruby was sitting there, Bettina's hand in hers, dealing from some inner strength that he didn't know was there. *Good on you, old girl. Keep her hooked.*

"And where has the brightest jewel in my crown been today?" Dilly, so busy with the family empire and so trusting, rarely queried Bettina about her day. She openly shared her discoveries with him and secretly wished they could speak more openly and meaningfully with one another.

"I . . . I've met a wonderful, wonderful woman, darling. She's kind of a therapist who deals in self-fulfillment."

"How did you meet her, love?"

"Well, I went to her to discuss what I felt was a personal failing . . ."

"A failing that I obviously have not seen or acknowledged."

"Oh, you're sweet. No, it wasn't a big thing. I just wanted to speak with someone who could be objective. Anyway, we've become kind of friends. Not like wonderful Lisa, but she is a very worthwhile person. At any rate, she's involved in a big project—her mission in life—and she took me out to see the first steps. Who knows? Maybe I'll even invest a little."

"She sounds like a good person. Someday I must meet her."

"Absolutely, love. And how was your day?"

"Tough. I had to convince a couple of our old vice presidents, who have not kept up with the changing technology, that they should take a golden parachute and bail out. Believe me, they're not going to suffer. One is leaving with two million dollars; the other with three and a half."

"My goodness, just because they were fired?"

"No, and they weren't fired. They just took early retirement. Both are in their early sixties but honestly aren't pulling their weight. One understood that; the other feels he's been dumped. I made it as easy and profitable as possible for both of them, but it's still hard."

"How is business—or the businesses—in general?"

"If the economy stays healthy, and I believe it will, we're heading for a record year. I made a couple of chancy decisions last year that have paid off big time. I have zero complaints—especially about you. Come over here, and let's neck."

"Neck? You mean, make out? I suppose you're the kind of boy who's going to try to put his hands where he shouldn't."

"Yeah, can't I cop a feel?"

"Cop a feel? Are you dating some shop girl on the side?"

"Why settle for vanilla ice cream when I live with Baskin-Robbins? Kiss me, you gorgeous married lady."

"I love you, Mr. Richardson. Let's not waste time talking. I have something to show you in the bedroom."

"I like you shy girls. Come back here."

"I'm hiding ... in the bedroom."

Kenneth had never been loving enough to even have sexual fantasies. So he was amazed to wake up and realize he had been dreaming about Bettina. She was beautiful, blonde, rich, and ... he wanted her. *Bad thinking, Kenny boy. Bettina exists for one thing—her money. Put her out of your mind.*

What Kenny wasn't seeing clearly was Ruby—she was on the edge and ready to go over. Hardest were the nights. Gila—her daughter, Gila—now grown and lovely, would visit her. She would say nothing, except "Why?" And then she would disappear into the darkness. And she looked exactly liked Bettina. Bettina was Gila, Ruby decided, sent back to remind her of her failings as a mother.

Those had been difficult times. Sent home from the hospital by the good doctor who had saved her life and Gila's, she had no money, other than the ten dollars he'd given her, and seemingly no hope. But she had a strong back and an honest work ethic and within two days had secured a cleaning job that let her bring the baby with her. Her Karl had died. He tried to leave a hooker without paying, and her pimp knifed him. Ruby felt nothing when she heard the news. Karl had been banished to her personal hall of ghosts.

Then tragedy struck. Ruby fell ill. Finally, a doctor correctly diagnosed her as having tuberculosis. She was immediately sent away to a sanitarium, and the baby was put in a foster home. Ruby never saw her child again. When she emerged from the sanitarium, she tried to locate the baby, but without money and proper legal advice, she failed. Faced with such hurdles, she gave up and tried to convince herself that the baby would be better in an American family.

Ruby tried to imagine what Gila looked like now. Maybe … maybe Bettina was truly Gila. She cherished the vague possibility and dreaded the pain they would cause Bettina. Perhaps suicide was a viable alternative …

The contract, fourteen pages long, certainly seemed to cover all contingencies. Bettina understood not one page. "Is all this legal stuff really necessary, Kenneth?"

"Absolutely, dear Bettina. We want you to have complete legal assurance that your money is being invested correctly. And in turn, we need to be able to prove that you have willingly entered into this agreement with us. This also spells out the payment schedule. Two million now. Three million eight weeks from now. And a final payment of four million sixteen weeks from now. Are you sure you can handle a nine-million-dollar investment? And have you discussed this with your husband? Is he going to go along with your decision?"

"He made it quite clear that my money is mine to spend as I choose. And I know we can do such important things and bring Madame's gifts to a world that needs her so very much. I've never felt so good about spending money."

"You're a blessed person, Bettina. I … I … oh, never mind."

"What, Kenneth? There's nothing that you and I can't say to each other. I feel very close to you. At first, I envied your closeness to Madame, but now I see that you and she both have big hearts, and there's room for me to be there too."

"That's a lovely way to look at it, Bettina. I know I shouldn't say this, but I understand that confession is good for the soul. I've ... I've become very attached to you. No, no, don't worry. I'm not going to make some ridiculous unwanted and unwarranted advance. I just realize that my affection for you as part of our project has blossomed into more than a business relationship. So pardon me for stepping out of line, and I'll never mention it again."

"Oh, Kenneth, I'm so very touched. And you know something? I've had intimate thoughts about you too. But it wouldn't be right, and ... oh, never mind."

Kenny, knowing the inherent dangers, leaned forward and lightly kissed Bettina's forehead, and tipped her chin up and kissed her, a long, gentle but sensuous kiss. He kept his eyes open, watching her. Her eyes were closed and stayed closed after the kiss ended.

Who are you Bettina? she silently asked her mirrored reflection. *Are you still Bethel? Bettina Richardson wouldn't let another man kiss her, so why did I? Was it something—or someone—I needed, that I wanted? What would Dilly say? It's all right, my darling. You want someone else? Take him. After all, you're Mrs. Dillworth Richardson, and you can have anything or anyone that you fancy. No, no, no, no, he wouldn't say that. It would hurt Dilly beyond repair. Besides, you love Dilly, don't you? Kenneth can't mean that much to you, or does he? I wish I could discuss this with Madame. But that's impossible. She will be repulsed by my thoughts and my actions.* Bettina couldn't look at herself in the mirror any longer. She sat on the edge of her bed, and tears fell. *For whom am I crying?* She wept harder.

CHAPTER *20*

There Are Few Places in the World That Caress the Inner Soul like the British Virgin Islands

The trimaran was an amazing boat. And Virgin Islands water was a wet miracle. Nothing could be that blue. Buoyed by a quickie swim course at the athletic club, as well as swim fins, Bettina kept up with the lovable Gutwillig clan, and Dilly saw a whole new side of Bettina—a young woman having lots of fun on a perfect vacation.

There's nothing to prove when you're out on the water. Clothing is simple—swimsuits, shorts, T-shirts, maybe a pareo tied around the waist for evening. The food, the conversation, and the fun was nonstop. Although Bettina had no experience with young teens, she became a fun-loving older sister to the Gutwillig boys, and Dilly found himself enjoying his time with both kids. Well-educated products of the best private schools, they pushed the adults to their intellectual limits.

Bettina and Dilly had the starboard hull to themselves, with two queen-size bedrooms and an ample bathroom. The boys had the port hull, and Lisa and Fred had the master suite, in the middle section. There was a dining area up top and a spacious interior dining room in case the weather turned. Stretched between the hulls were big nets—like oversized hammocks—and when sailing through some of the slightly rougher days, they'd all gather in the hammocks, and be thoroughly soaked and buffeted about.

There was no need to worry about makeup or hairdos. The look was au naturel, and Bettina glowed with sun color. In this natural state, she grew even more beautiful and desirable in her husband's eyes. Their lovemaking was silky, languid, and sometimes salty-tasting. Bettina's focus was on her husband and her loving friends, and other problems drifted away with the tides.

"Where are you, Betts?" Lisa was aware that Bettina's head was somewhere else. All the guys were on shore, exploring the caves in Virgin Gorda called the Baths. The girls were on the water hammocks, just partially submerged.

"Caught me. I don't know where I was. Now and then my mind goes south, and I—oh, I don't know. I go with it, I guess."

"You've had fun on this trip."

"Maybe the most fun I've ever had in my life. I love you guys so much. And if I thought I could have sons like Timmy and George and be as perfect a mother as you are, I'd opt for motherhood right away."

"You're sweet. And you look at us through rose-colored lenses."

"Not true—I see you as you really are."

"What? You know I'm a bitch?"

"Come on, Lisa. You know what I mean. You're my role model."

"Oh? You want to be 7.3 pounds overweight and a surly, witchy wife and mother—"

"Who is adored by her husband and sons ... and friends."

"You're cute, Betts. I'm so happy you convinced Dilly to take this week."

"It didn't take a lot of convincing. The combination of the trimaran, the islands, and you clowns was irresistible. And did I tell you how much I love you for including us. It's been pure magic."

One night, Lisa decided they would have amateur night, and everyone had one day to prepare his or her act. It threw Bettina into a panic. Act? Perform? Other than being Bettina Richardson every minute, she had never played another role in her life.

The boys were terrific. They did an old vaudeville act, the two of them playing ukuleles and singing "Ol' Man River" and segueing into a current rock selection. Lisa was a standup comic, and she was really funny, keeping the humor clean enough for the young teens but funny enough for the grownups. For instance, one sample: "One day God was flying around heaven, giving an impromptu inspection. He came to Saint Peter's gate, and Pete was there, looking pretty bad. 'Boy, Pete, you look lousy!' 'Well, if you hadn't had a day off in three hundred years, you'd looked wasted too.' 'So, take the day off—go play golf.' 'I can't. Who's going to watch the gate?' 'I will.' 'You? You, the man?' 'Absolutely. Give me your cap, and take off.' After about an hour, an elderly man arrives, walks near the gate, looks in, shakes his head, and walks back down the walkway, looking in all directions. He does this for about three hours, obviously looking for someone. Finally, God says, 'Good afternoon, sir. May I help you?' 'Oh, I don't know. I'm looking for my son. I was a carpenter, and they took my son from me.' Jesus looks at the old man, and tears spill down his cheeks. He reaches out his hand toward the old man, and says, 'Father?' The old man looks up at Jesus, and his tears begin, and he says, 'Pinocchio?'"

Fred played a forgetful minister, delivering a ridiculous sermon full of mistakes and plays on words—very funny. Example: "She's just a bird in a guilty cage."

Dilly was a foreign dictator but was really a pussycat, full of gentle and loving admonitions, while supposedly ripping a country apart. And Bettina? This past year she had secretly studied singing, never mentioning it to anyone other than Dilly. As much as it shook her to her roots, she decided she would sing. She took the opening song from *Sunset Boulevard*, "With One Look," and gently wafted those words over the quiet sea.

> With one look, I can break your heart
> With one look, I play every part
> I can make your sad heart sing
> With one look, you'll know
> All you need to know
>
> With one smile, I'm the girl next door
> Or the love that you've hungered for
> When I speak it's with my soul
> I can play any role

No words can tell the stories my eyes tell
Watch me when I frown
You can write that down
You know I'm right
It's there in black and white
When I look your way
You'll hear what I say

Yes, with one look, I put words to shame
Just one look sets the screen aflame
Silent music starts to play
One tear from my eye
Makes the whole world cry

With one look, they'll forgive the past
They'll rejoice I've returned at last
To my people in the dark
Still out there in the dark

Silent music starts to play
With one look you'll know
All you need to know.

It was a magic moment. Her sweet voice, with near-perfect pitch, filled the darkness. When she finished, no one spoke. Bettina thought something was wrong. Finally, after what seemed minutes, Dilly spoke.

"I'm astounded. I know you were taking lessons, but you never told me you could really sing. And your voice … its … it's something magic. Have you ever done this professionally?"

Lisa stood up and embraced her friend. "My God, where does all that come from? You made me cry. I loved that. I love you."

Bettina's smile said it all. She had never felt so accomplished, so loved. The Gutwillig men surrounded her with hugs and adulation. She couldn't believe it. Suddenly, she was Cinderella. No, better yet, she was Miss America, winning the talent competition.

Much later, Dilly made love to her as though it were the first time, as though he was just discovering who she was. Now, she was very still. Not moving. The only sound an occasional kiss of water against the hull. She whispered to the starry sky, visible through the open hatch above their heads. "I love you, Dilly. I love you so much." His breathing changed for a moment and then returned to normal. Bettina took his hand in hers and slept.

CHAPTER 21

What's Next for Bettina? For Dilly? For Ruby? For Marianne Farber? Who's She?

Marianne Farber hadn't slept soundly for a solid week. Why did she do this to herself? Why did she have to find her natural mother? She had known from the time she was a little girl that she was adopted and that her adoptive parents were good and loving people. Then one day, as so many adopted children had done before, she had to know. But now she was thirty-five years old, married, with a child of her own, and, according to the firm she'd hired, was going to meet her mother sometime this week. What if the mother had never wanted her? What if she was some fall-down derelict? What was the fallout likely to be for her own family, whom she cherished? Forget sleep.

Was this really happening? There she was, Bethel or Bettina, writing a check for $3 million. It felt good.

"Thank you, Bettina. Everything is moving along so much faster than we had hoped—thanks to you. It's so amazing that we've found each other. Madame needs you and me so much. I can't begin to tell you how touched and moved she is by your loving participation in the Center."

"How is Madame, Kenneth? I haven't seen her or heard from her for two weeks."

"Oh, I thought she told you; she went on retreat."

"Retreat?"

"Absolutely. When you give so much of yourself, you must take the time to regenerate. She's found a couple of retreats. One is run by an order of nuns. Life is Spartan there, but you have lots of time to analyze your own motives, the direction you're taking. I too have taken retreats now and then. It does something magical for your inner spirit."

"It sounds wonderful, Kenneth. I'd … I'd like to go on retreat sometime."

"I'll think about the retreats we know and discuss it with Madame. I might even go on retreat with you."

Bettina glanced at him from the side of her eye, but he was seemingly focused on something else. Maybe that would be all right. Maybe.

Kenny wished Madame was on retreat. She was in a hospital, recovering from a suicide attempt. He had twenty-four-hour nurses to help—and guard her. The previous Saturday night, while trying unsuccessfully to sleep, Gila—her Gila—had appeared and just stood there, shaking her head no. Ruby staggered to her feet, went in the bathroom, and found the bottle of sleeping pills. She took one, then two more, and then, in the next fifteen minutes, took all thirty pills. She fell to her knees to pray, the way they'd done when she was a child. "Forgive me, Gila. I only wanted to be your mother. Forgive me, Bettina. If you're truly Gila, find it in your heart to not blame me."

Kenny, sensing that Ruby was on the edge, went by that next morning, and when Ruby wouldn't come to the door, he got the super to come up with a master key. He found her, dialed 911, and prayed he wasn't losing his meal ticket.

"Uh, Mrs. Farber, we have some bad news." *Oh God*, Marianne thought. *It's got to be about my mythical mother.* "Come out with it, please."

"Your natural mother, whose name is Ruby Schmidt-Feller—"

"Schmidt-Feller?"

"Yes, ma'am. Anyway, she's in a hospital. Seems she tried to take her own life."

"My God. Is she ... going to live?"

"Yes, ma'am. Apparently they found her in time, and she's going to make it."

"I'm ... I'm glad. Thank you for bringing me this news, unhappy though it is. When can I see her?"

"The hospital thought she'd be strong enough tomorrow for you to visit. She's at Columbia Presbyterian, room 612. You can visit anytime. They suggest around nine in the morning is best."

"Thank you." *Ruby Schmidt-Feller. It sounds ... German, maybe.* She looked in the mirror. *This could be a German face. I never thought about that. She tried to take her own life? Why? Does she know I'm coming, and she's afraid to meet me?*

During her early days as Bettina, she dreaded visiting her parents. But now it was different. She was Bettina. Bethel was receding, a distant memory of a person who couldn't possibly understand Bettina. Instead of feeling repulsed by her parents, the new, gentled Bettina could appreciate them for what and who they were. "Hi, Maw, how're you doing?"

"Moishe, look who's come home. Come here. Bethel, baby, I'm doin' fine, and you must be doin' great. You look so ... so pretty. You turned out pretty good."

"Thanks, Maw. Yes, everything is great."

"Your husband is good to you?"

"He's wonderful to me."

"We'd like to meet him some day."

She cringed inwardly. "We'll try to make that happen. He travels a lot."

"Traveling salesman, right?"

"Something like that. Hi, Daddy."

Moishe had entered the room and just stood in the doorway, looking at this sophisticated-looking, beautiful young woman. *That's his Bethel?* "So hello, dollink. I didn't know you was comin' today."

"I didn't call. Just felt the need to see you both." Bettina had dressed carefully for today. Just a sweater and skirt, small jewelry, and a raincoat. To the practiced eye, it was all good goods. The Sokoloffs wouldn't see the money behind the outfit—it was too plain to be worth that much.

"So what brings you home, baby?" Ruth Sokoloff still wasn't sure she knew this new Bethel.

"Well, I know you don't like suspense, but I have a surprise for you."

"You're pregnant?"

"No, but that's not a bad idea. Meanwhile, I've been investigating retirement communities and have found one in Melbourne, Florida, that I'd like for you to see. I even went down there and looked at the houses and met some of the people, and I'd like to take you down there."

"Retire? I can't retire, we don't have enough money to do that. I gotta work."

"Daddy, you don't have to work anymore. I have enough money so you and Mom can retire to a warm, friendly place. I know how much you both hate the winter, and this is such a nice community, and you'll have lots of friends. Look, here are the brochures. Read it over, talk to each other about it, and I'll come back next week, and we'll plan a trip down there together."

"I don't know, honey. You know, we've been here a lotta years. Don't know if I could take a new place."

"You can try, Daddy. And you and Mom would love living in the warm."

Dilly was so single-minded about business and his husbandly obligations toward Bettina that he didn't even see that he was being hit on. Toni Sammis was a bombshell—body, brains, and beauty. As she confided to her best friend one day, "My eyes get me in trouble. I know whenever I see something I want, I'm gonna get it." And she saw something she wanted—Dilly. She didn't need his money. She was earning seven figures herself. She wanted his aristocratic body in bed.

"You mix a mean drink, Toni."

"Thanks so much for coming by, Dilly. I just wanted to discuss that merger with you, without any interruptions."

"It sounds good to me, right on the money. But after two of those drinks, don't ask me to make any important decisions."

"Hah. I'll bet with ten drinks in you, you could outmaneuver anyone."

"You see me through rose-colored lenses."

"Stay right here, Dilly; there's something I want to show you."

"Okay."

"I'll turn on the news so you won't get bored."

Ten minutes later, Toni called from down the hall. "Dilly, do me a favor and come here, please."

"Sure thing." He rose, walked down the hall, and walked into the only open door, where Toni was standing, wearing a negligee as transparent as possible, her hair loose and curling down to her shoulders.

She walked up to Dilly, who was stunned, put one hand around the back of his neck, and gently pulled his face toward her. With the other hand, she took his genitals in hand. She kissed him. He was still speechless. She took one of his hands and placed it on her breast. She kissed him again.

"Toni, I ... um ... uh ... this isn't what I was anticipating."

"So you don't always make the right decision?"

"I'm ... um ... very married."

"I know that, and I don't expect you to run away with me. I just want us to make love, right now."

"I don't know ..."

"Well, part of you knows."

Why did I allow that to happen? Flying back to New York the next morning, Dilly was angry with himself. *I don't need anyone but Bettina. And yes, the sex was good, but I didn't need it, didn't want it. I'm weak. I've cheated on my wife. I'm a pig.*

"Mother ... I'm Marianne, your daughter."

Ruby was lying there, her head turned to the wall. She turned back slowly and forced her eyes to focus on the handsome young woman with the kind face.

"How are you feeling now? The doctor told me you're going to be fine." She reached forward and took Ruby's hand. Ruby looked at her hand and put her other hand over her daughter's. Tears ran down her cheeks. Marianne cried too. "It's going to be all right, Mom. It's going to be all right." They sat there on the hospital bed, hugging and weeping.

Bettina's initial take on Teddy Catarsi was correct. He was a rotter. On two occasions when Dilly was out of town, Teddy had called Bettina to ask her to dinner. She flatly refused. She saw Teddy only at family gatherings or large social functions when Elizabeth—Dilly's sister, Teddy's wife—was at his side. The pity of it was Bettina loved Elizabeth but didn't want to be around Teddy at all. One evening, the butler's night off and Dilly out of town, the doorbell rang. *Strange*, thought Bettina, *the doorman didn't call to tell me who's here.* Knowing how secure their building was, she opened the door with confidence, and there stood Teddy. "Since the doorman knows I'm family, he sent me up."

"Good evening, Theodore. Shouldn't you be home, having dinner with Elizabeth?"

"She's off saving the nation's rainforests, or feeding children from a third-world nation, or maybe she has a lover. I just know she said it would be a late evening. Aren't you going to ask me in?"

"I would rather not, Teddy. I'm a bit weary and still have some homework to do."

"I heard you had enrolled in NYU. Why are you doing that?"

"Self-improvement, I suppose. I want to try to keep up with Dilly."

"You don't need any self-improvement, Bettina. You've got something that every woman would like."

"You're absolutely correct—I have Dilly. Thanks for stopping by, Teddy, but let's—"

"Let's try to be civil. I have some things I really need to discuss."

"Things to discuss with me? I am not the sage of this family. I'm an outsider, and if you have personal things to discuss, I don't think it would be proper to put them on my plate."

"Come on, Bettina." He forced his way into the room.

"I told you I have homework, and I'm tired."

"I'll wake you up." Teddy grabbed Bettina, pulled her roughly to him, and kissed her. She thought it the most unpleasant kiss of her life. His hands were everywhere, and Bettina thought, *Bettina could be raped but not Bethel.* Fortunately, she was wearing slacks and brought her knee up to his groin as hard as she could, and he doubled over, gasping for air. She thought about hitting him on the head with a vase but thought it would be too much violence for the family to understand. She picked up the phone and called the doorman. "Kevin, Mr. Catarsi has had an ulcer attack and is in great pain. Would you please come escort him downstairs and see that he gets in a car?" She opened the door wide. "Teddy, the doorman is coming to take you downstairs. I'll forget this happened, and it better not happen again." Moments later, the doorman appeared. "Oh, thank you, Kevin. Teddy, Kevin will help you to a car."

What's the old saying—if looks could kill? Teddy said it all with his expression. The doorman noticed it and wondered what had happened. He rather liked Mrs. Richardson. Unlike all the snooties in this building, she treated everyone like human beings.

When the hateful Teddy was gone, Bettina found herself shaking. She poured herself a small sherry and got her emotions under control. *Hmm, maybe Bethel isn't dead after all.* Maybe she could count on Bethel to help if she needed it.

Lisa Gutwillig had told the Junior League about Bettina's singing, and they wanted her to perform. The idea panicked her, but Lisa reassured her that it was for a good cause, and it was time Bettina came out of the closet with her newfound talent. In truth, Bettina had a good God-given voice, but she also had been studying diligently with a Mrs. Rajinsky, who, after years of singing in Europe, had fled Nazi persecution and settled down in New York, teaching discipline to would-be opera stars, Broadway wannabes, and cabaret hopefuls. She rather liked this Bettina Richardson. Obviously well-heeled, she wasted no time with idle chitchat about family or boyfriends or personal crises. She was there for a purpose, and together, they made good use of the time.

The annual Junior League Ball was the major fund-raiser of the year for all the League's activities. There was always entertainment, which was paid very little or performed for free, in exchange for the exposure to the rich. All the League officers knew that Lisa Gutwillig was the straightest shooter among all of them. And when she said that Bettina was a pure professional, they said fine, and no audition was necessary. They wanted her to sing two songs and, in case it was necessary, have one encore ready. She could have full orchestra accompaniment or just a pianist. Bettina chose the songs, and she and Mrs. Rajinsky brought them to a very attractive level of performance.

Mrs. R., as Bettina called her, was interested in this undertaking. "You know, Miss Bettina, that if you are a Maria Callas, it is enough to just stand there and sing, but I zink it vould be vise to plan some staging. This is theater, and you should let the trappings of theater enhance your performance."

"Yes, ma'am, I'd love any suggestions you can make. Since I've never ever been on a stage, any thoughts you have would be wonderful and very helpful."

"Vell, I understand zey have a curtain. So here's vhat ve'll do …"

Dilly had stopped punishing himself for the unnecessary Toni affair. She didn't count, and he deleted her from his conscious thinking. What mattered was Bettina and her growing influence on him and independence from him. He realized she was coming into a new period of her life. Part of it worried him, because he didn't want her to stray too far, but as a loving and giving human being, he applauded her "self-improvement" kick, as she called it. He was amazed she had agreed to the Junior League request and was touched when she said, "I'll try not to embarrass you."

"You never embarrass me, sweet bee. I am only envied because you are with me. What are you doing today?"

"Well, I'm going to spend a little of your hard-earned money, Mr. Richardson."

"Oh yeah, for what?"

"I'm going to buy a gown for my singing debut. Since I don't totally trust my own judgment, Lisa the Wonderful is going with me, and she is hideously honest about everything, as you know."

"Gee, I've never done it with a star."

"Well, before I become too famous, tonight I'll give you something to remember me by."

"I promise to not work late tonight."

"Kiss me goodbye, and go earn enough money for my gown."

Kenny had black-and-white photos of a corporate construction site and would show Bettina with great pride, pointing out which of the buildings in the Center for Self-Fulfillment that represented. Or, "This is the foundation for the medical clinic." Bettina had never felt so involved, so pivotal in the creation of a great work.

The night of the Junior League Ball, Bettina was surprisingly calm. She had chosen two songs from *Funny Girl*, the musical about Fanny Brice, so beautifully performed by Barbra Streisand. Since the show predated her years of attending theater, she relied on Mrs. Rajinsky for her handling of the lyrics, as well as staging ideas. One idea, according to Mrs. R., was part of *Funny Girl*, and Bettina liked it.

The curtain opened, and Bettina was sitting in the center of the stage, her hair piled high on her head, and herself bundled up in a white mink coat. Other than mink, the audience saw only her face and substantial diamond ear studs. Without any announcement, she started in with "My Man," and as she sang that lovely and familiar ballad, the spot on her gradually grew smaller and smaller and smaller, until all the audience saw for the last part of the song was her face. She finished, and before anyone could applaud, the music segued into another song introduction, and the face-sized spot started to open, revealing Bettina with hair down loose around her shoulders. As it opened more, it showed her standing there in a dazzling black sequined gown; the mink gone; the stool gone. She launched into, "His Is the Only Music That Makes Me Dance."

She finished to thunderous applause, a standing ovation, and someone brought two dozen roses to her. It was an emotional high like nothing before in her life.

The remainder of the evening danced by in a whirl of congratulatory smiles and hugs, and Dilly basked in her glow. It was sublime.

CHAPTER 22

Crisis Time: For Bethel, for Bettina, for Edwina, for Ruby, for Kenny. No One's Life Is Always Sunny. And When the Storm Hits …

"Edwina, rarely do you annoy me, but you're getting very close." Roland Richardson lowered his newspaper and looked directly at his wife, who was uncharacteristically pacing the rich Oriental carpet in the den.

"I'm telling you, Roland, Bettina is not Bettina. Her name is Bethel Sokoloff, a nobody from nowhere, and … and … and …"

"And you're annoyed that Ms. Nobody from Nowhere is doing a splendid job as Mrs. Dillworth Richardson. May I remind you that you were not social register when we married. I was smitten with your obvious charms, your wit, your intelligence and didn't give a whit for society's view of you. Obviously, society approved instantly. I think Bettina has had to jump a higher hurdle than you, but she's succeeding. She is winning everyone's approval on her own terms. Admire her for that. And most important, look at our Dilly."

"I hate that form of his name."

"Fine. Look at our Dillworth. He is more alive than ever in his past. There's a sparkle in his eyes, pride in his step."

"It sounds like every old boy's idea of a dream—to have a show-stopper on his arm so everyone will envy him."

"Oh, good heavens, Edwina. Dillworth isn't an old man. He's young, vital, and he deserves to have someone beautiful at his side. One thing for sure—this marriage isn't interfering with his business judgments. He's never been more right on. The family fortune is growing in Gulliver-sized leaps and bounds."

"Consider this, Roland. I assume there will be children. Since we are naught but a gene pool, can you imagine the genes this little street girl will introduce into our lineage?"

"Might be good to have a little bit of street fighter in the family. The genes I fear more in this family would be from Ted, Elizabeth's husband."

"What's wrong with him? Are you keeping something from me?"

"No, nothing has happened; it's a sixth sense I have about Ted. I don't think he is a man of moral courage and certainly isn't worthy of Elizabeth."

"Aren't you just being a father playing that old song, 'No One Is Good Enough for Daddy's Baby'? I can't imagine your being so ... so middle class in your thinking."

"Bullshit, Edwina."

"Really, Roland Hughington!"

"I'll say it again, Edwina, Bullshit. I'm tired of your tiresome references to 'class' and whether so-and-so wears it well and that a silk purse out of a sow's ear is still a sow's ear. Bullshit."

"I'm shocked. I'm not one of your call girls, Roland."

"I've wondered when you would bring that up, Edwina. I'm not stupid. With the advent of serious diseases, I gave up that little hobby. It was necessary. I was young, and you, if not frigid, were too busy deciding if you were doing 'it' properly. Sex shouldn't be a rehash of cotillion."

"I didn't know you had complaints about my ... performance."

"I never knew whether you enjoyed it, or if you were thinking about what to serve at the next boring dinner party."

"This conversation has gone to improper lengths."

"Oh, is that what Miss Manners says ... or does Emily Post still have the last word?"

"Letitia Baldrige is more current."

"I'll bet she never got her rocks off either."

"Really, that's quite enough."

"Fine, Edwina. I just caution you. Don't go for Bettina's jugular. You stand a very good chance of losing Dillworth forever." He picked up his paper and appeared to resume reading.

Edwina—stunned, furious—realized how people get angry and throw things. Of course, she wouldn't do that. She turned and left the room. Her husband of -thirty-six years watched her, his expression saying nothing.

"Mother, who is that man, and why does he upset you so?" Marianne had decided to unearth this problem, and today was the day. She and Ruby had taken a morning stroll through the shady streets where Marianne lived. Now, sitting in the sunroom, looking out across the back lawn bordered with Martha Stewart-inspired gardens, it was a quiet time. No one could or would interrupt them. She could see the question momentarily had unnerved Ruby, who gave her head a quick shake and hid her concerns with a quick, forced smile.

"He doesn't upset me, Gila—I mean, Marianne. I have a business relationship with him, and I want to back out, and he wants me to stay part of it and is willing to give me a lot of money if I go on. Guess I haven't decided how I want to play it."

"I disagree. It's evident to me that you don't want anything to do with him. You're not telling me the extent of this business relationship, and I want to know. We can't have any more secrets between us. What is your business relationship with that man, and why do you want to get out of it?"

Ruby sat there, silent, head down. Three minutes passed.

"Mom, I'm waiting." Marianne's voice was gentle, but she wasn't going to let go.

"There's a girl, a very beautiful girl, with a very rich husband. And … and she became you. She became my Gila, and I didn't want to see her hurt by Kenny and Warshon."

It took nearly two and a half hours to drag the entire story out of Ruby. Marianne realized she was sitting on a crime already partially committed, and unless the unmasking of it was handled properly, her mother could be indicted and sent to jail. That could not happen. *My dear God, what to do?*

"I don't know, Doc, I think the pain is from stress, but it's been two weeks now, and I'm not getting any better." The doctor said little during the examination but set up a couple of tests, a CAT scan, and a blood workup. Kenny didn't believe it could be anything. Hey, he was young; he didn't smoke.

"Did your parents smoke?"

"Uh, yeah, like chimneys. I mean, like, is that why I'm not feeling too good?"

"Not positive, Kenneth. But when we get the results of the tests, we'll have a better fix on what to do. Go do these tests right now, and come back to see me at 5:00 p.m. on Thursday."

"Okay, Doc, you're the boss." After completing the tests, Kenny walked through Central Park. *What the hell do all these people do for a living who spend their entire day jogging and walking through the park? New York City's backyard.* In less than an hour, he saw all those cross sections of humanity that make New York what it is—teeming, thriving, energetic, and completely screwed up. One old wino had a nice approach. He had a sign that read, "I need five dollars for a ticket to the boat show."

Kenny tried not to think about the medical exam. What if something was wrong, right now, on the brink of his becoming a multimillionaire? No, it couldn't be. *It's probably an allergy or something unimportant like that.*

Bettina heard the tears before her mother even spoke. "What is it, Mom? What's happened?"

"Oh, Bethel, baby, Daddy had a heart attack, and they put him in that intensive care at New York Hospital."

"Oh my God. I'll go immediately, Mom. Do you want me to pick you up?"

"I'll meet you there. I just came home to change. I was there all night. Honey, he won't die, will he?"

"No, Mom, he wants to live in the warm with you. I'll hurry."

The doctor wasn't expecting someone like Bettina to be the daughter of this rather simple and terribly ill man. The daughter was from another planet. She was perfectly put together, obviously rich or well-to-do.

"Is there anything we can do that we aren't doing? Money is not a concern."

"Not really, Ms. Sokoloff. Intensive care is intensive care … the quality doesn't change by virtue of a bank account."

"I apologize if that was a crass statement. I'm just so terribly worried."

"Not to worry. But if the expense isn't a concern, private-duty nurses are worthwhile, even in intensive care."

"Fine, please order them, and I'll pay you in advance. You said 'if' he gets through this phase. Is there some doubt in your mind?"

"I have to be honest with you. Your father is very ill. It's a toss-up whether he'll make it."

"Oh, God." Bettina sat down.

"Bethel, I'm here, and your sister is here too."

"Well, hello, sister." The voice wasn't friendly.

Bettina looked up to see her sister, Michelle, with a pinched, hard face, critically looking at her.

"Hello, Michelle. It's been a long time. Mom, sit down here, and I'll explain what the doctor has told me. Daddy is very ill."

"Is he gonna die?" The hysteria rose in her voice.

"They hope not, Mom. They're doing everything they can for him. And I've arranged for private-duty nurses to be with him around the clock."

"Isn't that a lot of money, Bethel? Does he really need that?" Michelle asked, referring to their father like he was a used car.

"The doctor said it might be helpful, so I'm doing it. The doctor said we really can't be with him right now. Every hour is crucial. Let's go downstairs to the cafeteria and have something."

"Your daughter is right, Mrs. Sokoloff. There's nothing you can do now but pray for your husband to respond to the medication. Go have some refreshments. When you return, Ms. Sokoloff, go the nurses' desk, and they'll have an up-to-the-minute report for you. I wish I had happier news for you, but don't give up hope. The human body is an amazing machine."

The hospital cafeteria was full of white coats and somber faces. Bettina insisted her mother have a toasted bagel with cream cheese and a hot tea. Michelle selected a sweet roll; Bettina settled for tea.

"I wouldn't have known you, Bethel … or have you changed your name too?"

Ignoring the query, Bettina answered pleasantly. "The folks told me how well you've been doing. That's a real responsibility to be the rabbi's wife and now a mother of three. I'm impressed. I just have a husband to take care of, and that's a full-time responsibility."

"You look none the worse for wear. That's some rock on your left hand. It's bigger than your nose, which seems to have shrunk since I last saw you."

Bettina saw the anger, the competitiveness, and the envy in her sister's eyes. "Yes, I have changed, Michelle. I didn't like the direction I was going in, so I shifted gears and turned my life around. I'm trying to be a better person and contribute something to society. But right this minute, all that matters is Daddy and helping Mom over this hurdle."

"I've always been around for them, Bethel. You can fill in now."

"I'm happy to do that, Mickey."

"Mickey? Huh, no one calls me that. I'm Mrs. Nussbaum."

"I'll assume I can call you Michelle."

"Girls, what's going to happen to me if Daddy dies?"

"Oh, Mom." Bettina put an arm around her mother. "Let's concentrate on Daddy's getting well."

"And if he doesn't?"

"We'll cross that bridge—together. Okay, sweetie. Let's think positive thoughts."

Kenny took off his Bill Blass sports coat and hung it up, thinking, *I'll be a well-dressed multimillionaire corpse. Cancer. No, lung cancer. One final gift from those scummy parents of mine.*

The doctor had said it all. "Your parents smoked a great deal, you say. Well, this looks clearly like a case of second-hand smoke causing a serious cancer condition."

"Am I as good as dead? Is that what you're telling me?" Kenny was pacing around the room, turning his head from side to side, as if looking for an emergency exit.

"No, Kenneth, 65 percent of all cancer patients these days survive cancer."

"And the other 35 percent are stuck in a box down in a dirt hole or turned into ashes in a big pizza oven. Which group am I, Doc? Do we have any answers? Hmmm?"

"We have lots of answers, Kenneth. Lots of tests, lots of procedures, lots of effective medicines. It isn't much fun, but the alternative is less fun. We have more successes than failures."

"I don't suppose this is something that can just be cut out, and get it over with."

"No, I'm afraid not. Besides, surgery is never a picnic in the park. But in this instance, the cure comes from chemotherapy and radiation, not surgery."

"Oh yeah, chemotherapy—that stuff that makes your hair fall out and makes you sick all the time."

"It's gotten better and better. There is little sickness with it, and yes, eventually, your hair will take a holiday, but guess what? It grows back, sometimes thicker and nicer than before."

"What if I choose not to do all the therapy and treatments?"

"I don't know you very well, Kenneth, but I'll be blunt. It would be much less painful and quicker to just put a gun to your head."

"Do I have to take your word for it?"

"Not at all. It's always healthy—no pun intended—to get a second opinion. I'll have my nurse give you a couple of names and numbers of respected oncologists, or you may go to whomever you choose. We'll give you a set of the test results so they may discuss them with you. The only advice I can offer is, whatever you do, do it now. Time, in cases such as these, is of the essence."

"Can I go now?"

"Indeed, you may. I'm sorry to be the bearer of this news. These are always turning points in people's lives—"

"Or deaths."

"One last point, Kenneth. You're not the first person to contract lung cancer and won't be the last. But one thing I know. Defeating cancer needs a brave, optimistic patient. I'll forgive you your defeatist attitude for the moment, but when you've had time for a reality check, summon up the man inside of you, and prepare to do battle—and win!"

"Very pretty speech, Doc. I'll try to remember. Thanks. Bye."

"Pick up the names of the oncologists from my secretary, as well as the copy of your test results."

"Yes, sir."

Doctors have been wrong—many times. He continued undressing. He carefully hung up the Calvin Klein slacks and arranged his Ferragamo loafers neatly side by side. He decided the shirt wasn't worth hanging up. Kenny stood there in his Hugo Boss jockey-style shorts and looked at himself in the mirror. He saw reflected a skeleton in a black hood. He crumpled to the floor and lay there in a fetal curl, weeping.

Bettina was wild with worry. No Kenneth, no Madame. It couldn't be ... They couldn't be... Madame wouldn't ... Kenny had heard all her calls on his answering machine. He just couldn't speak. Ruby was still holed up with her daughter, and he was too weak to face it all alone. The chemo was killing him. Or was it saving him? He decided he had to call her, or there might be legal and emotional ramifications.

"Bettina, dear Bettina, it's Kenneth."

"Oh, Kenneth, I was so worried. Not a word from you or Madame. And what's wrong? Your voice doesn't sound normal."

"I guess that book is right—'Bad things can happen to good people.' Madame became ill with a new strain of the flu while she was on retreat and is now recuperating with a woman whose life she saved. And I ... I have been diagnosed with a serious illness and am undertaking serious medical treatment to combat it."

"Kenneth, I'm so sorry. What can I do for you?"

"You are so sweet, Bettina. You can light candles."

"If you can't afford the best medical help, I'll get you someone."

"No, I do believe I have fine doctors. Everything depends on how I respond to the medicines. I finish this first phase in two weeks and, at that point, hope the Madame and I are both well enough to have an update meeting with you. I'm told that construction is moving right along, although it makes me nervous when I'm not there to add my two cents' worth."

"I'm just so relieved to hear from you. I won't bother you because I want you to concentrate on the medical process. And please tell Madame how much I miss her and am thinking of her. That goes equally as much for you too, Kenneth. I send you a warm hug and kiss."

"Thank you, Bettina. Your thoughts help me a lot." He hung up and thought, *They do help. She is very sweet, very good, loving, and—forget it, Kenny boy. She's way out of your league.*

Bettina had given her mother and sister a private number, answered only by Bettina. "Hello."

"He's dead."

"Wha … Michelle? Daddy is dead? Oh no." Bettina rose out of her chair, and the tears started to fall.

"Pull yourself together, sister dear. He didn't have much to look forward to."

"I couldn't disagree with you more, Mickey. He and Mom could have had some good years together, living in Florida. Poor Mom."

"No, poor Michelle, because I'll be stuck with Mom. God knows you're never around." Her voice was flat, with an edge of sarcasm.

"Why do you dislike me so much, Michelle?"

"What's to like?"

"Fine; if you like bile so much, go ahead and drown in it."

"Aha, the real Bethel comes out."

"No, you don't know me anymore. You know nothing about me. But you're right; I haven't been there as much as I should have been for our parents. But I'll take over Mom, so it shouldn't be a burden to you. Where is she right now?"

"I took her home. The doctor gave her a sedative, and she's napping."

"Thank you. How about Daddy?"

"Whatta you mean, how about Daddy? He's dead. They have him in the hospital morgue. We gotta make funeral arrangements. And who's going to pay for all that?"

"I'll pay for everything, Michelle."

"Oh ho, Mrs. Got Rocks."

"Goodbye, Michelle." *Hateful sister. But she's right. I wasn't there for the folks. I removed myself from them and became someone else. But now I can be there for Mom. It will be difficult. Besides blood ties, we have no common ground. I wish Madame were well. I need to speak with her. She'll help me come to peace with Mom.*

Teddy Catarsi's hatred for Bettina was eating him alive. "You know, Liz, there's a lot more to your brother's blonde bombshell than meets the eye."

The gentle Elizabeth was doing needlepoint and trying to analyze a dream she had had the night before. "Pardon me, darling. I'm not following you."

"I didn't want to mention this, but think I'm wrong not to tell you."

"Okay." She put her needlepoint aside. "You have my complete attention. What would be wrong not to tell me?"

"A couple of weeks ago, I got a message at my office to join Dilly and his missus at their apartment for cocktails. So I went, wanting to talk to Dilly about investing in one of my ideas."

"And?"

"And there was no Dilly. He was out of town. And his dishy little bride was there by herself."

"So?"

"So, after all the hellos and a big warm hug, she fixed a couple of drinks and proceeded to come on to me."

"Oh, no! I'm ... I'm horrified. What did you do, darling?"

"I told her to stow it and that inter-family foolishness is not the Richardson way. I had to physically push her off me."

"My poor Dilly. And poor you, darling. What a terrible position to be in. I can't imagine what got into Bettina. I don't see much of her but hear only good things about her involvement in organizations. And I know that my brother has never been so happy. Now what? I don't know whether this should be mentioned and to whom."

"I think you should tell Edwina."

"Oh God, no. Mother is too terrifying to deal with. Maybe I should speak with Dilly … or Dad."

"No, I wouldn't tell your father. He doesn't want to know about things like this. It would disgust him." Teddy wasn't blind to the fact that the elder Mr. Richardson wasn't exactly overwhelmed by his son-in-law's qualities.

"I can't bear it. Dilly loves her so. I'll have to think about how to broach this subject."

"Yeah, it's really a shame. I was … shocked."

Mitchell Jelline was perhaps the most respected attorney in Westchester County. "I wish I had a simple solution for you, Mrs. Farber. This isn't a pretty story. But since there's a legal contract between this woman, the man leading the scam, and the older woman you wish to protect, everyone is involved. The law, sadly, has many devices to protect bad people."

"But the older woman did not enter into this scam willingly. She has been coerced and frightened into compliance."

"It is conceivable that a court would be lenient with her, if her reluctance to be part of this deception could be proved. But meanwhile, what is happening to the victim? She has been taken for five million dollars up to now and another four million is yet to be paid; is that right?"

"Yes, Mr. Jelline, that is correct."

"Well, it seems to me that she should be told what is happening to her. If nothing else, it might cut her losses. She actually might have trouble recapturing the original five million."

"That seems hideously unfair."

"I couldn't agree more. The inequities of law in our fine country are one of its greatest weaknesses. It's sad."

"You've been very kind—and helpful."

"I don't know what your involvement is Mrs. Farber. I suspect it's more personal that you have communicated. However, this conversation will remain purely private."

"Thank you. I appreciate that."

"My pleasure. If I can be of further service, do not hesitate to call."

CHAPTER *23*

Bettina's Dreams Were Becoming More Complex, Bigger—Yes, Bigger. Then Why Was Life So Difficult? And Then She Remembered Who She Was ... and Wasn't

Last night was really something. She was a kid again. And Sam, her wonderful brother, was there. He was protecting her from street thugs, holding her hand when they crossed a busy street. Sharing an egg cream with her. So maybe they were poor. Maybe it was the Bronx, not Fifth Avenue. But Sam loved her and told her he'd always be there to protect her. Mickey, her stupid sister, wasn't there. She was never there.

Then, suddenly, Sam wasn't there. But Madame was there, holding her hand, protecting her. She was there at the Center for Self-Fulfillment, helping Madame to help all the people with problems. And there was—my God—Dilly, as a patient. "I have a problem. You see my wife, my Bettina, isn't really Bettina, and she doesn't really love me." And there was Kenneth in the background, laughing at Dilly. *Stop that, Kenneth. Don't ever laugh at Dilly.*

Is that Lisa? Yes. Lisa, over here, sweet friend. Why is she just standing there, shaking her head? She's fading—no, no, come back, Lisa. Why are you shrugging your shoulders?

Madame, I need your help. Madame, where are you? Where are you?

She awakened with a light coat of perspiration and a terrible thirst. *Did Dilly say I don't love him? Is that true? Why was Lisa shaking her head? Where were you when I needed you, Madame?* She tossed and turned through the rest of the night. She told herself, *It's only a dream, and it means nothing.* But she didn't believe it.

"Goddammit, Ruby, you're in it up to your ears. You can't back out now, I won't let you."

"You're wrong, Mr. Kenneth."

Kenny hadn't seen Marianne Farber enter the room. He started. "Stay out of this, lady,"

"No, I won't stay out of it. You can't force my mother to do anything more. I'm going to blow the whistle on you."

Kenny stood there, breathing hard, trying to think fast, to put this bitch in her place. "You do, and your mother goes down with me. Her name is on the contract, her *signed* name, so she'll be in the slammer. Nice thing to do to your mother, eh?"

"I don't think a jury would convict her."

"Hah, you don't think a jury would convict her. When our benefactor tells them how the 'Madame' told her about all the sad people she would be helping, when she tells the jury all the lies piled on top of lies that she told—hah. You'll spend the rest of your life behind bars, you stupid old bitch."

"Get out of my home, whatever your name is."

"Ruby, you know I'm not going to disappear. Your daughter is just going to send you up the river without a paddle."

"I said to get out, and I mean now."

Ruby said nothing but sat there, cowering, ashamed she had brought this problem to her daughter's door.

The train ride back to Grand Central was endless. Kenny weighed every option he had and some he didn't have. They already had five million, but Herman had taken his 40 percent of the total up front—$3,600,000, so there was only about $1,250,000 left. That wasn't even enough for legal fees. *Shit! There's another four million if I can string Bettina along for five more weeks. There's gotta be an angle.*

Bettina had lied to Dilly, a white lie, to settle her mother in Florida. "My mother had one sister who never got her life together. Anyway, she's surfaced, not in great shape."

"You can certainly bring her here. We have plenty of room."

"I wouldn't consider it, darling, not just for your sake but for mine. I've done some research and found an adult retirement community on the outskirts of Melbourne, Florida. It's a strong community of predominantly northerners, and when you need medical care or assisted living, they provide that. It's comparatively very little money, so I'm moving her down there. I'm going next week and will spend no more than three days, darling. Do you mind?"

"Of course not, sweet bee. I've been putting off a site visit to the Midwest plants. I'll schedule it for next week. Which days are you going?"

"I'm leaving Tuesday morning and will return early Friday."

"Perfect. I'll schedule the same, and that way we won't miss each other at home."

"You're so dear, Dilly. I'm the luckiest woman in the world."

"No, I'm the luckiest man in the world. Come here, and give your hubby a kiss, Mrs. Richardson."

"My pleasure, sir."

It had taken a lot of persuasion to convince her mother. But with the added incentive that Michelle and her children would come twice a year and that she would come twice a year and would bring her mother back at least once a year, she finally agreed to the move.

Packing her possessions for the move was harder than Bettina had figured. Mom wanted to keep everything, and most of it wasn't worth keeping. She finally came up with a plan. She'd store all of Mom's things in a nearby storage facility, and then she could start out with all new everything in Florida.

That was kind of fun. She settled Mom and herself in a good motel and that first evening went out and bought good, comfortable furniture for the entire house. It was a two-bedroom "modular construction," which translated to "two trailers joined together," but it wasn't at all bad. Almost 1,500 square feet, which was considerably bigger than the Bronx apartment, two bedrooms, two baths, a big screened porch, nice-sized living room, and a modern kitchen with dining area. Her mother was like a child at the circus, all wide-eyed and smiling. The second day all the furniture was delivered, and they were no sooner settled in than neighbors from next door and across the street came calling to welcome them. Her mother couldn't believe it. One couple had lived many years in the Bronx. It was a godsend. Bettina left her mom, not feeling guilty for the first time in many years. She promised to call her every night for a while. *Some things do work out. Amazing.*

Edwina had wisely decided to let the Bettina issue fade from center stage. She still smarted from Roland's attack. Instead, she decided to try a different tack. *If you cannot defeat the enemy, join them, or make them feel like a winner.*

"Bettina, dear, it's been too long since I've seen you, and I don't believe we've ever had the luxury of time alone."

Bettina looked at the phone with disbelief, all nerve endings at full alert. "What a surprise, Mrs. Richardson ..."

"I know I'm not the motherly type, Bettina, but you may certainly call me Edwina."

"Fine, Mrs. Ri ... Edwina."

"Why don't we do one of those 'ladies who lunch' things, and go treat ourselves to a fancy lunch. Let's see now ... how about tomorrow or Wednesday?"

"Tomorrow would be lovely. Wednesday, I have a long session with my voice coach and want to be in good form for that." Bettina rose from her private desk in the beautiful study that was *her* room, off limits to Dilly. She had been writing her mother, something she did religiously every week. She walked over to the window and looked out and down across Central Park. She wondered what this call was all about.

"Good. I'm going to make a reservation at Lipanisse in the Saint Regis, which gets rave reviews from everyone. How about twelve thirty, dear?"

"I'll be there—on time. Living with one Dillworth Richardson has made me an on-time person."

"It's a good habit. I personally loathe people showing up thirty minutes late and never with believable excuses. I think they just want to make an entrance. I won't keep you any longer, Bettina. But I'm looking forward to tomorrow."

"So am I ... Edwina. You're sweet to suggest it. Bye." *God save me. Two hours, at least, alone with Dilly's mother. What'll I wear? What'll I say? What if she unmasks me?* Bettina noticed her hand was trembling, and she was conscious of a serious headache creeping up from the back of her neck. *I don't know if I can get through this.*

"At first I didn't want to believe it, Dad, but the more I thought about it, the angrier I got. Yes, we all know Bettina is beautiful. And she has a beautiful husband—your son, Dilly; my darling brother, Dilly. And that isn't enough?"

"Calm yourself, Elizabeth, and tell me what's happened. I'm not following this conversation at all. What has Bettina done to upset you?"

Elizabeth was uncharacteristically pacing, trying to gather emotional momentum to place this squarely in her father's lap. "Bettina ... she ... she made unwanted advances on my Teddy."

An instinctual warning flag went up in Roland Richardson's brain. He knew—yes, he *knew*—it wasn't true, but Elizabeth didn't know that, and he would have to tread lightly and be protective of his daughter's fragile emotional state at this moment. "Tell me what happened or what you know of this incident."

"*Incident?* I don't think Bettina's inviting Teddy up when Dilly is out of town and then hanging all over him, with not-so-subtle commentary, is an incident! No, no, not at all an incident. It's ... it's gross and shameful. Yes, that's it; it's shameful. Poor Dilly. He thinks she's so wonderful. Now I wonder what's going on when he travels. Poor Dilly."

"I felt you were fond of Bettina, Lizzie." He used a form of her name her mother despised, but Elizabeth loved it, coming from her seemingly stodgy father.

"I am. Correction—I was. I just didn't figure her for that type of ... of home-wrecker."

"Obviously, this type of action is not savory and should not be condoned, but I don't think she has earned the home-wrecker label quite yet."

Elizabeth had quieted herself. She asked her father carefully. "You're not defending her, are you, Daddy?" She seated herself on the hassock at her father's feet and leaned forward on his knees, a physical liberty only a beloved daughter could take.

"No, darling. I'm not defending Bettina. Nor am I burning her at the stake. I am neither judge nor jury, especially when I have no tangible proof, and am hearing the story second-hand."

"You're not saying that Teddy has misrepresented the . . . uh, incident?"

"Absolutely not. But think of that game you played as children. If there were at least five of you, one would whisper a story to one of the children, who would whisper it to the next, and so on down the line. The final story was generally completely different from the original. I think you'd have to hear Bettina's version to be totally objective."

"Are you suggesting I speak with her?"

Mr. Richardson weighed his answer carefully, not wanting to expose his daughter to shock and hurt. "You might, but on the other hand, it might prove too emotional for you to handle the meeting with total calm. Although I've always made a point of staying out of any domestic squabbles, I may tackle this problem personally. I know I don't want your mother to get wind of this."

"I agree, Father. Mother might carry the news to extremes, although I'm not sure what those extremes might be."

Ruby waited until she was alone in her daughter's home and then telephoned Bettina. She knew her daughter wouldn't want her to make the call, and quite honestly, she didn't know what she was going to say.

"Oh, Madame, I'm thrilled to hear your voice. I've been so worried about you. Kenneth told me about your flu, and I wanted so much to come to your side and help nurse you back to health."

"Bettina, I felt your goodness and your love every day. And now I'm much, much better and feel it's important that you and I have some private time together to discuss . . . oh, things."

"What things, Madame? Give me a hint. Oh, I'm so happy, hearing your voice again." Bettina was smiling as broadly as possible, with tears of happiness in her eyes.

"No, no, Bettina dear, we need to speak face-to-face. I don't want to discuss anything over the telephone. It's just, oh, I guess it's too impersonal. And my feelings about you are anything but impersonal."

"As are mine about you. And I have important things to talk about with you. I'm going to tell you the total truth about my parents. Part of that story is very sad. While you've been ill, my father died."

"Oh, dear Bettina, I'm so terribly sorry."

"So am I because I could have and should have been there for him before it was too late. But I'm making up for a lot of lost time with my mother."

"You have no idea what that means to me. I have a story to tell you— about my daughter."

"You have a daughter? You never mentioned her."

"It's too long a story. And it may surprise you to know you played an important part in the story."

"Me?"

"Yes, you, sweet Bettina. But I told you I don't want to discuss all these things over the telephone." Out of the corner of her eye, Ruby could see her daughter's car pull into the driveway. "I'm going to have to go now, Bettina, but I promise I'll call soon, and we'll make an appointment to meet."

"I wish you didn't have to hang up now. It's been so long. I want more of you."

"And I want more time with you, Bettina. And it's coming; I promise."

"And how about the Center for Self-Fulfillment? Kenneth said there's progress but a bit slower since he's been so ill."

"Kenneth? Ill?"

"Yes, Madame, very ill. He didn't say what, but from what he said I gather it's serious. You didn't know?"

"I suppose he was keeping it from me because I'm older and wasn't in the best of health myself. Oh, I must run, right now, dear Bettina. Goodbye, darling."

"Goodbye, Madame. Do call me soon. And continue feeling better." *Strange*, thought Bettina. *Wonder what Madame wants to discuss? And why wouldn't Kenneth have told her about his own illness? Perhaps they aren't as close emotionally as I thought.* She forced her attention back to the lengthy letter she was penning to her mother. All the news from Florida was good. Mom had become much more social and sociable and had met a few other widows. She even played mah-jongg a couple of times a week. When they spoke on the telephone, it was hard to visualize the same depressed woman she'd known in the Bronx.

After six days of intensive radiation, Kenny felt more dead than alive and decided to use his illness to keep Bettina on the line. "Bettina, you were good to come see me, although I apologize for how I look. I didn't want anyone to see me this way. I know it's not a pretty sight."

"Don't be silly, Kenneth. It's now that you need friendship and support." But Bettina wasn't prepared to see how Kenny had changed. He had lost nearly fifteen pounds and hadn't been heavy to start with. His hair was gone, even his eyelashes. He looked slightly skeletal and many years older than he had just weeks earlier.

"The doctors tell me not to react too strongly to my mirror, that the hair will come back and so will some of the weight. But right now, not wanting or enjoying any food and feeling weak as a kitten, I wonder if they know what they're doing."

"You've got to trust your doctors, Kenneth."

"Oh, I do, Bettina. They seem to think we got started early enough to have complete success, but they're not willing to give me a clean bill of health yet. So I need patience—not my strong suit. But I'm trying."

"Poor Kenneth. I wish I could do something for you and help take away some of the pain or discomfort."

"Seeing you helps a lot. And thanks for all the magazines. How did you know I like Armani cologne? I'm sure we never discussed it."

"Honestly, I'm embarrassed to say it, Kenneth. I smelled it on you and recognized the scent because it's one my husband uses."

"Boy, I'd hate to have to keep a secret from you." Kenny managed as warm a smile as he could, and Bettina giggled in response. "Tell me about you, Bettina. What have you been up to for these past five or six weeks?"

"Well, there's a lot to tell you. I don't want to tire you, so promise you'll just wave goodbye when you have to rest."

"I promise."

Bettina launched into the story of her parents. Kenny was amazed she shared the story. He knew from the start she was hiding something. He tucked the information away in case he needed it later. When she finished the saga of her parents, she almost mentioned that Madame had called her but, in the last second, decided to keep that information private. Madame had specifically said she wanted a private conversation with Bettina, and that was enough for Bettina—keep the request private too. After an hour, Bettina felt that Kenny was tiring, and the nurses wanted to take blood, so she excused herself, after first giving him a hug and a promise to call every day. He told her he thought they would release him in a day or two, and he would call her.

CHAPTER *24*

Bearding the Lion: What to Wear for Luncheon with Edwina?

Nothing frivolous, nothing too showy. Black would be good. A color she never wore as a poor girl. She decided it would be gutsy for her to wear a suit. She chose a Jean-Paul Gaultier she had purchased in Paris. Black double-breasted, with well-defined lapels, with a long midcoat that reached about four inches above the knee. She wore a high-necked, heavily pleated Issy Miyake white blouse. Jewelry? A diamond crescent pin on the coat, just above the lapels. She loved that pin, especially since Dilly had picked it out for her. Smallish diamond earbobs and her wedding rings. Low-heeled black pumps. Black Gucci bag. Not bad. Bethel Sokoloff from the Bronx wouldn't have worn this, even to a funeral. But Bettina Richardson, with soft blonde hair that looked totally natural, looked terrific. And giving herself credit, Bettina knew it.

Edwina found herself startled at how good Bettina looked. She wondered if someone had dressed her. All classic, but the choice was perfect. She saw heads turn as Bettina walked through the restaurant. "I suppose you hear it all the time, Bettina, but you look very lovely today."

"Thank you, Edwina. I really only care if I hear it from our Dilly, but thank you for saying it."

Our Dilly. Strange that she'd say *our*. "And where is the darling Dillworth these days?"

"Today, he is either thrilling or killing a board of directors in Pittsburgh."

"Oh?" Edwina was amused by the comment. "What's going on? Not, I must admit, that I know or understand what the men in our family do."

"Please understand that Dilly doesn't include me in the business-decision process but quite often tells me what is going on in various companies."

Edwina realized, with a sudden pang, that Roland had never discussed corporate activities with her. Perhaps she should have insisted.

"In this instance, it's a company who desperately wants Richardson Enterprises to take them over. Depending on how well they present their act today, Dilly is going to say yay or nay. Whew, I wouldn't want to have to convince him, unless I knew I had the goods. He's tough. Fair but tough."

My God, Edwina thought, *she has a better working relationship with her husband— my Dillworth—than I possibly did with Roland. That's ridiculous. Remember who she is, Edwina. Remember Moishe Sokoloff.*

"And how have you been, Edwina? What have you and Mr. Richardson— I'm sorry; I just can't call him Roland—been up to recently?" Bettina sensed that things were moving all right. She casually half opened her napkin and laid it across her lap. Before Edwina could answer, the waiter appeared for a drink order.

"I'll have a dry sherry. Bettina? Do join me."

"All right. I'm not much of a drinker. I'll have a wine spritzer, light on the wine, please."

"Let's see ... what have we been doing? You knew we went down to the West Palm house for a couple of weeks. I had to get out of the wet, cold weather."

"I know; it's been dreadful."

"You've never been to the West Palm house, have you?"

"No, we just haven't had time. And besides, Dilly and I went away with the Gutwilligs for that magic week of sailing in the British Virgin Islands. Just thinking about it made the winter blues disappear."

"It sounds quite wonderful. Probably better for your age group; a bit too strenuous for me."

"If you like to swim, it's not too strenuous. I'll bring photos the next time we get together. The Gutwilligs are a marvelous family. I don't know what I'd do without Lisa. I smile the moment I hear her voice."

"She is a fine young woman. I knew her late mother very well. We all envied her Lisa when our children were growing up. She was, and is, a beautiful young woman, perfectly focused, a constant source of pride and comfort to her parents."

"Goodness, that sounds like Dilly and you and Mr. Richardson. I can't imagine him bringing you anything but pride and comfort all these years."

True, thought Edwina, *except for marrying you. Or did he make a mistake?* She found herself confused, rather liking this girl she had set out to destroy. *Don't jump to conclusions too fast, Edwina. Remember she's playing a role. What is she off stage?* "Tell me about your singing lessons, dear."

The rest of the luncheon continued with Edwina mainly asking questions, and Bettina laughing and smiling and answering her mother-in-law's probes … but not minding. She found herself not disliking Edwina, much to her amazement. They both had Dover sole, recommended by their waiter, and a small, perfect salad. No desserts. Young size-eight matrons and older size-twelve matrons never ate dessert. Nothing was worth the calories.

Edwina was submerged in an emotional whirlpool. She hadn't heard her husband walk in and was startled when he spoke. "How was your day, Edwina? I know you went out for lunch. Anyone I know?"

"Yes, dear, I had lunch with Dillworth's Bettina."

Dear God, thought Roland. "For what purpose?"

"What do you mean, for what purpose? She is part of the family, and I thought I needed to know her better."

"And?"

"Besides being exceptionally beautiful, I found her to be interesting and interested. I must confess she surprised me on many counts."

Roland came over, bent over his wife, and kissed her temple. "I'm happy to hear that, dear, very happy to hear that." He smiled as he left the room.

Edwina spoke out loud to herself. "You did surprise me, Bettina. You did surprise me."

Bettina was startled when her singing coach asked Danny Levin to sit in during Bettina's lesson. Besides admiring Bettina's obvious physical attractiveness, Danny Levin, Mr. Broadway to the theater crowd, was intrigued by her voice. "I know you're wondering who I am and why I'm here. I've known Mrs. Rajinsky for many years, and when she's excited about someone's talent, I pay attention. I produce Broadway plays, mainly musicals."

"You have my attention, Mr. Levin, but why would you be interested in me?"

"You have a voice quality that hasn't been heard on Broadway except in a few rare cases. I'd like you to start training for legitimate theater."

Bettina was completely flustered. She instructed herself to calm down and not look like an imbecile. "I'm very flattered, Mr. Levin—"

"Call me, Danny."

"Very well, Danny. But I've never appeared on a stage—"

"Except at the Junior League fund-raiser ball, and I checked you out with three different people at the ball who said you were a show-stopper. Hey, Bettina, you have the talent, and you have the looks. Maybe you can't act your way out of a paper bag, but it's worth pursuing. There are drama coaches, and you can learn to dance."

"Danny, I'm not a star-struck kid looking for a life in front of the footlights. I'm a happily married woman with social obligations and a family of in-laws that wouldn't understand my having a career in the theater. It's a lovely and exciting thought, but I—"

"No buts. Unless you have a dream and are willing to chase your dream, nothing will come true. I think it would be a shame for you to miss the opportunity of performing. And hey, understand I'm not suggesting that you go onstage tomorrow. I just think you should direct your studies toward the possibility of legit theater."

"Well, I'll certainly think about it. And again, I really do appreciate your encouraging remarks. Mrs. R., you're naughty to set me up like this, but I know you did it out of affection for me, and I thank you very much."

Later that day, musing on the conversation, Bettina realized that she thought and spoke differently now, and it all felt normal. What did she say to Mrs. Rajinsky? *"You're naughty to set me up like this . . ."* Saying something like *naughty* certainly was not Bethel, but she said it without thinking of what Bettina would say. She was Bettina. She was feeling good about herself.

Although she did not feel he was hostile to her, Bettina was nervous about Mr. Richardson's impending visit. He had called and requested a meeting. "I'll be in your neighborhood tomorrow, Bettina, and would like to stop in and have a chat with you."

"That would be fine, Mr. Richardson."

"Now, now, we're going to have to find another name for me."

"I'm sorry." Bettina laughed lightly.

"Well, I look forward to seeing you, my dear. I should be there around eleven, if that's convenient."

"Perfect. I'll see you then."

If I were Dilly's father, how would I like my son's wife to look during the day? She decided that classic was best. She selected a crew-necked cashmere sweater in charcoal gray and man-tailored slacks, also charcoal. A narrow belt with a small, tasteful gold buckle. Gold button earrings, a man-sized gold watch, no other jewelry except her wedding band. She pulled her hair back into a french twist. Lace-up oxford flats. Sensible but nice.

"My, what a lucky man Dilly is. What a pleasure to come home to someone as lovely as you."

"You'll make me blush, Mr. Ri—"

"Let's correct that first thing. I am not Mr. Richardson. You are welcome to call me Roland, although there's something else I would much prefer."

"What is that?" Bettina really liked Mr. Richardson. They were standing in the entrance alcove, with Mr. Richardson holding her hand in both of his. She could feel his approval of her in his expression.

"I want you to call me Dad."

"Oh, my God!" Bettina didn't expect that, and the enormity of the offer brought tears that splashed down her cheeks. "I'm sorry; you must think me a silly fool."

"Hardly, my dear." Roland Richardson also was teary. He loved this girl, and her reaction to his request was very endearing.

"My goodness, let me repair my makeup. A runny nose and smeared eye makeup isn't very attractive."

"Ha-ha-ha-ha. You may dry the tears, but you look perfect."

"Come in. Would you like some coffee?"

"That would be excellent."

Bettina indicated that he could sit on the overstuffed sofa, and she settled herself in the small wing chair at the corner of the sofa. "I can't tell you how touched and complimented I am to be allowed to call you Dad . . . Dad."

"The compliment is mine. I feel you have brightened this family. Dilly is more vital and focused than ever before. And much of that change is due to your presence."

"Thank you so much . . . Dad." Bettina, trying not to cry again, leaned forward and kissed Roland on the cheek.

He beamed. "This is going to sound very strange after all this loving exchange."

"What, Dad?"

"I want to talk about Teddy Catarsi." The cloud that appeared on Bettina's face was instantaneous. "I know this is an uncomfortable subject, but don't worry about it. I'm almost certain I know what happened, but I have to confirm my suspicions."

"Mr. Richardson—I mean, Dad—I can't discuss Elizabeth's husband."

"Oh, but you must, to clear your name." Her look of bewilderment was crystal clear.

"Clear my name? What? I don't understand anything." Bettina was wild with worry. After all this love, now there was something hanging over her head.

"I'll be blunt, so we can unravel this small mess. Teddy told Elizabeth that you made improper advances to him."

"That I *what?*" Bettina leaped to her feet, and her look of confusion changed to unmitigated anger.

Roland thought, *I wouldn't want to face her if the anger was directed at me.*

"That pig!"

"Calm down, sweet Bettina. Just sit here, and tell me everything that happened."

When she was finally able to speak and got her breathing under control, Bettina replayed that hideous evening when the detestable Teddy had shown up at her apartment. She left nothing out, including her knee to his privates. She finished, unable to look directly at Mr. Richardson, afraid he would censor her as being ruthless or common. And then she heard a strange sound and looked up.

Mr. Richardson was sitting there, laughing so hard that tears were falling. Bettina smiled and then couldn't help it; she started laughing herself. They howled. Just as they would stop, Roland would say, "And you kneed him in the balls," and they'd start again.

In the middle of this hilarity, Dilly walked in. He needed some papers he'd left locked in his desk. He couldn't believe it. His straight-up-and-down father and his beautiful bride, roaring with laughter. He had to smile at them, and when they saw him, they tried to get it under control. Dilly said, "Are you going to share the joke with me?"

And his father started laughing again, choking out, "You had to be there."

Bettina went to Dilly and gave him a hug and kiss. "Dad and I just got tickled about something silly."

Dilly heard the *Dad* and couldn't believe it. "Well, I'm glad my wife and father have such a good time without me."

"We probably had a better time than if you were here."

"Now, Dad." Bettina put her arm around her father-in-law. "You know that's not true ... but we did have a good laugh, and that's healthy."

"Well, I'm not going to interfere. I just need something from my desk. Good to see you, Dad. Let's have lunch one day next week. I'd like to bring you up-to-date on some of my current thoughts."

"I'd love to do that, son."

"I won't be late tonight, darling."

"Good. Don't have fish for lunch. We're having striped bass tonight."

"Great." He pursued her mouth and kissed her, smiling.

Roland Richardson cheerfully envied his son's love for his wife. It was the way it was supposed to be. He and Edwina just played the game. They never had this kind of relationship.

After Dilly left, Roland and Bettina sat there silently for a minute, each lost in private thoughts. The laughter was over. "I hate to break our reverie, but we still have a serious subject to discuss."

"Yes, we do. Oh, dear God, what must Elizabeth think of me? And what can I do to repair this? I can't go to sweet Elizabeth and tell her she's married to a pig. Oh, Dad, I'm sick about this. Please help me."

"I'm thinking of the best strategy. And frankly, I don't know."

Bettina was honestly distressed. Now that things were starting to go very well with Edwina and the darling Dad, she couldn't bear the thought of that bastard Teddy creating a family rift.

"Do nothing about this until you hear from me."

The last person she expected to see at the Waldorf Astoria was her sister, Mickey. "My, my, sister dear. Do you live here at the Waldorf, or is it just one of those places where you rich girls go for lunch?"

Indeed, Bettina had lunched at the Waldorf with the eight board members of the Junior League. They were interviewing her as a possible board member. Fortunately, she and Lisa had said goodbye to the others and were strolling through the Waldorf, discussing their impressions of the other women. She froze at the sound of Michelle's voice, with its unmistakable burden of a Bronx accent. She couldn't duck it, and Lisa wouldn't understand if she started running out of the hotel. She took a deep breath, tried to look pleasant, and said, "Hello, Michelle. This is my friend,

Lisa Gutwillig." Michelle looked at Lisa, who was wearing a beautiful mink coat. "Lisa, my sister, Michelle."

"That's some coat."

"What brings you to the Waldorf, Michelle?"

"My husband is here for a rabbinical seminar. All the wives were invited for the luncheon today. Big deal—dried chicken and mashed potatoes."

Lisa laughed. "All meals for big organizations are the same—dried chicken and mashed potatoes. I think I'd rather have a ham sandwich."

"Not if you're married to a rabbi."

"Oh, of course, no ham …"

"No pork, no shellfish—oy, at least we're reformed, so we don't have to keep a kosher kitchen. That's a real pain in the neck. Different dishes."

Lisa, sensing Bettina's emotional state, carried the conversational ball. "I know about that, Michelle. My sister-in-law married into a very conservative, religious Jewish family, and they keep a kosher kitchen. It's a lot of work."

Bettina smiled. "It's nice seeing you, Michelle."

"I'll bet."

"Nice meeting you, Michelle. I hate to pull you away, Bettina, but we're going to be late." They had nothing on their schedule. It was just Lisa, trying to get Bettina out of a clearly unpleasant situation.

"Oh, you're right. Say hello to Stanley, Michelle."

"What's the latest from our mother?"

"She's great. Very happy. I speak with her every week. She's a new person. I'm sorry, but we do have to run. Bye." And she and Lisa continued through the hotel. Neither of them spoke until they were about one block from the hotel. "I think I owe you an explanation."

"Hey, girl, you don't owe me a damn thing. Bettina, you're my best friend. When and if you want to talk about family, if ever, I'm always here for you, and whatever gets said stops right here. The only way two women can qualify as 'best friends' is if they have a completely private relationship. Whatever they say to one another doesn't get repeated—to husbands, manicurists, or anyone. But if you never mention today again, ever, I'm with you."

"I love you a lot, Lisa. And one of these days, I will have a story for you."

"I've always suspected you had more going for you than we products of finishing schools, nannies, and silver spoons. Now, we never finished dishing the dames at the luncheon." Lisa, dearest Lisa, was dropping the subject. Bettina was still safe.

Edwina didn't know why she wanted to see Moishe Sokoloff. Her own attitude toward Bettina was hazy. "My goodness, the tailor shop is gone? What happened to that nice Mr. Sokoloff?"

The woman who owned the Laundromat that replaced the tailor shop wondered why this lady, who obviously had big bucks, knew or cared about the old tailor. "Sokoloff died."

"He died? Oh dear. What happened to his wife?"

"One of her daughters has a lot of bucks and moved her to Florida."

"Well, I hope she's all right. I'm so sorry to hear about Mr. Sokoloff."

"Yeah, he was an okay man. His heart went phooey on him."

"Thank you for the information." *So, our Bettina has lost a parent. And she's taking care of her mother in Florida. How do I feel about all this? I don't know.*

CHAPTER 25

Meanwhile, the Ailing Kenny Was Still Alive and Had Prepared a Portfolio of Bogus Materials to Show Bettina

"Look at these photos, Bettina. It's the medical clinic in the Center. It's all really taking shape."

"Gosh, Kenneth, it's so exciting. What's this room going to be?"

The rec … uh … recreation room—all the exercise machines, a half-size basketball court, ping-pong, a steam room, sauna—nice, huh?"

"Nice is hardly the word for it. I'm so glad it's moving along. And how are you doing, Kenneth? You look much better."

"Feeling a little better every day. And my hair is coming back. I'm trying to keep my weight up and don't have any chemotherapy scheduled for another month."

"And the doctors are giving you good news?"

"Everything is good, and the tumor is shrinking, so I think I'm gonna beat it."

"Of course you will, Kenneth. And how's Madame?"

"Her health is fine now. She's just all wrapped up with the people she's staying with. They helped her, so she's helping them."

"How typical of Madame. If you speak with her, tell her how much I miss her."

CHAPTER *26*

Teddy Wouldn't Admit It to Anyone, but He Was Afraid of Roland Richardson

As head of the dynasty, Richardson could—and maybe would—throw Teddy out on his ear. It was worth putting up with Elizabeth to have all that Richardson money in the joint bank account. So he was shaken to see Roland walk in the door of his real estate "office," where he did little more than call his bookies, make lunch dates, and arrange extracurricular sex on the QT.

"Well, hello, Roland. What a surprise." Teddy's big smile might have fooled the average person, but Roland saw the fear behind the smile.

"Good afternoon, Theodore." He knew Teddy hated his formal given name. "Hello, Arthur," Roland greeted one of Teddy's eminently dislikable associates. "If you'll pardon us, I need to speak with Theodore privately," he said, clearly dismissing the man.

"Oh yeah, sure thing, Mr. Richardson." Arthur left as if on fire.

"Well, what a surprise."

"You already said that, Theodore."

"Okay, what's behind the surprise?"

"Bettina."

"I knew there would be problems with that lady. Poor Dilly."

"Oh, shut up, Theodore."

Teddy physically recoiled as though Roland had hit him in the side of the head with a board. "Par ... par-don me?"

"You keep your mouth shut and listen to me. I know what kind of man you are, Ted, and given my druthers, you would not be part of this family. But whatever the reason, our beautiful and dear Elizabeth seems to want you in her life. For that reason, and only for that reason, I am speaking to you and not to Elizabeth."

Teddy realized the danger of the situation, but he also knew the father would not attack him and risk his daughter's happiness. He knew it was a gamble but decided he'd counterattack. "And what, Father Richardson, does the blonde bimbo Bettina have to do with me, a loyal member of this family for almost eight years?" Teddy had moved out from behind his desk and seated himself on the window seat, with the panoramic view of Manhattan as a backdrop. He picked up a cigarette from a silver box on his desk and lit it with the Dunhill lighter. He took a deep drag and slowly exhaled, with a heavy-lidded expression of quasi-boredom.

Roland saw it all and analyzed Teddy's positioning. *He knows—or at least thinks—I won't expose him to Elizabeth. Maybe I can make him uncertain about that.* "If I ever hear you refer to Bettina in such a denigrating fashion, I'll make you eat the words, Theodore. This current crisis was created solely by you. Elizabeth told me about Bettina's so-called unwanted advances on you."

"That's right. She wants more than Dilly can give her, which isn't surprising."

"You're a foolish, foolish man, Theodore, tap dancing on very thin ice. I'm warning you to confine your comments to a bare minimum."

"Hey, Rolly, you're the one backing me into a corner. When cornered, I'm a wolverine—really nasty animals."

"An appropriate analogy. But I'm not interested in what kind of animal you are, I just want to tell you what you are going to do about this lie about Bettina that you told your dear wife."

"Lie? That cunt went after me."

"*Theodore!* You will not speak of *any* woman, especially the women in this family, in that manner. I will not tolerate it. This is my last warning to you."

"Okay, okay, I'll say no more. Tell me what lies Ms. Bettina has been spreading."

"You felt it necessary to tell Elizabeth that Bettina had invited you up to their apartment when Dillworth was out of town and then made advances on you. Elizabeth, a dutiful and loving wife, had no choice but to believe you. She was upset enough to discuss the incident with me. Since I believe I am a mature and careful judge of character, I didn't believe it and went directly to Bettina and confronted her with the story."

"Which of course she denied. What else could she do?"

"Her distress, her anger, couldn't have been fabricated. No, she told me the truth. She told me everything, Teddy Boy, including how she kneed you where the sun don't shine." Teddy was stunned that his father-in-law knew the entire story and would interject street slang into his commentary. "I even checked with their doorman, who told me you apparently had become ill with an ulcer attack and had to be helped downstairs and put into a cab. He said Mrs. Richardson had been solicitous of your health but felt you would be better off recuperating at home. Therefore, Theodore, my take on this tawdry episode is that you *hit on*—isn't that the vernacular these days?—you hit on Bettina, and she wasn't buying any of it, had to fight you off, and finally resorted to physically protecting herself."

"Look, Roland—"

"No, you look, Theodore. I won't tolerate any sorry excuses or any more lies from you. Here's what I want you to do. Go to Elizabeth, and tell her you've been thinking about that evening, and it was an exaggeration on your part. That Bettina had a bit of an attitude that evening, and you mistook her attitude as being a come-on, which indeed it was not. Tell Elizabeth it's not worth even remembering and that you apologize."

"Why should I do that?"

"If you don't, I will use all of my persuasive powers to convince my daughter to leave you, which of course would leave you penniless. And don't think I'm kidding, Theodore. In truth, it would pleasure me greatly to amputate you from this family. Agreed?"

Teddy looked down, tasting the bitterness of the medicine. "I don't suppose I have any choice in this matter?"

"For once, you're absolutely correct. And speak with Elizabeth soon. Tonight! I won't say it's been a pleasure seeing you, because it hasn't. Goodbye."

"Thanks for coming ... Dad." After Roland left, Teddy sat there, smoking, thinking about that rotten bitch Bettina. He spoke out loud to no one. "Bettina, I've just begun to fight. You're as good as dead." He smiled.

CHAPTER 27

"Darling, Will You Be All Right if I Go Away for a Few Days?"

Bettina leaned over Dilly and kissed the top of his head.

"Depends on who you're going away with."

"Oh, gosh, I was afraid you'd ask. He's a count or a duke or something like that. Unusual for a man that young to have such a big, old title. But I'm willing to forgive him the title because he's so terribly handsome, almost beautiful. But don't worry; it's all very platonic." Bettina was enjoying the game. It was a by-product of her newfound security.

"Fine, dear, go ahead, but first, *I'm going to kill him* . . . after I finish reading my newspaper."

"Honestly, Dilly, first things first. Do you have to finish reading the paper before you kill him?"

"Yup. Are you really going to leave me for a few days?"

"Yup. With Lisa. We're going up to Canyon Ranch in Massachusetts for three spa days."

"Why? I haven't noticed you getting porky."

"That's because I work at it, bones. Besides, three days of girl talk, and massages and facials and all that good stuff does a girl good."

"I will miss you, but I'm glad you're finally going to do something about those thighs, and—ouch! I take it back." Bettina was pummeling him with pillows. Then she sat down on his lap and kissed him, long and lovingly.

"Did Fred mind your going away?"

Lisa was driving their new Lexus. "Mind? He bought me new luggage and helped me pack."

"You are nuts, Lisa."

"And my children had a farewell party for me and said not to bother to call, that they were getting unlisted numbers. Nooo, my old sweetie knows I need to get away from that all-boy household now and then, and there's no girl on earth I'd rather commune with than thou."

The trip north was beautiful. The girls stopped for lunch at a beautiful country inn named Troutbeck in Amenia, New York. It was an English country house on hundreds of acres, and it was a perfect setting for the day. A smiling young innkeeper greeted them and escorted them into the Sun Room, with a wall of windows looking across the front lawn, accented by a row of two-hundred-foot-high sycamores planted in 1835. Lunch was delicious—a creamed asparagus soup served in a martini glass. Lisa had penne pasta with a vodka basil sauce; Bettina chose a blackened catfish. Iced tea with fresh mint, no desserts, and therefore, no guilt, as they began their three spa days.

Canyon Ranch in Lenox, Massachusetts, was very luxe, as were the prices. But ah, the sense of being pampered. There were seaweed wraps; Scottish baths; leg waxing; massages; pedicures; steam-room treatments; perfectly balanced, beautiful, low-calorie meals; and long, peaceful strolls through the extraordinary countryside.

"Okay, Lisa, I think it's time I introduced you to the real me."

"Hey, Betts, you don't have to say anything about the old you. Whatever or whoever you were helped make you the multimillion-dollar package you are now. I love the finished product and don't need to know how you came to be."

"I love you, Lisa, and I know you mean every word of that. But perhaps, as Bettina Richardson, I need to be able to confide in my best friend and be secure that the information won't come back to hurt me."

"That goes without saying. But please believe me; just because we ran into your sister doesn't give me the right to know more than that."

"I know that, but perhaps they're right when they say confession is good for the soul. I have fewer problems with my past these days because I'm feeling more comfortable, more secure in my new skin. But maybe in sharing that past with you, I can exorcise it even more."

"It's your call, friend."

They continued strolling through a fairy-tale forest, with patches of determined sun that made its way to the soft forest floor. Bettina said nothing for many minutes.

"My name is … was … Bethel Sokoloff. I am … was … a Jewish girl raised in the Bronx. My late father, who just died last month—"

"Oh, honey, you never told me about your dad."

"I couldn't at that point. Anyway, my dad was a tailor, and Mom took in sewing and cleaned houses. I had a brother who was killed in a holdup when he was nineteen. And you've met my totally charmless sister. In those days, I had such a nose—oy, such a nose—and chewed gum a lot. Utterly delightful. Anyway, one day I decided to do away with Bethel. So I started studying girls like you. I watched the way you walked, the way you dressed. I convinced a surgeon to give me a perfect nose. I drove a speech instructor nuts to get rid of the 'Brawnx ack-sent.' I read the right magazines, memorized the *New York Times* and *New York* magazine every week.

"Then, with new papers, new name, new nose, new voice, and a newly created background, I got a job at Tiffany's and moved out of the Bronx into a women's residential hotel. I thought Tiffany's would be the right place to meet Mr. Right, and I was right. One day, Dillworth Richardson walked into my life—bingo! I still can't believe he fell in love with me. And I fell in love with him. Love him much more now than in the beginning. Guess I was too busy polishing my new role during the first two years. It was tough sledding. Now, it's not so hard. Bethel has become Bettina. Other than dealing with my mother, whom I've moved to an adult community in Florida, I am Bettina Richardson. Poor, tacky Bethel has disappeared. How are you handling all this, Lisa? Are you ashamed of knowing me?"

Bettina had been speaking to the air, not able to look at Lisa. And now she turned to her friend and was pained to see Lisa standing there, tears streaming down her face. "Oh, Lisa, I'm sorry if you're that disappointed or angry—"

"You dope. Bettina, I'm crying because of what you've had to do. I love you, Bettina, more than I love anyone else in the world, except all my boys. My God, and you did all this without someone at your side to help you. I can't begin to tell you how much I admire you. I wouldn't have had the courage to do what you did."

"Oh yes, Lisa, you would have done anything to get out … Bethel saw nothing but unhappiness and ugly and desperation every day. And now, it's becoming nothing but a distant memory. But Bettina Richardson is trying to do something wonderful."

"What, Betts?"

Bettina told her about the Center for Self-Fulfillment and the Madame. She didn't tell her how she'd met Madame or mention the amount of money she had invested. It was all sugar-coated enough so Lisa could feel good about Bettina's participation.

The three days passed in a minute, and the girls packed and returned to their privileged lives in Manhattan.

Bettina called Dilly the minute she arrived back at their apartment. "Hello, my love, did you miss me?"

"I certainly did, Marilyn."

"It's Bettina, remember?"

"Oh yeah, Bettina. Marilyn is the brunette."

"Are we going to waste more time talking, or are you going to come home from the office as early as possible for some serious kissing and all that other stuff that goes with it?"

"Boy, if spas make you horny, I'm going to send you away more often. Yes, my darling, I won't be late. Why don't you call March and make a reservation for eight o'clock for dinner? And I'll be home before seven."

"Perfect. Kisses, lover."

"Back atcha."

CHAPTER *28*

Herman Convinced Kenny to Bring in a "Medical Expert" to Make Sure Bettina Didn't Get Suspicious

"I thought you'd enjoy meeting one of our leading psychologists. He's going to be in New York City next week, and I can make a date for you to meet with him, okay?"

"Well, fine, Kenneth. I certainly don't feel qualified to intellectualize the types of treatments we're going to be offering."

"I know that, Bettina. I just want you to feel part of the development process."

"Have you heard from Madame lately?"

"To tell the truth, Bettina, I'm a little concerned about Madame. She's making vague references to retiring."

"Really!"

"Yes, and frankly, I've been too busy to have a serious confrontational meeting with her. But I'll follow up on the situation."

"And please keep me in the loop as well, Kenneth."

"Absolutely. Anyway, keep Tuesday morning open, and I'll arrange a time and place for you to meet the good doctor."

"Terrific. Thanks for the call." She hung up and sat there, wondering what the problem was with Madame. That was the reason she was so deeply involved in the Center. Without Madame at the helm, did she want to be involved? And was it too late to become disentangled? She must call Madame soon, to have that private meeting.

CHAPTER 29

Danny Levin, the Broadway Producer, Had Requested a Meeting with Bettina. She Couldn't Fathom Why

"I know I told you to start studying for a legitimate stage life, but sometimes opportunities appear, not just knocking on the door but knocking it down."

"I think you're making me nervous, Danny." Bettina, Danny, and Mrs. Rajinsky, her voice coach, were all seated in Bettina's living room. Danny, wearing a "Broadway" suit, looked out of place. Mrs. R., with her more refined European background, was appreciating the subdued richness of the décor. And Bettina looked like Bettina Richardson, wearing ivory-colored gabardine slacks and an ivory silk blouse, belted and buckled in gold, and simple gold jewelry. She was all *Town & Country*.

"Hey, Bettina, there's a new musical that they're ready to cast, and there's a part that's so you—it wouldn't even take acting talent to play it. They should name the character Bettina Richardson. The girl must be young, beautiful, sing like an angel, and look like she's worth a few million bucks. Like I said, it's you."

"You're assuming too much. I might be a piece of lead on the stage. With lights, the roar of the crowd, and the smell of the greasepaint, I might get terminal jitters and die on my feet."

"And you might not."

"Bettina, dear." Mrs. R. hadn't spoken yet. "You would be amazed what adrenaline can do for you. I've known performers who were physically ill, and as their cue to enter the stage was spoken, their illnesses would disappear, the fire would come back in their eyes and their steps, and they would perform and make the audience embrace them with their eyes and hearts. I believe in your ability to do that also."

"I'm ... I'm very flattered ... and very confused. And of course, auditioning is no guarantee that I would get the part, so please forgive me for speaking as though it's a done deal. I just don't think I can put my wifely obligations aside for a career in the theater. My number-one role in life is to be Mrs. Dillworth Richardson. It's a very satisfying role to play, full of love and kudos. And, well, I'm babbling. Danny, you're very sweet to bring this opportunity to my doorstep, but—"

"No buts about it, Bettina. And I don't want you to dismiss it without discussing it with your husband. This is real, this is now, and I believe you would be brilliant. Please don't dismiss it out of hand, Bettina. It's truly a once-in-a-lifetime opportunity."

"You're both wonderful to speak so reassuringly to me about my talent. And yes, I will discuss it with Dilly. But in all fairness to you, don't hang all hopes on me."

"But you will think about it?"

"Yes, Danny, I will think about it."

They finally left, and Bettina sat there, dazed. *This can't really be true. Me, on Broadway? And even if I was offered the role, what does that do to Dilly? I know what Broadway schedules are like. Seven or eight performances a week, only Sunday and Monday free. And would I make a fool of myself, and in doing so, embarrass the Richardsons? Dear God, what am I to do? I need Madame.*

She picked up the phone and dialed. "Lisa, oh, I'm glad you're home. You're not going to believe this one, but I need to talk to you about it. Oh, do I need your point of view. You can come over here? Great, but I don't mind coming to you."

"No, I'll come over there. All the kids are home today, and I'm going to give them up for adoption and file for divorce. Can't wait to get out of here."

"Terrific. I'll rustle up some lunch for us. See you soon."

CHAPTER *30*

"Your Mrs. Richardson's Nose Is as Phony as Her Accent"

Teddy was thrilled. "How do you know that?"

"First, we tracked phone calls, and that lady made a lot of calls to the Bronx. Then we started with footwork. We talked to everyone in the Bronx, and found a doctor who did a nose for a Bethel Sokoloff. Showed him photos of her. He said yes, that's the one. He didn't want to tell us, but we reminded him that doctors don't do good work if their fingers get broken."

"Fabulous. What else?"

"We lucked into one more important person—a speech instructor, who beat the Bronx accent out of her. He absolutely identified her as the girl he taught—Bethel Sokoloff. And there's more stuff, more recent. We're not sure if she's playing around on the side or not, but she's been seeing a small-time con man named Kenny. They had meetings, there have been phone calls, and recently, he was in the hospital, and she went to visit him there. No one who was really straight would spend any time with this Kenny guy."

"What are they doing together?"

"We don't know … maybe nothin'. But we're watching that situation."

"Good work, fellows. I knew she was hiding a lot."

"Here's our bill. You owe us twelve thousand dollars for time and manpower up to now."

"You don't think that's steep?"

"No, we think it's exactly what you agreed when you signed this contract. We suggest you just pay it, mister. We're not the kind of people you want to owe money to. And do we continue? Three hundred dollars a day, plus fifty dollars an hour for each of our men on the street."

"Okay, let's continue another couple of weeks." *Ha-ha-ha! Well, Ms. Bettina, you're going to get yours. I won't be thrown out of this family—you will!*

The "doctor," a paid actor, had been well briefed and was very reassuring to Bettina. He spoke of some of the advances treating addictions and how the power of positive reinforcement with lots of feedback was absolutely the only way to go.

"How do you feel about the spiritual ties to the program, Doctor?"

"I think they're very wonderful, but I would be less than honest with you if I said that was my primary interest. I'm a professional health care physician. My focus must be patient health and treatment. Of course, a good spiritual attitude is going to help these people get back on their feet."

After the doctor left, Kenny insisted that Bettina linger a while so they could catch up.

"So, my lovely Bettina, how goes your life?"

"Magically, Kenneth. It's all magic. There are a few cracks in the marble sidewalk, but I'm handling those."

"And your relationship with ... what do you call him? Oh yes, Dilly?"

"Well ... that too has become rounder, softer, more complete. He's always been loving with me, but now I'm reciprocating from within. Dilly is a fine, wonderful person. And yes, I'm very much in love with him. You know something, Kenneth, all during your life you imagine what your great love affair is going to be like. How you will feel about that person. How he will treat you. And of course, it's always unrealistic. Nothing can be that good. And suddenly, you are faced with the reality of your life, and probably, at that point, your marriage either gels or you fall apart. Mine is gelling. Our love for each other is in the air."

Kenny had said nothing. He looked around the room, finally took a long breath, and looked back to Bettina. "I guess that means you and I . . . I mean, we . . . never mind."

"Oh, Kenneth, I remember the day we kissed. That was very sweet. But it never happened. I must be what I am, Mrs. Dillworth Richardson. You're very sweet, Kenneth. Please don't harbor any hostile thoughts about me."

"That would be impossible, Bettina. I have only the highest regard and respect for you."

"Thank you, friend Kenneth. Now, let's discuss Madame. I'm very confused and worried about her noninvolvement."

"So am I, Bettina. I'm still not sure of where it's all going to come out. She was ill but seems to be over the illness, but she still doesn't want to come back. I haven't given up. I'm going to see her next week and will make a very strong appeal. She absolutely should be part of it."

"Oh yes. It's not the same without her."

"Don't worry, Bettina; we'll be fine. And who knows? Maybe the problem will have gone away by this time next week."

"My goodness, I'm going to be late. I have a friend coming over to discuss a very interesting opportunity that's come up for me."

"Can I help?"

"Thanks, but no thanks, Kenneth. I might discuss it with Madame, if she were communicating with us. It's something quite interesting. I'll let you know what, if any, decision I make."

"Okay, sounds mysterious but interesting. It was wonderful seeing you today, Bettina."

"Well, I thank you. The doctor was quite impressive. I'm glad things are moving along. Oh, must run. Toodle-oo, Kenneth. So glad to see you looking healthier."

Edwina had her detectives track down Mrs. Sokoloff. At Edwina's suggestion, they had a woman operative meet with Mrs. Sokoloff about a possible retirement/health plan. She recorded her findings and sent a tape north. The detectives left it with Edwina, who played it one day when her apartment was completely empty.

"Hi, gentlemen. I met with that Mrs. Sokoloff, and here are my findings." Her voice was more Southern than not. But her pronunciation was clear enough to understand. "I'd say this little lady lucked out. She lived in the Bronx, in a kind of nothing apartment, for a lot of years. Then, all of a sudden, her husband kicks the bucket, and in steps one of her daughters, Bethel, who the mom thinks has married someone with big bucks. Anyway, Bethel not only takes care of hospital and medical expenses for Dad but moves her mom down to this fancy mobile home park.

"She buys her mother a 1,500-square-foot unit, really comfortable, and the daughter goes out and furnishes it all in just one morning. She said her darling Bethel calls her every week and writes her every week, and she said there's more money in the bank than she can spend, and she likes her neighbors and friends down here. Nothing but positive playback.

"That's about it. Oh, one more thing. I asked the mother if I could see a photo of Bethel, and she showed a photo of the typical Jewish-nosed New York Jewish girl. And she said, 'But she doesn't look like this anymore. Her nose is very small, and her hair is a soft blonde, and she just looks different—like a rich girl looks in New York.'"

Edwina sat there, unmoving. An hour passed, and she thought of this poor little woman with the rich, beautiful daughter, who undoubtedly was Dilly's Bettina. She had deceived Dilly. She had passed herself off as something she was not. Edwina spoke aloud to the empty room. "What do I do with this information? I don't know. I honestly don't know."

When in Doubt, Call Lisa. "Okay, If You Were Dilly or Edwina Richardson, How Would You Feel about Me Becoming a Broadway Star?"

"Gosh, Betts, why don't you ask me a hard question? What the hell do you mean about you becoming a Broadway star? You are full of more surprises than a belly dancer at a girdle convention. You're starting to make me nervous." Lisa was almost dancing around the room, unable to sit still.

"Well," Bettina said, making that a two-syllable word, "that's what's been offered, at least the possibility of it, and I'm stymied. Don't have a freaking idea of what to say. My initial response was 'forget it,' and I'm sure that's the correct answer, but I promised I would at least consider it and discuss it. So I'm discussing with my best and most important friend. And it's all your fault anyway, because none of this would have happened except for the Junior League Ball."

"All right, I've stopped hyperventilating and am calm enough to hear the entire, hopefully moral story."

"Oh, it's moral, you ninny." And Bettina took Lisa through the story about Mrs. Rajinsky and Danny Levin and his insistence that she try out for a new Broadway-bound musical.

"I'm so impressed, so cheerfully envious, I could die from it. I realize how little I do, how little I have to offer, when compared to you."

"If you ever say anything that stupid again, Lisa Gutwillig, I'll never speak to you. You are the best wife and mother in this entire world and the mover and shaker behind all the worthwhile organizations and charities in this city. This . . .thing that has come my way is all happenstance. Or pure luck. And besides, I'm not trying to one-up you; that would be impossible. I need you to help reassure me that just saying no is exactly what I should do."

"Mmmm, not sure I agree."

"How could I convince Dilly and his family that it's just fine for me to go on Broadway? They think a lady should never wear red because it's too showy. God, to have a Richardson on the stage, even though it's not vaudeville . . . doubt if they could tolerate it."

"You'll never know until you lay it on them."

"I realize all this is just pure nonsense. Danny Levin wanting me to try out doesn't at all mean the producers and director are going to jump at the chance of having a total nobody as one of the key players. And who knows? Maybe my real motivation here is fear. Fear of bombing badly or looking like the rank amateur I am, of embarrassing my family and friends."

"If you're looking for sympathy or reassurance for this fear crap, you're looking in the wrong corner. I'd say go for it, girl, and if you sense that Dilly—and screw his family—but that Dilly really would be pained for you to do it, that's a reason to say, 'Thanks, but no thanks.'"

"I don't know, Lisa. I love your point of view, but I don't know if I have the . . . the . . ."

Lisa had seated herself on the sofa next to Bettina and took both hands in her own. "The guts? You certainly do. Wish mine were as well developed. Granted, I don't face these magnificent challenges. Oh, honey, you only go through this thing called life once. This is just too good, too juicy, too uplifting to pass up. As you say, maybe they won't want you, and maybe the family won't be thrilled, but my gut feeling is that you will succeed, you will be a star, and we will all bask in the glow of your constellation. My God, I sound like a Dear Abby column. Forgive all the verbal shenanigans; you know what I mean."

"We'll see, Lisa. Thank you for everything. Seems I'm always saying that."

"Hah!" The two friends embraced and cheek-kissed.

Left alone for the afternoon, Bettina thought long and hard about telling Dilly about the possible tryout. Or would she do the tryout and then tell him? *I want Madame's point of view. Maybe I'll try to find her.*

Bettina had convinced herself that there wasn't the vaguest possibility of her getting the part, so she would go ahead with the tryout without discussing its ramifications with Dilly.

There was a week of everyday sessions with Mrs. Rajinsky, who had chosen two songs from *Sunset Boulevard*: "As If We Never Said Goodbye" and "The Perfect Year." She felt their range and strong emotional aspect would be excellent showpieces for Bettina.

Bettina applied herself diligently, telling herself she was only satisfying Mrs. R.'s need to have a student trying out for Broadway. It couldn't—and wouldn't—happen! Danny Levin sat in for three of these sessions. "Danny, I appreciate your interest, but you make me nervous, being here."

"What happens when you go to the tryout? You think the theater is going to be empty? Get used to people looking at you, appraising your ability."

"All right, all right, you've made your point. Do you have any constructive criticism, or have you finally come to realize that you've made a mistake, that I'm not star material?"

"I'm not going to tell you what I think and what I see. You're strong enough to feel what's working and what isn't. The only comment or question I have is about what you're going to wear at the tryout."

"Goodness, I hadn't given it a thought! Maybe, mmm, slacks, low heels, a comfortable silk shirt."

"Nope! Even though that's one of the costumes your character would wear in the show, I'd like them to see your body."

"I beg your pardon."

"Don't get your perfect little nose out of joint. I'm not asking you to strip. I just want you to wear one of those perfect little go-to-town dresses, a sheath, no more than knee length, so they can see your perfect legs, maybe some nice heels—not six-inch things; something you can stand and walk in comfortably. And, oh yeah, put on evening makeup."

"But it's for eleven in the morning."

"Yeah, but you're up on a stage, with a spot on you, and the makeup has to be forceful enough to stand up to lighting and distance."

"And how would you like my hair, Mr. DeMille?"

"Sarcasm doesn't break my bones. Wear it soft, not pulled back in the twist the way you have it today. The part you're trying for is the girl every mother wants her son to marry. She's soft, elegant, beautiful. She's vulnerable but not weak."

"My oh my, sounds just like my résumé."

"And she's not mouthy or sarcastic."

"Sorry about that. I just don't think of myself as all that perfect."

"Maybe you should. I gotta go. I'll be in the back of the house tomorrow morning. Break a leg."

"Thanks, Danny. I'm afraid I really will. I'll try not to embarrass you."

"Not a chance. Just listen to Mrs. R., and sing for her tomorrow."

CHAPTER *32*

Elizabeth Richardson Catarsi, While Bright, Suffered from the Same Intellectual Malaise That Affected Many Young Women from Overly Moneyed Families

She'd never had to really cut it on her own. There always were going to be funds available, trusts after trusts. But she was a good and loving human being. Perhaps her greatest weakness was her ongoing affection for her husband, Teddy, who had neither her moral fiber nor her innate sense of goodness.

Her smile illuminated a room. Her friends could trust her with intimate secrets. In her younger years, she flitted and flirted with one possible career after another. She was a gifted painter, but after a few years of study, when she was really getting good, she decided it was too lonely a life, too cut off from her friendships, and she put her easel and brushes permanently away. She danced on and off the stage of summer theater a couple of summers, but seeing the questioning look in her mother's eye, she fell into line, as was her predilection. Had she trusted her intellect, she would have been a poet. There was true talent in her soul and enough money in the bank to allow her to pursue such an ethereal career. But there was no mental mentor to help her understand and nurture that sensitivity in herself.

In truth, she really liked Bettina. Bettina was different from the rest of them, maybe more instinctual; there was something there. She couldn't put her finger on it, but she felt there was a worthwhile human behind the smooth blonde facade. Then, this Teddy and Bettina issue surfaced. She was outraged, later confused, and then, for a few tormenting days, concerned that the story hid a sexual interest on Teddy's part. She later decided that wasn't true. Teddy would not and could not want another woman when he knew he had her love, and Bettina wouldn't risk alienating Dilly for a liaison with another man.

Now Teddy has told her his impression that Bettina had hit on him was in error. That he was tense and angry about an office issue, and she was on edge about something personal, and he believes he interpreted her off-handedness as a possible come-on, and that it wasn't true, and he didn't want Elizabeth to cause any family uproar when it wasn't necessary. However, since that explanation, he had made asides about the "real Bettina" without any explanation. It was confusing, and she wondered whether she should just drop it, push it out of her mind, or seek the basic truth.

Bettina, on her part, after repulsing the repulsive Teddy, had shied away from Elizabeth, fearing that she'd say the wrong thing. Now, enough time had softened the incident, and she had called Elizabeth, suggesting they go to a matinee together, first lunching in the theater district. Elizabeth was delighted, having felt the distance grow between them. That day had arrived.

My God, Elizabeth thought, *Bettina grows lovelier every time I see her.* On this afternoon with her new "sister," Bettina was wearing a hunter-green slack suit, with a pale celery-colored shell blouse, her favorite diamond crescent pin on the lapel, and small emerald and diamond earrings. She had her glorious hair, pulled back tight to a spinsterish bun, which simply accented her perfect features, creamy skin, and bright smile. A large Chanel silk shawl with magnolias and green leaves was artfully draped around her shoulders and tied off-center. She looked perfect. Elizabeth too looked her part in a classic Chanel suit, all black and white, down to her spectator pumps and good pearls with a black-gold clasp. The two of them caught the eye of every passer-by, both for their beauty and their evident taste, style, and, yes, money.

Thai food was just right for midday—not too heavy, nicely spiced. The two of them chatted about their various activities. "Are you still studying singing, Bettina?" Elizabeth, as was everyone present that night, had been knocked out by her performance at the Junior League Ball.

Bettina considered discussing her current offer to try out for Broadway but decided she needed first to discuss it with Dilly. "Absolutely, Elizabeth. It's good for me—like daily exercise. It's another discipline that can't hurt me in the long run. And I do enjoy serenading myself in the shower."

Elizabeth truly liked her sister-in-law and was determined to make the unpleasantness associated with Teddy's original story fade into a forgotten past.

For the theater that day, they had chosen Christopher Plummer's tour de force as *Barrymore*. And indeed, Plummer was Jack Barrymore—drunk, disorderly, disrespectful, and very, very amusing. He was all alone on the stage, with only a prompter off-stage, a respectful voice who would respond with the missing words, when "Barrymore" would snarl, "Line!" Their relationship took on more color as Barrymore refused to present *Richard III* as he had been contracted, instead concentrating on telling stories, imitating his sister, Ethel, and his wheelchair-bound brother, Lionel. Now, half drunk, out of shape, he waxed poetic about his sex life ("What were you last in, Mr. Barrymore?" "Joan Crawford! No, it was some piece of MGM crap.") Bettina and Elizabeth roared at Plummer's pluperfect performance.

The two beautiful young women parted fondly, Bettina grateful that Elizabeth didn't press her for the real scoop on the Teddy incident.

CHAPTER *33*

Kenny Had Decided, with Herman's Consensual Advice, to Attack the Ruby Problem Head-On

"All right, Ruby. You've had time to recover, and now it's time to push on with the final chapter of our plan."

"What the hell happened to you, Kenny? You look awful."

"It doesn't matter. I was sick; now I'm better, and I'm living up to our agreement, and so are you."

Marianne entered the room. "My mother isn't going to do any such thing. You must leave right now, Mister Whatever-your-name-is."

"Stow it, lady. Would you like to see the signed agreement or view the tapes of your sweet little mommy tightening the noose on our pigeon? Besides, I'm not asking her to do a big favor. Your old lady gets half a million dollars for her part."

"I don't want the money, Kenny; it's dirty. I care about that girl and don't want you to hurt her."

"It'll hurt her worse to see you go to the slammer, because that's where you're heading, you old piece of shit."

"Do not speak of my mother that way."

"Lady, fuck off. Your mother has been scamming people for years, and this is going to be her last and biggest scam. Once we have the final payment, and your mom gets her cut, she'll never hear from me again."

"And if I just refuse to cooperate, Kenny?"

"I'll turn you in. My evidence shows you to be leader of the operation, and maybe I'll have to spend a few years behind bars ... I can afford it. But if they send you to the slammer, that's where you'll die. So I'm going to make an appointment for a reunion with Bettina this coming Tuesday. It's going to be at the Waldorf Astoria in a room booked with your name, Madame. It's for 11:00 a.m., and you damn well better be there, or the next knock on your door will be from the authorities."

"Forgive me for this intrusion into your private life, Mr. Richardson, but I must bring these checks to your attention."

"That's quite all right, Mr. Khan. As the family's banker for many years, you certainly have the right to red-flag something that looks suspicious. What do you have for me?" Dilly wasn't terribly concerned, only interested in what could prompt their ultraconservative banker to insist on a private meeting.

"Well, sir, these two checks signed by Mrs. Richardson come to five million dollars."

"*Wh-what?*" Dilly was so startled he jumped to his feet. "You have my full attention. May I see them, please?"

"Certainly, sir. We have verified the signature as being hers. Both checks have been honored. I apologize in that I had not seen the first check. It apparently cleared whilst I was on a family holiday. Although it is not unusual for large sums of money to be brokered in your family, this struck me as being somewhat odd."

"Hmmm, the Center for Self-Fulfillment. Sounds like a charity, which is fine—but five million dollars? Mrs. Richardson has unlimited access to ten million dollars, but I can't believe she'd spend this kind of money without discussing it with me first."

"I do hope you're not angry with me for bringing this to your attention."

"Quite the contrary. It is your job to do so, and it is my job to understand why this amount of money has been spent. I thank you, Jayson, for being forthright and confrontational about this issue. You have my gratitude."

"I'm relieved to hear that." Khan departed, leaving Dilly to some bewildering thoughts. Why would and how could Bettina spend $5 million without discussing it with him? *Perhaps I'll discuss it with her tonight, although I know she's in deep rehearsal for something that's scheduled for tomorrow. Maybe I'll wait a day and meanwhile try to find out something about this Center for Self-Fulfillment.*

He pressed the intercom to his secretary. "Lydia, please call George Canales in computers, and ask him to come see me, today, if possible."

CHAPTER 34

Bettina Said to Herself, "It's Just Another Morning." But Of Course, It Wasn't. This Morning She Was Going to Audition for a Broadway Musical

"Nonsense, Bettina," she said, speaking out loud to the huge, beautiful bedroom she shared with Dilly. "If you thought you had a squeaking chance, you would have cleared all this with Dilly first. You know things like this don't happen, so don't dwell on it. Just get out there this morning and try not to embarrass Mrs. R.—and yourself."

She took a little longer than normal with her morning ablutions, lazing about in the tub. She had had a pedicure (how funny; she wasn't going to show them her feet) and manicure the day before and decided she'd be most relaxed doing her own hair. Before shaving her legs, she rolled up some oversize curlers to enhance a couple of soft curls.

Jewelry. Well, Danny said to look rich. All right, pale, blonde, and rich. Pearls at her ears and a long strand of perfect pearls with a diamond clasp. The dress, a Donna Karen, in a surprising cold-weather color, a pale champagne beige, boat-necked, zipped up the back, long tapered sleeves, and just barely to the knee. On her trim body, it was perfection. And with everyone wearing black for these cool days, the pale was a standout color. Beneath it, pale panty hose and bone-colored lizard pumps. A single gold bangle around her left wrist, wedding band and engagement ring, and a small, delicate gold watch on the right wrist. She leaned over, brushing her hair forward, and then flipped it all back, and it fell in place almost perfectly. *Good, no high breezes today, so it'll stay in place.*

Bettina tried to remember having show business fantasies as a child, but the child she knew, Bethel Sokoloff, no longer existed. So now it was a childish fantasy being lived out in a purely adult environment.

She entered the stage door per her instructions, gave her name to the man at the door, and within two minutes, a handsome man came to greet her. "Good morning, Bettina. I'm John Moran, one of the show's producers. Danny Levin told us about you, and we're looking forward to your audition."

"Thank you, John. I feel privileged to be here."

John was cute—no, handsome. Kind of reminded her of the famous Gene Kelly. *Stay calm, Bettina. Ah, there's a familiar face.*

Mrs. Rajinsky appeared. "Hello, my darling Bettina. How are we feeling today?"

"I feel terrific. Somehow I didn't expect a reception at a tryout."

"Well, you had good advance press, Bettina." John had taken her arm and was leading her gently down a hall.

Bettina was trying to act as though this was all natural. It was the backstage of every movie she'd ever seen—narrow, dark hallways, now and then a star over a door, wires and fuse boxes and ropes. She had a shudder when she thought, *My God, what if it happens, and they offer me the part?* She almost swooned, thinking of Dilly and the family.

John Moran, a committed playboy who believed in variety as the spice of life, was fighting an internal struggle too. He said to himself, *I'm losing it, totally.*

Bettina felt his attraction to her, or was she just imagining it? It didn't matter; cute was cute, but she belonged to Dilly.

She heard a piano playing and a beautiful voice. As the stage came into view, there was a very pretty girl singing a wonderful ballad from a current hit show. Bettina was almost relieved. *There's no way I will beat out that girl. She sings beautifully, she is beautiful, and no doubt is an experienced actress.*

The other woman finished her song, and a few people in the black theater applauded.

"Bettina Richardson, please step out to stage center."

Bettina steeled herself, remembered she didn't trip when she had to meet Edwina the first time, lifted her chin, smiled sweetly, and strode out to the center of the stage with her best Madison Avenue healthy stride.

A man stepped into the small pool of light in the front row. "How do you do, Mrs. Richardson. My name is Gene Morales, the musical director of the show. Sitting here with me is Hunter Carlson, the director. And you've met John Moran, one of the producers. I see you've brought your accompanist. I'm not going to ask you about your theater background because I know there is none. However, people who understand theater believe you are just waiting to be discovered. Would you like to comment on that?"

"That I am standing here in front of you, knees not shaking, is reassuring to me. For me to believe that Broadway has just been waiting for me to emote, to sing, is a tough stretch. However, I'm grateful that others believe me to be talented enough. If nothing else, being allowed to be here today is a gift, and I accept it with heartfelt thanks and modesty."

"Nicely put, Ms. Richardson. May I call you Bettina?"

"Please do."

"Very well. You're on, Bettina."

"Thank you. Mrs. R., we'll start with 'A Perfect Year.'"

Mrs. Rajinsky started the piece, and Bettina began, her voice smiling in the spirit of the song, as Norma, the aging actress of *Sunset Boulevard*, tries to vamp and seduce the young writer. During a middle section, where there are no lyrics, she moved as though dancing with an invisible partner, laughing, and then returning to the lyrics. There was a surprising amount of applause at the end, Bettina aware of John Moran, still off stage, applauding loudly.

"Would you honor us with another selection?"

"My pleasure, gentlemen. Mrs. R."

The moody yet lyrical song "It's Like I Never Said Goodbye" drifted across the empty theater. It was a dramatic piece, allowing Bettina to almost whisper, and to belt, and to evoke pathos. She lost herself during the singing, imagining herself as the old actress returning to a movie set, where she hoped to be recognized. She did it flawlessly. The piece ended. There was dead silence and then even more applause. Bettina did a half curtsy, difficult in her tight sheath, and then lifted her head and smiled that sunny, warming smile that had become her trademark.

Gene Morales spoke first. "Bettina, it's difficult for us to believe that was your first audition. Perhaps Broadway *is* waiting for you. However, we're not going to offer you the part this very minute or perhaps ever. First, we must discuss you among ourselves. But we want you to be extremely proud of yourself, and please give your telephone numbers to John Moran, so we can find you quickly."

"Yes, thank you very much, Bettina. We will be in touch." That was Hunter Carlson, the director.

"Thank you, gentlemen. And thank you, Mrs. R. Goodbye, everyone. Thanks again." And Bettina exited the stage, where a beaming John Moran greeted her and took both her hands in his.

"You're magic, absolutely magic."

"Oh, thank you, John. This was very exciting and surprisingly pleasant. I'm sure everyone isn't handled this sweetly. Thank you very much. Here's my card with our home phone and my private answering machine."

John was wishing she was giving him a private number and insisting that he call her. But he knew that wasn't true. It didn't matter. He was smitten, and he knew it.

Bettina was dazed. It couldn't happen. She didn't want it to happen. Or did she?

"How was your day, darling? Didn't you have some singing event?"

"Yes, Dilly dear, I did. It was … okay. I'm not quite sure what it will mean. I'll keep you apprised."

"Would it help you to talk about it?"

"I don't think so. I'm quite tired tonight and don't think I want to dwell on it. If there's more to report, if it's worthwhile, I'll make a full report, *mon capitan*."

"I love it when you speak in foreign tongues."

"You know how clever I am with foreign languages. Chevrolet, lasagna, and *comment allez vous* is about the extent of my language skills. You're just making fun of it."

"I am not. I just think of French as the language of love, and when you say anything in French, even Chevrolet, I think of making love."

"You're a psychiatrist's wet dream."

"Come here, cherie, and kiss me. I'm an old Foreign Legion officer, home from the wars, and now I need the warmth of a woman."

"Why would I want an old Foreign Legion soldier who's probably wrinkly and maybe smells bad? I have an arrangement with this really cute, tall, blond guy with a sexy body … and he always smells delicious."

"And who is that?"

"You never look at yourself in the mirror. You are a really cute, tall, blond guy with a sexy body, and I am nuts about you. If I kiss you, will you promise to take advantage of me?"

"Count on it."

"Pucker up."

CHAPTER *35*

Hello, Roland. It's Teddy, Your Son-in-Law; Remember Me? Anyway, I Have Some Very Interesting News I'd Like to Share with You

Roland flinched at the hateful sound of Teddy's voice and knew intuitively that whatever news he had was driven by the need to hurt or belittle or cheat someone.

"Is it some juicy tidbit you can toss my way through the phone, or does it require a face-to-face meeting?"

"Oh, this one requires eye contact."

"Very well, Ted. Today isn't possible. You may come to my office tomorrow morning at ten. Be prompt. I have a full calendar."

"Not to worry. I'll be there ... wouldn't miss it ... Dad."

"So, Dad, I thought you'd like to know what I found out about your precious Bettina."

"Theodore, do not call me Dad. Even if I were your father, I wouldn't admit to it."

"Okay, okay, okay. But I thought a little reality check on the blonde princess wouldn't hurt."

"Speak your piece, and get out."

Teddy was trying to not overact to Roland Richardson's evident hostility. He hadn't realized how far he'd slipped in the eye of his powerful father-in-law. "Okay, Roland. Here's the scoop. Her name isn't Bettina; it's Betty Sorklov—"

"No, Theodore, you're incorrect. Her name was Bethel, not Betty, and her last name was Sokoloff."

"Wh-what? You know?"

"Yes, I know. What other old news do you have for me?"

"She's running around with a two-bit hoodlum named Kenny something-or-other, two-timing Dilly."

"That's pure lie, Theodore, and you know it."

"I know they've seen each other."

"Seeing one another, perhaps some relationship from the past, does not mean there is any kind of relationship. Bettina wouldn't do that."

"You mean Bethel wouldn't do that."

"No, Theodore, I mean Bettina. Her name is Bettina. Bettina Richardson. Her presence, her actions, and her obvious love for her husband all prove it. Are you quite through?"

"What's going on here? What's she got on you? Or maybe you're having a thing with her—"

"You loathsome pig. Get out, and I mean now. I suggest you tread very lightly around this family, Theodore. If I catch you stepping out of line just once, I'll have you exorcised from this family. Out, now!"

Teddy said nothing. He left. His anger swelled inside of him like a burning tumor. "Bethel … Bettina … I'll see you dead."

"I don't know what interest you have in this Center for Self-Fulfillment, Mr. Richardson. All I know is it doesn't exist."

"You're sure, Canales?"

"Yes, sir. With computer worldwide systems, we can check everything and anything, and that place does not exist. There's no incorporation or company papers filed in any of the fifty states or offshore. We did find a name by back-tracing the cashed million-dollar check from Mrs. Richardson. Here's his name: Kenneth Monroe. We have this as his last address. In fact, he recently received cancer treatments at Roosevelt Hospital and was released with a decent prognosis. We did not run a personal check on the man. I think you'd have to have a private investigator to do that, and I can give you the names of a couple."

"Thanks very much, George."

"And I know you didn't want it mentioned, so I personally ran the background check on the check so no one knows your missus was involved. My guesstimate is that someone is scamming her."

"I was just coming to that same realization. Thank you again for all your efforts. Greatly appreciated."

"Happy to be of service, sir."

CHAPTER 36

Kenny Was Setting the Stage for the Waldorf Meeting. He Had the Full-Scale Model on Hand, with Additions and Photographs Showing the Progress

He even had a folder full of recommended "clients" from doctors and some special requests from individuals to come to the Center. He knew Ruby was a loose cannon, and all he could do was instill the fear of prison, of dying without her daughter. Ruby was scheduled to arrive two hours before Bettina. *She better be there.*

"This is my last appearance, Kenny. You can explain me out of the picture any way you want. I don't want the dirty money from the deal. I just want out."

After hours of painful dialogue with her daughter, Ruby had decided this was the only way. She didn't want to go to prison. Now that she had found her Gila, sweet Marianne, she wanted the rest of her years to be peaceful and loving.

"You are beyond stupid, Ruby, but if you don't want your cut, so be it. But it's a damn good thing you came today. Now leave me alone for fifteen minutes so I can figure out a logical explanation for Bettina of why you're bailing out." He had figured something like this was going to happen and had a believable story ready.

"So, Bettina, what do you think about this model?"

"Goodness, Kenny, it's very impressive. And oh, Madame, I'm so glad to see you. So many things have happened to me recently, and I wanted to share them all with you."

"It's wonderful to see you again, child. My life too has taken a dramatic turn, as I'm sure Kenneth will explain."

"What, Kenneth?"

"The net net, Bettina, is that Madame has decided to retire. Her sickness frightened her, and during this period she's been reunited with a daughter she hadn't seen for years. Quite simply, she wants to spend more time with her daughter and relax and enjoy her golden years. The Center was going to require many, many hours. When she weighed that investment in time with the pleasures of being a mother and grandmother, familial ties won out."

"Oh, I'm so sorry you won't be part of it, Madame, but I certainly understand. You're earned the right to enjoy your life. Besides, you've done so much good for so many people in your life. Now it's your time."

"I wish that were true, Bettina."

Kenny flashed a warning look to Ruby.

"But it is true. I know it, and you and Kenneth know it."

"You're so very sweet, Bettina. You make me feel worthwhile."

"That's never been a question in my mind."

"I knew you'd understand, Bettina." Kenny sat down next to Bettina on the sofa. "Now I want to show you some patient—oops, pardon me—*client* candidates. And I have some résumés from doctors who want to join the operation."

For the next hour, Bettina read applications and résumés, examined the model, and was shown photographs of the construction progress. She was satisfied that money was being spent wisely, and at the end of the meeting, she wrote out the check for the remaining $5 million. She wondered why Madame seemed antsy, but perhaps it was because she was withdrawing from the project and was feeling the loss of involvement.

CHAPTER *37*

"Bettina, This Is Gene Morales, the Musical Director of …"

"Oh yes, Mr. Morales. I know who you are."

"Call me Gene."

"I'm almost afraid to have this conversation, Gene. Unless you're being especially kind and calling to tell me I need a lot more training and practice."

"We all need a lot more of everything to do our jobs well, Bettina. But in your case, I—we—think you are exactly right for the part of Cassidy Hunt, the bitchy, predatory heiress who is turned inside out by love. Well, what do you think? Bettina, are you there?"

"My God, it really happened. Oh, Gene, don't think me ungrateful. I'm just stunned. And although you're accustomed to people screaming with delight, I must discuss this incredible offer with my husband."

"Do you think there's really the possibility of his negating the offer?"

"I know this sounds ridiculous, Gene, but I don't know. My husband didn't marry a budding theatrical star, and I'm not positive he wants to be married to one. Will you allow me twenty-four hours before you give the part to someone who's probably more deserving than I?"

"No one is more deserving, but yes, I'll give you the time, Bettina. We think you will be extraordinary in the part. It was a unanimous decision."

"I've never been so complimented. Thank you again. And please don't think I'm ungrateful. You'll hear from me tomorrow; I promise."

"You're not asking about your salary and the terms?"

"Salary? Terms? Oh dear. I'll call you tomorrow."

"Fine. Goodbye, Cassidy—because that's who you are."

Bettina hung up and wondered who she was. Bettina, Bethel, now Cassidy? And dear God, what would her darling Dilly say? How would the family feel? She smiled to herself. *How nice that I care how the family will feel. They are my family now.*

"Dilly, something amazing has happened, or could happen, and I need to discuss it with you this evening when you come home."

"Sounds serious. You're not going to tell me something to destroy me, are you?"

"No, my love, but it is serious, and I can't make the necessary decision without your guidance."

"Are you just going to leave me hanging, or are you going to give me a hint?"

"No hints, no teasing, and I need to be looking into your beautiful eyes when we talk."

"I could get nervous hearing you speak like this, but you said this wouldn't hurt me."

"I would never hurt you, Dilly."

"I'll see you this evening, darling. I'll be there by sevenish." Dilly thought perhaps she was going to tell him about the $4 million. That would be serious.

CHAPTER *38*

We Want Bad Things to Happen to Bad People, Don't We? "Okay, Teddy Boy. We Got the Goods on the Blonde Bimbo, but That's Small Potatoes. You Owe Us $225,000, and We Want It Now"

Tony Manati wasn't someone you wanted to have threaten you. He was physically square—no neck, just a massive, cruel body, willing to inflict pain on the nearest target.

"Tony, you know I'm always good for my debts. I just need a couple of days, and I'll have your money, you know, like always." Teddy hoped his casual, easy delivery hid the fact that he was shaking and perspiring.

There was a full minute of silence while Tony sneered at Teddy. "I don't believe you. You're a sack of shit, and I don't want to deal with you anymore."

"Come on, Tony. You know I like doing business with you. I've just had a few horses run the wrong way. My luck'll change."

"Oh, so you think you're going to win what you owe me? Hah!" Tony looked across the room to one of his men, a measles-scarred monkey named Angelo. "I don't want to be bothered by this Teddy person anymore, Angelo."

Teddy panicked. "Tony, you ... you don't mean that. We have lots of business plans for the future."

Tony shook his head. "Teddy, you don't got a future." He left the room, and Teddy started to cry.

CHAPTER *39*

"You've Been Offered a Starring Role on Broadway? Is This Some Kind of Joke?"

Dilly was in a state of shock. Bettina singing onstage? He couldn't even grasp the idea. "I thought you were just studying singing as a hobby."

"I was, Dilly. This ... offer was never part of any plan; it just happened."

"And do you want to do it?" Dilly was conscious of hearing his own breathing.

"I don't know," Bettina almost whispered. "I do know I would never do anything that hurt you or the family. That's why I certainly didn't accept the offer. I told them I had to discuss it with you."

"Which means that you were considering saying yes?"

"Umm, yes, I guess so, even though I have trouble believing it myself."

"Are you that talented?" As he asked the question, he saw her on the stage of the Junior League Ball, her audience mesmerized. He remembered her singing on the boat that night in the Virgin Islands.

"I don't think so, but obviously ... someone does."

"I'm not saying you should or shouldn't do it, Bettina, but for how long do they want you?"

"The norm is to do a role for one year."

"How often?"

"There are performances every night Tuesday through Saturday, plus a matinee Wednesday and Saturday."

"My God, I'd never see you." His disbelief was being replaced by a growing pain.

"I couldn't bear that, Dilly. I'll turn them down." She said the words, but Dilly saw she didn't want to say them; she didn't feel them, didn't believe them. "Besides, what would your parents say?"

"Screw my parents."

"Dilly, that's terrible."

"I'm sorry—of course you're right. But it would impact more on me than my parents. Listen to me. I'm worried only about me, selfish me, not giving you the chance to be the star you are." His head dropped; he was exhausted. "What kind of part is it? Is she a decent person?"

"Oh yes, darling, it's a musical. And I play a grasping rich girl without much heart who becomes someone else because of love."

"You mean we would have to watch you make love to someone else on a stage."

"No, I asked. It's more about their budding relationship. I believe it's written where they finally kiss, and that's it. To tell the truth, I'm not worried about my singing, but it also calls for me to do some acting, and quite honestly, I'm not sure I have that ability. It doesn't matter, Dilly. I can see the thought of my being onstage is disturbing you, so I'll just turn it down."

"Do you have to call them tonight and tell them?"

"No, they don't expect to hear from me until tomorrow afternoon."

"Good. I need to sleep on it, if you don't mind. It's just too much for me to absorb all at once."

"I understand, darling. And don't let it worry you. It doesn't matter. What matters is that we're together and happy."

After an uneasy, nonchatty dinner, Bettina retired to her bath, and Dilly made a phone call to his father. "Hi, Dad. Can we meet tomorrow morning, first thing? Great. I'll come to your office by nine thirty."

CHAPTER *40*

The Final Chapter for Teddy
"Dilly, Oh God, Dilly, Teddy ... Teddy ..."

His sister, Elizabeth, was hysterical, crying and screaming.

"What is it, sis? I can't understand. What's wrong with Teddy?"

"Oh my God, Dilly! He's ... he's dead. Teddy is dead. They killed him."

"Are you at home?"

"Y-y-yes."

"Stay where you are, Elizabeth, I'll come over right now. Bettina!"

"Yes, darling."

"There's some terrible emergency. Teddy has been killed."

"*What?*"

"Elizabeth just called, hysterical. I'm going over there."

"I'll come with you."

"Okay, but we have to hurry."

"Give me two minutes."

Moments after they arrived, Edwina and Roland Richardson walked in the door. Elizabeth, shaken and drained, threw herself, sobbing, into the comforting embrace of her father. Her mother was ashen and worried about her child.

"Lizzie, darling, can you tell us what happened?" Roland's voice was gentle and soothing to the bereft young woman.

She sobbed out the words. "The police received an anonymous call to go to Teddy's office, and when they got there, they found him sitting at his desk, dead, shot two or three times, and a note pinned to his chest saying something about not paying his debts. Oh, Daddy, what am I going to do?"

"Right now, you're going to come home with your mother and me and stay with us as long as you like. Then your brother and I will meet with the police and find out what they know, if anything. All the hysteria in the world won't bring your Teddy back. Let's just concentrate on your welfare and your state of mind."

"Liz ..." Bettina spoke for the first time, and Elizabeth turned to her sister-in-law and saw the tears on Bettina's cheeks. She went to her and embraced her. They stood there, the two young women, silently weeping and consoling one another. "Look, Liz, Dad is right. Their home is the best place for you. But then you can come and stay with us. Dilly and I love you and would be very happy to be able to take care of you."

"Thanks, Betts. I know you mean it."

"I do, sweet Liz. I do."

Edwina watched the exchange closely and felt the closeness of the two, realizing that Bettina was, indeed, a Richardson. The realization startled and pleased her.

"Dilly, is our meeting at nine thirty tomorrow still on?"

"If you can handle it, Dad."

"Absolutely. I'll see you there. It's good to see you, Bettina. I wish it were happier circumstances."

"How true, Dad. Elizabeth, let me help you pack a few things, okay?"

"Yes, yes, that would be fine." And the two of them left the room.

"Roland"—Edwina had a specific question for her husband—"recently you commented that you worried about Teddy and/or his influence on this family. Was this the kind of thing you were referring to?"

"Obviously, I wasn't thinking of anything this extreme. I had become aware of Theodore's involvement with unsavory types. I knew Elizabeth wasn't aware, so I said nothing to her. We must tread lightly on this because we mustn't hurt our Elizabeth, no matter what. Ted didn't and doesn't matter. Elizabeth matters, and we as a family can help her through this terribly sordid happening."

"Gosh, Dad, I had no idea Teddy was not on the straight and narrow."

"Dillworth, I don't believe it would have even been possible. He was not a man of substance or value. Let us all agree in this room that we will say nothing to the police or press regarding our feelings about Theodore. Only that we lament the loss."

Dilly and his mother both nodded in agreement. And Dilly added, "And I'll make that very clear to Bettina as well."

CHAPTER 41

"So, Dad, What Do You Think? Can We, as a Family, Live with Bettina as a Broadway Star?"

To his father's eyes, strong, competent Dilly looked like a frightened teenager, wondering whether he was going to make the team.

"Well, heh, heh, heh—that Bettina is just full of surprises. Was this something she's always worked for and dreamed about?"

"Noooo, she told me, and I believe her, that it's something that just happened. That she didn't believe it herself, except that the offer is quite real."

"I think to say no to her, Dilly, does a disservice to her and to you."

"Really?"

"Yes. This is a most unusual opportunity for Bettina, and yes, it will impact your lives together. But it will also establish Bettina as a strong and important person in her own right, which I believe is important and is more reflective of your marriage. I like your marriage, Dilly. I like the relationship the two of you have. It's a better and more honest relationship in many ways than my own marriage. And don't look concerned. I don't have a mistress on the side. Your mother and I are mentally and emotionally joined at the hip, but you and Bettina are what a marriage should be—partners and best friends. Besides, her accepting the part doesn't mean the show will have a long run, or that she will succeed, although frankly, nothing she does will surprise me. I'm assuming she'll be great and do us all proud—especially you."

"God, Dad, you surprise me. I couldn't just say yes last night, and Bettina told me three or four times that she'd turn it down because she could see I was bothered by the prospect. But I agree with you. It's a growing experience for me."

"I think in view of this terrible mess that Teddy has left us with that she should ask the producers to not announce her involvement in the show for a few weeks. I want this ugliness to have faded so it won't give the press the opportunity of joining the good and beautiful with the bad and ugly."

"Thanks, Dad. I think Bettina really wants to do this, but she was even concerned about how 'the family' would feel. Do you want me to tell Mother before Bettina accepts the part?"

"No, I'll tell your mother. And I don't think she'll be troubled by this turn of events. Bettina is winning points with her on a regular basis."

CHAPTER 42

But Kenny Was Still Alive. Marianne Didn't Trust Kenny to Not Involve Her Mother and Finally Succeeded in Getting Ruby to Go to the DA and Sign Up as a State's Witness in Exchange for a Small Sentence, If Any

O nce the DA heard the entire story and the amount of money that had exchanged hands, he put another plan into action. He promised Ruby that if she'd do it, he'd practically guarantee that she did no time behind bars.

"You want me to do what?" Ruby turned white. "I . . . I can't go in and get confessions from Kenny and that Herman animal."

"You're not going to get confessions from them, Ruby. You're just going to get them to talk, and you'll be wired, so that every word they say will be there in court to sink those two bastards."

"Marianne, I don't know if I can go through with this."

"Yes, you can, Mom. For both of our sakes. I want you free of this connection. We have some wonderful years ahead to make up to each other."

"I'll tell you, Mr. Richardson, we're dead certain we know who erased your son-in-law. That's the good news. The bad news is that unless someone fingers him, we don't have enough to take him into court."

"Would his name mean anything to me?"

"No, sir. It's just a racketeering thug named Tony Manati. Obviously, your son-in-law played with dirty friends."

"Obviously. So what's next?"

"A lot of routine police work and see if we get lucky and find someone who wants to talk. You know how the courts are. Unless it's open and shut, some greasy lawyer will get it thrown out of court. Sorry to tell you, but I believe in telling it how it is."

"I understand perfectly, Inspector. We thank you for all your efforts."

"I don't think this is some kind of vendetta aimed at you or your family, Mr. Richardson."

"Nor do I. My late son-in-law was a man with an affinity for bad judgments. This is one of those judgments that's come back to kill him. Thank you again. I won't take more of your time."

"Anytime, sir. Obviously, if you hear something, let me know immediately. Here's my card with office and cell phone numbers."

"Fine. Thanks."

The inspector watched Roland leave—erect, dignified—and wondered how a piece of shit like Ted Catarsi had become part of that family.

CHAPTER 43

Bettina Threw Herself into Rehearsals as if Her Life Hung in the Balance

Hunter Carlson, the director, was a calm, soft-spoken dictator. But he always allowed enough room for the individual to fine tune the action, the phrase, and the expression. Bettina worried that her nonexperience would annoy or slow the process. But the rest of the cast, all pros, treated her as a peer and never referred to her nontheatrical past. They became a large family in short order. Like most families, some were closer than others. There were squabbles, disagreements, and some quiet romances. Her costar, Carl Michaels, was a lanky, handsome fellow with a quick grin, a scattering of freckles across his nose, and a booming baritone voice that filled the theater. He also had loose hands and a roving eye but had been told by Gene Morales, the musical director, and John Moran, the producer, to keep his hands off Bettina, or there would be hell to pay. He knew and respected both men too well to disobey. Bettina thought him charming and "so polite and sweet to me," she told Dilly.

Besides group rehearsals, she had private dance lessons for the musical numbers and a drama coach for all the nonmusical numbers. Unable to judge her own progress, she just worked harder, trying to justify their faith in her. The truth was, Messieurs Moran, Carlson, and Morales were all thrilled with their ingénue. She was magic onstage, and the extra classes were having a profound effect on her performance.

The days turned into weeks, the weeks into a few months, and opening night, preceded by a couple of dress rehearsals, was just a week away.

CHAPTER *44*

The Meeting at the Waldorf Was Set Up around Bettina's Rehearsal Schedule. Ruby Arrived Early for a Strategy Meeting with Kenny and Herman

She had never been so nervous. What if the sweat running down her neck set off one of the wires and she was electrocuted? What if Kenny or Herman found out she was wired? They might throw her out the window. And the meeting was on the twentieth floor.

"Ruby, you're looking very well, very expensive, very well cared for."

"Save the niceties, Kenny. You know and I know it means nothing. I'm here because you gave me no choice."

"Cool it, you two. We all know why we're here." Herman was part of the meeting, acting the role of project coordinator. He, at least, was clean today, in a conservative suit, nails manicured, hair trimmed. In Ruby's eyes, he was still a poisonous snake, a cobra in a nursery. "We have the full-scale model of the Center for Self-Improvement. We have all the budgets and estimates on appropriate letterheads and notarized. I have some dummy newspaper articles praising the future Center and its lofty ideals."

"That's brilliant, Herman. I like the way you think."

"Thank you, Kenneth. That's why you brought me on board."

"I still don't understand why you thought this rich lady—our Bettina—would buy it."

"*Our* Bettina, Ruby, doesn't come from rich. She was just a little girl scraping her way through life, kind of like you and me. So, since she's living a fake life, she's ready to buy into anything that gives her stature, a reason for being. And that's where you come in."

"And this is where I go out. I did my part, Kenny, and I'm backing out. She knows; you told her I'm not going to be part of this make-believe Center."

"True, but she needs to know that all the plans have your approval."

"What plans? The plans to rob her of millions of dollars to build a make-believe Center?"

Kenny snarled at Ruby. "If you say anything like that, I guarantee twenty years in the slammer for you, you old sack of shit—guaranteed."

"I know, I know, Kenny. You made that perfectly clear. I won't blow the whistle on you crooks, but I'm not going to gush about this crap either. If Bettina asks me a question, I'll answer positively but nothing over the top. And let me ask you something. What happens, oh, six months from now when Bettina realizes that nothing was built, that there is no Center?"

"The money will be out of the country, and she'll be too embarrassed to tell her husband what a jerk she's been. And aren't you interested in what your cut of the money is, Ruby?"

"No. It's dirty. I don't want any part of it. I don't need it. I'm not going to die hungry. How much longer do I have to stay around you two? The air stinks in here."

"Shut up, you old turd. Kenny may have to put up with you, but I don't."

"Hah. You can't kill me 'til you have the money."

"Tell her to shut up, Kenny, or I might kill her."

"Both of you knock it off. Bettina ought to be here in a few minutes, and I want us to be calm—and ready."

Five minutes later there was a knock on the door. Kenny opened it to reveal a beautiful and glowing Bettina. "Wow, Broadway is doing something for you that cannot be ignored."

Bettina beamed and smiled warmly at Ruby. "Thank you, Kenny. Oh, Madame, how wonderful to see you." The women embraced.

CHAPTER 45

"I've Never Understood That Break-a-Leg Stuff, but You Know All of My Love and Good Wishes Will Walk Out on That Stage with You Tonight"

"I know, my darling Dilly. You've been so wonderful and understanding about the hours and hours of rehearsals. I feel like a neglectful wife."

"Not at all. You've been there for me and with me. You've been a wonderful sister to Elizabeth. And tonight, all of New York will know what a very lucky man I am." With tears in his eyes, he gave her a long, soft kiss and put her in a limo for the theater.

Dilly watched the limo pull away, full of trepidation about tonight. He did believe she would be wonderful. *And if the show is a huge success, what does it do to Bettina? What will it mean to our marriage? And on a more serious note, when do we discuss the $9 million she's given away to what appears to be a scam?*

CHAPTER 46

"Ruby, Thanks to You, We've Got 'Em Where We Want 'Em. Now We Want You to Turn State's Witness, and They're Dead in the Water"

"Does this mean that Bettina will get her money back?"

"All that they haven't spent."

"Good. I'd like that."

"You honestly like this patsy?"

"Patsy?"

"That's a term for someone who lets herself get suckered by someone else."

"Yes, I do like her. She's a good and decent human being. I never wanted her to be hurt."

"Well, you're doing the right thing, Ruby. We got a question for you. Did this Bettina lady ever mention her husband or bring him into the mix?"

"No, never. I'm pretty sure he didn't know anything about this."

"Well, we think we ought to involve him. We just aren't sure whether to do it without telling the wife or telling her first and then him."

"Don't look to me for advice. This is all out of my league."

CHAPTER 47

Opening Night on Broadway Is the Stuff That Dreams Are Made of ... or Nightmares, Bettina Thought

What if she blew it? Spaced out? Forgot lyrics? *Hey, negative thinking never got anyone anywhere.* Annie, the makeup expert, dropped by. "Hi, Betts, lemme see. Hmm, you don't need my help. I'd put just a dash more rouge here; lemme rub it in. But you've got the idea. It's more than nighttime makeup, or it'll get lost with all the stage lighting. Yeah, that's it, gorgeous. Break a leg, Betts. You're really great."

Deep breathing will help. You know your lines, your dance steps. It's just another dress rehearsal. Knock, knock. "Yes, come in."

"Flowers, Bettina, beautiful flowers."

"Oh, they're beautiful. Is there a card?"

"Here 'tis."

"Oh." Bettina's eyes sparkled with tears. The card read, "Bettina, we're all very proud of you and proud that you are a Richardson. We'll be cheering for you. Love, Edwina/Mom."

At that moment, John Moran stuck his head in through the open door. He saw the hint of tears. "Hey, Bettina, are you all right?"

She turned and flashed that winning star-of-the-show smile and said, "John, I've never been better. I'm going to make you proud of me tonight."

"None of us has any doubt about that, Bettina. You have our love and admiration." As much as he wanted to crush her in his arms, he leaned forward and gave her a brotherly kiss on the cheek, smiled, and left.

She looked at the flowers again, alongside some spectacular roses from Dilly, and smiled. "Thank you, Edwina. You give me the courage to win."

"Ms. Richardson, the overture is starting."

The curtain opened on an office scene with a couple of men making semicrude passes at Cassidy, Bettina's onstage character. They left, and she sang the opening number, about how much more money she'd have if she had a dollar for every time a jerk made a pass at her. She was rich, she was tough, and she wasn't very vulnerable. The thunderous applause at the end of her first song startled her. She resisted the normal urge to acknowledge the applause with a bow and stayed in character. The story continued, introducing new characters, new opportunities, a funny sidekick, and a series of well-crafted songs. The first-act closing number, when Bettina meets her nemesis and for the first time shows a crack in her armor, left everyone in the audience laughing and crying and cheering.

The audience doesn't realize how busy you are during a show, with costume changes, freshening makeup, a hair change at one point—it's a real push. But Bettina was now part of it, playing a role in life custom-made for her. It seemed in no time the play was coming to an end. Would she, Cassidy, succumb to her emotions? She dismissed him—Doug was his name. And as he was leaving the stage, the audience sat frozen in silence. She spoke. "Doug." He stopped, and slowly turned around to face her. She looked at her feet and lifted her head to speak to him. "Take ... take me with you." He smiled, and they both walked toward each other as the final curtain came down.

With the romantic theme song filling the theater, there were many curtain calls, and when Bettina came out, the audience, as one, stood to its feet, cheering. She partially fought back the tears and then let them fall, as a bouquet of roses was placed in her arms. She curtseyed as elegantly as the royal presence she now was.

Dilly, his parents, and his sister, Elizabeth, were standing there. Dilly was unable to cheer but was crying with a combination of joy and fear at his wife's new position in life.

His mother squeezed his arm. "We shall never forget this moment. Never."

CHAPTER 48

Goodbye, Kenny

"Anything you say can be used against you."

"Just a big, fat minute. Who are you arresting and for what?"

"Mr. Kenneth Monroe, you are charged with false representation and extorting ten million dollars from Bettina Richardson."

"I'll call my attorney."

"You have that right."

Meanwhile, across town, police were handcuffing Herman Warshon, who knew better than to struggle. His lawyers would have him out in a heartbeat. You win some; you lose some.

"So that's the way we see it, Mr. Richardson. Your wife didn't realize she was being scammed, and hopefully we've ended the scam in time to retrieve most of the money."

"Thank you, gentleman, for coming directly to me. Since my wife has just opened in a Broadway play—"

"Yeah, I read about her. She's like the toast of Broadway."

"Right. And because of that I may not tell her this right away until there's more progress. But I applaud your efforts and appreciate all that you've done, and we will certainly cooperate in any future efforts to jail these people. By the way, how were you able to break the case?"

"We were lucky, sir. There was a woman who was part of the scam, and she decided she really liked your wife and didn't want her hurt. She came to us with the entire story."

"Remarkable. I'd like to meet her at the appropriate time, and if she needs some legal representation, I'd be happy to provide that with no charge to her."

"Thank you, sir. I know we can set up a meeting."

Dilly fixed himself an aperitif and sat down for yet another evening without his celebrated wife. He thought about her and how she could have been duped into believing the scam. Was her life with him so empty that she needed to be involved with this Center of Self-Improvement? Surely there was no attraction to the men involved—or was there? He thought about her throwing away $9 million and felt a wave of anger wash over him. What now?

What now? Bettina was thinking as she struggled to get away from the attractive arms of John Moran, who was holding her too close and too tight. "John, stop it this instant. We're not teenagers. This isn't appropriate, and John, I'm not available."

"Bettina, I'm in love with you and have been since the first day you walked into this theater. I want us to be together. I know you're married, but your life is show business, and that means life with me."

"No, John, my life is Mrs. Dillworth Richardson, not Cassidy, the character onstage you love. Now stop kissing me, stop holding me—*I mean stop it*—and right now."

Her sharp command forced John to release her. "I'm not sorry, Bettina. I want you, and I know you would love me if you'd let yourself."

"You're very attractive, John, but you're kidding yourself. I'm not even remotely inclined to become entangled with you or anyone else. In spite of this phenomenon called Broadway in my life, I'm very clear about who I am supposed to be—Mrs. Dillworth Richardson."

"You can't turn your back on passion, Bettina. Every man and every woman needs a passionate relationship to make them whole."

"And what makes you think my husband and I have a passionless relationship?"

"I've seen the two of you together. There's more courtesy than caring, more of a settled relationship than raw desire."

Bettina knew there was an element of truth in what John said, and she admitted he overflowed with charm and sex appeal. She admonished herself. *Don't even think about it, Bettina. You're not Bethel, and Bettina wouldn't risk all for sex.* "You can think what you like, John. The fact remains nothing is going to change. I'm flattered that you feel so strongly about me and hope it won't hinder our professional relationship."

"I'm not going to stop loving you." And without warning he pulled her to him and kissed her long and deep. She didn't fight it. Then he left. She felt the warmth creep into her face, and much to her annoyance, she wept.

Kenny, smarting in defeat, was trying to damage Bettina as much as possible. "You don't think for a minute she gave us that money just for some do-gooder cause! She was hot for me. I gave her the kind of sex her deep-pockets husband wouldn't or couldn't do. She wanted me all the time. Couldn't have enough of me."

Dilly had read these transcripts, and now, besides being mystified that Bettina could throw away that much money, he became angry, and his anger festered until it broke open. "When you get home after tonight's performance, we have to have a serious talk."

"Fine, darling. Is something wrong?"

"I don't want to get into it on the telephone. Just come straight home. Don't waste any time with the theater crowd."

"I always come straight home, darling. You know that."

"Do I?" And he hung up.

Bettina was troubled. That didn't sound like Dilly. There was anger in his voice. About what?

A knock at the door. "Curtain in five minutes, Bettina."

Concentrate on the play. Whatever Dilly wants will come out when I get home. Put yourself into character. Be Cassidy.

"Dad, thanks for letting me come over. Will you excuse us, Mother? I need to discuss something with Dad."

"Certainly, Dillworth."

"We'll be in the library, dear."

Once settled, a glass of brandy for each, Roland looked at his son expectantly. "Speak, Dilly. I can see the wheels turning."

"I hardly know where to begin. For starters, I don't think you know I gave Bettina ten million dollars of her own, early in our marriage, because she was afraid of what Mother would do to her if something happened to me."

"An impressive sum. You gave it without strings, I presume."

"Absolutely. Hers to do whatever she wanted."

"And she's done something with it."

"Oh, yes. She's allowed herself to be scammed by a couple of con artists, and she gave all the money to them to build a 'Center for Self-Fulfillment' or some crap like that."

"That's sad but not tragic. There must be a reason behind it. And can some of the money be recovered?"

"I can't believe you're so calm about it. We haven't discussed the reason behind her involvement, and she doesn't even know that I know. Yes, most of the money can be recovered. But there's a new twist that I particularly hate. The main con artist told the police that the reason she gave the money was that she was sexually involved with him. That he provided her with the kind of rough sex that her 'deep-pockets old man couldn't provide.' I don't know why he would say this if it weren't true."

"Do you think you're being fair to Bettina?"

"Fair? What's fair? Giving away ten million dollars? Sleeping with some hoodlum?"

"The money is one thing; the sexual alliance is another and is only alleged and by a person without a moral foundation. Don't you think you owe Bettina the right to explain these allegations?"

"We're going to talk, tonight, when she gets home from the theater."

"Don't do it when you're so full of anger, Dilly."

"Why do you always defend her?"

"I don't know. I guess I care deeply for her and believe in my heart that she is deeply devoted to you. That she gave the money away was probably because she believed it would do something worthwhile. I honestly believe she wouldn't do anything that would purposefully pain you."

"But that's not all, Dad. It gets worse. They've also told me that her real name is Bethel something-or-other and that her past is an invention, totally false."

"I know."

"*You know?* My God, my own father knows a deep secret about my wife and doesn't share it with me?"

"I would have told you in time. I was hoping she would eventually tell you herself."

"Jesus Christ!"

"Give her the benefit of the doubt, Dilly. She has too much value to you and this family for you to discard her out of hand."

"I don't know what I'm going to do, Dad. I'll call you tomorrow and tell you what was said."

"I would appreciate that."

"Don't mention this to Mother. I don't think Bettina is her favorite member of the family."

"I think you're wrong. Your mother has the intellectual and emotional capacity to admit her wrongs and to forgive and move on. She may see Bettina even more clearly than you."

"Good night, Dad."

"Good night, son. Remember Bettina loves you. And therefore, you can hurt her terribly."

"Do you want to talk about Kenny and Herman and the Madam?"

She was surprised Dilly knew, but why did he sound angry? "I wanted the Center to be nearly finished when I told you. I wanted you to be proud of it and of me."

Dilly looked at her incredulously. "Proud? Proud that you allowed yourself to be swindled out of nine million dollars?"

"Swin … what … what? What are you talking about? Madame wouldn't cheat me. She couldn't; she wouldn't." Bettina was sobbing, not understanding, unable to accept the words.

Dilly always went to her, but his anger held him back and then threw him over the edge. "Not just swindled, but apparently you and this Kenny person have a … a physical relationship. You've been fucking him."

Bettina recoiled as though slapped. "No, no, no, Dilly. I've never—oh God, no!"

"Can I believe anything you tell me? Isn't Bethel your real name? Aren't you just some Jewish girl from the Bronx?"

Bettina thought she might die. Her careful facade, Bettina, had become her skin. She no longer was acting; she was that person. She looked blankly at Dilly, reaching out to him but not seeing anything. The pain in her heart and head was throbbing. She remembered nothing after that. Blackness.

She didn't know how long she was out, but as she slowly came to, Dr. Blakely, the family physician, was sitting at her side. "There now, Bettina, come back to us, slowly, carefully. Everything is fine."

She opened her eyes slowly and, after a few minutes of recuperative silence, said, "No, nothing is fine. Ever again."

"Now, now, Bettina. I don't know what brought you to this point, but I'd opine it's too much stress, you working hard on Broadway, and coping with some of the recent family problems. I know the murder of Elizabeth's husband affected you deeply. I'm giving you a tranquilizer that will let you sleep peacefully through the night. There's no performance tomorrow, and we'll call the producer or director and tell him you may miss a couple of other performances. But we'll wait and see how you feel tomorrow. Is there anything you want to discuss with me, dear?"

"No, Dr. Blakely. Thank you for being here. I apparently passed out?"

"Yes, and it frightened Dillworth. He'll be glad to hear you're going to be all right. I'm sure he's waiting in the living room. Would you like him to come in?"

"I think not, Doctor. I think sleep is the best thing for me." *Besides, Dilly won't want to see me, a Jewish girl from the Bronx who gave away $9 million to crooks and supposedly slept with one of them. Oh, dear God, he did say all that. What can I ever say to him? How can I explain?* And then, thankfully, the drugs took over, and she slept.

CHAPTER 49

The Aftermath: Roland, Bettina, Dilly, John, Lisa

"What, Roland? Bettina did what? Ten million dollars! I hate hearing this. I believed her, I accepted her, and now she's done this to us?" Edwina was shaking her head and walking in a circle.

"Simmer down, Edwina."

"Simmer down! She really fooled me."

"I'm amazed you're jumping to this conclusion. Yes, I do believe Bettina was scammed out of the money but also feel in my heart that she acted on good impulse. Too, I am deeply concerned about what Dilly said to her last night. He was, quite frankly, out of control, unable to intellectualize and rationalize but instead accepted the word of felons and attacked her. He called me and said the doctor came by and gave Bettina a tranquilizer. I know the absolute rule has been for us to butt out of the children's business, but in this instance, I think we should break that rule and make our presence felt."

"I'm sure you're correct, Roland. I'm sorry for judging her so harshly right now, but I still wonder if she ... if she ..."

"If she what, Edwina?"

"We know she isn't what she led Dilly to believe. Maybe everything she's said and done has been a lie."

"Of course you could be right, dear, but deep down inside, I don't believe it. Bettina has earned the right to be a Richardson and to be treated accordingly."

"Yes, Roland, I will withhold my judgment." Edwina was silent for a few minutes. "I believe Bettina has been somewhat of a cathartic for this family."

"How true."

"Your acceptance of her before any of us, except, of course, Dilly, annoyed the hell out of me."

"Why, Edwina, I've never heard you speak so colloquially. I find it rather appealing. In fact, after all these years together—not all of them perfect but none of them boring—I can honestly tell you I think you are one of the most remarkable and appealing women in the world, even sexy."

Edwina couldn't help herself. She blushed. "Why, Roland, what brought on this adolescent approach? I must say, it's rather sweet. And I feel I owe you an apology because I ceased being the 'Sweet Eddie' you married and became only Mrs. Roland Hughington Richardson."

"Hah, so you remember my nickname for you."

"I've never forgotten it ... Rolly."

"I've never forgotten Rolly either. Come here, and give me a kiss, girly."

"You smooth-talkers always have your way."

"Are you still feeling poorly, Bettina? Ever since you were sick, your performance lacks passion."

"I'm sorry, John. I know you're right. I'll try to recapture Cassidy."

"Somehow, I think your illness wasn't just a physical thing. I think something happened to you that knocked you out emotionally. Is it too egotistical for me to think part of it was my telling you how much I love you?"

"No, dear John, that wasn't the cause. But you're right; I have an emotional hurdle to get over. And it's a tough one."

"You want to tell me? I listen real good."

"No, John, I do not want to tell you. You're hardly objective." She admitted to herself she wanted to talk it out with someone but not with

John, whose attractiveness was ever present. "I promise you'll see a real improvement in my performance. But thank you for being here. It's helped me already, just to admit there was a problem."

"There's nothing I wouldn't do for you, Bettina."

"I know that, John. Thank you."

Once assured that Bettina would indeed recover, Dilly immersed himself in business matters, working endless hours, racing across the continent and the world, pushing, prodding, and manipulating. "Bettina, I didn't get to speak to you last night ... I'm in Paris."

"Oh my goodness, Dilly. Is everything all right there?"

"Just a business problem with our European branch."

"I can't think about Paris without remember the magic of our first trip, that first time you took me to Europe. I'll think of that tonight during the performance, and hopefully I'll do a better job than I've been doing."

There was an awkward trans-Atlantic pause. "How are you feeling, Bettina?"

"Fine ... darling. I guess the stress of finding out I had been cheated and being generally worn out from performing just got me down. I hope you're able to recover the money. The police have spoken to me, and I told them I would be happy to cooperate, and they seemed to indicate that most of the money was recoverable. I am so very sorry, Dilly, I thought I was doing something good for humanity. I'm a very foolish young woman, and I hope you'll be able to forgive me in time."

"We'll discuss everything when I get back."

"Fine. I hope you can come back soon. This house is too big without you."

"Goodbye, Bettina. Take care." His formality hurt.

"I will, Dilly. Think of us in Paris, please. Bye." She sat by the phone, not moving a muscle, barely breathing. Finally, minutes later, she spoke to the empty room, "I love you, Dilly. Please don't stop loving us."

He didn't stop thinking about Bettina but, totally out of character, fueled by his anger and an unrealistic belief that she very possibly had cheated on him, he allowed himself an unscheduled liaison.

"That was very nice, Mr. … umm, whatever your name is, but it had all the warmth and intimacy of a mercy fuck. I won't complain because I was feeling lonely, and I'm not a professional, and you are as clean and lean naked as you are nattily dressed. That I am probably ten years your senior doesn't seem to bother you."

"Must we analyze all this? And no, your age isn't apparent, nor does it matter. I apologize if I was not as touchy-feely as you might have liked, but perhaps that is my manner."

"I doubt it. Behind that corporate facade, I sense a fire, passion unleashed, and somewhere, there's a woman who has demanded and received that from you. I congratulate her. But I won't make you tarry this evening. You've done your duty and satisfactorily. I doubt if you'll want a recommendation, and if you knew my name, which of course you can find by checking on my hotel room, you would forget it by tomorrow."

"As much as I find this type of intimate chat a bit distressing, how is it you're so smart? I confess to everything. I am the cold, heartless, passionate ax murderer you have described. I have never consciously cheated on my wife and did it out of a sense of revenge."

"Did she deserve it, ducks?"

"I thought so. No, I think so."

"But you aren't sure, so therefore you haven't given her the benefit of the doubt. You have been judge and jury. Obviously, you are righteous, pure of heart, and undeserving of such treatment from her. Which of course did not stop you from having a little on the side."

"You needn't rub it in. I'm feeling … oh hell, I don't know how I'm feeling."

The woman, English, with that expected creamy complexion and soft eyes and hair, leaned forward and lightly stroked his cheek. "I think you're probably one of the sweetest men in the world. Go home and listen to her with your heart."

For the first time since they had met in the hotel cocktail lounge, Dilly smiled, leaned forward, kissed the side of her mouth, and said, "Thank you, Doctor. I hope I'm able to take the medicine you're prescribing, but I'm not sure that I can. However, I will think about it."

After he left, Eleanor Sherrington sat in her bed. She smiled and said to the empty room, "What a lucky girl you are, whoever you are. What a lucky girl you are."

There was a telegram from Lisa Gutwillig waiting for Bettina when she returned from the theater that night.

"I know you don't get up 'til ten—stars must get their beauty sleep— but at 11:00 a.m. tomorrow, I'm coming over to find out what the hell is going on with my most important friend in the whole world. The only acceptable cancellation would be a no-money-back session with a plastic surgeon, which wouldn't hold water as an excuse because you look like all the 'after' photos."

Dear, darling Lisa. Bettina smiled and reread the note, wondering how much Lisa knew. *It doesn't matter. If I can't share it with Lisa, I can't share it with anyone.*

"Okay, Betts, what *is* going on? My darling Fred, who misses the most blatant hints, especially of anything of an emotional nature, said he had to call Dilly regarding some corporate murder the two of them are involved in. He asked how you were and said, 'Dilly sounded so distant about Bettina. He could have been talking about his secretary.' I know you don't want to hear that, but you are not a woman to be distant with or about, and I suddenly felt that besides all those cheering crowds, you might need one more person in your corner. I'm appointing me."

"Oh, Lisa, the sky is falling—on me—and most of it is my fault. You know Bettina Richardson is a faux person ..."

"Bullshit. The truest and best aristocrat I've ever known. Most of them are aristocraps."

"Darling Lisa, your friendship makes my heart beat faster, but don't be blinded by it."

"Are you telling me you did something really bad and did it consciously?"

"No, absolutely not."

"Okay, then speak."

Lisa was silent as Bettina told her about meeting Madame and then Kenneth and the Center for Self-Fulfillment. The $9 million she entrusted to their care. The horrible realization that she had indeed been scammed. That Madame, however created she was, was not a bad person and, in trying to protect Bettina, allowed herself to be wired to trap the criminals and had turned state's witness. That Kenneth, wanting to take everyone down with him, said Bettina was in it for the sex with him, which he spelled out in court in graphic terms. That Dilly, who had never come to the court proceedings, read the court transcripts and decided he believed Bettina was sexually involved with this meaningless hoodlum.

"He believed what? That ... that screaming asshole."

"Lisa, I can't believe you called Dilly ... that."

"Well, he is one. How can he be so smart on the one hand, and one of the dumbest human beings I've ever known on the other? What happened when you discussed all this?"

"We didn't discuss. I came home from the theater one night, and he laid it all on me—being scammed. I hadn't known until that moment. He told me Madame was a scam artist and so were the others, that I had given away nine million dollars and allowed myself to 'fuck' another man. Oh yes, he also acknowledged, without my being prepared for it, that he believed I was fucking the other man because hadn't I lied about everything, even my name? That I was really Bethel, a Jewish girl from the Bronx."

"What did you say to him, sweet Bettina?"

"Nothing. My system closed in on me. The internal computer died, and I passed out cold. Spent a couple of days in bed, more dead than alive; went back to work, not performing very well, I might add; and would come home to an empty apartment. Dilly was traveling all the time or at home, sleeping in a guest bedroom."

"Fuck him."

"Lisa, I can't pretend I've never heard or used that word before, but somehow it's not you."

"Listen to me, friend. I've never had a friend who mattered more to me. I'd bet the head of a son that you've never slept with anyone else but Dilly since you found Bettina Richardson inside of you. Why don't you come home with me? Move in with us. I'll give you that far wing, which is quiet and private, and we won't interfere with your theater schedule and won't insist that you see us at all, unless you'd like some company."

"You're wonderful, Lisa, and I do love you and appreciate all that you do for me. But somehow, I've got to see this through. I don't think running away is the thing to do. I don't know how it's going to end, but I'm going to try to win Dilly back. I can't lose him, Lisa; it would kill me."

"All right, Betts, I won't insist. But if Dilly tries to play hardball with you, please call me. If he's so stupid he doesn't realize what he has and who you are, I'm going to make sure you get out of this marriage with mucha bucks—ten million will be chicken feed."

"Please don't say it, Lisa. This isn't about money. Bethel Sokoloff needed money. Bettina Richardson needs love."

"Okay, okay. Can I take you to lunch now?"

"No, thank you, darling. We girls who give our vocal cords a workout every night spend quiet days, eating lightly. I may have a massage this afternoon, perhaps indulge in a pedicure. You know, girl stuff."

"Fine, Betts. Please call me on a regular basis."

"Cross my heart."

The weather had turned. From brisk fall, it suddenly was biting winter, with icy winds whipping across town from one river to the other. Even properly layered, anything exposed burned with cold. Bettina didn't even feel it. Still numb from events of the past week, she strolled through frigid Central Park, peopled only by the hardcore runners and joggers. Even the street people had disappeared to escape the relentless chill.

The masseuse, a Swedish woman with masculine hands and strength, kneaded the pain from her muscles and, to her own surprise, brought her to a level of sleep. After a lengthy bath, a pedicure, and a manicure, she finally felt like the beautiful, genteel woman she represented. She looked at herself in the mirror. "How do you do? I am Mrs. Dillworth Richardson, formerly an awkward Jewish girl from the Bronx. Now, as Bettina Richardson, I am the toast of Broadway, cheered by thousands, loved by no one." She sat there for almost an hour, until it was time to leave for the theater.

"Mr. Richardson, have you always been so lily white? Have there been no transgressions in your own behavior?" Dr. Bell, the analyst, was personally enjoying this case. He understood the shock to the younger man's system, finding out his wife wasn't the person he thought she was, discovering she had given away millions of dollars, and being semiconvinced that she was having a love affair with another man—a criminal at that. It was a plot that books are written about. Maybe he would write one in the future.

"While I was in Europe a few weeks ago, I picked up a woman in the hotel bar and slept with her."

"And?"

"It just made me feel guilty. The woman accused me of being judge and jury of my wife."

"Was she right?"

"Possibly."

"That's an interesting answer. Why 'possibly'?"

"Because I'm listening to a felon's story, discounting her own claim of innocence. I ... I ... oh hell, I don't know."

"You don't know what, Mr. Richardson?"

"I don't know what or who to believe. She duped me. She isn't the girl I thought I married. Her name wasn't Bettina; it was Bethel. That's not even her nose. I don't know who she is. If she could go to such lengths to trap me, why wouldn't she sleep with this other man?"

"I think it might be helpful for you to separate these incidents that have caused your emotional estrangement from your wife."

"How's that?"

"Well, her transformation from Bethel to Bettina had nothing to do with the scam artist or the nine million dollars. She had decided that being Bethel was a road to nowhere, and through a great deal of diligence, hard work, and a lot of chutzpah, she made that transformation happen. To her everlasting credit, it was done so well that you were captivated by her charms, fell in love, and married her. Right?"

"Yes, sir."

185

"Next, she convinces you that your mother was going to throw her out, so you gave her money, a lot of money, with no strings, to protect her, just in case."

"Right."

"The felon still hadn't entered the picture."

"Then, according to your wife, feeling the need to do something worthwhile, something, she says, that would make you proud of her, she invests in this Center for Self-Fulfillment, which has been brought to her door by two scam artists, one of whom is the felon. But what I'd like to know is how and why she got involved with them in the first place. I understand she received a letter from a fortune-teller type, and she felt it was speaking to her heart. You must remember, Mr. Richardson, since your wife was living a lie, she was easy to lie to."

"Yes, she told me the first letter and all the subsequent letters seemed to understand who she was, why she was frightened, and why she was so alone."

"But you felt none of those fears?"

"No, I thought she was doing very well and, if anything, we were growing closer every day."

"That's an enviable position, Mr. Richardson, one very few men ever enjoy."

"What is?"

"Growing closer to one's mate day by day. The truth is, most people in the world couldn't say that."

"I suppose you're right."

"I know I'm right, Mr. Richardson. And as beneficial to my bank book as a continuing long-term analysis would be, I suspect sooner, rather than later, you will realize that whatever happened is yesterday's news and that it would be best to come to grips with it and forgive and forget. Your wife sounds too valuable to be summarily dismissed. However, let's continue for a few more sessions until you have a clear and comfortable fix on your own point of view. Until Tuesday, I wish you good, productive thoughts."

"So, Mr. Monroe, how did you attract Mrs. Richardson into your scheme?"

"I did nothing to attract the lady. She came to us. She asked us if she could be involved and what she could do to help."

"And what did you tell her?"

"I told her about our idea for the Center for Self-Fulfillment."

"Which was a totally phony concept."

"Objection. The concept of the Center has not been established as false."

"The jury will ignore the last comment about the phony concept."

"How and why were you involved with Herman Warshon?"

"Herman was a good generator of ideas. Kind of a developer. And he had always wanted to do this Center for Self-Fulfillment because he thought it would help a lot of people. He just didn't have the necessary financing. When I told him we had a potential investor, he became part of the team. So we took the lady out to show her the land where we would build, told her some of our ideas for the place, and she insisted on investing, uh, I think it was five million dollars to start with."

"I believe it was three million, Mr. Monroe, but what's two million dollars to a Christian do-gooder such as yourself? And then what happened? Did you start construction right away?"

"No. We had to have plans drawn and a model of the Center made. We had to enlist some doctors who would be part of the operation."

"Sounds very impressive, Mr. Monroe, if it had been true. *But the truth is, you did none of those things.* You just phonied up more papers and convinced Mrs. Richardson to pay out nine million dollars to you and Mr. Warshon. And that Center would never have been built."

"That's not true. Herman and me ... we, uh, we were just getting permits together when you people forced this hysteria."

"Do you realize how easy it is for us to check whether you applied for permits? You're lying under oath, Mr. Monroe. I suggest you try honesty for a change."

"Objection. The prosecution is harassing my client."

"Overruled."

With six members of the crew felled by the flu, the producers closed the show for one week. Bettina took advantage of the break to spend some time with her mother. "Mom, tell me about your new life here in Florida." Bettina was delighted, seeing her smiling mother, happy in a bright turquoise two-piece polyester pantsuit.

"Oh, Bethel, it's grand here, really grand." Bettina silently choked on *Bethel*. "I've got super friends. We play cards, mostly mah-jongg, and go to movies, and when there's a big party, we all go together. Mr. Snyder asked me to dance at the last party. There was a one man-band playing, and he was really super."

"You look wonderful, Mom. Can I take you shopping while I'm here? I'd love to buy you whatever you want."

Bettina's mother sat quietly, eyeing her daughter. "You've been awful good to your old mother. And goodness knows you've bought me more things than I've ever had in my entire life. And you send me a big allowance. You're a sweet girl, Bethel. I don't need anything else."

"Has Mickey been down to see you?"

"Yeah, but it wasn't as good as I expected it to be."

"Why, Mom? Mickey was always close to you."

"Oh, I think she's still close, but most of the time, she seemed annoyed with you. She kept calling you Big Bucks and Got Rocks, and I said it doesn't matter if you're doing well. You deserve it. But she was unhappy most of the time. I think she's jealous of you. You got out of the Bronx, and I don't blame you. I just thank you for getting me out of the Bronx."

"I'm sorry Mickey feels that way, Mom. I'll try to contact her soon and see if we can't close the gap and be sisters again."

"That would be good. I'm beginning to think you can do anything you put your mind to."

Bettina spent four days with her mother. Took her shopping, trying to influence her choices, even took in a couple of movies. They would dine early. Her mother showed her all her favorite places, with Early Bird rates for dinner. They kept the conversation on familiar ground, mainly about her mother's new setting. Bettina found her mind wandering, missing the intellectual stimulation of New York and her friends. The four days felt more like two weeks but were worthwhile. Bettina sensed her mother was glad she was leaving so she could return to her new friends and her new, happy life.

"Bettina, dear, how is your mother doing in Florida?"

"Edwina, how wonderful to hear your voice. I'm sorry I haven't called lately. Besides coping with the show, I've had a lot on my mind, all of which you know about. There are many things I need to say to you and somehow believe it will be all right."

"I can't think of anything you'd say that wouldn't be all right."

"Here's a spur-of-the-moment thought. I still have this weekend free. Could you leave sweet Roland and come to the country with me? I never go to our country house in Jersey, and it's a lovely place. We'd just have a couple of days away to talk about life and stuff."

"How soon do you want to leave? It sounds terrific."

"I'll pick you up at four o'clock—okay?"

"I'll be ready. What fun, and Roland will completely approve of our girls outing."

The trip through New Jersey horse country was scenically pretty, even with a winter landscape. And Edwina wanted to know everything about Bettina's mother and her new life.

"You know, Edwina . . ."

"You realize Mom or Mother is an acceptable option."

"Yes, I do, and I can't tell you how much that means to me. I think, just to keep me honest with myself—for a change—that I'll call you Edwina, so I don't desert my actual mother."

"Good thinking. Now continue with the story of your mom."

"It's amazing, Edwina. It's as though a new person has emerged from the old person. The moth becoming the butterfly. A woman, more embittered than not, burdened by life's hardships, reluctant to smile, now greets every morning with sunshine in her expression, laughter in her voice. Truly amazing."

The country place in New Jersey was a converted barn with a private lake. Inside, old beams soared twenty-four feet, and great slabs of glass overlooked countrified lawns and gardens, now covered with a postcard snow. The kitchen was Bettina's favorite. In her new life, she had taken to cooking and experimenting with food. This was a cook's kitchen, with granite counters, state-of-the-art appliances, and glassy views of gentle hills and nosey deer.

"Edwina, since we're on holiday, and I don't have to sing tonight, and our men aren't here to keep tabs on us, how about having something risky?"

"Risky? Bettina, Edwina Richardson hasn't done anything risky in a hundred years."

"Well, this won't make the *Post*, but it could be fun and maybe give me the courage to tell you all that is in my heart and mind."

"All right, dear. What is it?"

"A perfect margarita."

"A what? A margarita? As in Mexico, tequila, that kind of thing?"

"Absolutely. We had a Mexican houseman, and he taught me how to make them. You game?"

"Game."

"All right. Let me squeeze some fresh limes. It takes one part lime juice, two parts Triple Sec—purists say Cointreau, but I think Triple Sec is fine—and two parts tequila—good tequila. Put it in the blender with about five cubes of ice. Blenderize it for about ten seconds. And pour it over rocks, without salt on the rim, because we don't need that much salt. Voila!"

"Oh, my goodness. I can tell these are indeed risky. But oh, so good."

"Before I have too many of them, like one more, I'd like to talk about Bethel Sokoloff and why she did what she did."

"Fine, darling, but I want you to know you don't have to spell it out for me. I've known for a long time. But, foolish and controlling as I can be and have been, I was wise enough to see the good that you brought to this family. You are Bettina Richardson. You've proven it many times. Roland, being wiser and more temperate than I, saw your great quality before I did, but I can cheerfully tell you that I am your friend."

"Your love and approval make me cry, Edwina. But I thank you. And I do want to tell you what it's like to wake up and know there will be no light and shadow to my day … just gray, just boring, endless nothing. That was my life, so I decided to do away with that person, become someone else. No, I wasn't counting on snagging a Dilly Richardson. I would have been content to end up in a split-level ranch house in Long Island if I truly loved the man at my side. Luck, timing, and fate brought me Dilly. At first, knowing I was deceiving him, I worked at playing the role, and then, much to my own astonishment, I became that person.

"And then this stupidity about the Center for Self-Fulfillment. Of course I was dumb. An accident waiting to happen. A scam, who therefore could easily be scammed. But I thought if I did something big and wonderful that Dilly—and you—would look up to me, and I wouldn't have to feel inferior in my new skin. Oh, the scammers were clever, but then they spend all their time figuring out how to be clever, and I was eager to be taken. Can you imagine how powerful it felt to be able to write a check for millions of dollars? Bethel Sokoloff writing a check for millions—wow!"

"But you weren't Bethel Sokoloff, dear Bettina. You were and are Bettina Richardson, and you acted from your heart. As you now know, it wasn't wise to do that without consulting Dilly first, but it's understandable. Now my main concern is how Dilly is treating you. Your fath ... Roland told me that Dilly has been very hard on you."

"Gross understatement. He believes everything the crook said about me, that I was sexually involved, and all kinds of nonsense. I know Dilly can't believe that, but ... oh, maybe I don't know. Maybe he does believe."

Edwina studied her daughter-in-law, liking what she saw. As usual, the look was perfect. Bettina was wearing a silk cream-colored turtleneck with a suede hacking jacket, and tailored camel slacks. But it wasn't clothes that made the woman. This beautiful and, yes, complicated girl was under attack. And for once in her adult life, Edwina felt the situation was completely out of her control. "Roland and I know you are not guilty of any of the serious charges. Your only crime was not believing in yourself enough so you could see through those disgusting people. We know you will rise above this, and I have faith that Dillworth will come to his senses." Edwina reached out and hugged Bettina.

"Edwina, I love you and Roland so much. I can't begin to tell you. Well, all this emotion calls for food. And since we've had margaritas, I thought we'd have something uniquely Mexican for dinner."

"Oh dear, isn't Mexican food all hot and kind of Tex-Mex?"

"Not at all, Edwina. We're going to have chicken breasts stuffed with *cuitlacoche.*"

"Stuffed with what? And how do you pronounce it?"

"Cuitlacoche. Wheat-la-co-che. It's the black fungus that grows on corn."

"Black corn fungus? Sounds … just … delightful."

"I promise, Edwina. You'll like it."

CHAPTER *50*

The Lawsuit!

"Mrs. Schmidt-Feller, tell us in your own words about Kenneth Monroe and how you became involved with him."

"I was phony baloney, barely earning a living doing palm readings and telling fortunes. So, this Kenny fellow—"

"Kenny?"

"Mr. Monroe, but I call him Kenny."

"Proceed."

"Anyway, Kenny comes along and offers me big money—you know, like fifteen hundred dollars—if I become the voice of the future for this cockamamie scheme he's got working. So he sends out one of these letters telling people we know how they're feeling and can help them get over their problems, and wow, a lot of people—I guess a lot of people are unhappy with their lives–send in twenty bucks for a reading from me. And I couldn't predict what I was going to have for lunch that day.

"One of the letters really gets Kenny's attention. You know, the paper was edged in gold. And it's from this lady named Richardson. He gets all excited and makes a date for me to meet this lady. He changes my outfit, my hair, and rehearses me like I'm going to be a stage star. And this lady—and she really is a lady—comes to the Waldorf Astoria. That's how important this deal was to Kenny; he actually sprung for the Waldorf Astoria."

"Please go on, Mrs. Schmidt-Feller."

"Anyway, this lady—oh, such a lady—comes in, and I instantly see the face of an infant daughter I had to give up. And I know I wouldn't let nothing happen to her."

"But you continued being part of the operation."

"Yeah, but I wanted to protect her. If Kenny would ever tell you the truth, he'd tell you I wanted to protect her. She was so ... so, umm, real and caring and gentle, you know."

"What did Mr. Monroe—Kenny—and his partner, Mr. Warshon, want from Mrs. Richardson?"

"Bucks. Money. She was nothing to them, just a bank account."

"And what was your role, Mrs. Schmidt-Feller?"

"I was the shill, the main attraction. I had to convince her that the Center for Self-Fulfillment was the real thing. I had to convince her that her welfare was the most important thing to me. And it was."

"Explain that."

"Her welfare is what mattered to me. I loved her and wanted to protect her—from them."

"And why didn't you warn Mrs. Richardson about their scheme?"

"I was afraid. Kenny said he'd kill me if I blew the whistle. And Herman scared me even more than Kenny."

"Mrs. Richardson, Mr. Monroe has told the court that you were a scam artist, that you falsely represented yourself to your husband, and that, in truth, you were Bethel Sokoloff from the Bronx. Is that true?"

In that instant, Bettina was once again eleven years old, sitting in their grimy kitchen, something unpleasant-smelling bubbling on the stove; the ever-present TV blaring in the small, airless living room; her father in his undershirt, sprawled out, having his first of three beers—no more than three. Her mother was ironing and complaining about old Mrs. Meyer downstairs.

"If it wasn't bad enough to hear her damn dog barking all day, she never walks it, and you can smell her apartment as you walk by. Her family should put her away in some old-folks home."

"Knock it off. I'm trying to watch television. Who gives a crap about Mrs. Meyer and her stupid dog?"

"Mrs. Richardson, I asked you a question."

"Pardon me. My mind wandered. Yes, it was true. I was not the person I said I was."

"Did you, in fact, grow up in the Bronx?"

"Objection. My client is not on trial, and this line of questioning has no bearing on the case."

"Your Honor, we disagree. We will show you why Mrs. Richardson's facade had a great deal to do with the so-called scam perpetrated by Mr. Monroe and Mr. Warshon."

"Overruled. You may continue."

"I'll repeat my question. Did you, in fact, Mrs. Richardson, grow up in the Bronx?"

"Yes, I did. I was born and raised in the Bronx."

"What did your parents do?"

"My father was a tailor and had a small dry-cleaning business. My mother cleaned houses when she worked."

"But it's my understanding you presented yourself as an orphan, left penniless by a plane crash."

"That is correct."

"Isn't that pure deception on your part?"

"Yes, but I didn't like the options offered to Bethel of the Bronx. So I created a more acceptable young woman."

"Don't you think you cheated your husband?"

"No."

"Explain that."

"He wanted an attractive, loving, caring wife, and I was—and am—that. My past had no bearing on our relationship. It was not an attractive past, and I didn't want to burden him with it."

"We understand your husband gave you ten million dollars with no strings attached."

"Yes, he was very generous."

"Do you expect us to believe you weren't part of a plot to cheat your husband out of the nine million dollars?"

"Objection. Mrs. Richardson has not been charged with any crime. The prosecution is leading the witness and trying to lead the jury on a wild goose chase."

"Members of the jury, you may omit that last statement by the prosecuting attorney. Mr. Meltzer, do not go down that path again."

"Yes, Your Honor. Mrs. Richardson, how well did you know Mr. Monroe and Mr. Warshon?"

"I never met Mr. Monroe until the meeting at the Waldorf Astoria, which was arranged for me to meet the Madame. I didn't meet Mr. Warshon until many months later."

"Ms. Sokoloff—"

"Objection! Our client's legal name is Bettina Richardson. The prosecution is harassing the witness."

"Mr. Meltzer, I don't want to have to tell you again."

"Yes, Your Honor. All right, Mrs. Richardson." His voice was layered with sarcasm. "Why would you believe this Madame DeSantis, when it would be evident to anyone that they were trying to scam you?"

Bettina sat quietly and very straight, her hands folded in her lap. She raised her head to its full height. "Mr. Meltzer. Even though I had everything and more than a person has a right to have, I wanted more. I wanted, I think, to believe in my heart that I was Bettina Richardson. Madame—and I don't believe she's a bad person—spoke warmly and intimately to me, to my inner thoughts. I felt that if I helped her, I would help myself and gain new respect from my husband."

"And that's it? Based on that, you forked over nine million dollars? So you could believe in yourself?"

"Objection, Your Honor. Our client did not hand over ten million dollars to these individuals. She believed she was funding a charitable and useful plan, this make-believe Center for Self-Fulfillment."

"Mr. Meltzer ..."

"Yes, Your Honor."

Edwina sat directly behind Bettina and thought what a pig the prosecuting attorney was and how she'd like to crush him. *Poor Bettina. But she's handling herself as a Richardson.*

"What made you think these people were legitimate?"

"They showed me the property, architectural plans, and photos of the work in progress. I was introduced to doctors who were going to be part of the operation. I had no reason not to believe them. And I felt deep down that the Center would do good work for many needy people. If you had told me back then that they were phonies, I wouldn't have believed you. I'm still hurt by the realization. And still don't believe that Madame DeSantis—or Schmidt-Feller, you say—was trying to gyp me out of anything." Bettina looked over at Ruby and smiled warmly at her.

Newspapers, especially the *New York Post*, were having a field day with the case. "Bethel from the Bronx, Now Bettina, Wearing Bill Blass." "Fortune Teller Convinces Society Girl to Fork Over Ten Million Bucks." "Broadway Baby from the Bronx Acts Her Way into Society." Bettina was horrified, but again, Edwina and Roland told her the silly headlines meant nothing, to ignore them. Dilly was mortified. The show, already a sell-out, now had people clamoring for an opportunity to see the multimillion-dollar scam victim. Meanwhile, Bettina recaptured the energy to bring the audience to its feet every night.

"And Mr. Monroe, what about your declaration that you had a physical relationship with Mrs. Richardson?"

"You bet I did. She was hot for me. Said her old man had lots of money but wasn't rich where it counted."

"Objection. Hearsay. And from a liar at that."

"Overruled. You may continue, Mr. Meltzer."

"Thank you, Your Honor. And where did these trysts take place, Mr. Monroe?"

"All over. Now and then at hotels. A couple of times at her apartment. She was hot. And she knew the money was going into private accounts and that one-third of it was hers to keep, and her husband wouldn't know anything about it."

"Your witness."

"Mr. Monroe, besides the fact that we are going to prove without a doubt that you lie about everything—and under oath at that—I'm curious about your self-deception."

"Huh?"

"If you ever looked in a mirror, Mr. Monroe, you would realize no woman could ever be interested in you." The spectators laughed.

"Objection. Badgering and insulting the witness."

"Sustained. This is not an appropriate exchange."

"Yes, Your Honor. I apologize. Back to you, Mr. Monroe. You say Mrs. Richardson was keeping some of the money in her own account, but of course that is pure fabrication on your part. You still had most of the money—money she thought was going to a good cause, another out-and-out lie. And now, for the so-called sexual involvement. I'm going to give you an opportunity to partially save yourself, Mr. Monroe, and confess to that lie."

"Objection. He's provoking the witness."

"Sustained."

"There's nothin' to confess. She wanted me, and I gave her what she wanted."

"Ever hear of DNA tests, Mr. Monroe?"

Kenny tried to look blasé but wondered what they could prove.

CHAPTER *51*

Finally, Dilly Couldn't Take It Anymore

Dilly sank even lower into a depressive rage as he read the day's transcripts from the court. He figured it must be true. *The man isn't backing down. Why would he lie about it? What does he have to gain?*

"Bettina, I realize all of this has been very hard on you, hard on all of us. But not only are you not the person you said you were but quite possibly have had an intimate relationship with that Kenneth person. I'm sorry, but my feelings about you have changed. I think it would be best if we separated."

"Please, Dilly, don't do this to us."

"I shouldn't do something to us? And what do you think you've done? You've made our family a laughing stock. I ... we have been publicly humiliated. The Richardsons have become nothing but fodder for gossip columns, thanks to you."

"Dilly, how many times can I say I'm sorry? If your parents can forgive my stupidity, why can't you? I love you, Dilly. Our marriage is all-important to me—"

"Don't worry; you won't be penniless. You'll have plenty of money."

"This isn't about money. I want us—together."

"No, no, no, no, I'm sorry, Bettina. I want out. Even though this is my apartment, I will move. I'll have my attorney draw up an agreement, and I suppose you should hire your own attorney who will try to gouge as much money as possible out of me."

Bettina sat there, looking at the fine Aubusson carpet, seeing nothing, remembering a line from one of her stage songs: "I never knew my life was empty until you walked through the door." She didn't hear the rest of Dilly's farewell speech, didn't see him leave with his suitcase. She sat there for a couple of hours. The doorman called to tell her the car to take her to the theater was waiting downstairs. She went to the theater, numb.

John, still carrying a bright torch for Bettina, was acutely aware of every emotion and nuance reflected in Bettina's face and movement. He knew something heavy had happened. "Betts, whatever has happened, remember I'm always here with a shoulder you can lean on or cry on."

Her voice was so gentle; it didn't even sound like her. "Thank you, John. I'm very fortunate to have you nearby. I've done nothing to warrant your support. But it sure helps, and I do appreciate it. Now scoot out of here so I can finish my makeup and concentrate on being Cassidy." John left, and she looked in the makeup mirror and said, "And when you finish tonight's performance, Bettina Richardson, you will go home to an empty apartment and start a new role—the divorcee, a single, unwanted woman, dropped by your husband because you were, and probably are, stupid." Somehow, the professional in her came to the forefront, and, buoyed by an adoring audience, she electrified the theater. Drained after the performance, she returned to her dressing room and sat in front of the mirror, trying to decide her next steps.

"Bettina, I'm not leaving until you tell me what's wrong." John's voice came out of a dark corner of her dressing room, where he was seated.

Bettina leaped to her feet. "My God, John, you scared me to death. Thank goodness I don't have a heart condition; it would have been all over for me."

"I'm sorry for the scare, but I was afraid you wouldn't let me in, and you can't keep me out, Bettina. I love you, I want you, I know I can take care of you."

"We've been over this before, John, and you know I'm married."

"And I know that something is wrong, very wrong, and I want to make everything right for you." He had moved over to Bettina, who had fallen into her chair. He put his arms around her and rested his chin on her head, both looking into the mirror. "Give me a chance, Bettina. Without you, I have no value, as a man, as a professional. I love you completely."

Bettina leaned back against John, and he kissed her temple, the bridge of her nose, her lower lip. She said nothing. He finally let go, afraid this was her final rejection. He stood straight. She observed him in the mirror, and then Bettina stood. She reached out and laid her open palm on the side of his face. He leaned in closer, still closer, and they kissed, softly, gently, and finally passionately.

"I don't want us to be on the floor in the dressing room. I want soft lights, and music, and champagne." He was almost whispering. Bettina nodded and smiled, so grateful for the promise of his love.

Lisa Gutwillig made Bettina her number-one project in life. When legal papers appeared from Dilly's attorney, Lisa had her prominent attorneys review it all and return it, heavily weighted in Bettina's favor. Bettina never read the papers. She knew they discussed money—her future money— but did she deserve that? Yes, Dilly had abandoned her, but now she had abandoned Dilly.

The weeks turned into months, and suddenly her one-year anniversary in the show was a reality. They wanted her to stay, but John wanted her to quit so they could have some time together to travel. She agreed; one year was enough, and she was gratified when a big-time star signed on as her replacement. The farewell party from the cast and crew was one of the warmest and most endearing things that had ever happened to Bettina.

CHAPTER *52*

Knowing She Had Gone to Paris with Dilly, John Chose London as a First Destination

They stayed in the Athenaeum Hotel on Green Park, which felt like a private men's club. John knew London well and took Bettina to the small clubs and restaurants that only London insiders know. She loved the pomp and pageantry and easily fell into the role of tourist, enjoying the civility and courtesies of the British. She particularly enjoyed *Two Gentlemen of Verona* at Shakespeare's open-air Globe Theatre in Bankside. And she felt right at home in the chumminess of the good pubs, like the Grenadier in Belgravia and the Blue Post in Soho. After four days of London, with brilliant theater every evening and spectacular dining, John's next surprise was a car trip to the Cotswolds.

Bettina was enchanted with the gold-toned stone walls bordering vivid green fields and pastures. He had selected one famous inn, the Broadway, as their home for a few days. The first morning, he suggested she try the "special" porridge, which unexpectedly featured a shot of Kahlua poured into the middle of the porridge. The days were gentle, with long country walks and afternoon stops for scones with clotted cream and strawberries. The nights were passionate, beyond what Bettina, or Bethel, could ever have imagined. John's deep love was reflected in the most moving and satisfying lovemaking in Bettina's eclectic history. Dilly was … well, fading from the front of her memory as she found herself caught up in the fire and romance of a true love affair. Perhaps Dilly had never loved her. Perhaps she was just a beautiful icon on his arm.

"So you see, my darling and beautiful Bettina, I too was not born with a silver spoon in my mouth. It was a barely likeable, brawling Irish clan, with all the adult men big drinkers, caricatures of Irish men. And Mother, long-suffering, was no great bargain herself. She brought whining and complaining to a new level of professionalism." John had never spoken of his past to anyone, he realized, but now he wanted Bettina to have it all. He left nothing out, and she was breathless from each chapter.

His young years were hardly more memorable than hers. Instead of the Bronx, they had lived in Queens in a large, ill-kept apartment, with many visiting siblings from the old country sprawled out on sofa beds in the living room. He shared a room with two brothers, who bullied and ignored him. He considered running away many times, but the thought of confronting the family with his dreams seemed too risky, so he stayed, he tolerated, and he looked for the first exit available.

"I finally decided the only way out was through the church. And although I was hardly a goodie-goodie, I had a reasonable acceptance and understanding of the Father, the Son, and the Holy Ghost, amen, and decided I could do good things for the world as a priest. Oy, such an experience. I entered a seminary with a rosy view and a clear conscience. But this particular seminary—and I'm not pointing fingers at all seminaries—could have been called the semen-ary. There was an active group of homosexuals in the school, who failed miserably to indoctrinate me. I thought, fine, that's their problem, and I could ignore it and learn my lessons so I could become a worthwhile priest. But then one day, one of the important monsignors in the school called me in for a conference regarding my progress, and the old fart put the make on me. That did it; I was out of there, first taking a hard-line stance, telling the monsignor that if he made up any bullshit about my behavior or lack of attention to my studies that I'd blow the whistle on him and the entire damn school. I think his report to my parents was something about my being a fine student—I had all A's at that point—but that I had too worldly a view for the necessarily restrictive life of a parish priest. He went on the say that I would do very well in private industry and, therefore, reluctantly released me from my young and well-meant vows. What a crock. It sadly turned me away from the church for a lotta years, and just recently have I found myself returning to the fold. Once Catholic, it's difficult to ignore that influence."

"Are you saying I should convert?"

"Absolutely not. I like you just the way you are. You are my personal religion. I may build a shrine to you."

"Shame on you, John. Beware of false gods, and God knows I've been pretty false."

"*Real* takes on a new meaning when applied to you. Oh, Bettina, there is nothing in the world that we can't have—together."

Meanwhile, the case against Kenny and Herman gathered steam and pushed them into a corner with no escape.

"Ladies and gentlemen of the jury, we thank you for doing your job so admirably. Mr. Monroe and Mr. Warshon, a jury of your peers has found you guilty on all counts of extortion. Sentencing will be one month from today. Court is adjourned."

Dilly read the headlines, which came as no surprise. But it still didn't clear Bettina of her possible sexual involvement with the man. However, he had been surprised to read she had left the show. Many times he picked up the phone, thinking he'd call her, but never completed the call. It didn't matter. Bettina, or Bethel, was old news. He had gone out a couple of times but found excuses to not be involved. Sex was overrated in his troubled emotional state.

"Dillworth."

"Yes, Dad. How are you?"

"I'm fine. More important, how are you? And where is Bettina?"

"Where, what?"

"Where is Bettina? She left a brief message on our answer machine saying she was going abroad with a friend and would call us when she returned. She thought she'd be gone a couple of weeks. We thought perhaps you knew where she was and how she's doing."

"No, Dad, Bettina and I have nothing to do with one another. Sorry. I can't tell you her whereabouts."

"I'm sorry you're not communicating with her. You know how I feel about this split of yours and wish you would reconsider."

"Right this minute, Dad, I don't see a reconciliation."

"More's the pity. I'm afraid that someone will come along and see what a jewel she is and snap her up."

"If that's what the cards hold, so be it."

The elder Mr. Richardson pursed his lips and stared at his son, saying nothing for a couple of minutes. "Am I missing something, son? Is there another element in this mess? Another woman, perhaps?"

"Good heavens, no, Father. And why am I being made out as the ogre in this melodrama? Bettina, or Bethel, whoever she is—"

"Bettina is her name, as you know so well."

"Very well, Bettina, is the one who brought down our house."

"Only your house, apparently, son. It was an unfortunate set of circumstances, but your lack of generosity quite appalls me."

"Well! Pardon me for breathing. Excuse me, Father. I must get to work. Thanks for your call, even though I didn't particularly enjoy the conversation."

Roland sighed. "Goodbye, Dilly. I didn't mean to offend you." And both men hung up, both tormented by the loss of the same woman.

John's final surprise was the trip home to New York—a penthouse stateroom on the *QE2*. Bettina was enchanted with shipboard life. As John said, it was "a total abandonment of responsibility." You could open your mouth, and someone arrived with food and drink. But it was fascinating. It was a busy city. There were early morning exercise classes, which Bettina attended and even pulled John out of bed one morning to join her. There was a pampering spa, with massages and steam baths; a beautiful library; first-run movies; a nightly cabaret show; betterment lectures by traveling semicelebrities; even a 5:00 p.m. "Friends of Bill W." meeting, which John told her was Alcoholics Anonymous. John had insisted they have a private table for meals, although one evening, two well-heeled couples came up to them and praised Bettina to the walls, saying they had seen her performance a few months ago. She was slightly embarrassed, but John glowed as she handled her now public fame.

Their stateroom was beautifully designed, with a king-size bed, ample room for luggage and all their clothing, a desk for writing, a beautifully appointed sitting room, and an outside balcony. Bettina left the door to the balcony open every night to hear the ocean. It was all too short a trip—seven nights, with a couple of stops along the Spanish coast before crossing the Atlantic to New York. Arriving in New York at 6:00 a.m., Bettina was outside on the ship's boardwalk, thrilled to see the Statue of Liberty and her beloved Manhattan welcoming her home.

That morning, she thought of Dilly for the first time in long while, wondering if he thought of her and missed her and wondering how she felt about him. She wasn't sure, and besides, no one could ever replace John.

CHAPTER 53

"My, My, Amazing What a New Nose, New Name, and New Background Can Do for a Girl."

"My famous sister. Everyone in the old neighborhood asks about you, and I know you're eager to know how they're all doing." Mickey's voice, besides dripping with sarcasm, was overlaid with contempt.

"Hello, Michelle, or do you prefer Mickey?"

"It doesn't matter what you call me, Bethel; pardon me—Bettina."

"Can't we start over, Mickey? I know you and I weren't close growing up, but I have no bad memories of you."

"Hey, rich or poor, it's nice to have money. Are you going to keep some of the family bucks now that you're on the street? At least that's what the gossip columns say."

"I guess I missed those columns. I've been ... away."

"Yeah, I know. One columnist said you were seen in Europe with somebody named John something-or-other."

"How have you been, Mickey? Have you spoken with Mom lately?"

"Nice change of subject, Sis. Yeah, I spoke with Mom and just have to listen to her sing love songs about all that you do for her."

"We're not in competition about Mom; you know that."

"Yeah, but you can certainly do a lot more than I can, the newly soon-to-be-divorced wife of the rabbi."

"What? I … I find that hard to believe. What happened, Mickey?"

"The bastard's been having an affair for over a year, and she has enough bucks to convince him to dump me and the kids. To think I put up with all that lousy sex for that many years."

"Let me help you, Mickey."

"I don't need any help. I need money."

"Fine, I have money and can help you."

"It's just a loan."

"No, consider it a gift. Would fifty thousand dollars help you get resettled?"

"You'd give me fifty grand?"

"Yes. If that will help, I'll send you a check, or if you give me the name of your bank and account number, I'll have it put in your account."

"Okay. But it's a loan."

"Whatever you want it to be. I understand what it's like to be dumped, Mickey. My husband doesn't want me anymore either. It's not a good feeling."

"Men are shits."

"Sis, when things have settled down for you, please call me, and let's get together. Maybe we can even go down to visit Mom together. That would make her very happy."

"Okay, Beth … Bettina. I'm sorry I'm …"

"Hey, Mickey, let's not be sorry about anything. Let's just be sisters again." She heard Mickey quietly crying. "Now give me that bank account number so we can get you settled again." She hung up and saw much of her life passing in front of her. *Crazy Michelle, who marries the rabbi, now just your soon-to-be-divorced sister. Both of us under an emotional gun. Wonder why it should be this way. Is life supposed to be a constant trial? Are there no easy routes?*

"You make me nuts; you know that? I just bought a book of poetry. Poetry! My God, I've lost it."

"I think that's sweet, John. Thank you for calling to tell me. Are you going to read me some poems or merely memorize them so you can hypnotize me with your sonorous tones and then, when my defenses are down, do all those things you boys like to do?"

"You sound like you know about those things pretty well."

"Take it from me, kid; I could write the book."

"That's fine by me, as long as you include a chapter or maybe just a paragraph about me."

"That's not good enough. I would dedicate the book to you because you taught me the only things worth knowing or remembering."

"Do you mean that, Betts?" His voice softened almost to a whisper.

"Yes, I do, John Moran. I realize I never knew anything about love until I met you. Come over here right now, and maybe I'll prove it, shameless hussy that I am."

"It's only two in the afternoon."

"Sounds like the right time to me."

"Bettina, I've been thinking."

"Wow, Lisa, that must be a new and exciting experience."

"Wh—? Well, my God, Bettina, you must be feeling better."

"About everything, my darling and best of best friends. I'm head over heels."

"Oh, honey, I'm so happy for you. Who is this prince?"

"I thought we might all have dinner together, if you think Fred wouldn't feel it's too difficult, being such a close friend of Dilly's."

"Noooo, I don't think Fred would feel that way, but hey, it doesn't hurt to ask. Wow, you're in love! Dilly is the biggest jerk in the world."

"You know something, Lisa? I'm so full of inner peace and contentment I can't be angry with Dilly. It killed me at first, but as they say, some things are fated. And if this is my fate, then I am the luckiest woman in the entire world."

"May I ask the name?"

"Absolutely. John Moran."

"Wasn't he something in your Broadway show?"

"Right, the producer, or at least one of the producers. I knew how he felt, but he always respected my marriage. Suddenly, I didn't have a marriage to be respectful of, and he sort of swept me away. It's all fairy-tale stuff. I didn't know things like this could really happen."

"Nothing that happens to you, Betts, is an accident. You deserve it. Now, when can we sit down and have a serious talk? I know you've been ignoring all the legal papers, but I haven't, and I think you should know exactly where you stand ... basically in a field of clover."

"Lisa, where would I be without you?"

"Probably queen of some exotic country. I just wanted to make sure the lawyers didn't try to shortchange you. If Dilly wants to be an idiot, I want him to know it's an expensive proposition."

"Okay, friend, how about coming here tomorrow for lunch? I'll have something ordered in so we'll be private. Doesn't sound like the kind of conversation to have with other ears in the room."

"Perfect. I'll be there by twelve thirty."

The telephone ring at two in the morning slapped Bettina into apprehensive consciousness. "Yes?"

"Bettina, its Edwina. Forgive me for waking you, but I'm so frightened."

"What's wrong, Edwina? Is it Dad?"

"Yes." Her voice cracked with tears. "Roland has had a stroke. They've taken him to New York Hospital, and he's in ICU. I'm here but frankly don't know where to turn."

"I'm on the way, Edwina. I'll be there as quickly as possible. What floor are you? Do you want me to call anyone for you? Is Dilly coming over? And Elizabeth?"

"Dilly's somewhere in Europe. And Elizabeth is up in someone's ski house, and I don't have the number."

"I think you should call Marcella; she always has Dilly's schedule with her. No, never mind. I'll call her and tell her to find Dilly. I know he'll rush back. Try to stay calm, darling. I'm on the way."

She was out the door in five minutes, and a cab was waiting. When Edwina saw her, she burst out crying, and Bettina held her one-time enemy closely, murmuring reassurances.

"My God, Bettina, without … you know, I mean … married to someone like Roland … so strong, such a piece of steel … I never imagined him even being ill … but a stroke … it can have such debilitating effects."

"Let's try to think positively. The doctors are the best in New York, and it all depends on the severity of the stroke. With physical therapy and our love, I know Dad will recover."

"Mrs. Richardson."

"Yes, Doctor. This is my daughter Bettina."

"How do you do, Ms. Richardson?"

"How is Dad? Please tell us the extent of the damage."

"We can't determine yet the damage. Fortunately, he has a strong heart, and his general health has been excellent. At this moment, he's sleeping, heavily sedated. Understanding that no one looks his best when sleeping with sedation, I thought you might want to look in on him. You can only stay for a couple of minutes, and then I thought you might do best to go home and get some rest."

Bettina held Edwina's hand tightly, and they tiptoed into the room. Edwina gazed lovingly at her husband and then spoke softly. "Rolly, darling, Bettina and I are here. We're going to see you through this. We love you and need you."

Bettina didn't try to hold back the tears; she just murmured, "Yes, Dad, everything is going to be fine. And don't worry about Eddie. I'll take good care of her. We love you."

As they left the room, Edwina said, "I didn't know you knew about 'Eddie.'"

"One day, Dad told me. I thought it was very sweet. And Marcella told me that she would find Dilly … Eddie."

"Well, you're welcome to call me that any time, sweet Bettina."

The phone jolted Bettina out of sleep.

"Bettina, what's happened with Dad? I didn't want to call Mother until I spoke to you. Marcella said you were racing over to the hospital."

"Oh, Dilly, I'm so glad to hear your voice. Mom—Edwina—needs your presence. Dad had a stroke, and the doctors haven't determined how much or how lasting the damage is. Fortunately, his heart is strong, but strokes often leave partial paralysis or speech impediments. I'm going back to the hospital first thing in the morning, but I told the doctors to call me at any hour if there's any change."

"I'm glad you were there for Mother. What's the doctor and nurse situation?"

"Excellent. Remember Dad funded an entire wing of the hospital, so besides around-the-clock nurses, there's a doctor staying in the room, monitoring the machines as well as vital bodily signs. When can you come back? I think having you here would do more for Mom than anything."

"I'm booked on a flight at two today, which takes me to London, and I'm changing to a New York flight, arriving around 7:00 p.m., your time. Marcella's sending a car for me. And how are you, Bettina?"

"Fine, Dilly. I left the show."

"Yes, I heard, that surprised me. What brought that on?"

"Mmmm, I was tired of the weekly grind and felt I needed some time to deal with my new situation in life."

"Well, according to my attorneys, you've had time to deal with our separation agreement."

"Actually, I haven't even read one page from the attorneys. I only said for them to do what's fair. Please get home quickly and safely. Edwina needs your strength. And I will be with her every hour."

"Thanks, Betts. I've got to run. See you later."

Bettina hung up and said, "Goodbye, Dilly." And it hurt her to say it.

"Good morning. I am Dr. Kurish. Mrs. Richardson, how are you doing?"

"Thank you for asking, Doctor. I'm holding up. This is our son, Dillworth, and our daughter Elizabeth, and you met our other daughter Bettina last night." His mother's use of "daughter" referencing Bettina did not escape Dilly's notice. "How is my darling Roland? Can you give us a prognosis?"

"Unfortunately, strokes are difficult to predict in the earliest stages. However, he did receive proper treatment within the first three hours, which is crucial, and besides that, he is a very healthy man for his age."

"What are the chances my father will end up paralyzed, which he would hate?"

"Again, Mr. Richardson, I can't honestly say one way or the other. In truth, I'm encouraged by what I see. With this level of medical care, and the support of an obviously loving family, and whatever therapy is required, he may well emerge from this stroke with very little to remind him of this debilitating event. We will continue to monitor him around the clock and will keep all of you informed of any change. Mrs. Richardson, we also have arranged for a room here in this hallway, for you or any member of the family, to use as a place to rest during the day or even to spend the night. I assure you it isn't necessary to keep a bedside vigil with your husband; that is our obligation. This card has all the telephone numbers you need to access us at any hour of the day or night. I want all of you to think positively, and we shall do everything in our power to help your husband and father through this."

"Thanks very much, Doctor. My mother and all of us appreciate your comments."

"You're welcome. I am always here first thing in the morning and late afternoon to early evening, should you want to speak with me personally. Now go home and rest. Call Dr. Rashkoff around 1:00 p.m. for an update."

"Well, children. Now what?"

"Edwina, our—my apartment is closest to the hospital, and I'd love to have you stay there with me."

"Oh, goodness, Bettina, that wouldn't be too much of a bother?"

"You know it wouldn't, and it would please me very much. Elizabeth, you know you're welcome too, but I understand your plate is a bit full."

Elizabeth, enjoying a love interest for the first time since her husband's death, smiled warmly at Bettina, thinking how fortunate she, Elizabeth, was to have such a sterling sister. "Thanks, Sis, I'll just come over now and then and mooch a lunch or dinner off you."

"Nothing would make me happier."

Dilly realized he was the outsider. They were the family, and Bettina played a major role in keeping the family intact. "That's … that's good of you, Bettina. I'll worry less about Mom if she's with you." Bettina smiled at Dilly, warmly, without irony.

Life slowed to a crawl, revolving around doctors' reports, Roland's physical therapy, and maintaining Edwina's health. Bettina threw herself lovingly into this new microcosm, embracing both parents with an open heart, as well as her sister. If there was any awkwardness, it was with Dilly. "How have you been, Bettina? Do you miss the applause?"

"Sometimes I do miss it. The show forced me to adrenalize myself every evening, to leave what problems I might have in my dressing room, and focus on being Cassidy, who wanted the audience to love her. The applause is such a strong approval system. But at the same time, it was exhausting. I was drained after every performance."

"Dad told me you went away for a while. Where'd you go?"

"England. I loved London and visited the Cotswolds, and then as a special treat, I sailed home on the *QE2*. I now understand why people like cruises. You unpack once and pack once. At any rate, it was a good change of scene, but as always, I was glad to come back to New York. And you, Dilly? You were in Europe, on business, I suppose. What else is going on in your life?"

"Oh, nothing very interesting. You know old workaholic Dilly. I did spend some time in Istanbul on this last trip. A fascinating city. I remember it years ago, when it was smaller, kind of dark and mysterious. And now it's fourteen million people, a European capital. But it is fascinating with the mosques and palaces, and I quite liked the food."

"Is it exotic—the food, I mean?"

"No, not really. Reasonably sophisticated. They offer too many little first courses, which tend to fill you up, but once I got on to that and just ordered an entrée, it was excellent. I especially liked one restaurant named Kores. They pick you up in a boat and take you across the Bosporus, a wide, busy river, and you dine beside the water. Excellent. And the people in general were very cordial."

"Sounds great, Dilly. It's nice that you can still be excited about a new destination, considering how much travel you have under your belt."

"True. But travel is good, if for no other reason than it makes you glad to come back to the States. Well, it's nice to catch up. Thank you again for all that you are doing for Mom and Dad."

"You don't have to thank me. They are wonderful. I love them both. And whatever I can do for them is a labor of love."

"That I am missing you is gross understatement. I've tried to stay out of your hair because so many people are hanging on to it and you."

"There hasn't been a day, John Moran, when you haven't been with me, at my side, holding me, bolstering me as I try to bolster all the family. And family or no family, I'm spoiled and need to have you . . .um . . . closer than the telephone allows."

"Are you suggesting that we try to physically get together?"

"If we don't I'm going to go committably insane."

"I've never done it with a crazy woman."

"We can be a lot of fun, if handled correctly."

"Do you see an opening in your schedule?"

"Yes—tonight! Mom has scheduled an overnighter at the hospital, so I'll be alone. Will order dinner sent in and will expect you here by nine o'clock."

"I'll check my diary and see if that's possible."

"If you have other plans, other than going to your mother's funeral, you're dead."

"Aha, as luck would have it, I'm free at nine tonight."

"I can't wait. I love you. Goodbye."

"Dillworth, I know I've been a pushy and, at times, demanding mother. And I've tried to stay out of your business. But I have to ask you: are you really finished with Bettina?"

"God, Mother, I don't know. She hurt me so much. I can't seem to put it behind me."

"As you know very well, I wanted to kill her off from day one, but now I'm one of her strongest supporters. She's gotten me though your father's illness. And when he sees her every day, there's a smile and a twinkle in his eyes. And he loves it that she's there, sweetly nagging him to do everything necessary for the physical therapy to work. She's really a superb woman, and you would benefit having her at your side."

"I know how you feel, Mother. But Lisa Gutwillig, who *used* to be a friend of mine and has spearheaded the multimillion-dollar settlement for Bettina, said to me the other day, 'You deserve to lose her, Dilly. Now she has someone who loves her with more love than you're capable of giving.' So it sounds to me as though Bettina is very much involved with another man."

"I'm sorry to hear it, darling. Not surprised but terribly sorry to hear it. I had hopes that you would get back together."

"Mother, I promise you I'll try, but it may be too late."

"Will you really try, Dilworth? I mean, really? Take out all the stops, fight dirty, even make a fool of yourself."

"My God, Mother, what's gotten into you? That doesn't sound like you. Take out all the stops, fight dirty—"

"These are desperate times, son. I do believe Bettina was and still can be a miracle in your life, and I grieve to think you may have lost her."

"But she—"

"Don't rehash what happened, Dillworth. I just hope it isn't too late. If another man has entered her life, she may not be available to you ever again." Edwina crossed the room to her son and put her hands on his shoulders, facing him. "But I'd sure as hell try to win her back."

"This is going to be my very last glass of champagne for a long, long time." Bettina had kicked off her shoes and curled up on the plush down sofa, next to John.

"Why, my beautiful sprite? Are you, who never drinks much of anything, going on some special diet?"

"Indeed I am. Big health kick is in the cards."

"You're in perfect health, perfectly beautiful, and I don't want you to lose even a pound."

"No chance of that happening, my love."

"Oh, why am I not following this dialogue?"

"Maybe because you haven't ever been knocked up."

"Becau ... because ... what did you say?" John stood, his arms raised like a revivalist preacher.

"You're trembling and stuttering. And stop weaving around like that. What kind of father image is that going to be for our child?"

"My God, we're pregnant!"

Bettina loved John's reaction. She smiled seductively. "I think you're off the hook about carrying the child. Yes, my darling John, we are pregnant. We are going to have a baby in approximately eight months. Are you going to make the kid legitimate, like with a married mom and dad?"

"Are you asking me to marry you, my darling, darling Bettina?"

"I guess I am, but I kind of thought you were supposed to take the initiative."

"Will this do?" John knelt and, holding Bettina's hands in his, with tears brightening his eyes, said, "Will you, Bettina, take me, John, as your lawfully wedded husband, so I can spend the rest of my days loving you and our child or children, and ... what else am I supposed to say?"

"You've said it all. And yes, of course, John. I am yours." A kiss never lasted so long, never meant so much.

CHAPTER 54

Dilly Is More than a Memory

"Thank you for agreeing to see me, Bettina."

As always, the Sister Parish elegance of his former Manhattan home soothed him.

"It's always good to see you, Dilly. Come in." Bettina led Dilly into the library, always his favorite room, with fourteen-foot-high ceilings and a beautiful and valuable library, documented and filed and accessible by handsome sliding ladders. They sat on the sofa upholstered in an Oriental carpet. "Would you like something to drink, Dilly?"

Dilly thought that Bettina looked even more beautiful than in his memory. She glowed with good health and managed to look dazzlingly chic in a soft white silk shirt with poet's sleeves, deep red slacks, a gold belt, simple gold jewelry, white flat shoes, and her hair soft and falling around her face. "Oh, no thanks, Bettina. I'm fine."

"By the way, Dilly, even though you moved out of this apartment, and I believe it was awarded to me in the separation agreement, I think you should take possession again. It is very much you, and you should be living here. It's a perfect reflection of your taste and orderliness. I feel as if the furniture misses you."

"That's very sweet, Bettina, but I couldn't possibly live here unless ..."

"Unless what, Dilly?" She wondered why this conversation was taking a toll on Dilly. He was breathing more deeply than normal and was chewing on his lower lip.

"Unless you would live here with me. Please don't say anything for a minute, Bettina. I'm a very stupid man, and I did and said things that hurt both of us. And I've had to turn myself inside out to see what kind of man I am. There's only one sure thing in my life, and that is you, loving you, being with you, taking care of you. Are you all right, Bettina?"

Bettina had turned to stone, both hands clutched, as if in prayer, below her chin. "Oh, Dilly, I prayed so long that you would come back to me, and when you didn't, being vulnerable, I let myself fall in love with someone else."

"Do you have no love left for me?"

"Yes, I do feel love for you. But I couldn't hurt John."

"*Hurt John?* But you're not married to him."

"Nor am I married to you."

Dilly embraced Bettina, holding her tightly to him. "I won't take no for an answer, Bettina. You know how much I loved you and will love you that much more now. Give me the opportunity to prove that. I won't push you for your final answer right this minute, but think of all we've meant to one another." And he kissed her gently, then passionately, and then turned and left her standing alone.

Bettina wept.

"Oh, dear God, Lisa, why does it all have to be so difficult?" I know I have no right to bitch at anyone or anything but myself, because I did this all on my own."

Lisa was sitting there, smiling at her beautiful friend. "That's just so much bullshit, Betts."

"Lisa, I think I'm a bad influence on you. You never spoke like we Bronx girls speak."

"Triple—no, make that quadruple bullshit. You didn't do anything all on your own. And we are not going to rehash the scam. Big fucking deal. Even a court of law and a jury of your peers found you guilty of nothing.

And now, Dilly, who was the dopiest dope of them all, suddenly wakes up and wants his 120-pound emerald-cut diamond back. Tough shit."

"Lisa, Henri is going to throw us out of here if you don't calm your mouth."

"Let's talk about what has really happened." Lisa grinned that warming, embracing smile that she reserved only for her husband, her children, and Bettina. She leaned forward so she could brush an imaginary hair off Bettina's forehead. You're preggies? You got knocked up by a man who adores you. You have enough money in your bank account to buy a third-world country. Hey, I don't see any problems here."

"I adore you, Lisa Gutwillig. Without you, I can't imagine where I'd be."

"Let's get one thing clear; you know, dicks on the table."

"Lisa!"

"Sorry, it was a line from a book I liked. The only question that you must answer in your own perfect head is this: Are you still in love with Dilly? Or are you sure that John Moran is everything you could ever want? Be honest."

"Be honest. Be honest? God, Lisa, then maybe I should call myself Bethel. Am I capable of honesty as a simple virtue? Tell the truth! What the hell is the truth? I can remember not caring whether Dilly lived or died. Then, somewhere along the way, I guess I fell in love with him, so when he left, I died. I remember too how much I feared Edwina, for fear that she would know I wasn't really Bettina and tell the truth. Yet now she supports me for being who? For being what? And John Moran? Sent to me by my guardian angel? Maybe he fell in love with Cassidy, watching me be her every night onstage. Is he honestly in love with a real person? I think I'd better think this out carefully."

Lisa, cautious, caring, watching her friend, said, "I think you're being much too hard on yourself. And yes, you do have to answer that question for yourself. Having a child is the most dramatic role you'll ever play, and it influences everything you think and do, now and forever. What was it that Gabriel Garcia Marquez said? Something like, 'When an infant wraps his tiny hand around his father's finger, the man is trapped forever.' And you know something, Betts? Once you've created those people and carried them 'til they're ready to breathe on their own, you forever want to breathe for them. Nothing or no one means more. They don't compete with a loving husband, but inside yourself you know that if the choice was you or them, you'd take the pain, you'd take the gun, you'd take the surgery. And you feel it all over every time you peek in to see them sleeping with the angels every night."

"Lisa, we're both crying."

"And you didn't even have a drink."

"Okay, friend. I'll be honest with myself, and I'll let you know where I am."

"I'm proud of you for offering yourself to Bettina. That's certainly the nice way to do it. Just hope it was in time."

"Thanks, Dad. She didn't say, other than not wanting to hurt this John person. Christ, I hate the thought of losing her just because I was so proud. Why didn't you slap it out of me?"

"I tried, but you weren't buying it. Although this cannot be our cross to carry, if you like, your mother and I will stick our noses into this mess. Bettina knows we love her, and maybe we can help direct her back to your arms, hmmm?"

"It can't hurt, Dad. Nothing ventured ..."

CHAPTER 55

Bettina Wanted to Reach Out and Embrace All the Women Sitting in the Obstetrician's Waiting Room. Look at Us. All of Us Here Because of Love

"Hi, I've not met you before. I'm Andrea Mitchell, here for the fourth kid."

"Wow, you don't look like you've had three children, not with that body."

"You know Lottie Berk exercise classes? They are masochistic episodes of pain, but they keep me trim. I don't want to give my husband the excuse of being married to a cow."

"You're great, Andrea. I'm Bettina Richardson."

"Ah, yes, I thought you looked familiar." Bettina looked down, hoping it wasn't because of the lawsuit. "Hey, forgive me. It's just that I saw you on Broadway, and you were magnificent. And I was so sorry you had to go through that legal crap, but you came out of it as the star that you are. I'm envious. My talent ends in the kitchen and, now and then, in the bedroom."

"I'm sure you're downplaying all of your skills. Certainly, being easy to know is one of your strongest suits."

"This is your first pregnancy?"

"Yes, and I'm so excited."

"Well, you'll love Dr. Moore. He's such a gentleman, but he always knows everything. Sometimes he tells me how I'm feeling before I can put it into words. And all the babies were perfect. He's perfect, even though I'd love to redo this waiting room. I've been in vets' offices with more appeal. But decor notwithstanding, he's a jewel."

"I love to hear all that. I liked him the first visit, but it's all so new and a little scary. You're just who I needed to know."

"So far, so good, Bettina. This first trimester can be—not always but can be—physically assaulting, but follow this diet and these easy exercises."

"Thanks, Dr. Moore. I feel fortunate to have you in my corner. But everything is, well, healthy and normal?"

"For the moment. I won't kid you, Bettina. Pregnancy is usually 100 percent successful. But it's a totally new experience for your body, and there are lots of internal adjustments to be made. Just take it one day at a time. Goodness knows you personally are in splendid condition—don't smoke, thank God; not drinking. . . . I foresee no problems."

Bettina loved to visit Edwina and Roland's giant corner apartment in Olympic Tower. Their forty-second-floor three-bedroom home looked north over Central Park, west toward New Jersey, and downtown to the famous New York skyline. Where many of the Olympic apartments were stark and modern, theirs was eighteenth-century English, with three matching camel-backed loveseats upholstered in a rich chintz around a massively simple glass cocktail table at Edwina's signature twenty-five-inch height, and everywhere, Oriental carpets of astounding value and subtlety, to say nothing of museum-quality art on the walls.

"Bettina, darling, forgive your meddlesome in-laws, but we think you understand where our hearts are as far as you're concerned."

"I trust you both with my life; you know that."

"Okay, here's where angels fear to tread. Oh, goodness, Roland, I'm too nervous to even speak of this. Please take over."

"This is a momentous event, Bettina, Edwina asking me to speak on her behalf."

223

"Knock it off, Rolly. Just do as I've asked."

"Yes, my love. Bettina, darling, the subject is Dillworth, or Dilly, as you rightfully named him. He finally came to and realized that the best thing that ever happened to him was the beautiful faux aristocrat who wowed him and wowed Broadway and won friends and admirers everywhere, including her in-laws. He does love you through and through and wants you to try to forgive him and let him once more plan a dramatic and loving life for the two of you."

Bettina leaned forward and grasped their hands. "For the three of us."

"The three …?"

"I'm expecting a child."

"From this John someone," Edwina almost whispered.

"Yes, Edwina, from John Moran, who has asked me to marry him."

"My, my, my, this does put a different spin on the situation."

"Yes, it does, Dad, and I hope you both don't hate me for this."

"Understand something, Bettina. Roland and I could never and will never feel anything toward you but love. But we also understand obligations. A child is a tremendous obligation. And if the child was conceived in love, perhaps that is the only logical option. We're older and perhaps more selfish, and we want to keep you in our arms and at our sides forever."

"No matter what happens, Edwina, that won't change; I promise you. This is that famous rock and a hard place that I am between. It would be easy, frankly, if I could hate Dilly, but that's impossible. And I do think I love John. He's really a fine man—generous of spirit, loving, and kind."

"As much as it hurts me to say it, Bettina, I—and I'm sure Edwina agrees with me—have no doubt of his quality. You wouldn't allow yourself to be involved with someone lacking emotional and mental value. However, I do hear you say you 'think' you love John. Does that leave a door ajar for Dilly?"

"I don't know, Dad. I didn't tell Dilly I was expecting a child. When he knows that, perhaps this issue won't exist. That's a tough proposition for a man, to find his one-time wife pregnant with another man's child."

"What if he doesn't care, Bettina?"

"I don't know, Edwina. I don't begin to know. Do you really think that's possible?"

"Like you, I can't answer that, darling. Well, Roland, let's leave Bettina to her thoughts. We know you will make the right decision, and we want it to be the right decision for you. Don't decide for us—or for Dilly. You must take care of number one and the child, and … oh dear, I'm crying. Maybe I've always wanted a grandchild." The two women embraced, crying and laughing.

Rolly stepped forward to embrace them both. "Enough farewells, Edwina. I may start crying in a minute. Good night, our darling Betts." He hugged and kissed her warmly, and she left.

Bettina wandered up Fifth Avenue and entered Central Park, loving the statuary, admiring families together, husbands and wives, with their children, sometimes accompanied by their other child, a dog. She tried to envision herself in these tranquil familial scenes. She saw herself with that unknown child, sitting on a beach, building sand castles, building dreams. She thought of the divorce rate and the tedium of raising a child. She thought of sex with John, wondering how long before it would lose the heat and become just another night with the same old body. She wondered about sex with Dilly, if it could ever matter, if their love could ever be what it should have been.

"Beth … Bettina, how do you face the world when you've been dumped by a man?"

"Oh, Mickey, for a while it's impossible. I cried myself to sleep so many nights and still had to go and perform on Broadway, feeling scooped out." Bettina had invited her sister to join her for lunch at the Boathouse in Central Park. She insisted Mickey have a cosmopolitan, while she had a mineral water with lemon. "I was grateful to have to perform because I could become that character and stop being that dismal marital failure Bettina Richardson, also known as Bethel to a select crowd."

"I went to see you, Sis. You were sensational. I wasn't speaking to you back then, but I wanted to stop people in the lobby and say, 'Hey, that's my baby sister. Isn't she great!'"

"That's sweet, Mickey. You know psychologists say the most important relationship in a family is sisters, not parents and children, or brothers, but sisters. I think we should work on making their predictions true."

"I'm game. God, you're great to open that possibility to me."

"Sis, we girls gotta stick together. Besides, it will make Mom the happiest woman on earth."

"She already is, thanks to you. I've got to do more for her, and I promise you, I will. Now, tell me why you're not having a cocktail, and can you also tell me how to make this delicious thing you ordered for me?"

"Okay. First, how to make a cosmopolitan. Start with Absolut Citron, a little cranberry juice to give it a rosy glow, just a dash of fresh lime juice, and a sweetener, like Triple Sec, about the same as the cranberry."

"You're not giving amounts."

"Well, you just do it by trial and error; you'll figure it out."

"Fine, and now, why aren't you having a drink? Are you on a diet, and if so, why?"

"Well, Mickey, from everything I've read, I get a very strong impression that you shouldn't drink or smoke if you're pregnant."

"*Pregnant! I'm thrilled!* Oy, who's the father?"

"He's darling and handsome and loves me and wants us to get married right away. His name is John Moran, and he's … I don't know, a one-of-a-kind prince on a white stallion. It's all very exciting, Mickey."

"I'm going to be an aunt! Can an aunt have another cosmopolitan?"

CHAPTER 56

"Betts, My Love. Remember How Much You Loved the _QE2!_ Well, It's Time to Pack Some Glad Rags Again Because We're about to Set Sail"

"But, John, we can't go now."

"Why?"

"Well, after 9/11 and all the other things ..."

"The war and the world won't end if we leave for ten days."

"But is this the time for Americans to go abroad?"

"Probably not, so we're not. We're going to go on a Silver Seas ship, the _Silver Cloud_, with fewer than three hundred passengers, to Philadelphia; Baltimore; Norfolk; Charleston; the Amelia Islands off Jacksonville; Freeport, Grand Bahamas; and Nassau. Except for Nassau, it's all under American flags, and it will give us both the change of scene we need, and give you time to read and relax. And we can dance every night—well, you know the drill."

The ten days and nights were cathartic for Bettina. She visited the Museum of Fine Art in Philadelphia, marveling without deep understanding of the fine collection. She vowed to spend more time studying the museums and taking a couple of classes. She also went to Longwood Gardens and loved a lily pad at least six feet in diameter. The next port, Baltimore, had the newly created inner port city with a fine aquarium. "I've rented a car for us in Norfolk, so we can drive to Williamsburg. It's beautiful, and it's a wonderful statement of early America." But it was Charleston that appealed to Bettina. An incredibly beautiful old town with colonial charm, packed tightly, no spacious lawns, but oozing with Southern and historical appeal. The afternoon was spent at an old plantation, where appropriately costumed "colored folk" entertained their visitors, and rum punch and fruit juices were served.

Life on the ship was easy. With only 268 passengers and just as many staff, the service was extraordinary, the food excellent, and the amenities— like Bulgari soaps and shampoos, and engraved personal stationery—made them feel spoiled and cosseted, something everyone needed after the horror of the attack. The other stops weren't exciting. The Amelia Islands off Jacksonville, Florida, were flat, hot, a place for golfers. Freeport, Grand Bahamas, was another port worth missing, and finally Nassau. The colors of the buildings were fun to see, but it was time to get home, and Bettina and John were happy to board their flight for New York.

As they disembarked at La Guardia, Bettina was startled to see her sister-in-law, Elizabeth, who apparently was there to greet her. "Liz, what a surprise. How did you know where I was? Oh, of course. Edwina and Roland had my itinerary and knew how to find me. Your being here frightens me a bit because you don't look happy."

"Let's get your luggage, and then I'll talk to you in the car."

"Elizabeth, I'm John Moran."

"Hello, John. I look forward to meeting you under a different set of circumstances."

"Betts, darling, why don't you and Elizabeth go ahead. She needs to speak with you, not with me. I will get our luggage and bring yours to your apartment. Wait for me there."

"Are you sure, darling?"

"Absolutely. Now run along."

The two women turned away, with Elizabeth holding Bettina's arm firmly. "That's really a good man to be that sensitive and to make that fast a decision."

"What is going on, Liz?"

"Let's get in the car first. Here it is."

"All right. We're in the car. Now tell me."

Liz looked at Bettina and tears fell, and finally she whispered, "Dad is dead."

"Oh, God, no." Bettina felt faint. She wept openly. "What happened? And how's Edwi ... Mom?"

"Mom is doing okay. Just in pain. Dad had another stroke two days ago, but this one took him away. They were having dinner, having a loving conversation, much of which they attribute to you, and he just went away."

Bettina thought her heart would break. Roland's acceptance and love for her had carried her through the hardest days of her life.

"I know how much Dad meant to you, Bettina, and vice versa. I'm sorry to bring you this news but didn't want you to read about it or hear it via telephone. I wanted to try to find you, but Mom wouldn't hear of it. She wanted you to have this time with John and time to try to heal after the attack."

"I'll go to her this afternoon. Selfishly, I did want my child to know Roland. He was ... is ... such a wonderful human being, a Gulliver in a world full of tiny, unimportant people."

"In spite of the sad news, you look wonderful, Betts; beautiful and peaceful and relaxed. I take it you and John had a great trip."

"Oh yes, Liz. A trip full of small pleasures. A visit to a museum, a tour of a lovely Southern city, delicious food, albeit too much of it, good conversations with interesting people, and John, as always, taking care of me like I'm some fragile China doll, which you know I'm not."

"We all need that kind of loving care now and then. I'm so happy that you have John, and I still think my brother deserves the dunce cap of the year."

"Don't be too hard on Dilly. I brought a lot of pain to his world and can't blame him for overreacting."

229

"Maybe at first. But when Mom and Dad both voted in favor of you, he was just being stupid. Water over the dam. It looks like you have a super guy, as you well deserve."

"Thanks, Liz. But now we must focus on Edwina. What can I do to help her?"

"Just by being there. You are as much her daughter as am I. Your presence will make everything less painful."

Edwina, always so strong, so centered, seemed lost. "You know, Betts, we had fallen in love all over again, and when he came out of the last stroke, I thought, *Oh, thank you, God. Now we can spend the rest of our lives together.*"

"And he did, Eddie. He spent the rest of his life with you, loving you. And now it's the first day of the rest of your life, and you're going to have to go on. No one expects you to be 100 percent for a long time. You need time to remember all the good stuff."

"And God knows, there was a lot of that. Humpf. Good stuff. So much more of that than the bad stuff. You're right, as usual. I'll work on it. If I'm feeling lonely, can I hang out with you?"

Bettina laughed. "Hang out with me? You can move in with me if you'd like, or vice versa. I love every minute with you and suspect we can find a lot of things to do and talk about."

"No, I won't move in . . . well, maybe for a few days, and then I want to get used to being Edwina, alone. It's important to learn alone, how to do it, how to keep it positive. But you'll help me, won't you, darling."

"Arm in arm."

CHAPTER *57*

Life, with All Its Complexities, Goes On

"Mr. Moran, just lie still. Try to not let the MRI noise bother you. It's important so we can see what's going on in there."

"I've changed my mind, Doc. I don't want you to know what's going on in there. Just give me a tune-up and a lube job, and let me out of here."

"Now, now, John, just hold still. Here we go."

"Bettina, it's Dilly. Mom told me. You're pregnant!"

"Yes, Dilly, pregnant. I just couldn't tell you the other day. And then Dad passed away and ... I don't know; there never has been a right time."

"Can you tell me about the baby's father?"

"Certainly. John Moran was one of the Broadway producers. A good and kind human being. I know you'd like him under different circumstances."

"Dumb question. You love him?"

"Yes, Dilly, and not just because he's the father of my child. He rescued me—lovingly."

"When I was drowning you ..."

"Don't think of it that way; please, Dilly. We were apart. And I had no reason to believe we would ever be getting back together again. Did you?"

"No, I guess not. Too stupidly stubborn."

"No, just too hurt by what seemed to be disloyalty on my part."

"Well, I want you to know that I am here for you, for whatever."

"I can't tell you how much that means to me, Dilly." She replaced the phone ever so gently and spoke quietly to herself. "Let's not cry, Bettina. Let's try to accept the reality of right now. You loved him, you lost him, you gave your love to someone else. You're going to have that someone else's child. That is what you want, isn't it? Isn't it?"

"Mr. Moran—"

"Call me John, David. Mr. Moran sounds like an undertaker—no pun intended."

"All right, John. How gentle and evasive and even hopeful do you want me to be?"

"Give it to me right between the eyes."

"Some cancers are curable."

"Mine isn't, I presume."

"You presume correctly."

"Then this meeting is over, right?"

"Wrong. There are treatments that can prolong your life."

"Like simmering vegetables instead of boiling them?"

"Like giving you enough time to be with the people you love. Enough time to make peace with yourself, perhaps with your enemies, and hopefully enough time for your loved ones to accept the … the …"

"Finality of this trip."

"Yes, the finality of this trip, as you call it."

"Okay, Doctor, you win. Give me all the delicious details so I know what to pack."

"Lisa, my beautiful John is abandoning me for a full week. He said I couldn't go to the male stripper bars, but he didn't say I couldn't take my best friend away. Can you get away? I'll treat you to a week in Acapulco."

"Acapulco? Have you been gorging your pregnant self on tortillas? Why Acapulco? And yes, I'll accept. This winter weather is turning me into an old piece of leather."

"Why Acapulco? Mmmm, best winter weather in the world, or so someone told me. And Continental has one nonstop flight a week on Saturdays. And I understand the hotels have restaurants and beaches that are lovely and that it's safe, and—"

"The Montezuma's revenge isn't the deadly kind."

"No, I'm told they've taken care of that. Water is ultravioleted clean of bacteria. Ice cubes are all sanitized. You come home weighing more, not less, than when you went. Besides, with all the talk of terrorism and the economy, I'm becoming mentally stalled and need to jump-start my life again. Anyway, will Fred let you go, and will your little guys go nuts without their mommy?"

"Yes, I can go. Mommy needs a break. And I think they all need a break from Mommy."

"*Señoras, a que hora ... perdón*, at what hour would you like to dine?"

"Oh, goodness. After that late and ample lunch. Is the dining room still open at nine o'clock?"

"It doesn't open until nine. We Mexicans are used to dining very late."

"How about ten o'clock, Lisa?"

"Count me in, but first things first—a siesta—so I can dream about my margaritas ..."

"You self-indulgent swine, swilling tequila while I have mineral water."

"Hey, you're the one who got knocked up, not me."

The concierge never changed expression but thought how coarse these beautiful American women spoke.

The week hurried by, a blur of wonderful food, of usually quiet beaches, time to talk about life and stuff, and time to catch up on reading some of the newest literary finds. "What was your favorite book this week, Betts?"

"I guess it has to be *The Lovely Bones* by Alice Sebold. Can't believe I could enjoy a book about a murdered teenager. Very, very thoughtful and thought-provoking. Although I also love the Elizabeth Berg novels you brought. She's amazing. I could finish reading one of her books, think about it for an hour, and pick it up and read it again. That *Talk Before Sleep* and *Until the Real Thing Comes Along* were wonderful. I found myself laughing and crying.

What talent. And there's something very involving about anything by Anne Lamott. This latest, *Blue Shoe,* is ... well, charming is the wrong word. You just care about everyone in her books. Did you ever read her *Traveling Mercies?*

"No, that's a novel?"

"Not really. It's the story of one woman's relationship with her God."

"And that's really worth reading?"

"I think it's worth carrying around all the time. Promise me you'll read it. You'll fall in love with this brilliant woman, who happens to be a single mom and lives in northern California and teaches writing in one of the universities up there. She's priceless."

"Okay, Betts, how did a little girl from the Bronx become so literary-minded?"

"I was so scared during the first couple of years as Bettina that I took every course I could take, went to lectures, listened, and somewhere along the way, became a reader. It's changed my life. But enough of my finely tuned literary mind—God, I can't even say that without choking. What was your favorite book this week?"

"I'll cast my vote for Myla Goldberg's first novel, *Bee Season.* It's really something. A must. But that book by Anita Shreve, *The Last Time They Met,* is also a book you must read. Part of the novel takes place in Kenya, and you can smell it. It almost frightened me."

"Mr. Richardson, thanks for agreeing to see me."

"One can hardly resist the opportunity to see one's ex-wife's lover. And I understand congratulations are in order, that you and ... Bettina are expecting a child."

"You're extremely generous of spirit, Mr. Richardson."

"Call me Dilly, please ... John, if that's all right with you."

"Very much so."

"Besides, John, I know you did not steal Bettina from my ... arms, my bed, my life. I opened that window of opportunity for you, and you wisely climbed in and took your treasure."

"Life takes so many unexpected turns ... Dilly."

"Does it ever."

"I know I don't have to tell you what Bettina means to me. By shedding her old skin and becoming Mrs. Richardson and Bettina of Broadway, she allowed her extraordinary qualities to emerge. Enough of this, I'm speaking of her as one would describe a rare orchid. Bettina is a beautiful woman, richly deserving of a heroic man who can give her the kind of care and adoration she merits."

"That is, obviously, you, John, and all I can do is give my blessing to your union and try to profit from my own mistakes."

"No, Dilly, I'm afraid it isn't me."

Dilly was stunned and haltingly said, "You do not love her, as I am assuming she loves you?"

"Oh, I do indeed. But she's going to need a man who will be beside her for many years."

"I'm not totally following you, John."

"Four days ago, my doctor told me, as we would say in the theater, that I was going to have a short run ... maybe not even six months."

"Surely he said there's an 'X percent' chance of your beating whatever is attacking you?"

"I asked that very question, and he said no. My cancer is a very special one-of-a-kind that refuses to be cured. All he can do is delay it for a few months, so I have time to leave my life in order and give the people— correction, the person—I love a chance to get used to the idea."

"My God, John, we've only known one another for minutes, but this hurts. What can I do to help you?"

John walked to the window of Dilly's handsomely rich office, with gleaming antiques on the two solid walls, A couple of museum-quality impressionist paintings, four wing chairs around an antique cherry Queen Anne table, all harmonizing with a softly toned Isfahan carpet and a skyscape of towering glass and steel, backed by the Hudson River. He said nothing for what seemed like a very long time. He turned toward Dilly with an apologetic smile. "I can't keep this a secret from you-know-who. I sent Betts away to Acapulco this week with her great friend Lisa Gutwillig. But now comes the reality of the situation. Forgive me if I say something stupid now, Dilly. I'm hoping you'll help me figure out how to do what I have in mind."

"Mom, do you think we're out of our minds, agreeing to meet with Bettina's John Moran to discuss some private issue? I'm worried we're doing something that could hurt Bettina."

"I understand your qualms, Elizabeth. But all I can tell you is this Mr. Moran was almost eloquent in asking for this meeting. I can't even tell you precisely why I agreed to meet—and he wanted you to be here too—but some gut instinct told me to say yes. Dilly called and said to meet with him too."

"Somehow I feel it isn't going to be a happy and uplifting exchange."

"We don't know that. But if we can be of some help to Bettina, I know you would want to join me in doing whatever is required."

"Definitely, Mother. Bettina forced us to reinvent ourselves as a family, and we came out of it much better than we were before."

Edwina smiled and took her daughter's hand in her own, and they sat there quietly, until Edwina's houseman, Reginald, appeared to announce Mr. Moran's arrival.

Clothes may not make the man, but they certainly don't hurt. Edwina liked John Moran at face value. His expression was open, not guarded; his smile warm without merited intimacy; and the Savile Row tailoring accented gracefully his sturdy well-kept body. An hour went by in a matter of minutes, with John doing most of the talking. He tried to stay seated most of the time, now and then asking permission to move about the room while collecting his thoughts. Elizabeth thought to herself, *My God, what a strong man this is. A good person.*

"Now, let us recap all that you have shared with us, John, and I will call you John, and please call me Edwina. You are—forgive me—dying, and you have no doubts about the finality of the doctor's opinion."

"That is correct."

"And loving Bettina as you do, as we all do, you want our support of her, which goes without saying, but also to help her make a transition back into Dilly's life? And he knows how you feel about this?"

"Yes, Mrs. ... Edwina and Elizabeth. And I told him I wanted to meet with the two of you, and he agreed. In truth, had Bettina not become pregnant, I thought there was at least a fifty/fifty chance of her returning to Dilly, if not more. Not because I loved her less or he loved her more, but her loyalties to Dilly were still there. I knew that, accepted it, and thought only the consistency of my feelings for her might help her make the ultimate decision. But now, I know I'm not going to be here for Bettina and this child who will be born out of love. I felt completely inadequate explaining my perspective on this to Dilly and was hoping he wouldn't throw me out on my ear, but he too lived up to all the superb qualities of character that seem to be the gold standard of your family. I want to know that when I have passed this way but once, that our Bettina and that child will be loved and cherished."

"What did Dilly say, John, when you told him?"

"Elizabeth, your steel-edged aristocratic brother shed some tears and said, 'I would never stop loving Bettina, and if she can allow me to be her lover and father of her child, I would be forever grateful. Just tell me what I can do to make these coming months easier for the two of you.' So, Edwina, Elizabeth, Bettina's prince, as she once described Dilly, gave his loving approval. Will you both join the cast of this play within the play?"

"Hello, my darling. Do you like the new tan me?"

"You look like honey but sweeter. Hi, friend Lisa, how was Acapulco?"

"If I hadn't been stuck with this pregnant cow, I probably could have scored. I think those Latin men like fleshy women."

"She's been like this all week, John, just vulgar, slutty, and common, and I've loved every second of it."

"You two are perfect together. I promised your better half I would take you straight home, Lisa, and will assume that none of the men on this plane are expecting to accompany you."

"Naw, it'll be fun to go home and scare Fred."

Bettina was all smiles, loving her friend, thrilled to see her John, knowing their child was happy and healthy and growing day by day. She thought, *Life doesn't get any better. I'm so lucky.*

Orderly by nature, Bettina immediately emptied her luggage and starting sorting laundry and things for cleaning and storing some other items. She thought, *John is quieter than normal. But that's all right. We don't have to always be entertaining one another.*

"Bettina, darling, let's play a game."

"A what?"

"Well, it's kind of a game."

"All right, although so far I don't think I like the game."

"Okay, just hear me out. What if I left you? What would you do?"

"I knew I didn't like this game. You're not saying you're involved with someone else?"

"No, no, no, no, no. Just focus on what I'm saying. Suppose I was in a plane that was terrorized."

"This is a terrible game."

"We live in a terrible world, and I just want you to realize all the options in your life and the life of our child."

"I think I would die if something happened to you."

"No, that's not acceptable. You have a child to raise. And certainly, money isn't going to be a problem. After a time to mourn me, what would you do?"

"I can't. ... I can't answer questions like this. I am in love with you, John."

"What about Dilly?"

"What about Dilly?" She sat there, weeping. "Why are you saying all this?"

"Look at me, Bettina. You know I love you more than life, more than anything on or off this earth. But I'm not going to be here when our child is born."

"I ... I don't understand anything, John."

"Darling, a couple of weeks ago, I had a very bad headache."

"I remember."

"And I went to see Dr. Bearnot, who had a brain scan done."

"Oh God, John, don't tell me this."

"I'm going to die, Bettina, anywhere from two to six months."

"It can't be true. We're just beginning our life together. There are doctors around the world. We'll find the best."

"No, darling, it's the truth. I'm not going to make it. But I'll do everything I can to delay it, so you have time to prepare yourself."

"Prepare myself? John, you are my anchor, my knight in shining armor, the father of our child. Without you, I'm empty. I'm … I'm …" Bettina thought, *This isn't happening. It's just a bad dream. I'm not going to be cheated out of John's love.* She went on emptying her bag, putting jewelry where it belonged. She felt faint.

"Sit down here, darling, and look at me, and let me hold you." John gently put his arm around Bettina and led her to the sofa in their bedroom, and they sat down, sinking into the soft down, surrendering themselves to the softness, hoping it would shield them from the pain.

Bettina's voice was barely more than a whisper. "Doctors have been wrong many times before. We should have a second and a third opinion. You didn't go to Mayo Clinic, which you always said was the best."

"I'm sorry, darling, I did have two opinions here in New York, and Dr. Kurish sent all the scans to Mayo, which confirmed their diagnosis. All they can do is prolong my time on earth. Can miracles happen? Of course they can, but they said to not expect any miracle. It's written on the wall; my days are numbered. So … let's the two of us try to make the most of that time and make all the decisions that will make it easier for you and our love child."

"Mother, I don't know what to say. You met with John yourselves. You know what is happening. What happens next?"

"Oh, Dilly, my God. John Moran is very brave and certainly not selfish. There was no 'poor me, poor me.' We honestly believe that his sole concern is Bettina and the child."

"I totally agree, Mother."

"Can you honestly tell me how you feel about Bettina and their child?"

"I think so. I know there won't be another Bettina for me, and I certainly can love that child, and who knows? Maybe it would lead to our having another child—ours—in the coming years."

"The big question, Dilly, is how do you think Bettina feels about you?"

"Can I join in?"

"Sure, Sis."

"I think Bettina still loves you or feels very strongly about you, Dilly. Not sure I would after the way you dumped on her, but you were her Prince Charming. The hard part, as I see it now, is how to be there for Bettina without taking *anything* away from John's illness or her love for John. That may prove difficult at times, Dilly, but if you want to end up with Bettina back at your side, that will be an absolute necessity."

"That's very insightful, Elizabeth, and I quite agree with you".

"Thanks, Mom. Dilly?"

"I hear you. I'm going to be walking a thin line."

"If you'll let us, we'll help you keep your balance."

"Thanks, Sis, I love you and Mom for your caring and good advice."

CHAPTER *58*

Until Someone You Love Goes through Cancer Treatment, You Can't Conceive the Indignities, the Pain, the Hope or Lack Thereof

Bettina insisted on accompanying John for the initial treatments until he forced her to not come. He said it made him nervous. And in truth, it did. He didn't want her to see him failing. The very best oncologists in Manhattan were treating John, courtesy of Dilly, who insisted when he began his treatments to use all the facilities that were available to the Richardson family. John mentioned Dilly's generosity to Bettina, who was surprised. Dilly hadn't mentioned anything to her that he was helping.

"What a treat to have a family lunch." Bettina smiled lovingly at Edwina, Elizabeth, and Dilly.

"John gave his blessing on having you join us, knowing that today was going to be one of those long treatment days. How is your dear John doing, Bettina?"

"Oh, Mom, it's all so painful. John pretends—and he is pretending—that it's all fine, but it's not. He's losing weight and is furious because he has so little energy. He's busy writing something, but I'm not sure what."

"Betts, we know you're doing everything possible to help John. But today, we want you to eat a solid meal."

"Liz, you can see I'm becoming pear-shaped or maybe avocado-shaped."

"And it's very becoming, Bettina."

"Thanks, Dilly. You know, I've never been to the Four Seasons. It's so beautiful. I love those chains instead of drapery fabric."

"Besides beautiful, Betts, the food is knockout."

"You look so wonderful, Bettina. You must be enjoying a healthy pregnancy."

"I am, Dilly, and Dr. Moore is just terrific. And I've made a new friend there, Andrea Mitchell. She's terrific."

"I know her, Betts."

"You do, Liz?"

"Yes, they have three or four children, and her husband, Arthur, is a peach."

"Oh, I know Arthur Mitchell too, Bettina. He's with GE Capital. If it's the same Arthur Mitchell, he's a fine human being and a brilliant businessman. Good people to know, Bettina."

"Thank you, Dilly, I feel so fortunate to have the friends I have. God knows Lisa Gutwillig is pluperfect."

The flawless waiter brought one exquisite dish after another, the bone marrow soup being especially remarkable. Bettina felt loved and protected and realized that the family considered her as one of them. How could she be so lucky?

Dilly fought to keep his comments neutral, the look in his eyes saying nothing about how he felt.

Besides the necessity of the cancer treatments, John was ever mindful of the boring monotony of being prodded and poked, of lying still while vile liquids poisoned his body. He tried to maintain an objective view of the proceedings but found himself dreading each subsequent action. He knew the conclusion was carved in stone; he was going to die. But if this bought him enough time to leave Bettina on more level ground, he would do it.

"This coming Wednesday marks my thirtieth day of treatment, and to celebrate my anniversary, the medicos have given me a week off. And I have a plan for the week."

Bettina, who inwardly was desperate, facing the loss of her child's father and someone who had cushioned her life with love, was outwardly trying to be warm and gentle with John, but she was frightened. "Good, darling, a week of no treatments sounds wonderful. We'll do whatever you want to do."

"Great, pack. We're leaving Thursday evening for a week in my ancestral country."

"Ireland? We're going to Ireland. But can you … I mean, do you have the energy to travel."

"Absolutely, so let's go."

Dilly was keeping his distance, afraid of crowding Bettina, and proving himself to be a generous and giving human, helping John with moral support and enlisting special cancer specialists.

"Dilly, you've been that proverbial pillar of strength during all this mess. I want you to know how much I appreciate it. And by the way, I have next week off from treatments, so Betts and I are going to Ireland. How about coming to dinner Tuesday night? I know it will feel strange, coming as a guest to your own apartment, but I want Bettina to understand how important you are to me and to remember how important you were to her."

"Well, all right, John. I think I can handle it."

"Terrific, Dilly. God, I never realized how manipulative I can be. We'll see you Tuesday, around seven o'clock? Don't be shocked at my appearance. I'm becoming a shadow of my former self."

Dilly hung up, thinking, *You're a brave man, John Moran. I wonder if I could tough it out as well.*

"Bettina, dear Bettina, I don't know whether you'd ever want to see me again, but I've wanted so much to speak to you."

"Oh, Madame, how wonderful to hear your voice."

"Dear Bettina, I'm not Madame. I'm only Ruby Schmidt-Feller."

"To me, you will always be Madame. And I know you weren't behind those hideous people. My, how gullible, how stupid I was. I realize now, looking back, that when you sent me a note one day, you were trying to warn me, but I was blinded by my own efforts to be something I wasn't."

"But from everything I understand, Bettina, you are indeed that wonderful, loving, giving human being. I've followed all your accomplishments with much pride. Would it be too much to ask if I could visit you someday? I would like so much for you to meet my Gila—I mean, Marianne. It was seeing you that made me focus on the child I thought was lost forever, and somehow I believe that my thinking of her helped her find me."

"Nothing would please me more, Madame. I'm going away this coming Thursday but will be gone only a week and will call you when I return. What is your telephone number?"

"You've invited Dilly to dinner? I'm speechless."

"I didn't think you'd mind, darling. And Dilly has been wonderful from the beginning of this new passage in my life. He's brought more big-time medical minds to give me their pieces of mind than I could have ever attracted. I feel very important at that hospital, and I'm sure it's because Dilly has said, 'Fix him!' Or something like that. Come on, give me smile and a smooch, and tell me I'm right for feeling grateful."

"You're a perfect idiot, but you're my perfect idiot, and of course you're right. I know Dilly has been quietly helping, and I too am grateful. Lessee now, what to serve for dinner ..."

"Choose something he likes. You know I prefer things administered intravenously."

"Ho-ho-ho, so very amusing."

"If I'm that funny, laugh a little."

Bettina kissed and hugged John and went to the kitchen to discuss a menu with the cook. She was still stunned that John had invited Dilly. But she assumed everything would be all right. *Dilly certainly knows what's going on, and, well, why worry about something out of your control?*

Dilly thought he had never seen Bettina so beautiful. Now, obviously pregnant, she seemed to glow from within. Despite the concern in her eyes when she looked oh-so-adoringly at her husband, the young self-created girl he had married had come into her own as a woman of substance and valor, with an elegance that seemed to be from the manor born. He also realized, to his chagrin, what a superb man John Moran was. Perhaps he was dying, but he managed to be a warm and welcoming host, and Dilly found himself admiring John's intellect, never having focused on that part of the man before. The dinner, the conversation, the relationship of the four of them couldn't have been better. Bettina had wisely, Dilly thought, invited his—and her—sister, Elizabeth, whose open affection for Bettina, John, and her brother was soothing and satisfying.

CHAPTER *59*

John Had Booked a Morning Flight on Aer Lingus, from JFK International to Shannon, Ireland

As they flew over the craggy west coast of Ireland, with the unending patchwork of fields, Bettina was struck by the powerful and enchanting spectrum of greens. *It's true*, she thought. *It's magical-looking. There's a leprechaun hiding behind every rock.* John had rented a comfortable sedan, and they drove through twisting and curling country highways to a lovely small inn, facing the Lakes of Killarney. Bettina was entranced by the beauty. Exhausted from the flight, they had a light supper and retired to their room, reading their books of the moment. John's choice: *The Cabinet of Curiosities* by Preston & Child, a fascinating and historically based thriller set in New York City. Bettina was reading *Never Change* by Elizabeth Berg. The story was a little too close to home, about a woman caring for a man she loved, a man dying of cancer. But somehow it was helping Bettina.

Ireland proved itself to be a land of small and simple pleasures. None of the exotic dazzle of the world's capitals, this was a country of bucolic splendor, and Bettina was charmed by John's delight in the minutiae of his ancestral home. He was not—fortunately, she thought—an Irishman "back on the ole sod." He was a handsome, albeit a bit wan, Yank, visiting Ireland.

A day of driving, along with a fine lunch in a roadside restaurant, brought them to Kanturk in County Cork, the town of his ancestors. Bettina was thrilled as they drove through the village at five in the evening, and the cows were coming home, being herded down the main street of the village. A short trip to the outskirts brought them to their destination, a beautiful Irish manor house set on three hundred acres, with stables, a quiet river alongside, and a huge, endless front lawn, broken only by a tennis net strung over one patch of grass.

Assolas was the name of the house. And from the moment the smiling innkeeper with the lilting brogue opened the door, Bettina felt totally at home and at peace. There was a friendly scent of a peat fire and somewhere an unrecognizable aroma, which turned out to be fresh loaves of Irish soda bread. The Bourke family owned and operated this eight-bedroom home. Eleanor Bourke, wife of Hugh and mother of four, immediately bonded with Bettina, and John became as one with Hugh and found himself living in and managing the home, at least mentally.

From lawn tennis at ten at night, with no outside lights, to lazy strolls across country paths, every day was devoid of tension. The problems of the world were somewhere on another planet.

"Where are you going, my love?"

"I'm just after going to the village with Eleanor."

"You're *just after* going to the village? Suddenly, my wife is Irish?"

"Well, darling, when in Rome, you know. And you know I love being here, John. The Bourkes are so very dear. And I love their kids. They've done a sensational parenting job. Hope we … I … **we** … can be as successful."

"There's no doubt that you will be a fabulous parent. No doubt."

Eleanor navigated the curling country roads expertly, stopped now and then by a donkey-drawn milk cart, but unlike a statesider, never impatient. She was a gentle woman, nearly six feet tall, with a narrow smiling face framed in soft red hair. She ran her ancient home with a velvet touch, somehow always in touch with her four children and, from Bettina's standpoint, seeming to defer to her dear but not terribly effective husband. Bettina thought, *I could learn a lot from this woman.*

"Bettina, my mother, who is considerably more au courant than myself, tells me you were a famous Broadway star. You must find Kanturk a wee bit sleepy, and one wouldn't be blaming you for it."

"Oh, friend Eleanor, Broadway is a million miles away from here. Right this minute, the gentleness of Kanturk is precisely what the doctor ordered." And without warning, Bettina started to cry.

"Mother of God, Bettina, what is it?"

"Eleanor, my darling John, whose ancestors hailed from this region, is dying of cancer. The doctors say there's no chance he'll pull through. So, every day, I try to say, '*Good* God, another day,' but I know it's one less day I'll spend with John Moran."

Eleanor's eyes brimmed with tears. "I'm so sorry, Bettina. What can I do to help?"

Bettina smiled warmly at her new friend. "Your welcome, your affection is everything we could possibly ask for."

"Bettina, I'm certainly not going to dwell on John's future because it's out of our hands. But I do want you to know that our door is always open for you and your baby. Someday, come back to us. I feel a strong attachment to you and want to know your baby—and John's baby."

"It's a deal, Eleanor. Thank you very much. Now, let's think of happier things. Like what can we have for dinner. I have a hungry person growing inside of me, and I want him or her to be very healthy."

The flight home was smooth enough, and Aer Lingus first-class service was very first class. "And what did you think of my homeland, love? Too many leprechauns, too little pizzazz?"

"I loved Ireland, John, and especially Eleanor Bourke and everything she represents. I loved seeing your face light up, especially that day when you met your distant cousins. They were so cute, trying to determine how real you were."

"And whether I'd leave them some money."

"You did leave them some money. I saw you do it, and I'm glad."

"It took some doing. I gave them twenty thousand dollars in traveler's checks, having identified some of their financial problems. They told me it might be a while before they could get started paying me back. And I told them that it was good for me to share with my ancestors and that no payment was expected. It did leave them speechless. But thank you for coming with me, love. And now the piper must be paid, whatever the hell that means. It's time to return to Dr. Death."

"Don't say that, darling, please."

"I apologize. Time to go back to daily cocktails. Wish they'd make them taste like a negroni. Hey, I'll tolerate anything that gives me more time with you."

"And maybe this new series of treatments will help you turn the corner and start getting well. Let's think in terms of getting well."

"Absolutely, darling." Although he knew it was futile. *How long do I have? Months? Probably not; probably just weeks. I've got to get Dilly back in Bettina's life.*

Bettina felt she was living two simultaneous lives. Every moment of every day she was the wife of John Moran, hoping that this week's treatment would help him turn the corner; at the same time, not really believing it and berating herself for the negative feelings. And then she was Bettina, the mother-to-be, full of another life and planning the brightest future imaginable for her yet-to-be-realized child. *You've come a long way, Bethel,* she reminded herself one day, knowing that Bethel was no longer part of her fiber. She had indeed become Bettina Richardson Moran, and as such was envied, protected, and admired from all corners.

Dilly was trying to reinvent himself, at once striving to keep John Moran alive, because he knew that would make Bettina happiest, and at the same time wondering if Bettina would take him back once John had gone to his glory, an unavoidable conclusion, according to all the medical reports.

John, besides dying a little every day and trying to not burden Bettina and the baby with his pain, was trying to reinforce the positives in the memory of Dilly, knowing that Dilly would and could take his place, thereby ensuring Bettina a sheltered and loving environment.

"Oh, Bettina, my dear, this is my daughter, Gila, or Marianne, as she is now called. Thanks to you, we were reunited. Marianne, this is the beautiful Bettina."

"Madame, and you are Madame to me, you are too sweet. Marianne, I'm delighted to meet you. Your darling mother gave me a sense of being societally conscious, even if we were both being manhandled by those dreadful people. But your mother was wonderful and tried to protect me."

"Mom has told me so much about you, and even if the circumstances were a bit convoluted, I'm so very grateful because it brought back my mother to me and has made my life so much more complete."

After they left, Bettina sat quietly, glowing with the joy of seeing mother and daughter back together, and then, feeling strong family ties, picked up the phone to call her sister and turned it into a conference call with their mother. The three of them laughed and chatted about nothing special but knew the specialness was knowing and loving one another. *Life is good*, Bettina thought. *Now if only God would protect my darling John.*

CHAPTER **60**

"All Right, John, What Do You Want to Know?"

" I would like to know the truth, oh master of my destiny. I've come to think of all you white coats as vultures in drag waiting 'til I'm just an appetizer."

"Thank you for that warm and appealing imagery. Vultures, my, my. As doctors, we're accustomed to being called heartless money-grabbers, sawbones, and other charming labels, but vulture is new."

"Yeah, yeah, just tell me what my veins look like these days—polluted rivers full of industrial sludge? And my once-boyish head of hair? Does that stay gone forever, or do I even live long enough for it to come back? Is my cancer like one of those horrible wildfires out in California? It simmers down and is contained for a while, and then a high wind picks it up and dumps it in new neighborhoods. Is that me? Come on, don't pull your punches. I need to know when this castle that was my body is going to be consumed. What are your stethoscopes saying to you?"

"We're saying you have a lot of questions, and we don't have a lot of black-and-white answers. It's sometimes harder to deal with people of your social and intellectual level because you've already answered many of your own questions. You just know too much."

"Hey, I can revert to another class if it makes you happy. I tried middle class for a long time; some of it was very amusing."

"Very funny, Mr. Moran. Okay, truth you want; truth you're going to get."

"All right, Lisa, here comes your dummy friend with an impossible hypothesis. Don't laugh too hard."

"Why do I think this is not going to be even minimally funny? Go on; lay it on me."

"It's hard to start because this is a new thought that's nagging at me, and I have no right to think it, but somehow it keeps coming back and interrupting my dreams."

"You're killing me, Betts. And it better not be one of those stupid meaningless dreams I had; you know, like doing it with the concierge in the hotel in Mexico. It felt so good in my dream I felt guilty when I woke up. But Fred is safe; I won't go back to Mexico without him at my side."

"You had a sex dream about the concierge? You unmitigated slut!"

"Only a dream slut. And you and your hypothesis?"

"Okay, hear me out. I have this funny feeling that my darling John is actively trying to get Dilly back in my life, and I mean in my life, not just as a friend."

"My God, for real? How do you know?"

"It's all stupid, or maybe it isn't. John just makes every effort to have Dilly at the house for dinner, or he mentions what Dilly has done and how great Dilly is, and ... and ... and ... and I can't disagree, but there's something about it that seems a wee bit forced to me."

"Forgetting the forced part, Betts, how do you feel about having Dilly as a presence?"

"God, Lisa, I don't know. Yes, I loved Dilly, but he was yesterday, and now my life and my baby are John. And I know John is dying. I accept it privately. I just haven't been able to tell him I know and whether it's okay or not. It's okay; I can deal with it."

"Christ, you're even stronger than I thought you were. But it is an interesting premise. And John is, from my viewpoint, such a generous human being it could be for real. If he feels he is dying and thinks he can protect you and the baby by having Dilly step into his role, I ... wow, I don't know what to say. How do you feel when you see Dilly?"

"Oh, he's just sweet Dilly."

"I mean, you've forgiven him for being an asshole?"

"Lisa, give the man a break."

"Maybe I will in the future, but he's still kind of on my S-list. But now you make me wonder how Dilly feels about all this or wonder if he has any idea of what's going on."

"That's a tough one. I've caught Dilly looking at me with such tenderness, but then maybe it's sympathetic in nature."

"I dunno, Betts. Once he realized what an immense jerk he had been, he wanted you back, big time. And yes, I know he's been very helpful with John's illness. Something inside of me tells me you may be right. *Now* what?"

"Mother, this may be a strange conversation, but I have decided to bring you into the loop because I value your analysis and advice."

"My goodness, Dillwor—Dilly, I'm quite stunned. I've always been gratified that you've tolerated my well-meaning probes into your personal life all these years, but I never kidded myself that I might be one of your chosen advisers."

"Maybe I'm finally wising up, Mom, seeing you as the wise—"

"Don't you dare say wise *old* anything."

"Wouldn't dream of it, darling. I just know that all we've been through in recent times—your support of Bettina and vice versa—has opened my eyes to what a great dame you are."

"I like that *great dame* stuff. Now, come on; lay it on me."

"Lay it on you? Mother! You're becoming really—"

"Yes, I know. I won't say common, just allowing myself to be a wee bit more contemporary, in touch with the language and all that good stuff."

Dilly smiled at his mother and walked around her, eyeing her with a suspicious smile. "Is it really you, Mother, or aha! Admit it; you're a phony dressed as my imperial mother."

"Knock it off, kid. Come talk to your mommy."

They laughed and locked arms and sat down on the satin-upholstered overstuffed sofa. "Okay, Maw."

"Let's not get too colloquial, shall we?"

"Agreed, Mother dear. Okay, here's the story. John Moran, whom I have come to appreciate and admire, wants me to be there for Bettina when he … dies … and he is dying. And he wants Bettina to eventually fall back into my arms as my wife. It is a generous turn of events, but … well, I'm not sure who I am today or tomorrow. Thought you might shed some light on the shadows in my head."

"Whew, tell me this is the hard question, not the easy one."

"Oh, the hard question for sure."

Bettina studied her son, realizing that with maturity he was even more handsome and every inch an aristocrat. "Obviously, this does not come as new news to me. I liked John Moran when I met him, and he made it very clear the reuniting of you and Bettina was part of his overall plan. He's very courageous. However, there are two huge considerations here, in no particular order. One: how do you feel, if given the opportunity, about becoming Bettina's husband, and father of Bettina and John's child? And two: how does Bettina feel about once more becoming a Richardson?"

Dilly stared ahead where a treasured Matisse hung on the wall. He said nothing. Two minutes, maybe three; the silence was, Edwina realized, deafening.

"I can't answer the second question, Mother. But I believe I can honestly tell you that I would welcome having Bettina back at my side, as my wife and lover and confidant. And that child would be raised as my own, and perhaps we'll be blessed—isn't that the word everyone uses?—with our own child or children. And how do you feel about how I feel?"

"What was Rhett's line to Scarlett? 'Frankly, my dear, I don't give a damn.' All that matters to me is what you want and that you don't get hurt wanting it. Of course I'm lying. I do give a damn, but you know I am predisposed toward Bettina. She's done more for this family than any ten psychiatrists. I think the bigger question is, how does she feel? Obviously, loving John means she will have to mourn his passing. And you'll have to give her plenty of space to do that. Then, and only then, when she can put aside the veil of sadness and loneliness—and believe me, I wore it when your darling father left me; pardon me, left us—can she consider the other options in her life. You're a beautiful option for her and one I believe she knows she can trust."

"Even though I threw her love aside?"

"Phooey, that's all old news. I'm sure she feels all the goodness and protection of you during these hard days. It's not going to be easy, Dillworth, and you're going to have to be more patient that you might ever imagine."

"We always knew, as did you, John, that your condition wasn't fixable. In truth, your willingness to cooperate, your desire to have more time with your lovely wife has kept you as a billable patient longer than we might have imagined."

"I'm glad you left the billable part in that comment. Almost makes you sound human. Just kidding, Bobby; don't give me that look. I know you all have done marvels with this disposable body. But even though I'm not sitting here in abject pain, the party is ending, is it not? Closing night has been posted, as we would say. Only X performances left."

"Something like that, John. But even at this point, I can't say go home and kiss your ass goodbye; you're heaven-bound this Wednesday. The human spirit and the need to relate to someone else are very powerful forces. You could hang on for—I don't know—even weeks, a month or more."

"I know I can't ask what I want to ask. But when the lights are really going out in this theater formerly known as my body, I know you can't just turn off the master switch, but can you try to put me in a condition where Bettina doesn't have to deal with me in pain and wasting away? I don't want her to remember me that way."

"I understand, John, and we'll do what we can. You're a brave man. A very nice man. We've come to love you in spite of your repeated slurs on our professional vows."

"If I wasn't afraid you'd like it too much, I'd kiss you."

Dr. Robert Cohen, a man of innate dignity, leaned forward and hugged John and kissed him on the forehead. He whispered to the grinning John Moran, "Don't tell my secretary about us."

"Dilly, it's Bettina."

"I'd know your voice anywhere. What can I do for you, Betts?"

"I need your advice, Dilly. May I come to your office? I'd suggest lunch, but you're too busy, and I'm honestly not in much of a mood to go out."

"Absolutely. If it's an emergency, I'll get rid of someone from today's list."

"No, no, no, there's no emergency. What is convenient for you, Dilly?"

"How's eleven tomorrow morning?"

"Perfect; I'll be there. Thank you, Dilly."

At the end of the day, Dilly barely remembered the business crises and opportunities of the day, so strongly was he focused on tomorrow's meeting with Bettina. He admonished himself to not build up his hopes too high—to not play all his emotional cards during the meeting. But she had called and needed him. Just thinking about it gave him a rush. He could feel himself blushing.

"Bettina, there are things about me I've never shared with anyone."

"And you're going to share them with me? Are you sure that's wise or necessary … Mom?" Bettina grinned fondly at her mother-in-law, still not quite believing that Edwina Richardson accepted her as a friend and equal. More than any hurdle she had faced as Bettina, Edwina had been the highest and hardest.

"God knows I don't want to diminish my all-powerful image in your eyes, but … I don't know … I guess I want you to know the real me."

"Oh, you're going to tell me your real name is Harriet Slotsky, and you're from Queens? Of course, if you are truly Harriet, I would and could understand perfectly, being the former Bethel Sokoloff from the Bronx."

"To tell the truth, my darling Bettina, I don't think there was anything wrong with Bethel Sokoloff. I think that Bettina was there all along, just waiting for the right door to open. By the way, I realize I never told you about my undercover work and how I came to know your real father." Bettina was amazed and enthralled that Edwina would tell her the story of her going to meet her father and discovering who Bettina had been. "I liked your father. There was a simple honesty about him. I'm sorry he passed away. I would have liked to know him better."

"It's an interesting thought. Obviously, I was dishonest with my parents, never telling them who I was or had become, and I feared Dilly's reaction to meeting the in-laws. Even now, thinking about it makes me uneasy. As it now stands, Mom is happier than she's been in years, and even my sister and I get along, and today I'll tell you about my sister, the divorced wife of the rabbi."

"Fine, but first I want to introduce Evelyn Langford."

"I've never heard the name. Who is she?" Bettina was practically giggling like a schoolgirl, sitting there in 21 Club, holding Edwina's hand, both warming each other with heartfelt smiles.

"You're looking at her."

"Evelyn Langford?"

"My parents named me Evelyn, and I legally changed it at age twenty-three to Edwina. And although my parents were hardly poor, they weren't the classiest act on the block. Both were self-centered social climbers. I, on the other hand, was a flawless human being—" She started coughing. "I can't even say that kiddingly without choking." A sip of water calmed the cough. "I had decided my parents were something to be tolerated, not celebrated, and I concentrated on building a formidable mind and a healthy, trim body. I had inherited—I can admit it now—a need to be in a higher social stratum."

"I've never heard how you met the darling Rolly. I always assumed you were just both from the correct side of the tracks and met through your families."

"No, no, no. I joined a Young Republicans group and aligned myself with a couple of worthwhile causes, such as Save the New York Library, and worked for autistic children. Through one of those groups—I think the Republicans—someone invited me to a cocktail party, where I met Roland. You talk about playing a role, Bettina love. Hah, I was auditioning for the Academy Award. I wanted to be beautiful, intriguing but not too sexual, brilliant and incisive, and the girl you wanted to take home to meet Mom. Roland was on the rebound from a proper young woman of blue blood lineage, and he found me interesting and appealingly not so perfect. At any rate, one thing led to another, and after a decent engagement period,

I became Mrs. Roland Richardson, or Edwina the Great, a title I didn't bandy about."

"To me, you were born Edwina Richardson. You scared the holy hell out of me."

"That was the idea. How dare anyone else have the nerve to play the same role I played—and win my darling Dillworth. And I can tell you now, it was the luckiest thing that ever happened to Dillworth ... and to us. I was a lucky girl, Bettina, and because I had empowered myself to be Edwina, the titanium ice queen, I could have lost Roland along the way. But you helped me—us—to regain our footing, and for that and many other gifts, I'll always treasure you."

"No, I'm the luckiest girl in the world because I have you."

"And now what's next, darling? I know you are losing your wonderful husband. What can I do to help you through this period?"

"I'm just now accepting the fact that John is dying, and I'm trying to be as gentle and loving and supportive as humanly possible, right to the very end. But I'm also going to see Dilly tomorrow, to ask his advice about what to do, if ... God, Edwina, I can't even say it. I'm acknowledging that it's happening. I know John isn't going to recover. But I guess until the moment comes, one doesn't accept the reality of it, does one?"

"No, you don't. But I'm here, Bettina. Not just as Edwina but as your other mother and certainly as your friend."

"So Betts, this is the Jack Thomas I told you about. Isn't he cute? So goyim—look at that nose—and absolutely loaded with money."

"Bettina, I'm delighted to meet you. Will you tell your wretched sister to stop introducing me as the rich, cute goyim with the small nose? I adore Michelle—"

"Call me by your nickname for me!"

"I adore Mike. She's a hurricane of fresh air in my studied, predictable life, and I love her dearly."

Bettina was laughing so hard she could barely choke out the words. "Oh, thank you for making me laugh." She embraced them both. "I'm so happy to meet you, Jack, and Michelle, uh, Mike has been singing your praises for days."

"And I'm happy to meet you, Bettina. I saw you onstage and know what you're going through right now. If there's anything I can do to help, you have but to ask."

"That's great, Jack. It's wonderful to feel the support of another member of the family, and I understand that's in the plans."

"Absolutely. I told him, no wedding ring, no more nookie. Why buy the milk when you can get the cow for free? Or did I get that wrong?"

"Bettina, does she ever calm down, or should I just get some strong tranquilizers?"

"You're just hearing a well-known song . . . 'A Sokoloff in Love.' Besides, once we hook 'em, we get very tranquil."

"Betts, geez, hook 'em? He doesn't know I hooked him. He thinks it's all his idea."

"Actually, it was my idea, Bettina. She had decided that marriage was for rabbis and their rich parishioners, and I had to really work to convince her."

"Will you be my matron of honor, Betts?"

"If we can get Omar the Tent Maker to make something big enough in champagne lace to cover this humongous belly. You both make me so happy."

That evening, after John had his medications, they were served a light dinner of fresh wild salmon, grilled with a little garlic and olive oil, and a tomato and cucumber salad. "Betts, I know these are things you don't want to talk about, but we have to be realistic. Tomorrow I'd like you to sit down with me and Harry Clark, who is my attorney and executor of my will, and discuss some of my own investments, which are sizeable."

"Darling, since neither one of us married for money, wouldn't it be simpler if all members of your family were left everything. All I need is you, and I have the beautiful pieces of jewelry you gave me. And I need all the photos of your life to share with our child."

"That's all well and good, but no; no one in my family deserves anything. As a courtesy, I'll leave some money in trust for all the nieces and nephews, but I want you to have everything else. Much to my surprise, my estate is worth around nine and a half million."

"Good Lord. You've been holding out on me, Moran. I could have bought—oh, I don't know what, since I have everything in the world. I'll do whatever you say. But are you saying this because you've given up all the medical treatments?"

"Wrong! I'm still doing everything and anything just to stick around so I can tell everyone, 'See that beautiful blonde chick with the kid in the oven? She's mine.'"

"Yes, she is, John—yours."

After John became too weary and went to bed, Bettina sat quietly in the den and, without warning, saw a replay of her life. Bethel, with that nose, with a self-pitying peer group; all with parents beaten down by the daily necessity of earning a living. Bethel, just skimming through school, never stimulated enough to care. Bethel, with the never-fashionable wardrobe, always carefully mended by Daddy, the tailor. And there was Sam, her beautiful brother who was going to do great things until the neighborhood took him down, turned him into a punk, and killed him. And Michelle, now Mike, who really scored with the guys.

And who was Bethel's first? *Oh, Stevie Gelman. Not a bad kid, just empty like the rest of us. Thank God, he didn't get me pregnant. I remember it hurt; it wasn't fun. I never really liked doing "it."* But surely someone must have mattered; someone gave me something to chew on besides our daily bread. *Oh, I had forgotten Jane Prettyman.* What a teacher. She taught biology. She faced the untidy gray and blank group with a caring smile. Yes, Jane Prettyman was maybe the first person to give her an inkling of who she might become. *When I was having trouble getting through her course, she kept me after school and taught me how to study, to write things down, to make verbal associations so I could remember things. And then we would have a chat about life and stuff, and she'd ask me how I felt about something and then make me defend my own statement. I wasn't just dumb little Bethel Sokoloff. I was a future member of some kind of society. There had to have been others who didn't summarily dismiss me, but it's Jane Prettyman I remember most of all.* But that was all back in the Bethel era. None of that happened to Bettina Richardson. What was the ad campaign? You've come a long way, baby.

"I'm glad to see you, Bettina. It's been a long time since you visited the office."

"In the beginning, I never came because I felt your business associates would see right through me. And then life got so busy with the stage play and my stupid personal drama. I didn't have time to come and sit watch you move the world."

"Moving the world isn't terribly important when you're not moving it for someone." He almost regretted the words with their hidden emotion but was relieved to see Bettina wasn't reacting. She had some other agenda today.

"Dilly, I know John is dying, and"—she lowered her head as tears filled her eyes—"and when it happens, I don't know what to do with funeral arrangements, and all that stuff. I'm sure as Bettina Richardson I could figure it out, but this is going to be John dying, and I don't think I'm going to be able to call the right shots."

"You don't have to, Betts. I'll be there. As unpleasant as it is to think about it, unless John has made some specific requests in his will, there will be some decisions to make. To tell the truth, the John I have come to know and admire doesn't leave loose ends. Speak to, um, Harry, his attorney, or better yet, I will speak with Harry so you don't have to do that."

"Thank you, Dilly. I suddenly thought, I can't do this. On a much happier note, I had the most loving luncheon and heart-to-heart with your glorious mother. We are all so fortunate to have her in our lives. My only sadness when I'm with her is missing your dad."

"I quite agree. I conjure up Dad now and then to chat about the meaningful issues in my life, and his advice is always good."

"And loving." Bettina smiled and stood up as gracefully as a woman nearly eight months pregnant could stand. "Thank you again, Dilly." And she leaned forward for a cheek-to-cheek hug.

"Mrs. Moran ...Bettina ... it's Dr. Cohen."

"Oh, God, it's John, isn't it?"

"Yes, Bettina. During this morning's treatment, John had a heart seizure. He is still alive, but his condition, well, you know what his condition is. We have him in intensive care and thought it would be good for you to come to see him. And I suggest you bring a family member with you."

"Thank you, Doctor. I'll be there as soon as possible."

Bettina sat there weeping, trying to accept the reality of what she already knew. John was dying. After a minute or two, she thought, *Who do I need to be with me?* And picked up the phone and dialed. "Hello, Edwina."

"Hello, darling. What's wrong? I hear pain in your voice."

"I need a close friend and a mother to come with me to the hospital to say goodbye to John. Will you meet me at the intensive care unit on the eighth floor? I'm going to leave here in five minutes."

"I will be there, darling. In fact, let me come over with the car and driver, and we'll go together. I can be there in ten to fifteen minutes."

"I'll be downstairs waiting. Thank you." And Bettina wept.

Even though she was prepared, in that she knew John was dying, the actuality of it was beyond comprehension. Dr. Cohen gently explained that there was a point in the final days of any illness when the various pumps and generators and valves that maintained the patient weren't enough. "We are transfusing your husband, and it's conceivable that he will come to for a brief time. I know it's difficult, but you could sit by his bedside for a while."

It was hard, but two hours later, Bettina and Edwina were rewarded. John's eyes fluttered, and he focused on Bettina and smiled. He whispered, "Hi, love. You shouldn't be here. You should be at home, resting. Oh, and hi, Edwina. You brought our favorite mother-in-law. I'm glad."

"Hello, darling." Bettina leaned down to softly kiss John. "You Broadway babies are all so dramatic."

"Yeah, life is just one curtain call after another. Listen to me, Betts. I know I can't talk long. I didn't believe I could be as happy as you've made me. And now I want you and our baby to go on being happy and loved and know how much you did for me."

"Oh, John, look what you did for me."

"Yeah, knocked you up. Gosh, I want to see that baby."

"You will, darling; oh God, you will." Bettina was weeping openly, trying to keep a smile.

"Do me a favor, Betts . . ."

"Anything, darling."

"Give Dilly a chance. He still loves you very much. Edwina knows that too, right?"

"Yes, dear John, I do know how Dilly feels. We'll have to give them time. Bettina must make the right decision for her life and your child. I love you too, John, and will say au revoir and leave you and Bettina alone." Edwina kissed her fingertips and tenderly touched John's forehead. She left the room.

"She is one great broad. Am happy she's in your corner, Betts. Ohhh . . ."

"Doctor, please help."

The doctor gave John an injection. "This should help, John. Stay with us."

"Mmmm, thanks, Doc. Good, glad I won't be around to become a drug addict. Betts, before I met you, even though you thought I was just a happy-go-lucky man around town, I had decided to pull the plug on myself. I mean, who gives a shit about success if there's no one to share it with? Who cares about rich apartments without someone to share the riches and have fun redecorating it. I cared about nothing and no one. And you made me whole. And now I'm leaving, maybe for a better place; let's not worry about it. Just make your life and our child's life happy and full of love and promise. I love you, Bettin . . ."

"John, oh God. John, it will be so hard without your love." In the background, the machines drew a flatline, and a flat sound, and John was gone. Bettina Richardson Moran had too much inner fiber to physically fall apart. "Goodbye, darling. Come see our baby." She walked carefully out of the room into the arms of Edwina. The two of them, erect, dignified, tears falling freely, walked slowly toward the exit.

CHAPTER 61

Baby Time: It Overshadows Everything and Anything Else

"What do you mean am I going to the hospital with you when you're in labor? I'll be there so you can yell at me and call me all kinds of names."

"Lisa, I could never call you names!"

"Hah! You never had a baby. I remember threatening Fred that he would never get me in his bed again. Nothing like passing a watermelon through your crotch."

"Lisa! Are you just trying to scare me?"

"Didn't I turn around and do it a second time? Hey, it smarts a bit, sometimes a lot, but it's the fastest forgotten pain in the entire world. Would there be so much overcrowding on the planet if it wasn't tolerable? Trust me, Betts, it's going to be fine. Dr. Moore said your baby is primo healthy; that's all that matters. Look, my loving best friend, I know it's tough. It's just been one month since John headed for his big stage in the sky, and you're doing terrifically. And this baby is going to be all the best medicine in the world."

"Funny; I don't feel terrific. I find myself crying because one of John's favorite anchormen is on TV. I cry at any music we shared. It's only the baby that keeps me going. Damn it, John. Why did you have to leave us? I know

I'm being stupid, Lisa. No one can have it all forever. And God knows I've had enough good in my life, no complaints, but oh I miss John. I'm sorry; forgive me."

"Forgive you for what? For having a heart? For loving someone more than life itself? I know, baby. I see all your pain, and you need to feel it, and you need to mourn. But at the same time, you're going to need to celebrate a birth of an extremely important and meaningful man in your life. Meanwhile, she said, adeptly changing the subject, how's Dilly doing?"

"He's, um, keeping his distance but calling me every couple of days. Since we know it's a boy child, he and his sister, Elizabeth, have sent over a complete wardrobe, which I'm sure cost enough to support a small country. But they're being very sweet. But to answer your unasked question, it's way, way too early to worry about Dilly's influence in my life. I'm glad he's there and know I can lean on him. But I think I have to learn to be the Widow Moran and take charge of myself."

"No one can manage you better than you, Betts. Look where you came from. See yourself on that Broadway stage. Imagine what it took and takes to be Bettina Richardson Moran. If I were a betting woman, I'd bet it all that you would win, place, and show."

"You make me better than I am, but I love you Lisa Gutwillig. Without you, I think the day-to-days would defeat me."

"Hey, Betts, it's your sister, Mike. Guess who's arriving tomorrow to surprise you? Maw. Thought I'd give you a heads-up. She said she wanted to see you pregnant and might even stay through the birth. How does that sit with you?"

"Oh, Mike, I love that idea. Is that going to interfere with you and Jack? She can stay here; there's plenty of room."

"No, it's fine. We have a guest room, and she knows all about Jack. Besides, even though I know you love her and vice versa, you don't need the South Bronx cluttering up your space."

"You're dreadful, but I'm sure you're right."

Bettina awoke with a physical jolt and thought she had wet the bed. Then she realized her water had broken. *Why does it usually happen in the middle of the night? Why can't it be sometime between 9:00 a.m. and noon?* She started timing the cramps, but they were too far apart to call anyone. *Stay calm, Bettina. If you could win over Edwina Richardson, if you had the nerve to step out on a Broadway stage, you can get through labor.* When the cramps were just under five minutes apart, she was already packed, and called Lisa, who had threatened her with all kinds of obscure curses if she didn't tell her it was baby time.

Dr. Moore was affiliated with NYU-Tisch Hospital. Bettina hoped all women were treated as sweetly as she. The nurses were encouraging and helpful and said the doctor had been notified and would be there long before she was due. Except for the remindful dose of pain, Bettina could have laughed because Lisa arrived with arms full of yellow roses, four books, magazines, and a CD player with earphones and some of Bettina's favorite shows and albums.

"I mean, Lisa, ohhhh, ouch, do you think we're going on a cruise?"

"You never know. I just want you to have some things to pass the time."

"Oh, ooouuu, I think I'll be able to pass the time."

A nurse bustled into the room. "Yes, sweetie, you'll pass time with your breathing. Remember Lamaze. Breathe deep; that's my girl."

"Do all you nurses take happy pills? Is that it?" Lisa was toying with the nurse, trying to keep Bettina calm.

"Absolutely, love. Why don't you breathe right along with her, and then you won't be able to talk so much."

"Not bad. I wonder whatever happened to that sweet, devoted image we had of Florence Nightingale."

"Aw, she got thrown out with the bedpan drippings."

"Drippings? Yuuch! Sounds like a roast leg of lamb."

"It does, doesn't it? Might cook one tonight, but first you and I are going to help this sweet lamb with her breathing. Breathe in, Mrs. Moran."

"Call me Bettina."

"Okay, Betty."

The nurse finished checking all of Bettina's vital signs, clucked over her a few more times, and left to check on some of her other mothers.

"Okay, Betty, give it your all," Lisa said in a low, masculine voice.

"Lisa, if you start calling me Betty, I'm going to start calling you Elizabeth Ann—in public."

"Okay, Betts, it's a truce. She was really very sweet—Florence, I mean."

"Yes, they've all been, humph, whew, in, out, they've all been very nice."

"It's going to be such fun having a baby around; there's just nothing like it. Of course, you'll have those days like Anne Lamott describes in *Operating Instructions*, a journal of her son's first year."

"I love Anne Lamott but never read that."

"She's the only person in the world who can make caring for a baby both poignant and hysterically funny in the same breath. I'm not quoting her, but she'd say things to her infant like, 'Okay, it's been fun, but you can go now. I don't think I want you as my roommate forever.' At least that was the idea, not exactly what she said."

Minutes became hours, and Lisa performed, read aloud, sang songs, and encouraged breathing. Six hours passed in an instant, and with the contractions just one minute apart, Dr. Moore appeared.

"Well, my beautiful Bettina, how are we doing, or are you still speaking to the male race?"

"My friend Lisa hasn't given me a chance to rant or rave or swear off sex forever, but right this minute Tom Cruise wouldn't have a chance with me."

He laughed warmly. "How about me, Lisa? Do I have a chance to help you bring this future president into the world?"

"Anything you say, Doctor. I'm at your disposal."

Lisa, her eyes filled with tears, said to the doctor as Bettina was being prepped, "I mean, Doctor, is she all right? Just tell me she's going to be all right. I couldn't bear to have—"

"Lisa, calm thyself. Bettina is wonderful, and as far as I can see, it's going to be easy and normal."

"That's easy for you to say; easy and normal means a lot of pain. I just hope she can take it."

"I think she'll surprise all of us. The woman I've come to know is strong and capable. You're welcome to join us in the birthing room."

True to the good doctor's opinion, Bettina amazed herself by concentrating on breathing and thinking about her new son. It was a textbook birth, with happy tears from Lisa as well as the nurses. And Lisa was right. It's the fastest forgotten pain in the world. The following afternoon, Bettina, having nursed her son, was resting in her bed, looking out to a sunny day, filtered by venetian blinds, and the East River of Manhattan, busy with strong currents and boats traveling in both directions. She looked soft and golden, with barely any makeup, her hair soft, with tendrils falling in front of her ears. A book was at her side, *The Marrying Game* by Kate Saunders, an English woman. It was charming, full of promise, yet surprising.

"Bettina, am I interrupting? We just had to come see you." Dilly had arrived, handsome in navy flannels, a white turtleneck, and a military blue peacoat. His face flushed from the cold, he was extremely handsome, and his smile couldn't have been warmer.

"And we weren't about to let him have all the fun. Hello, darling." Edwina, carrying a shopping bag full of gifts, came to Bettina's bedside and leaned down and hugged her closely.

Elizabeth was right beside her. "Hi, Sis. You've brought a beautiful boy into the world. We admired him from behind the nursery glass wall. What's his name? It just says Baby Moran on the percolator, but we figure he's got more than that on his papers."

Bettina was so happy to see them, to know that these beautiful women considered her part of their family. Does one get any luckier than this? She beamed at them and said, "His name is John Roland Moran."

Edwina gasped and couldn't hold back the tears. "John Roland ... oh, thank you, darling ... John Roland. I promise we won't nickname him Rolly."

"If his personality is that big, it would be fine."

Dilly, surprised to find himself teary-eyed, said, "That's wonderful, Bettina. I know Dad would be pleased."

"I'm sure he is pleased, Dilly. I figure Roland, Dad, is sitting there in the corner watching us, hoping we won't be too maudlin. I just loved Roland so much and owed him so much. I thought, what better gift could I give my son than the memory of Roland and what he stood for."

Dilly was painfully aware, even while sharing this euphoric memory of his father, that he was feeling that old tug in his groin, wishing he could be alone with Bettina. He had not felt so much sexual longing since their separation. He wondered if Bettina felt his aura, his wanting her.

"Okay, Betts, how did you feel to see Dilly melting in front of you?" Lisa was holding the reading light on Bettina. "Fess up."

"You want truth or some vague open-ended statement about my inner self?"

"I may frow up. By the way, you may as well start talking like an idiot. Even though you don't mean to, you find yourself speaking to children as if you're a kid without all your marbles. It's always, 'See the too-too,' never something like 'Jeesus, look at that diesel rocketing along the tracks.' But to answer your question, anything but the truth is completely void, and I will delete it."

"Yes, Dr. Brothers."

"I think Joyce is yesterday. Dr. Laura Schlessinger is more today."

"All right, Dr. Laura. What's that song from *Chorus Line*? 'Nothing, I felt nothing, da da dah, da da da da da da da da dah.'"

"Nothing?"

"Give me a break, Gutwillig. My—what did you call them? Oh yes, my nether parts—have taken a real licking—"

"That doesn't sound bad."

"Beating."

"Still not terrible."

"Is it possible you can be serious for just a minute or two?"

"Two minutes; the clock has started."

"Immediately after childbirth, I can't imagine any woman wanting to do the old horizontal mambo in the sack. So, that's just for starters. My hormones were taking a siesta and my G spots had gone into hibernation. But besides all that, my mind is totally on my new son, and at that moment, I was thrilled to be considered one of the Richardson women. I would have rather had Elizabeth crawl in bed with me than Dilly."

"Hey, hey, doubles your chance for a date on Saturday night."

"Two minutes, remember? Anyway, I *was* in love with Dilly, and it's certainly conceivable I could be again. But now? No way. Not quite sure what's going on in my dopey not-quite-naturally-blonde head anymore, but I'm feeling … I don't know. I'm feeling like I need to see if I can fly on my own. Besides which"—and Bettina's eyes moistened, and her total being softened—"I'm still very recently the widow of a man I really loved. Once I faced the reality of John's impending death, I started reading about grief management, and most experts say, although it's not a rule, that you need about two years to bring yourself back to ground zero. I'm sure that John Roland Moran will help me get back there sooner rather than later, but that's where I am."

The two friends hugged and rocked back and forth.

"Harry, this is Dillworth Richardson. I wanted to thank you for handling all the details of John's funeral."

"My pleasure, Dillworth."

"Are there any concerns or complications with John's will? I just want to make sure Bettina isn't hassled in any way. She's so thrilled with her new son. I don't want anything to get in the way of that experience."

"No, there are zero complications. Since John knew so long in advance that he wasn't going to be around forever, he had everything completely tied up in a very neat package. Also, there are no family complications. He left 'enough' to the few relatives there are, and the will is so ironclad. It would be impossible for anyone to challenge. I realize you have a special place in Bettina's life; John was very clear about that. But I promise you as John's attorney and lifelong friend, I will also make sure she is fine. I think she's one helluva woman and was happy John had her in his life."

"She is indeed, Harry, and thanks again. You know you can call on me for anything at all."

Harry hung up the phone and realized he wished Bettina didn't have Dillworth Richardson waiting in the wings. He had always been crazy about her from the minute she and John became an item. That was the only secret he ever kept from John.

"Hello, J. R. I'm your auntie Mike, the nice sister, your Jewish aunt. And this is your Jewish grandmother. Say, *Grandmuther.*"

"May I point out that your nephew is only one week old, and already you're bringing ethnic conflicts to the table?"

"Ethnic, smethnic, Sis. He's gotta know where he comes from. Whatcha think, Maw? Isn't he gorgeous?"

"Oh, Beth … Bettin … uh, sweetie, he's wonderful. I'm so proud of you and happy for you. But this house, or apartment, I guess it is—how can you afford to live here without a husband to pay the bills?"

"Don't worry, Mom. He left me enough money to be completely comfortable. But fortunately, Johnnie doesn't know or care how much is in the bank account. He just wants his mommy to hold him and sing to him."

"I used to sing to you girls when yous was little. Row, row, row your boat, gently down the stream … do you know that one?"

"Yeah, Maw, we remember. Isn't it great to see Sis holding a beautiful baby in her arms. Wow, it blows me away."

"You're no stranger to making babies, Mike. And how are the siblings anyway?"

"All three are fine. It took a lot of self-control on my part not to destroy their phony father, but instead of feeding the anger, I got wise for a change and kept his image reasonably untarnished in their image."

"Good for you, Mickey, Mike; that was the smart thing to do. So many people caught in ugly breakups leave their children with permanent scars."

"So! What's next, Sis? I know the loss of your wonderful John must be killing."

"It is that, Mike, but young John here is keeping my focus positive. Guess what? I'll get through it, and no amount of mourning in the world will bring John back to me. The best thing I can do is to keep his memory and image alive in this little guy."

"I love you, Sis, and I've got to say it. You really are Bettina Richardson Moran."

The sisters lovingly embraced, their mother delighted, if not a bit confused by the elegance of the surroundings. Everything was fine.

John Roland's first year was an emotional roller coaster for Bettina. From moments of wanting to "give him back," followed by serious guilt trips, to the unmatchable high of loving her baby more than life itself, Bettina was coming to grips with the realities of life and the loneliness of single parenting.

CHAPTER 62

Suddenly, the Love of Your Baby Isn't Enough

"I can say this only to you, Lisa. I think I'm getting a little horny."

"Aha, so you aren't just the flawless icon I've set you up to be. You're just as randy as the rest of us."

"Probably more flawed, if examined closely enough."

"So sex sounds good in your head?"

"One minute yes; the next, absolutely not. Part of me agrees with the wag who said sex is proof that God has a sense of humor. And the other part of me wants to be devoured by a man."

"A man named Dillworth?"

"Uhhh, not sure. That might mean love talk, love thoughts, all that love stuff. Maybe just sex would be better."

"Any candidates?"

"I was invited out to dinner the other night by Harry Clark."

"John's lawyer, right?"

"Yep. And if I was reading him right, he would have cheerfully crossed the line between counselor and client."

"Soooo? As I recall he's a good-looking cat."

"Very. Sort of an unsexy George Clooney–type, and it's either very good tailoring, or he has a good body hidden in there."

"Okay, what are you waiting for? Call him. Invite him to a beautiful tête-à-tête for two. Candlelight dinner, soft music. After dinner, tell him you have a sore spot on your neck, and ask him to rub it with oil, and hand him a bottle of the new KY warming lubricant."

"For God's sake, Lisa. Why don't I just serve him oysters on the half shell arranged in a heart shape on my lower belly?"

"That would work too."

"Bethel, who didn't really like sex, could do that. Bettina, who has learned to love meaningful sex, isn't sure she can do all that."

"Men love high-class whores. Put yourself back on Broadway, and put on a performance." Lisa pranced around the room, playing to the invisible spotlight. "Now, here she is, the new, improved, sexier-than-ever Bettina, the most fuckable girl in the world."

"If Fred heard you say all this—"

"His old Thompson would be harder than a dinosaur bone."

"Honestly, Lisa."

"I'm right, and you know—or should know—I am. I'm going to leave you to your own thoughts, and I hope they're hot and horny. I like the idea of Harry. He's not married, is he? Or gay?"

"Divorced, and my Gay-Dar says he's a straight arrow."

"Go for it, girlfriend. And keep me posted. I just love real-life porn."

"You're impossible, and I love you. Go. I'll let you know."

"Harry, it's Bettina."

"Hi, Bettina. What's happening?"

"Other than motherhood, not much. Which leads me to the reason for this call. I'd love to have you over for dinner—not a dinner party; just the two of us. That was fun the other night. I felt like an adult for a change."

"That's great. When?"

"How's about this Sunday evening, say sevenish?"

"That's perfect. May I bring the wine?"

"No, you can't. I'm cooking *and* selecting the wine."

"Wow, a home-cooked meal. It's sounding better every minute."

"You're sweet, Harry. I'm looking forward to it."

"Me too."

Going through the morning mail, Bettina was amazed to see a letter with a return address of the state prison, with "Kenneth Monroe" printed above the address. She looked at the envelope for a full minute or more. She rang Emerson to bring her some tea to the morning room and sat down to read the letter.

Dear Bettina:

I doubt if this is a letter you'd expect or want to get, but before you throw it away, give me a minute to apologize. Here in prison, even though I wasn't an alcoholic, drug addict, or gambler, they suggested I join one of the twelve-step programs, because the lessons learned apply to anyone with problems. And I know I have problems. Problems with authority, problems with honesty, problems with lack of work ethic, problems with lack of caring about other people. Anyway, I've been learning a lot about myself. In looking back to our big effort to scam you out of all those greenbacks, I realize it wasn't difficult because you were a scam to start with, so you were a willing victim. By the way, you were right what you said in court; old Ruby never wanted to hurt you or scam you. I don't know what the connection was, but we had serious arguments about what was going to happen to Bettina Richardson. So anyway, this twelve-step program has one step where you're supposed to write or talk to someone you've hurt and apologize. So that's what I'm doing. I apologize for cheating you. I apologize for the lies and the pain it cost your marriage. I can't undo those things, but who knows? I'm up for parole in eight years, and maybe I'll come out as a new, better person. I won't write you again, and I'll certainly never contact you, but I did want you to know how I feel.

Respectfully,
Kenny Monroe

Amazing, thought Bettina. *Maybe there's a shred of decency in Kenneth. Hopefully, that shred is in all of us. Well, it's a chapter closed, and I must not let it be an emotional barrier to my future.*

Dilly thought he was losing his mind. Always incisive, always focused, he felt himself drifting, and he replayed every minute of his life with Bettina. He remembered the moment in Tiffany's, his first sighting. He remembered their first sexual encounters, or did he? And was it—of course it was—all role-playing on her part. But he bought into it, hook, line, and virginal timidity. Was he still angry he had been so thoroughly deceived? No, she more than made up for her facade. He found himself visiting bars, not overdrinking—that would be too disgusting—but sitting on well-appointed bar stools, wishing other customers wouldn't speak to him, smiling but looking away from a too-talkative bartender. If no one knew him as Dillworth Richardson, an industrial and financial Goliath, he could work on being Dilly and try to determine how Dilly could become the man that Bettina Moran needed to make her life whole again. It was a formidable task.

Meanwhile, Bettina was always warm and friendly and smiling when she saw him or spoke with him, but he didn't feel she would rush to the bedroom or even kid him about the possibility of a liaison. It was different now. Standing between them were his stupidity, the memory of John Moran, and now John Roland Moran, whom, Dilly admitted to himself, he loved and envied because he was enfolded in Bettina's arms around the clock. Yes, an enviable position.

He did all the right things. He was giving Bettina her space. He sent flowers and notes about things he knew interested her, and he gave baby John a million-dollar stock portfolio for his first birthday, which floored Bettina. She knew he could afford it but wasn't used to anyone thinking so grandly. She said, "I love you for doing that, Dilly. I won't say you shouldn't have done it, but it was very dear and very unexpected." All nice but nothing intimate. What to do? And when to do it? And what if she didn't want him in her life? It was too painful to carry that thought.

Saturday—a pedicure, a manicure, a facial. Bettina emerged from Elizabeth Arden's salon feeling ravishingly beautiful. Until she was a member of that world who could pamper their bodies, she didn't realize the sensuous pleasure of having perfect toes, for instance. She laughed to herself, thinking how the old Bethel would have guffawed and said, *You're kidding!*

"Tomorrow night is your dinner with Harry, yes?"

"Yes, Fred. Harry Clark has been John's lawyer and friend for a few decades."

"I know Harry."

"You do, darling?"

"Yes, Lisa, and you met him once, four or five years ago; very classy guy with a sterling reputation. Have never heard a negative word about the man."

"Mmmm."

"That's all you can say, Betts? Mmmm?"

"What else do you want me to say, Mrs. Gutwillig? Whoopee?"

"Why do I think I'm not in the conversational loop about Mr. Clark? You both must know something I don't know."

"Darling, of course we both know things you don't know. You're a man, clueless—"

"And you both are conniving shrews, planning the downfall of a gallant man." Throwing down his napkin on the table while trying to twist his orderly face into a mock scowl, Fred had joined the game.

"Put a sock in it, my love. Winter is coming. I want someone around who's going to keep Bettina warm."

"I think I'll call Clark and warn him."

"Do you know who's going to be sleeping on the sofa, even on his birthday and Father's Day?" Lisa leaned into her husband, nose to nose.

"You see what's she's like, Bettina, using sex like a carrot on a stick?"

Lisa licked her husband's ear. "Like a carrot on a stick? Gosh, Fred, you just turn me on with all your phallic imagery."

Bettina stood and dramatically threw her hands out in front of her. "Both of you stop it. I have no specific plans to attack Harry Clark tomorrow night. I think he's an interesting and attractive guy, and I'll enjoy his company."

"No comment, but five'll get you ten, Frederick, that she's gonna nail him."

"Nail him? My God, Lisa, if I didn't know better I'd think you were raised in the gutter. But then"—he reached over and kissed Lisa—"I've always liked guttersnipes."

"Okay, you win. You can do with me as you like tonight."

"May we refrain from discussing our personal life with our good and true friend, Mrs. Moran?"

Bettina was laughing with them and, as always, loving them for making her part of their family.

"By nature, Bettina, I am not timid or shy. But I find myself mentally stuttering. And it's not just because of the perfect food. My God, where did you learn to cook like that? I've never had pork stuffed with brandied prunes. And those vegetables, what did you call them? Chowoats?"

"Close but no cigar. *Chaotes*—chy-o-tays. It's a Mexican root vegetable. Kind of tastes like potato, but it's really a vegetable. Glad you liked everything."

They were sitting comfortably on the overstuffed sofa, sipping a very fine cognac. "That's gross understatement. Now ... my God, I'm trembling like a high school boy. Bettina, I ... I would like our relationship to be more than it is. I have strong feelings about you ... uhh ... sexual feelings. How about that?"

"I'm flattered, Harry. I'm not going to play games with you; I've had similar thoughts about you." Bettina looked incredible tonight. A silk mauve shirt picked up her eye color and allowed just enough of her nearly flawless body to show. Deep-purple velvet slacks and embroidered slippers completed the outfit, along with some diamonds casually placed at the ears, a tennis bracelet on her wrist, and a diamond dinner ring. Her hair was pulled back, except for tendrils that floated around her face. Harry had never seen a more beautiful, impossible-to-resist woman in his life.

They leaned toward one another and kissed, and the kiss continued for a long time.

How they got to the bed Harry wasn't sure, but suddenly they were there, skin to skin. He knelt and kissed her on those most private lips. Then he was inside her with his tongue. He was in and out and finally below in that emotional mine field between, then kissing that red rim with his tongue. Bettina was almost holding her breath. Never had this happened; she was lost in his passion. And then he moved back up, and she felt his tongue move up her torso and nursed her breasts. She had never felt so lustful, so wanton, so wet with need. Finally, his mouth came back to hers. After minutes—or was it hours?—she nudged him up on his knees and had him move forward, with his knees pushed into her armpits, his ample manhood in front of her. She leaned forward and nibbled the end and, with hands on his ass, pushed him into her mouth more. Although she had never participated, she had him kneel over her face and tentatively tried to return the gift he had given her. Did they speak? Bettina didn't remember a word passing between them.

There were sounds, sighs, moans, and heavy breathing, and there he was again, his mouth on hers, on her neck, whispering—or did she imagine it?—"I love you, Bettina; oh God, I love you," and finally he was inside of her. She arched up to meet him, and he didn't rush. Bettina lost count of the orgasms. Three, maybe four, and finally, he murmured, "Oh, now Bettina, I'm going to be part of you; oh God, oh yes," and he shuddered, and a falsetto sigh escaped from somewhere inside of him. They didn't move for many minutes.

Finally, Bettina spoke. "I thought the first time wasn't supposed to be very good. After ten times, I don't believe it would ever be better than this." She was stretched out beside Harry, one hand lightly circling his relaxing cock. She realized that as much as she had loved Dilly and John, she had never felt so seductively peaceful as she did at this moment.

Harry smiled at her and kissed her forehead, her eyes, her nose, and lips. "Thank God for my active imagination. Without being able to anticipate your moves, I've made love to you at least ten times before tonight. But nothing can replace the reality of you. I can honestly say to you, Bettina, that I have never in my life had a sexual—no, a love experience—like this. I won't do that dumb male plea for reassurance, like *how'd I do?* I know you were there with me. I love you, Bettina. I know that may be too fast, but you have to know where I am where you're concerned." Bettina didn't know what she was going to say.

A cry from J. R.'s nursery brought Bettina to her feet. "Saved by the *yell.* Excuse me, my beautiful, naked lover. There's another naked male in my life, and I can't neglect his needs."

"I won't even be jealous. I'll just lie here and luxuriate in my thoughts of you."

She was gone for almost thirty minutes. Harry hadn't moved. His eyes were closed. Bettina studied him, realizing she was powerless over her feelings about this kind and beautiful and sexy man. His eyes opened. He smiled and reached out a hand and tenderly pulled Bettina back to the safety of his adoring embrace.

There was more lovemaking, each moment a new revelation. Finally, they slept. As the first glimmer of dawn threw a soft light across the bed, Harry awakened and whispered to his sleeping goddess. "Darling, as much as I would like to just spend the entire day right here, I should get up and get out of here before your staff arrives. And ridiculous as it sounds to me right now, I'm going to work today, which may be impossible. There's no room in my head for legal procedures, only you—you, forever."

Once dressed, he knelt beside the bed and kissed Bettina's hand until her eyes fluttered open. "Oh, I'll get up and fix you some coffee."

"Shhh, go back to sleep, my love. I will speak to you at midday. Don't move; just sleep. I love you." He kissed her gently and was gone.

Bettina lay there, thinking. Suddenly, flooded with peace, saturated with love, her eyes and mind drifted back into sleep.

"Hi, Betts. So tell me I win the five bucks from Fred. You nailed him, right?"

"I don't think I've ever acknowledged until this moment how totally vulgar you are, Lisa."

"Hah! I knew it. Is he good in the sack?"

"I am saying nothing."

"Which speaks volumes. Attention world: friend Bettina has someone to do the ol' in-and-out with. Oops, bad English; someone with whom she can do the ol' in and out."

Bettina was trying not to laugh but finally caved in under the infectious mouthiness of Lisa. "Enough, Lisa. Let's just say Harry is very special."

"That good, eh? On a scale of one to ten, would you give him an eight or better?"

"You've had my last word on the subject."

"Wowee, takes your breath away, hmmmm? Maybe he gets a ten and a lifetime membership."

"Honestly, Lisa—"

"Okay okay, not another word on the subject. Hey, wanna take a drive today? We could go visit a stud farm—"

"Lisa!"

"I promise. I'm just happy to hear some happy in your voice."

"You're right; there is happy in my voice. He's quite a guy."

"Oh, poor Dilly."

"Let's not go there. I'm having enough trouble accepting this new, um . . ."

"Influence? That's as good a word as any."

"Right. It's enough to accept this new influence in my life. Change of subject. I have two tickets to this Wednesday's matinee of *The Boy from Oz.*"

"Oooo, that's the musical about Peter Allen, the Australian singer/composer who was married to Liza Minnelli?"

"Yes, would you care to be my date?"

"Done. And lunch is on me."

Harry felt he even looked different. Wrapped in the confidence of love, he knew there was more spring in his step, his chin a touch higher, his smile brighter. Flowers were delivered to Bettina every few days. Gentle phone calls, chilled champagne, one dinner was only caviar and oysters. And the relationship grew, physically and emotionally. Bettina was in love, she knew, with her son. And Harry's nonstop affection left her feeling sun-touched, warm, and glistening.

"Bettina, it's Dilly."

"Oh, Dilly, how nice to hear from you. It's been two weeks at least. But I'm not complaining. I know how busy you are, and goodness knows I never knew what busy was until I had a baby."

"How is young John Roland? Behaving himself? Does he have you wrapped around his little finger?"

"Ha-ha, he owns me. I've never felt so male-dominated in my life and never enjoyed it so much. He's really a good guy, Dilly, full of laughter and love. It's all good. And you, sweet Dilly? How are you doing?"

"As usual, proving that workaholics don't get in any trouble but also don't have a great deal of fun. Which segues into my next comment. Betts?"

"Lay it on me."

How I would like to lay myself on you, Dilly thought. "Very well. I have the use of a sixty-five-foot sloop for the next couple of weeks, complete with captain and crew, and would like to invite you and little John to come with me on a cruise up the Hudson River. We'll pick a day we know is going to be perfect weather, and we'll have a picnic on board." Bettina hesitated, and Dilly sensed it. "Betts, I'm not trying to compromise you, or goodness knows I don't want to be rushing you …"

"Stop, Dilly. Forgive my slow uptake. I was just digesting the thought of a day on a boat with the baby. But I understand you're saying we'll choose a perfect-weather day, and there are no concerns."

"And if you'd feel more comfortable, I'd be more than delighted to invite Lisa and Fred to join us, since we joined them in the Virgin Islands."

"That would be sweet, Dilly, as long as it doesn't interfere with your plans."

You bet it interferes with my plans. I want to be all alone with you and hope you'll fall in love with me again. "Not a bit. It'll be fun. I'll clear a couple of days with Fred, who sometimes has a very tight schedule, and then get back to you."

"Great, Dilly, it sounds very charming and something totally new to think about." Bettina hung up and sat there thinking about Harry. *Am I being unfaithful to him? Noooo.* Dilly had been her husband and had acted superbly during her loss of John and had set up the baby with the beginning of a personal fortune. *It's just a day's outing with friends. Or is it?* She hadn't forgotten her suspicions that John had consciously set up Dilly as his successor. *Where does that leave Harry? And my God, where does that leave me?*

"Hello, darling, it's John Roland's other grandmother."

"Edwina, how wonderful to hear your voice. I've been missing you."

"And I've been missing you. I know how busy mothering is, so haven't dragged you out for a girl's lunch."

"You don't have to drag me anywhere. I'll come running. What day is best for you this week?"

"Tomorrow would be perfect."

"Tomorrow it is. Let's meet at Santa Fe on West Sixty-Ninth Street. No, they moved to West End Avenue; I think around Seventy-First."

"I remember their margaritas."

"And good food. How's twelve thirty?"

"I'll be there. Kiss J. R. for me."

It will be wonderful to see Edwina. But what do I tell her if she asks about Dilly or anyone else, for that matter?

Later that night, with the passionate Harry deep inside her, pumping his love into her, she thought about tomorrow's luncheon and wondered what the hell was happening to her. She returned to the present and gave her physical all to Harry.

"I never thought age and pregnancy improved anyone's looks, but you're more gorgeous than ever."

"Wow, when your mother-in-law ladles it on like that, she must want something."

"Nothing like having a compliment thrown back in your face like a dead fish."

"Oh, you know me; a million laughs, Edwina. But thank you. I feel fine, and John Roland thinks I'm the most beautiful woman in the world, so that probably helps."

"Hmmm. I know it's none of my business ..."

"You're right."

"But you also look like a woman in love. Could that be?"

"I was hoping you wouldn't ask. But I have no secrets from you, Edwina. There is a very fine man who is courting me efficiently and romantically."

Edwina dropped her eyes, took a breath, and quietly asked, "Does that mean Dilly doesn't have a chance?"

"No, my darling Eddie, it doesn't. Were I able to banish Dilly from my conscious thinking, the new suitor could run away with me. But I'm hesitating, not wanting to cause him any unnecessary pain, and truthfully, I'm not sure where I am in my head with Dilly. I still love Dilly on some level."

"Then you've forgiven him?"

"Totally. I think he had more to forgive than I. And we just made a date to go out on a boat with baby John, and Lisa and Fred and their guys. So, no, love, Dilly hasn't been shut out of my life."

"I'm glad to hear that. Also, although I think you know that, I'm not going to say anything to Dilly about your other suitor. I know you'll make the right decision for yourself and John Roland. Now, let's talk about something vitally important. Should I eat the spicy crusted shrimp or the Southwestern meatloaf, washed down with a margarita?"

"I don't think those choices would make us the poster girls for the South Beach diet."

"To hell with diets. Most women would sell their souls for our bodies."

"I love you, Edwina. You make me so glad to be Bettina Richardson Moran."

"And you make me glad to be Eddie!"

"Good afternoon, ladies."

"Good afternoon, Mark. How about two margaritas on the rocks, *sin sal*. We'll order when the drinks arrive."

CHAPTER 63

And the Men in Orbit around Bettina?

"You're going where with Dilly?"

"Calm yourself, darling. It's a one-day outing on a boat, and Lisa and Fred and their sons and my son are coming with us. It's not a Caribbean cruise."

"It's hard to be calm. I know what Dilly wants. I wish you weren't going, and I'm sorry I just said that."

"Don't be nervous, my love. You know Dilly feels some sense of stewardship with me and my son. He's been a perfect gentleman with me every minute. I couldn't think of any good-sounding reason to say no, especially when the invite includes all the Gutwilligs."

"I know, I know. You're right, and I apologize."

"You don't have to. Your angst is very sweet and complimentary. I haven't had anyone be jealous of me in a very long time. Come here and kiss me."

"Yo, Dillworth, how're they swingin'?"

"Guillermo, you nut case, how've you been? Haven't seen your pitiful face for more than a year." The two men embraced, grinning widely at each other. Guillermo Barron had been Dilly's roommate and favorite friend in graduate school, and through the years they had managed to keep in touch, including one another in wedding parties and even some joint business deals. Dilly had total faith in Guillermo as a trusted friend.

"Well, I tried to stay out of your face during all that hoo-hah in the press about your beautiful ex. I honestly felt sorry for her and think she got the short end of the stick. I knew you had your reasons for ending the marriage, but I was sorry to see it. Betty?"

"Bettina."

"Yeah, Bettina was a collector's item. She was great onstage, and I thought gave you something you didn't always have."

"Oh really, dumb Mexican? Just what was that?"

"She turned you into a human being. You were always a perfect machine, but she made you realize there's more to life than making $4,912 per minute."

"Thank you, Doctor, for your kind analysis. What's putting you on this particular soapbox?"

"I was at Grenouille for dinner the other night with my current poke and suddenly saw, through the floral arrangement, your Bettina, looking like the zillion-dollar beauty she is, being very obviously attended to by an adoring hombre. They looked mighty fond of each other. I'm sorry to tell you all this. I can see from the expression on your face it's not welcome news. But I thought maybe you'd want to know or maybe not give a shit."

Dilly sat down and stared at his feet for a couple of minutes. "I do give a shit, Gui; I'm still very much in love with Bettina. Obviously, someone that beautiful doesn't sit around without someone else going gaga over her. Damn, maybe I've been too slow to react. I was giving her time to get over her husband's death."

"Whoa, I didn't know she was remarried and widowed."

"With a baby son, a little over one year old."

"What happened to the father?"

"The big C. A terrific guy—John Moran, theater producer.

"I know the name."

"I really liked him, and John wanted me to reenter Bettina's life. I hope it's not too late."

"Could kick myself for bringing this news to your door."

"No, you're still the best, Guillermo."

"That being true, you wanna run off to San Francisco and marry me?"

"Naw, you weren't that good. Besides I'm against marrying third-world people."

"That's my wise-mouth friend, Dilly. Anyway, *hermano*, let us not be apart this much. I will call you. Which in Mexican-speak means hell could freeze over before I call, but that's not true. I miss you. You were the first gringo who ever treated me like anything but a dumb gay Mexican."

"Well, that's because I felt so sorry for you."

Guillermo, laughing, hugged Dilly and kissed him on both cheeks. "Here's my card, *pendejo*, within the month I want to hear your voice."

"Done deal, amigo."

Guillermo left, and Dilly stood looking at the Manhattan cityscape outside his window and tried to formulate his next plan of action.

"The itsy-bitsy spider went up the water spout. Down came the rain and washed the spider out. Out came the sun that dried up all the rain, and the itsy-bitsy spider climbed up the spout again. Oh, you don't like that one, J. R.? How about your mommy singing you a song? Okay, let's curl up in the rocking chair, and I'll sing you a favorite of mine.

Red and yellow and pink and green.

Purple and orange and blue.

You can sing a rainbow, sing a rainbow,

sing a rainbow too.

Listen with your eyes, listen with your eyes,

and sing everything you see.

You can sing a rainbow, sing a rainbow,

sing along with me ...

Red and yellow and pink and green,

purple and orange and blue.

See? You can sing a rainbow, sing a rainbow,

sing a rainbow too.

Mmm mm mamma, mmm mm mm

mmm and sing everything you see.

You can sing a rainbow, sing a rainbow,

sing a rainbow too.

Okay, my beautiful young man, just sleep, my love, and dream all the happy dreams there are to dream." Bettina gently deposited J. R. in his crib and stood there gazing with wonderment at this incredible gift. Her reverie was interrupted by the distant sound of the doorman's intercom.

"Yes, Patrick. What is it?"

"Ah, missus, thought I should tell you that Mr. Dillworth is on the way up to your floor. Ah, um, please pardon me for pointing it out, but it appears as though he's had a trifle too much liquid refreshment."

"Thank you, Patrick. I appreciate your discretion, and it will not be mentioned to anyone what you said. But thank you."

The doorman hung up, thinking, *That's risky, but somehow, I know it'll be all right with Mrs. Richardson. She's not like all the others in the building. She's a real lady.*

The front door chime rang softly, and Bettina opened the door to find Dilly, walking and talking too carefully and obviously smashed.

"Hi, Betts. I just felt like I had to see you. Is it too late or anything?"

"No, of course not, Dilly. I just put J. R. to bed, and I was going to settle down with a book. Do come in. Would you like a coffee or anything, Dilly?"

"No, no, no, no, Bettina, nothing. I just want to talk, I think."

"Okay, I've learned to be a good listener."

Dilly walked in far too carefully, staggered just for an instant, and swung around, all smiles, and deposited himself on one of the large sofas. He said nothing for what seemed a very long time, trying to gather his thoughts and find the words. "Bettina, would you ... could you please come and sit here with me?"

"Of course. Are you sure you don't want a coffee or water or—"

"Nothing, just ... you."

Bettina wasn't sure where she was going. She was glad she had dined very lightly and had drunk only tea with her dinner. "All right, I'm here, and now what?" As she seated herself, Dilly grabbed her and kissed her passionately. She neither returned the kiss nor physically fought him off. Once she caught her breath and her composure, she smiled warmly at Dilly and said, "You said you wanted to talk, Dilly."

"I've talked to you every day for a year and a half. I've hoped that you were hearing me, that you would find room for me in your life again. I didn't want to push you because of John, and I liked John very much; liked him very much. But don't fall in love with anyone else, Bettina, until you've given me ... given us a chance to put our love back together." Dilly had half slid onto the floor and was on his knees, his face buried in Bettina's lap.

Bettina was trying to not hyperventilate. "There's so much at stake, Dilly. I think we need time ..."

"We don't need more time. I need you." Dilly stood and powerfully pulled Bettina to her feet and was simultaneously kissing her and touching her and removing her blouse.

"Wait, Dilly. We should wait ..."

"No, Bettina, I need you now." He had managed to remove her blouse and unzipped her slacks and was pulling them down.

Bettina thought, *This is what rape is about, but this is Dilly, whom I loved, and oh God, what is happening?* The sex was unlike anything Bettina Richardson or Bettina Moran had known. The body was familiar, but he was someone else, a dockworker with an aristocrat's body, a trapeze artist capable of making his body do impossible twists and turns. He possessed her; she thought she would scream out, *Fuck me!* He was everywhere, burning inside of her, and she was fighting nothing. His mouth, his tongue, her mouth, her tongue were everywhere. They rolled from sofa onto the carpet, and he physically owned her. She was crying, gratefully?

"Uhh, oh God, Bettina, yes, now. Oh, Bettina, I cannot live without you." And he slept. With his sex drive gone, the alcohol and his emotional being took over and let him sleep.

She lay there, half under him, realizing he was sleeping. After a long time, she wondered, *Did I sleep?* She eased herself out from under Dilly and brought a pillow for his head and a blanket to cover him. She wrapped herself in a soft robe and took a pillow and blanket to the sofa beside the sleeping Dilly, so he wouldn't be alone when he awakened.

Dawn. Dilly thought, *Where am I? Oh God, naked, on a carpet; oh God, Bettina's carpet. Oh, I remember. She'll never speak to me again.* Painfully, he cracked open one eye to see Bettina not three feet away, sleeping on the sofa. *Why is she here? Did*

I injure her? He tried to raise his head but couldn't. Too much pain. He closed his eyes and, somehow, internal struggles notwithstanding, fell back asleep.

"Good morning, Dilly."

"Ohhh, oh, good morning, Betts. Do I have to speak? Are you speaking to me?"

"Shhh, quiet, and drink this."

"You're not giving me a bloody Mary, are you?"

"No, Dilly dear, it's everything a spicy bloody Mary has, with a raw egg mixed in it, but no alcohol. It will help you recover."

Dilly drank it slowly, hoping it didn't trigger nausea, and was relieved when it didn't. "I'm not positive what happened last night but have a pretty good idea. Am I being dismissed forever from your life?"

"I could never do that, Dilly. You gave me a life and the opportunity to really be Bettina. I'll always be grateful."

"I guess it's not your gratitude I want but something considerably more."

"That's understood. But it's a process, and you're going to have to let me get there on my time, even though last night cannot be ignored."

It pained him to ask her. "Was it terrible? Did I violate all principles of decent or acceptable behavior?"

"Yes."

"Oh, God."

"And it was the best sex I've ever had, including all my time with you. You were an animal in heat, and whether I was happy about being your bitch at that moment, I surrendered myself to you. Just glad no one showed up to throw a bucket of cold water on us."

"Wha ... what? You mean that? I mean, about the lovemaking?"

"Yes, I do, Dilly. What remains to be seen is was it lovemaking, or was it just necessary sex? The fact is that when I covered you last night, I remembered all the reasons I fell in love with you—I'm ashamed to say, *after* we were married."

"But—"

"No, let me finish." Dilly was sitting on the floor, the blanket wrapped around him, his hair sticking out in every direction. Bettina thought he looked like a little boy, all messed up, so unlike her Dilly. "I've gone through a lot since our separation. A lot of sadness for my own stupidity, then anger at your understandable anger. Then the darling John came into my life and once again, I was the princess you created by making me a Richardson, by letting me not be Bethel, by allowing me to maybe make a fool of myself on the Broadway stage. Has there ever been a luckier woman in the world? And when you're that happy—and make no mistake about it; John made me very, very happy, in different ways than you, in case you think I'm comparing you to John—I thought the happiness would go on forever, especially when I knew I was pregnant.

"John wasn't supposed to die. And all the money in the world, which I seemed to have, courtesy of attorneys and the Richardson fortune, couldn't save me. I died inside, and probably, if not for John Roland Moran, I would have given up right then. But I carried on, made a baby, became a good mom. I've been smart about keeping wonderful Lisa by my side, and you'll never totally believe how much Edwina continues to enrich every day of my life. I've even made up with my edgy Jewish sister, Mickey.

"And I'm only human, Dilly. John had left me a wonderful and loving farewell letter, explaining that he had set you up to come back into my life, and I was trying to figure out if that was what I wanted. Meanwhile, being only human, I became lonely for someone close to me, and another man has stepped in to fill that need."

"I know there's someone. A friend of mine said he saw you dining at Grenouille the other night, and there was a man obviously adoring you. I won't ask you who it is and feel too stupid sitting here, naked and disheveled, to make a dignified stand."

"Thank you for not asking, Dilly."

"Am I too late? Are you totally, committedly in love with the handsome stranger?"

"Yes, I do love him." Dilly cringed inwardly, wanting to reach out and pull Bettina to him. "But I haven't told myself that this is the man I want to be with forever, even though he's too important to summarily dismiss. But"—Bettina kneeled on the carpet and embraced Dilly—"I know you're important to me and always will be."

She pulled back and looked at Dilly and saw the tears overflowing in his eyes. She wiped the tears away and kissed him tenderly on the mouth. Smiling and a little teary herself, she said sweetly, "Now get up off my living room carpet, you slob. You may go into the guest room and shower and make yourself presentable. There's shaving equipment and a toothbrush and all that stuff in there. Fortunately, Emerson has today off, but the nanny will be coming in less than an hour. If you'll pardon me, I must go see to my son's welfare. With any luck, I'll have time to put myself together before he wakes up. I'll take the sofa and floor linens to the laundry room."

Dilly stood up, totally naked, trying to look reasonably dignified. Bettina couldn't help but giggle. "Thank you for that, Bettina. Nothing like giving a man confidence." With that, Bettina started choking with laughter, and so did Dilly. He kissed her on the top of her head and strode forcefully out of the room, first scooping up his clothes, which were thrown about the living room.

A long, warm shower was, as always, restoring to Bettina. She was humming one of the many songs from *The Boy from Oz*, which, besides energetic and entertaining, was also very romantic. She thought about her night with Dilly and smiled and thought of their conversation this morning. She had never seen Dilly cry. And they were tears of joy. *He loves me. And I love him, right? And where does this leave Harry? Too many conflicting thoughts. Concentrate on today.* After careful makeup and a quick brushing, her hair fell into place, much to her amazement. She put on a white silk blouse and navy slacks and some favorite jewels Dilly had given her—a sapphire ring and a double strand of pearls from the South Pacific. Very beautiful and very Bettina. She went into the nursery to tend to her handsome son, who was making early morning sounds.

When the nanny arrived, she found the señora having coffee in the living room and a tall handsome man holding her charge, the baby John.

"Good morning, Estela. This is Mr. Richardson."

"Buen dia, señor. Would you like me to take the little gentleman?"

"May I keep him with me for a few more minutes, Estela? Is that all right, Bettina? It's been so long since I've held a baby, I've forgotten how wonderful it feels."

"Of course, Dilly. I'll call you, Estela. Meanwhile, help yourself to some breakfast. Johnny has had his bottle, so he's not starving yet."

Dilly was entranced with this small smiling bundle. The little hands so strong. Now riding Dilly's knee like a horsey, the small active package looked right into Dilly's eyes. Dilly felt himself melt. *Is this what fatherhood feels like? Why didn't we do this right away?* He tore his gaze away from the baby to look at Bettina, who, as usual, was more beautiful than any other woman he could imagine.

"Um, where do we go from here, Bettina? Can I come calling? I know if you had a father I'd ask him for your hand in marriage. But since I've just snuck in the back door, will you let me come in the front door and compete for you? It's difficult to accept that there's someone else, but I'm older and smarter now, and I'm willing to take the challenge and take my chances."

"That's asking a lot of yourself, Dilly. I hate to put you in that position."

"I have no choice. Unless you're willing to give him up right here and now, I will battle him for you. I love you, Bettina. You know that, and you know nothing would make me happier than to be your husband, your lover, your best friend—again."

After Dilly left, Bettina thought, *It's true; what tangled webs we weave. It would be easy to just say yes to Dilly. Or would it be? Would I be able to just forget all that Harry has come to mean to me?*

For the next four weeks, Bettina felt she was back on Broadway. She was constantly onstage, every minute. Always the mommy, and once a week, locked in the passionate, loving embrace of Harry Clark, and without his knowing, which suffocated her with guilt, making love with Dillworth Richardson a few nights later.

CHAPTER 64

When in Doubt, and Women Know This Better than Men, Turn to Your Friends

"You may wonder why I've called this meeting of the Bettina Board, or maybe we should call it Getting Bored with Bettina." Sitting in the living room were Edwina, always flawless-looking, wearing Chanel today, and smiling at her darling Bettina. Next, Lisa Gutwillig, in slacks, a silk T, and a wrinkly linen jacket with sleeves pushed up, always loving and approving her friend Betts. On the sofa, an unlikely duo, the two sisters: Bettina's sister, Mike, looking better all the time, today in perfectly pressed jeans and a well-fitted cotton sweater in marine blue. Next to her, Dilly's sister, Elizabeth, who had always loved Bettina, today looking soft and beautiful in a white silk suit. Bettina was dressed more quietly than normal: a short-sleeve cotton-knit sweater and black tailored slacks and flats. Small gold earrings; only a wedding band.

"Hah," said Lisa, "you couldn't be boring if you were reading the Bronx telephone directory."

"And," added Mike, "she could read it with the correct accent, right, Sis?"

"Roight!" The women giggled at her mispronunciation. "Anyway, I've invited you all here because you are the women I love most in my life and hopefully will continue to love and influence me."

"You know that's true, and I'm sure I speak for all of us, Bettina."

"Thanks, Eddie. Your understanding of me has kept me going at many turning points in my adult life. Anyway, I've been very carefully avoiding all of you for the past four weeks, other than carefully thought-out phone calls, because I didn't want your advice yet. I'm going to tell you something about myself that's difficult to tell, and I'm hoping you don't come down on me too hard."

"Like what, Betts? We're going to have you stoned?"

"Maybe, Lisa."

"I can't imagine … but never mind; cut to the chase."

"Okay." Bettina told them about her romance with Harry Clark. How loving and dear he had been, kind and good and handsome and sexy, and that he loved her and wanted her. She then told them that Dilly had reentered her life, leaving out the drunken sex scene but allowing as how she and Dilly were once again seeing one another intimately.

"Like I said, I'm hoping you won't be too judgmental, since I'm toying with the heartfelt affections of two men, one of whom"—she turned to Edwina and Elizabeth—"is of particular importance to you. By the way, Dilly knows there is another man who was courting me before he was. He accepts that and has been generous and loving in his acceptance."

"I, for one, love it, Bettina. It's Dilly's fault he lost you."

"Oh, Elizabeth, darling, that's history. Bettina forgave Dilly ages ago, and so must you."

"You're right, Mom, I apologize. But I do think it's great for you, Bettina. Gosh, to have two handsome hunks in love with you at one time—what a rush."

"It is a rush, Elizabeth."

"As self-appointed best friend, why didn't you tell me about Dilly?"

"Because, Lisa, I didn't want you to call me the town whore and make me nervous about this ménage a trois. I had to find out how I felt before I shared it with anyone. But I'll never keep a secret from you again. Okay, now comes the really big news."

The four women—Edwina, Lisa, Elizabeth and Mickey—sat silently, each running all they'd been told through instant replay in their minds.

"I'm pregnant."

"My God, Betts!" Lisa was the first to scream out and leaped over to hug Bettina.

"Oh, darling, I'm so happy for you." Edwina tearfully embraced Bettina.

"Me too, Sis," said Elizabeth, hugging her warmly.

"Wow, Sis," said Mickey, "you really know how to hold an audience." She hugged and kissed her sister. "But here's the sixty-four-thousand-dollar question. Who's the lucky papa? We noticed you didn't say."

"Who's the lucky father? The man I'm going to marry."

"And," said Lisa, grinning ear to ear, "that is …"

Bettina took her time, looked around at each of these wonderful women, smiled, and said, "I don't know."

"*What?*" "But …" "Don't know?" "Oh dear!"

"That's right; I don't know."

"Can they do a DNA on the fetus and tell you?"

"I don't think so this early."

"So what are you going to do, darling?"

"I'm going to wait and see who I bring into this world—a Richardson or a Clark. And then, if he's still up to it, I will marry the new daddy."

"And meanwhile, friend, what do you tell your two lovers?"

Bettina smiled, took a sip of her iced tea, and said, "I'm not sure. Any suggestions? I'm listening."

"Oh, simple," said Lisa, jumping to her feet. "Listen to me, Dilly … or is your name Harry? I think there's something you oughta know. As good as you are in the sack, you know, a girl can get, well, maybe bored a little. So …"

"Lisa, you clown. I'm not about to say anything that could or would hurt anyone's feelings."

Mickey added, "How about drawing straws or flipping a coin? Heads or tails. Both sound kind of sexual to me."

"Sis, you are as bad as Lisa. Eddie, are you going to say something, or are you never going to speak to me again?"

"Mmmm, I'm trying to walk in your shoes, trying to imagine myself facing lover number one and lover number two and having to choose. I can't! What will you do, my darling Bettina?"

"Whatever you decide, Bettina, I'll be happy to stand up for you."

"Thank you, sweet Liz. Right this minute I feel drained of ideas. Just trying to think how either man—both wonderful—might react!"

"Sis!"

"Yes, Mike?"

"I know this is unusual, but I have an idea."

"Shoot."

"What if we, just the two of us, go away together, maybe to visit Mom for a few days, and see if we can talk our way into a level playing field for you?"

"I love the idea, Sis; let's do it."

"Sounds smart to me, Bettina. Meanwhile, you know how to find me if you want to share a new point of view."

"Thank you, Edwina. Don't be surprised if I knock on your door."

"Nothing you do surprises me ... anymore."

CHAPTER 65

A New Venue Might Work: Sister, Mom, Balmy Florida

"I never thought I'd see this day. The two of you, arm in arm, sitting in my living room. I'm knocked out. Are you both real?"

"We couldn't be realer, Maw. It's me, your Michelle."

"And me, Mom, Bet ... Bethel. And you look wonderful."

"How could I not look wonderful? Melbourne, Florida, is not the Bronx. And Florida's winter is something I could only dream about. Whatta you want for dinner?"

"A Jewish mother never changes."

"Being Jewish has nothing to do with fixing dinner."

"You're right, Mom. But don't fix anything. We're taking you out tonight. Meanwhile, if you don't mind, Mickey and I are going to take a walk. We have some things to hash out—together."

"I don't mind nothin', Bethel. Go do whatever you want. I'm gonna take a nap so I'm ready to go out tonight."

"Let's drive over to the beach, Mike. It'll probably be empty today. Too cool for the locals."

"This was a good idea, Betts. Bare feet in the sun and sand and the edge of the water clears the mind."

"Oh, and how did you arrive at that, Doctor."

"Well, it's better than a bare ass at the beach, because then you get sand in your stuff ... and that does *not* clear your mind."

"Okay, clear mind speaking now."

"I am all ears, Sis. Speak."

"It's extraordinarily difficult to love two men—simultaneously. But were I not pregnant, I could never choose between the two of them!"

"Can you explain or describe the difference between the two of them, Beth ... Bettina?"

"Mmmm, I think so. Harry, while as passionate as any man I've ever known, is immaculately gentle. When we're together I feel as fragile and valuable as one of those bejeweled eggs from Russia. He offers himself as a gift to me. He blesses my body. His touch is silken. His mouth anoints me. Somehow, he is feather-light, and suddenly he's inside of me, touching every cell. I am Eve; he is Adam; we are inventing this thing called sex between a man and woman".

"You're making me wet."

"Mickey!"

"I can't help it. My Jack is great in the sack, but he's never going to teach a master class in how to do the ol' horizontal mambo. Mind you, I'm not knocking it—or him. But we are not Adam and Eve ... we are just man and woman. And Dilly?"

"Dilly was the prince I had always dreamed would sweep me away. And maybe because I was a fake me, I didn't concentrate on all that he was and could be. But now, suddenly, I am me, Bettina, and maybe he is seeing me for who I really am, and the sex is, uh, animal-like. He's all over me, capturing me, forcing me to the ground, dominating me, pumping up every hormone I've ever had to the bursting point. I never knew how much a tongue can do. Or how deep a ... penis—there, I've said it—how deep a penis can penetrate. My backbone feels it. I don't just have an orgasm; it's a red-hot geyser. I almost scream when it happens, and who knows? Maybe I have screamed."

"And growing up, I thought I was the sexy sister. Boy, how wrong you can be about yourself."

"But you know something, Sis? When we're through …"

"When you're through with which one?"

"Either. I get up, wash up, and go back to being Bettina, mother of John Roland. He's the male who really owns me."

"I get it. Only a mother knows the meaning of true love. The kind of love you'd give your life for. And you feel it too, Betts?"

"Completely. I can watch him sleep and forget every problem or concern I have in the world. He is my world. I honestly loved being pregnant, knowing he was growing minute by minute, that I was nourishing him with every healthy meal I consumed. I couldn't believe I was creating another human being. And I loved John, who planted him … now there was an exceptional man. God, Mike, how can I have ended up so lucky? To have married Dilly. To have been loved by John. And now to have both Harry and Dilly begging for my love. If ever I complain about anything, slap me and remind me—no woman alive has ever had so much."

"I'm envious. But not in a mean way. I got over that. You're my baby sister who did good, and I'm proud of you. But we still haven't come up with an answer. Who's ring are you going to wear? Who will be Daddy? Dilly? Harry?"

"I don't know, Sis. I hear so many voices in my head, all full of love and needing me, wanting me, pushing me—gently, I might add, but pushing—pulling, and just when I think I have the answer, the *wrong* buzzer rings, and I'm back at the beginning. Too bad the laws won't let me love two men at the same time, because I'm somewhere in the middle—deeply loved … and lost—at the same time."

"Besides the obvious fact that two men are begging for your love, you're luckier than most. I believe that most all of us stumble through life looking for a life jacket that will carry us through this storm called life."

"That's very philosophical, sister dear."

"Hey, I became a philosopher after that schmuck husband of mine dumped me for that moneyed bitch. Although I've been thinking I should send her a thank-you note for saving me from a lifetime of being taken for granted, to say nothing of lousy sex."

"Now, that's looking at the bright side."

"Right! But we haven't solved the number-one problem. You haven't made a choice."

"Yep. So let's go home and be loving sisters and daughters, and tomorrow go back to reality. Besides, J. R.—"

"Who?"

"J. R. John Roland, of course ... probably, hopefully, misses his mother's touch. I sure miss his."

CHAPTER 66

Medical Science Steps in to Tell Bettina
What Her Heart Wants to Know

"Youre positive this procedure will not harm my baby."

"I promise on the head of my mother."

"Did you really say that?"

"Mmmm, yeah, I think moms-to-be relate to that kind of promise."

Bettina giggled a little. "You're right."

"Now, hold perfectly still. Think of a sunny beach."

"It's snowing outside."

"Nevertheless, think of a beach, and the water is quiet, no waves."

"I see something. It's a sand crab."

"Fine, concentrate on the crab. There. All done."

"You're kidding!"

"I never kid about DNA procedures. Now you can wash up, dress, and go out for a nice lunch, and then come back to see me by two o'clock. and we'll have some news for you."

"That easy?"

"That easy."

"Okay, that was a very long hour and a half. And while that was happening, I opened every door of my life. I had fortunately forgotten some of the stuff I had shut out. But now and then, I was reminded of all the good stuff that fell in my lap. I'm a very fortunate woman, Doctor. If you ever hear me whining about how life is treating me, don't let me get away with it."

"Bettina, knowing you has only been a pleasure. Your first pregnancy was a doctor's dream; you were ideal. And I know this baby will be also. Would you like to know the father's name?"

CHAPTER **67**

If You Think Secrets Are Hard to Keep, Try This One on for Size

"Okay, Betts, I know you were going to the DNA doctor. And pray tell, what did he say?"

"Ummm, it's a secret."

"*What?* A secret? Surely he told you whose DNA is a match."

"Yep."

"Sooooooo?"

"So, it's my not-so-little secret, but I want to live with it for a while and decide how and with whom I share."

"My feelings are hurt; you know I keep secrets."

"Yes, I do know that, Lisa love, but humor me for a little while, while I figure out what the hell I'm going to do."

"No. I'm going to say no to you for maybe the first time. As you know so well, there is nothing you can't tell me. And because I know it's a secret, terrorists couldn't pry the information out of me with water-boarding or, uh, maybe bamboo shoots under the fingernails."

"Ouch."

"Well? Am I still your best friend or your ex-best friend?"

"All right, Lisa, Best Friend Lisa. I won't say the name; I'll just write the first letter of his first name."

"Oh, baby. Promise me you'll tell me what he says when you tell him."

"I promise."

CHAPTER 68

How Do You Tell a Man He *Might* Be the Father of Your Child?

"Hello, Dilly ... thank you for coming by."
"Wild horses couldn't keep me from your door."
"That's cute—wild horses?"

"That's kind of a sex symbol. Anyway, I'm here. What's on your mind, and does it require things like clothes, or can we get down to basics, the way we came into this world—bare-ass naked?"

"Honestly, Dilly, you were never so, so ..."

"Honest? Forthright? Pushy?"

"Yes, *pushy* is the word."

"Does that bother you?"

"Not a bit. I think it's kind of cute. But I do have something to discuss with you. And it's not easy."

"You know you can have your way with me, Bettina, so be gentle."

"When the darling John Moran died, you were ready to step into his dual role—husband to Bettina, and Father to John Roland."

"With such pleasure, it cannot be measured."

"What if I were to throw you another curve ball?"

"Dillworth Richardson in the batter's box, ready to face Bull's-eye Bettina, with the deadliest eye—and mouth—in the majors."

"You better sit down, Dilly."

"Now you're making me nervous."

"Remember when I told you I was pregnant with John's child?"

"Mmmm, yes, it was a kick in my belly, and I was so full of guilt for having made it happen in the first place. But I got used to J. R.'s existence, and I think he's very special."

"I wouldn't disagree for a second. He's overwhelmingly delicious."

"And you're worried, Bettina, about the thought of having another baby?"

"Nooooo, not a-tall. I never would have believed what a baby in my arms would do to me, mean to me, make me promise to be a better me. My John Roland inhabits my every thought."

"I'm hoping you can save some thoughts for me."

"I know that, Dilly, and I can't think of you without smiling, inwardly and outwardly."

"So, what's the news?"

"You have been overly generous, accepting the reality of another man in my life, and hopefully have realized I'm not comparing the two of you."

"I won't say I've loved the idea of Harry Clark, but I know none of this would have ever happened had I been as smart as I should have been. God knows my parents were wiser—faster—than *moi*. But you still haven't delivered your newest missile."

"Okay, Dilly. Here it comes—what if I were once again pregnant?"

Dilly shut his eyes and bent over. "Am I not the father?"

"Does it matter?" Bettina put her hand on his shoulder.

"God, Bettina, you are playing hardball, aren't you?"

'Yeah, Dilly. Too hard? Am I being cruel? Bettina Richardson wouldn't be cruel. Bethel Sokoloff might."

"Huh. I forgot about poor ol' Bethel. You gave that girl a stylish burial."

"Wow, thinking back, I'm amazed anyone could be that stupid."

"Who are you kidding, Bettina? Out of Bethel's unhappiness with herself, you created the most appealing woman in the world."

"And you've actually forgotten her? She's no longer the eight-hundred-pound gorilla in the corner?"

"Au contraire, she's that flashy hummingbird flitting around outside our window, checking her exquisite alter ego."

"You make me feel good about me."

"You have every right in the world to pat yourself on the back, Mrs. Richardson. But besides your self-approval rating, you won over the toughest judge in the entire world—Edwina Richardson."

"When I think back to that first meeting, I still tremble. And still can't believe that Eddie calls me her daughter and considers me a best friend."

"To say nothing of the thousands of theatergoers who adored Cassidy and her struggle to find real love, living behind a facade of shallow nothingness. I'll ask the question one more time, Bettina. Am I the father?"

"Please don't hate me for this answer, Dilly. I'll tell you on Monday."

"So, I'm going to have the longest weekend of my life. It's Friday, 7:45 p.m., and I can come back and see you Monday? If so, I'll be here by 6:00 p.m. Does that work for you?"

"Yes, forgive me for this delay, but it's necessary."

"I suppose intercourse right this minute is out of the question, but perhaps a meaningful kiss would be acceptable."

"More than acceptable. Necessary."

"I pray this is not a goodbye kiss."

"Good night, Dilly, dear Dilly. Good night, my sweet prince."

CHAPTER 69

Two Outs, Bases Loaded. Harry Clark, No Pushover, Steps Up to the Plate. The Pitcher Steps Up to the Plate and Wonders What the Hell Her Pitch Is Going to Be

"Do you realize it's been five days since I've seen you, touched you, knelt at your altar? This is a command appearance. What's on your mind? I kind of love being ordered around by you."

"Harry, you're like having a fairy godfather—"

"Wait, I don't like the 'fairy' part. I know I'm not a hairy, smelly linebacker, but I hope the 'fairy' reference doesn't mean more than an adjectival description of a good, helpful man in your life."

"You make me laugh, Harry. After all our times together, I wouldn't dream of putting you up as a candidate to lead the LGBT campaign in Manhattan. Don't worry; I see you as I see you—Harry Clark, one of God's goodliest people, loving and generous, and oh, I don't want to hurt you."

"Wha-what are you talking about—hurting me? You couldn't hurt me if you broke a vase over my head—and please don't prove that to me."

"I have something very serious to tell you, Harry. I did tell you that Dilly has been calling on me."

"Yes, you did, and although I kind of wished you were remaining platonic friends, I'm really not naive. I assume you've done more than have an occasional dinner together."

"You assume correctly. This doesn't speak very well about me, because Dilly also knew I was seeing you—intimately. We, he and I, just never discussed Harry Clark."

"So why are we having this discussion right now? And why does that question make me nervous?"

"Ready? Here it comes. I'm pregnant."

"Oh, dear God, and Dilly is the father?"

"If he were, could you handle it?"

"You mean raise the child as though I were the father? The way I was willing to do with John Moran's child."

"That's ... it."

"I would like to lie to you and say, 'Yes, yes, yes—I don't care if you are pregnant with an unknown donor from the sperm bank. I want you to be mine and mine alone.'"

"But ... you said you'd *like* to lie to me, but there's a *but* somewhere in there."

"Yes, Bettina, there is. I've always felt Dilly's presence—finally kicked him out of our bed—but he was in there too in the beginning because I knew you cared about him and knew how much he cared, and cares, about you. Hey, I just thought of something—what if *I am the father?*"

"But if you're not?"

"I guess Dilly wins. I could fight with his memory but not with his child. You do know how much I love you, Bettina?"

"Heart and soul, Harry, and now, even more than ever. Your generosity and selflessness are sterling.

"So ... it is Dilly's child?

"It is."

"And you are a Richardson. Edwina and Elizabeth made that very clear to me. And although I will never forget you, never for a minute, I will, in the current vernacular, take your name off the speed dial on my cell and try not to compare every woman in the world I chance to meet with you. Goodbye, Bettina."

"Harry, I won't forget you. Nor will I diminish the thought of you as only a past sexual fantasy, although you more than qualify. Thank you for every minute that you shared with me. You gave me a new feeling about myself when I couldn't find me. Thank you. And may I kiss you goodbye?"

"Thank you, Bettina. Dilly is most fortunate. I won't ask if he deserves you. You chose him and turned his eighteen-karat-gold life to pure platinum. You are a treasure. Goodbye. I promise not to call."

CHAPTER *70*

It's Monday, 6:05p.m. The Doorman Said Mr. Richardson Was Heading Upstairs. Bettina Opened the Door and Was Waiting for Dilly

"Before you say anything, Bettina, I want you to know that unless the thought of my raising his child makes Harry suicidal, I want us to be together forever and raise both children and, God willing, maybe another one, if you're willing."

Bettina smiled from her heart. She took Dilly by the hand and led him over to the sofa and said, "Sit down and calm down, Dilly."

"I have only one question and none after that: Is Harry going to be part of the baby's name?"

"No, darling Dilly, I think *her* name will be … Edwina, but we'll call her Eddie."

"Ed … *Edwina?*"

"Mmmm. Come kiss Eddie's mommy, Daddy."

Printed in the United States
by Baker & Taylor Publisher Services